UNIQUELY STELLA

Uniquely STELLA

a novel by

DEBORAH M. MENENBERG

Copyright © 2020 by Deborah Menenberg

www.deborahmenenberg.com

Edited by Linda Franklin
Cover art by DLR Cover Designs
www.dlrcoverdesigns.com

This story, while fictional, is based on actual events. In certain cases incidents, characters, names, and timelines have been changed for dramatic purposes. Certain characters may be composites, or entirely fictitious. This story is created for entertainment purposes. Opinions, acts, and statements attributed to any entity, individual or individuals may have been fabricated or exaggerated for effect. The opinions and fictionalized depictions of individuals, groups and entities, and any statements contained herein, are not to be relied upon in any way.

All rights reserved. No part of this book may be reproduced or transmitted in any form or by any means whatsoever, including photocopying, recording or by any information storage and retrieval system, without written permission from the publisher and/or author.

Publisher: JAT Trax Studios | www.jattrax.com
               PO Box 230151, Tigard, OR 97281-0151

ISBN: 978-1-7362318-0-7

1 3 5 7 9 10 8 6 4 2

To

LaVerne Stella Kossler and Donna Marie Dickenson.

I am who I am because of you.

PROLOGUE

2016

The first thing that invaded Rosie's thoughts when she pushed open the attic door was not the screech that made her wince or even the mustiness escaping from the small space. No, she grimaced with the realization that she had not needed to spend the last hour looking for a high-powered flashlight. Rosie squinted as she squeezed into the compact enclosure. The sun's brilliance cascaded through the alcove window at the far end of the attic. Dust particles danced around in an eerie glow of yellowish light.

Rosie groaned slightly as she tried to stand up, annoyed that her age was catching up with her never-ending expectations to move with youthful exuberance. She had retired two years ago, and Medicare was just around the corner. Rosie didn't particularly worry about age as much as she did those extra pounds that had crept onto her petite frame over the last decade. She still *felt* young and healthy even though a few gray hairs occasionally made her surreptitiously rush to the drug store to purchase a box of instant hair color glamour, hopeful that no one would notice. Today, she had used a clasp to hold back her strawberry blond hair. The jeans and sweatshirt were a perfect combination to wear in this dusty old attic in her mother's log house.

"I knew you would arrive before me!" came an irritable voice from the bottom of the stairs.

Rosie rubbed her eyes and shouted down the opening toward her sister, "I can handle this on my own."

"Laddie doesn't think so," Maddie replied.

The puppy bounded up the ladder steps, ears flopping. Once he reached the attic floor, Laddie rolled, causing even more dust to fly. Rosie crawled over to him and wrapped her arms around his neck. "Settle down, Laddie boy. Come help me find those hat boxes."

"I'm coming up," Maddie shouted.

Do you have to? Rosie thought to herself.

"I still don't understand why Mom would want Aunt Veronica's hat boxes," Maddie whined when she poked her head through the opening.

Although Maddie was almost seven years younger than her sister, she exuded an air of dominance and superiority. She was a no-nonsense woman who expected order and structure in every part of her life, including her own personal style. Her hair was professionally cut in a short bob with no strand out of place. Her designer clothes were impeccably displayed on a solid middle-aged body. Rosie often mused that her sister's elegant grooming reflected perhaps a subconscious cry for attention rather than what made sense for the occasion.

"I agree."

"We agree on something?"

"Well, there's a first time for everything."

It had been two weeks since the sisters had moved their mother and the woman they had always called Aunt Veronica into the two-bedroom cottage at Whispering Winds Senior Retirement Village. They were convinced they had gotten everything. Most of the remaining items were approved to be sold at the garage sale or would be donated.

Rosie put a hand through her hair and looked at Maddie in confusion, "Do you know why Mom was so upset about our forgetting the hat boxes? She acted as if they were the most important items in the house."

Maddie shook her head no. "Does she want to start wearing some antiquated hats now? Hats like Veronica's have been out of style for more years than I can remember. Not only that, but I thought Veronica liquidated all her inventory with the sale of her craft shop."

Rosie shrugged, "Maybe she hid a few in the attic as keepsakes."

"Mom said she hoped the hat boxes would jolt our memories. I have no idea what that means."

"Maybe she wanted to recapture her own memories. Mom is becoming increasingly confused. You know it was her decision to move to the retirement home. She told us it was time. Being eighty-nine years old, her memory isn't as sharp as it used to be."

"Let's find those stupid boxes and get out of this messy room. It gives me the creeps," Maddie shivered as she gazed around.

"Look!" Rosie exclaimed. Laddie was at the far end of the attic. He appeared surprisingly tall as the light cast a long shadow behind him. He stood on his hind legs with his front paws on a wooden shelf.

"What do you see, Laddie?" Maddie asked as she got up and gradually headed toward him. "I don't like it back here. There are probably a colony of spiders and other creepy crawlers."

Laddie jumped down with something indistinguishable hanging from his mouth and brought it straight to Rosie. "Drop it, smart puppy." Rosie smiled as Laddie dropped a large tattered leather collar at her feet. She picked it up and read the faded words on the attached tag, "Merlin, EL6-1562."

"What does that mean?" Maddie asked.

Instantly, tears came to Rosie's eyes. "You must remember Merlin, our dog?"

"Of course I do," Maddie said, "I meant the other part."

"That was our phone number in San Jose. I can't believe I still remember something Mom had me memorize so long ago."

"How can you remember that but not what you did last week?"

"Maybe what I did last week isn't important." Rosie smirked as she again stood up and walked with Maddie over to the shelving unit.

Maddie automatically took charge and tried to reach toward the back. "Don't just stand there; find me a stepstool or something. I think I see the hat boxes."

Rosie pushed over a solid wooden crate and set it next to the shelf. Maddie stood on it a bit unsteadily as she reached toward the items wedged against the back wall. "If I get bitten by a black widow spider and die, I will never talk to you again!"

"Stop grumbling and just pull out everything."

"Some dead thing could be in whatever's up here," Maddie moaned. "You should climb up. Why do I always have to do your dirty work?"

"Mine?" Rosie hollered back. "This wasn't my idea."

"Well, I am doing this for Aunt Veronica and Mom, not you!"

"Fine. Just find the darn things. All of them, too." Rosie kept Laddie close by her side.

"Here, take this one." Maddie held a hefty hat box in her hands and heaved it toward the front of the shelf. She lifted it down to her sister.

"Good heavens, this is heavy. Were hats heavy in the olden days?"

"There are a lot more – hang on." Maddie pushed each one into Rosie's waiting arms.

"Take them downstairs to the living room. We can open the boxes there and try on all the ridiculously heavy hats," Maddie directed.

"I can't wait to tease Aunt Veronica about them."

"Don't you dare. She and Mom always loved those silly things. You would hurt her feelings."

"No, I wouldn't. Aunt Veronica has a wonderful sense of humor."

"Well, you better get used to wearing them because Veronica and Mom said that we needed to know about these hat boxes and do whatever we thought was best. I'm not sure what she meant," Maddie said.

"Do they want us to open an antique hat shop?"

Maddie grinned, "Or a craft shop?"

"No way. I'm retired, you know! I just want to travel and write my stories."

An hour later, Rosie and Maddie sat on the carpeted living room floor, surrounded by numerous colorfully designed hat boxes, their lids tightly secured with tape and glue. Some boxes were labeled "Stella," others "Veronica."

"What are you doing?" Maddie shrieked. "Don't try to tear them open with your hands. Use a knife and be gentle!"

"Why? We need to pry the lids off, and we'll undoubtedly toss the boxes anyway, so what difference does it make?" Rosie said.

"Let me do it. You will destroy the delicate hats inside."

"Oh, for heaven's sake, hurry up and open them. This junk still must be transported to their cottage. I don't have all day and traffic is miserable!"

"I still don't understand why they're insistent about calling a simple ticky-tacky box house their cottage. It doesn't look anything like a cottage to me."

"Something we can agree on," Rosie added. "Here's a knife. Be careful or you will cut yourself and blame my sweet Laddie."

"No, I will blame you!"

Rosie watched intently as Maddie put the blade between the lid and the round shape of the heavy cardboard hat box. She gently pried the lid away from the sides. Once it was completely untethered, she glanced at her sister, "Are you ready?"

"Pull away!"

Maddie lifted the lid off and gasped.

They all stared noiselessly – even Laddie. Maddie put a hand over her mouth as if she were afraid to breathe. Rosie took the box and tipped the contents onto the floor. Countless papers scattered the surrounding area. Letters, envelopes, lists, small notes, notepads, numerous full-sized notebook pages, school assignments, postcards, an old diary, and a couple small journals flew about the living room like the dust particles in the sunlit attic.

Without speaking, Maddie grabbed another box and frantically tore off the lid. Rosie did the same. They turned the boxes over simultaneously and dropped identical items into the growing pile on the floor. They proceeded doing the same thing with the rest of the boxes until hundreds and hundreds of items spread around them, until they were drowning in a sea of paper.

The sisters gazed in speechless stunned wonder, broken only when Laddie jumped up and barked. A brisk wind blew open the front door, causing a lone piece of yellowed paper to rise into the air. Laddie raced around the room until he caught it in his mouth.

"Laddie, come. Drop it," Rosie simply said.

The tiny parchment floated to the floor. The sisters looked at each other as if the note had been destined to fall from the heavens. Rosie opened the single sheet of paper and gazed at it for what seemed like an eternity.

Unable to wait any longer, Maddie said with more intensity than she meant, "Well, what does it say?"

Rosie read the words out loud as her eyes burned with fresh tears.

"I am sorry."

Part One

Chapter 1
1946 – CHICAGO, ILLINOIS

The memories of snow from the past winter had evaporated long ago. Although the afternoon was bright but a bit chilly for early July, Stella didn't care. She couldn't remember a time when she had been more excited. Only 19 years old, Stella was beyond ready to start the adventure she had yearned for all her life. She bounced down the twelve steps of her childhood brownstone home in North Chicago, in a hurry to get to her father's furniture shop. She had been performing this exact same routine quite often over the years, but today was different. She was going to tell her dad she was leaving the only home she had ever known to go on an unfamiliar journey without a time agenda. Yet Stella could not have imagined how this journey would become part of the puzzle that would ultimately change the focus and mindset of her country – maybe even her world.

The family's only bicycle continued to hug the black wrought-iron fence that enclosed a tiny rectangular plot of grass at the very bottom of the steps, as it had the day before when Stella left it there. As Stella jumped off the last step, she twisted her head around to sneak a final peek at her ma's possible wrath. Riding her bike when she was wearing her widely pleated, plaid school uniform skirt was one thing, but it was quite another issue to try to maneuver the dusty old vehicle while wearing a brand-new skirt and fitted suit jacket. Stella loved fashion. She always wanted to be ahead of the fashion game, but finances kept her on a lower level playing field. The runway fashions of the day were well beyond her current dreams. Today was special, however, so she dressed in her finest attire.

"Stella!" Ma screeched from the doorway at the top of the steps. Stella heard her but tried hard to pretend she couldn't. Avoiding the confrontation would be easier. Frances Kluskowski secured her apron strings a bit more snugly to her round, petite frame. Loose strands of graying hair escaped from the scarf tied in a tight knot under her soft chin. Stella wondered if her 40-year-old mother ever agonized about the lifetime behind her while her future was running away. Or did she only worry about her daughters? She knew her mother suspected something. Ma stood at the doorway with a raised eyebrow and a slight grin on her face.

"What are you up to now, Stella?" Ma cried out.

Feeling a bit guilty, Stella shouted back, "It's okay, Ma. I must go get Dad's beer. I'm late." She quickly jumped on the bicycle and pedaled eagerly down the empty road.

"Tell your dad dinner will be ready at six tonight. Don't be late. Why are you wearing your best outfit on that dirty bicycle? Don't ruin it. The outfit, I mean, not the bicycle. Do you hear me?"

Lost in her own thoughts, Stella only vaguely heard her ma's words as they drifted off in the soft breeze. She couldn't help but muse about what had brought her to this decision. Had it only been a year since the war ended? It truly didn't seem so long ago that she was standing at a long table soldering one odd part to another at the Red Flyer Wagon factory, which had been converted to make items specifically for the war effort. Along with many of her school friends, she had left high school a year before graduation to do whatever she could to help end a horrible war. She also knew she would be able to keep her earnings. Ma told her to use the money to follow wherever her path might lead – just be sure to go in the right direction. Stella knew her parents wanted her to finish school, so it felt odd when they allowed her to work at the factory. A year later, the war ended, and Stella headed back to school, graduating only last week – June 28,

1946. While pedaling down the alleyway, she changed her mind once again. Maybe she wouldn't tell her dad at his shop. No, tonight at dinner would be better. She would tell both of her parents and her sisters at the same time. Stella hadn't changed her mind about when she would leave, however. The train would depart later this evening and she would be on it.

Joe's tavern loomed ahead. The building, the business, and even Joe hadn't changed in a dozen or more years. To Stella this place always felt more like a community meeting hall than a beer joint.

"Stella!" Joe yelled from the doorstep of his tavern. "You're late again. You better hurry. You know how your father feels when you go racing around the corner to his shop, spilling half of his lager along the way." Joe O'Malley was a little past middle-aged with a belly that jiggled and a few wisps of hair on a mostly bald head. He held a broom in both hands and only pretended to sweep the sidewalk in front of his establishment.

Stella stopped abruptly and jumped off her bike. She watched Joe lean his broom against the wall as he wiped his hands on his apron. "It's fine, Mr. O'Malley. I'll be careful. I promise."

Joe ambled back behind his bar and pulled the handle to cautiously draft a full pint of beer.

"Thanks, Mr. O'Malley. Dad said he'll be around later this evening to square up with you as always."

"I know, my girl. And he'll be complaining that I cheated him once again. You be careful now. Steady as you go."

Stella held the full mug of beer in one hand while she maneuvered the bicycle with the other. Just as soon as she careened around the next corner, she glanced carefully around before licking all the foam off the top.

Dad was standing at his workbench hammering some upholstery nails into a handmade chair of his own creation. Stella enthusiastically opened the door and jumped up as high as she could to ring the bell. She loved to hear that bell ring every time someone entered the shop as if it were telling the world this little shop had a soul and would always be alive with excitement.

"Hi, Dad."

"Hey, how's my sweet girl? What do you have there for me?"

"Oh, Dad. You always say the same thing."

"I see that swindler, Joe, has done it again. I have a good mind to..."

The sound of the bell interrupted Dad. People were frequently coming and going from his shop. When Stella was young, she often wondered why so many of them would be interested in having furniture built. Maybe they only came to chat with Dad. Yet he wasn't especially interesting. Dad and his companions usually went into the back room, but he always refused her requests to also go back there. Now she knew better, but also knew better than to express her opinions.

Both Stella and her dad looked up as Officer McMurray entered the room. She frequently wanted to ask him if he owned any other clothes because he wore the same tattered police uniform every time she saw him.

"Oh, my. Who is this lovely lady? Hey, Stanley, this can't be your charming girl? When did you grow up to be so beautiful?" Officer McMurray chuckled.

The bell rang, interrupting the lighthearted fun. A man in a tweed suit and bowler hat hopped into the room and swung Stella around in a playful circle. He glanced over at the police officer and said, "Hey now, Mac. You leave off. This pretty little thing is destined for greatness – me!"

"Is that something you might want to mention to your wife and three children, Harry?" Stella teased, smiling all the same.

"Oh, darling. They'd welcome you with open arms," Harry continued. "I'm headed to the back room for umm...the necessaries."

No sooner had Harry exited through the backroom door than Bob the baker rang the bell. Ben the butcher followed right behind him. They had shops down the road not too far away and habitually came by when she visited. Both men's attire had once probably been starched clean white full-length aprons.

Now they both appeared to have their respective by-products stamped haphazardly all over themselves, clearly proclaiming their chosen careers. Stella wasn't convinced that Bob and Ben were their true given names, but they appeared to love that she had been addressing them that way since she was a child.

Bob saw Stella and gently patted her cheek, leaving a dust of flour in his wake. He glanced over at Stanley and said simply, "So how did this marvel of beauty come from a guy with a mug like yours, Stanley my man?"

"Surely God works in mysterious ways!"

Bob pondered before he answered, "Only God could figure this one out and he's not talking!"

Everyone laughed except Stella. She wondered if this was a compliment or blasphemy.

While everyone lightly bantered, Stella could hear the telephone ring off and on in the back room.

"Who is answering the phone, Dad?"

Without missing a beat, Stanley looked at his daughter lovingly, "Is that a new outfit, my girl?" he queried while wrinkling his brow. "You look quite classy for a short ride to this old, dusty workshop. Oh, wait. Do you have a date?"

"A date?" Ben and Bob questioned simultaneously. "Have we met this scoundrel? Bring him around for the once over. Hey, Stanley, you didn't tell us your girl was dating. She's way too young."

Stella jumped in before they could say any more, "That phone keeps ringing and ringing. Is someone going to answer it? Your business must be doing well, Dad. I suppose people need furniture."

Everyone stopped talking and focused on the back door. "Yes, well. Oh, I'm sure it's probably just Harry," someone answered.

"Yes," Officer McMurray said. "I better go help him."

"We need to go back there to do whatever is necessary," Bob and Ben laughed again while Bob playfully pushed Ben through the back door.

"Dad, why won't you let me go back there? I've never been. I often ask, but you always say..."

"The back room is no place for a sweet little thing. It's much too cold and dark and dirty."

Chapter 2

1946 – CHICAGO UNION STATION

*F*IFTEEN MORE MINUTES AND THE STREAMLINER TRAIN WOULD BE departing Union Station in Chicago for San Francisco. Stella sat uncomfortably in her the third-class coach carriage seat. She had never known such excitement mingled with fear. If butterflies could truly exist in one's stomach, then hers most certainly were having a flying competition. She fiddled with the clasp on her handbag, which she had kept securely on her lap. The man opposite glanced her way, giving a slight nod and a quick tip of his hat. She turned her head to stare out the window. Her thoughts whirled like a sandstorm. Particles of previous conversations and feelings were swirling around, dancing this way and that, as if they did not know where to settle. Out of the imagined storm, she sensed a bit of a commotion. Stella looked up and saw a strikingly beautiful woman of about her age walking hesitantly down the aisle. She wore a crisp white skirt with a matching white suit jacket that contrasted dramatically with her silky dark skin. What caught Stella's attention was not the woman's discomfort or even her color, but rather the hat on her head. This creation wasn't something she had seen in the department stores or the fashion magazines. She knew that for certain. The hat suited this young woman as if it had been made for her alone. Sitting snugly and slightly off center to frame her face, the hat matched the thin striped velvet line of her fitted suit jacket. The brim rippled with a matching solid velvet braided band encircling the entire hat. Stella stared at it intently, wondering where she had found such a unique fashion statement. The young woman went to each seat and asked if she could sit down. At each encounter, she was either ignored or told emphatically to move on. The man across the aisle quickly dropped his paperback book and reading glasses on the seat next to him and turned to gaze out his window.

Stella continued to focus on the hat, her curiosity prompting her to blurt out, "Where did you get that hat?"

"I made it," the woman replied softly, with a bit of embarrassment.

"That is the most unusually intriguing fashion accessory I have ever seen. Do you own a hat shop?"

"Oh, goodness gracious, no," she grinned. "May I sit here?"

"Yes, of course. I'm sorry. I should have offered right away. I just can't get over the intricate design and exquisite detail. You are very talented."

The young woman looked almost sad as she answered, "I doubt many others would think so, but thank you."

Stella pulled the glove off her right hand one finger at a time. The woman now sitting next to her pulled her glove off one finger at a time. They both held out their hands simultaneously and shook hands, laughing as they did so.

"My name is Stella Kluskowski."

"Glad to make your acquaintance, Miss Stella. I am Veronica Rose Boyd. My dad calls me Rosie, but when I became a teenager, I told everyone I wanted to be called Veronica because I believed it made me seem more grown up. Rosie is a sweet name, but..."

Gently staring, Stella interrupted her, "Veronica it is. You seem like a very mature young lady."

Veronica chuckled as she pulled the hat pin out of her pinned-up hair and put the hat on her lap, neatly putting the pin back in the hat. The women were getting settled as the train whistle blew, causing them to jump. They studied each other with mock expressions of nervous excitement and laughed again. The conductor shouted something neither could quite make out. The noise of the engines and the wheels on the track combined to elicit the women's unexpressed inner desire for adventure. Stella could barely contain herself as her outward joy mingled with inner apprehension. She didn't know which way to turn or what to do next. Veronica must have felt the same way. She looked around nervously and said matter-of-factly, "I guess one can't jump off the platform now."

"Especially since we're not even on a platform," Stella grinned as she took Veronica's arm and squeezed it playfully.

The train jerked ahead, gaining speed as it progressed. The conversations in the carriage lessened to an unintelligible murmur. Stella sighed as she noticed the other passengers. The elderly lady in the front row knitted. Behind her sat a middle-aged couple. One read a newspaper while the other leafed through a magazine. Others quietly chatted amiably or gazed out the window. The man across the aisle pulled his hat down over his face and leaned against the window. In just a few moments, his gentle snores competed with the hum of the train.

"I recognize you, but I don't know from where," Stella squinted quizzically at Veronica.

"Maybe it's my height. People often tell me I look like someone they know because of my height," Veronica answered.

"You're short?" Stella mused.

"I haven't quite reached the five-foot mark yet," Veronica joked, looking at her with a playful glint in her eyes.

"I usually tell people I am five feet, although I doubt the five-foot mark will ever be within my reach," Stella chuckled. "So, have we met?"

"Actually, I'm pretty sure I've seen you as well, but certainly not in a crowd," Veronica replied as they both laughed once again.

"I know it wasn't at my all-girls Catholic high school."

"Heaven's sake. My mama would turn over in her Baptist grave."

"Oh, I'm so sorry, I didn't mean…"

Veronica broke in, "Oh, no. My mama's not dead. She just acts like it sometimes."

"I know what you mean. I always thought that my mother wished she had been born in another era. Maybe even mine. She was quite eager that I go on my journey. When I left the factory, she didn't even care if I went back to school. She just wanted me to 'follow my destiny,' as she put it."

"That's it!" Veronica exclaimed. "The factory, of course. I could never forget that. You came to my rescue."

"Now I remember. Certainly not as dramatic as you make it sound. Being annoyed, I only spoke my mind. My mother and dad admonish me about opening my mouth when it should stay closed. My dad is frequently telling me that I tend to speak before my mind has a chance to catch up. He thinks that I should only talk when given permission and absolutely not talk back to any kind of authority." Stella winced when she added, "I never quite learned his lesson."

"It's a good thing you didn't, I'd say. You saved a lot of us that day."

"Well, I doubt it. I do remember standing in line waiting for a job which, to be honest with you, I didn't really want."

"Don't be sly now," Veronica continued, "You watched the whole episode unfold with eagle eyes and cried foul at just the right time. You stood in the line of young white women. An elderly man at the desk had the women sign some papers and have their pictures taken one at a time; then he gave each of them their badges almost immediately."

"Being the next one in line, I noticed the other line a short distance away from us dispersing," Stella added.

"It was the line of young black women and I was at the front. The man at the table claimed they had no more jobs. He told us to all leave. As I turned to walk away, I noticed you were watching. I saw you turn straight to the man in front of you and say..."

"She can have my job!"

Veronica continued, "Yes, but not before you declared loudly to that man and everyone else in the vicinity that he was a fool.

You persisted that they had tons of jobs open and claimed they were eager to hire because you had read it in an ad. You had everyone spellbound when you announced that President Roosevelt signed a proclamation stating the war factories could not discriminate against someone because of their race!"

"The crowd of women of all races was getting upset, too. I remember," Stella said, "Do you know that there was even a woman in a wheelchair?"

"Yes, you even yelled out that they should allow her to work, too. It was only fair that if you were to suffer, so should everyone!" Veronica laughed. "I couldn't believe it when the man pointed to me and said to you, 'If you are so eager to let every Tom, Dick, and black Harry work, then she can have your job!'"

"That's when I said it was perfectly fine with me. 'Give her the job you were going to give me,'" Stella said.

"You actually said since there was no Tom, Dick, or any kind of Harry around, they should be grateful they had all of us women willing to sacrifice our time and energy to the war effort. You even babbled on about composing a letter to the War Department when a supervisor came over and whispered something in the man's ear. He told everyone to line up and get processed."

"I suppose we won some sort of victory that day," Stella said.

"It didn't feel like a victory once we all started working. My goodness, it sure was dull work!"

"You can say that again. Do you have any idea what we were doing?" Stella asked.

"Do you really think anyone would tell me?" Veronica sighed, "Heavens no, but I got paid. With the little I got, I gave Mama some and the rest I tried to save for whatever came next. I did buy some materials to make a few hats."

"Are you going to try to sell your hats?"

"I'd like to, but they are expensive to make. And I'm not exactly in a circle of acquaintances that would be willing and eager to buy one. So I thought I would try San Francisco. Maybe I'll marry a rich man and he'll set me up for business in my own shop," Veronica chuckled.

"Well, a girl can dream."
"But can you even imagine a rich man who looks like me?"
"Short?" Stella smiled.
"You know, I wouldn't even care if he was white!"
"Mercy!" Stella joked.
"Well, as long as he liked hats, who cares?"
"I heard hats are all the rage in San Francisco."

The steady rhythm and hum of the train caused drowsiness amongst many of the passengers. Time slipped by without notice. The easy camaraderie the women experienced solidified their new friendship.

Veronica glanced briefly at Stella, then returned her gaze to the hat resting on her lap. Cautiously she asked, "So, what brings you out on this unknown journey?"

Stella was bolder and eager to chat, "I'm not totally sure. It wasn't sudden. I've wanted to explore ever since I can remember. I've always felt this overwhelming desire to travel and experience exciting adventures. Ma told me that there must be someone very special inside of me and I needed to follow my destiny. She wanted me to go because she said she never could. I thought it odd when she said that she wasn't allowed to and now she was allowing me. But my dad wasn't happy at all. He said there was only a fool in me. My place was at home. I should find a husband that wouldn't beat me, if possible, and become a housewife. And I should just stay in Chicago. My dad and my ma had a big argument just before I left. I couldn't listen to it anymore. I left without saying goodbye. I'm so worried that I'll regret it someday. Maybe I'm foolish. I don't even know where I'm going or what I'm going to do. Isn't that silly?"

"No. I understand," Veronica nodded. After a long, silent pause, Veronica took a deep breath as if she was inhaling some inner strength. In a quiet, solemn tone she continued, "My parents fought tonight as well. I didn't leave because of an overwhelming sense of desire or destiny, but rather a sense of urgency. Mama told me to get out quickly. My father was on his way back from the tavern. A neighbor had raced up to our apartment and told her that Pa was drunk as a mule and fierce. When he drinks, he can become violent. Mama used to put extra powder on her face sometimes in the morning after a big argument. Or she would bake more than usual and flour would be all over her including her face, arms, and hair. I thought she did it to cover any bruises she believed she might have. I'm not sure, but even at a young age I did know he hit her. Sometimes I would see a trail of dried tears run down her drawn, powdered face. I was frightened. I just couldn't stay and watch this age-old story continue. I fled like a coward. Now I, too, fear that I will regret my choice someday. Mama stuffed the little money she had hidden in the sugar jar into my pocket as she pushed me out the door. I ran to the train station and didn't look back." A tiny tear slid down Veronica's cheek.

Over the next few days, Stella and Veronica became fast and empathetic companions. Their fiercely loyal friendship would last a lifetime.

Chapter 3

1957 – CHICAGO, ILLINOIS

Over a decade had passed since Stella had bicycled up to her dad's furniture shop that eventful day. She now stood where she had all those years earlier. These days the door was locked and the windows boarded up. The printed sign that once proudly proclaimed *Stanley's Handmade Furniture* was faded and the lettering cracked as if someone had unsuccessfully tried to pry it off. It all looked so dark, dirty, deserted, and oddly cold, but today was bright as the sun lathered the sidewalk with warmth. Stella took a tiny handkerchief out of the sleeve of her new blouse and wiped a small circle on the window to enable a glimpse inside. Ghosts that were mere memories swirled around her mind vividly recreating the scene of a time she hoped she would never forget.

Stella shifted the bag of groceries from one hip to the other as she cautiously climbed the twelve steps to her parents' house. She was shocked at her own feelings of excitement laced with dread. How could anyone have such opposing emotions? How could she feel happy at being home when her father was dying? She had gotten a telephone call from her mother not more than a week ago stating her father had been diagnosed with stomach cancer and wanted desperately to see her. She wanted to see him again, too, more than she realized, but uncomfortable fear overwhelmed her. She fretted about what she would say to him. Would there be a look of disappointment on his face? Yet each day since her arrival she had sat close to him, holding his hand for a few hours while he slept. Ma urged her to wake him so they could talk. Stella only shook her head no.

The moment she reached the last step, Ma opened the door. It still squeaked as it always had. For some reason this irritated her. Why didn't they oil it? Why had they never installed a working bell?

"Stella, there you are. What took you so long? I only sent you down to the corner grocery to buy a few items for dinner," Ma scolded.

"I'm sorry, Ma. I wanted to swing by the furniture shop. Why didn't you write me about Dad closing the store? What happened? Why didn't he sell it? Why did he let it go to ruin?"

Ma shook her head and said, "So many problems; so many questions. We'll never get dinner on the table at this rate. Your father is eager to see you. Go talk to him now."

Stella took a deep breath, "How is Rosie?"

"She is amusing your sisters. They're supposed to be watching her, but instead Rosie is performing for them. For a six-year-old, she is quite a character, our Rosie."

"And the baby?"

"Rosie is trying to teach her how to blink. If I didn't know better, I'd think she's succeeding. But surely, that must be impossible. Poor thing," Ma sighed.

The door to her dad's bedroom was slightly ajar. Surprised at her own hesitance, Stella took a few deep breaths before she quietly knocked. Not detecting any noise, she counted to ten in her head, took another breath, and walked in. Propped up with three sturdy pillows behind him, Stella's dad stared at the open doorway with eyes half closed. He was unbelievably thin. The heavily lined and extremely pale face of her beloved father scared her. Stella stood frozen as she fought with all her might not to give in to hysterics. What should she say? What should she do? The lump in her throat threatened her ability to talk. Her eyes ached with emotion, but she would force herself not to cry. She would be brave.

"Rosie, you little scamp, is that you?" Dad's tinny voice scratched at the air, surprising Stella.

"No, Dad," she said as she took a few steps toward him. The overwhelming determination it would take to walk up to his bed and take his hand confused and saddened her. Why was she so frightened?

"Stella? Is that you? Come closer so I can see my sweet girl. I've missed you so much and now you are here. I hope I'm not dreaming," her dad spoke with great deliberation and so softly she had to strain to understand his words.

"Yes, I'm here, Daddy. Every day for a week, I poked my head into your room, but I didn't want to wake you. I guess I was afraid. What can I say? I'm so heartbroken. I…" she couldn't continue.

"Oh, darling. Time waits for no one. Where did I hear that from? I think it might have been Rosie," Dad beamed and gazed at his daughter.

Stella was incredulous. "Rosie? Wait a minute, I'm confused. You looked at me in the doorway and thought I was Rosie? I don't understand. When did you meet her?"

The elderly man in his sick bed broke through his frail demeanor and grinned pensively, "She looks just like you. Every day she comes running into the room and jumps up onto the bed to wake me up."

"Oh, no. I'm so sorry."

"Why? I love it. You may laugh, but when I first saw her, I thought I was dreaming about you. She is quite a character, our Rosie!"

A heartbeat later Dad choked out, "Come here, Stella, my darling girl. I want to talk to you."

Stella took his hand but focused her attention downward. Her eyes were slowly filling with tears that she didn't want him to see. "I always wanted to explain why I went away. But the days went by and I felt I let you down and...oh, I don't know."

"My dear girl. You are here now and that means the world to me. Why was I able to reach the end of my days before realizing what is truly important in life? Living with so many regrets and remorse is never easy. Stella, I want you to understand that the choices you make are lifelong commitments that you must face willingly, or the consequences of your actions may very well haunt you until your dying day. Please don't let my foolish actions influence your decisions in life."

"I don't understand, Daddy."

"Please just humor this old man. I'm not sure how it's possible to be so excited you are here with me now and angry that you were gone for so long. Time passed us by without a care in the world. Maybe I worry too much. Are you happy? Have you been happy? I want to believe all is well in your world. I missed you terribly. I do have a question for you. Why didn't you come back? I always thought that you had this itch to travel, but once you got it out of your system, you would come home to stay." Dad blinked his eyes and sniffed.

Handing him a handkerchief that was resting on the bedside table, Stella could only nod.

"Children grow up," he continued, "that's what happens. Dads must let their children move on eventually. I didn't want to accept that reality."

"I came back home to Chicago to marry Richard. Remember?"

"Yes, of course, but you left a few days later. That was seven years ago."

"I wrote now and then," Stella tried to explain.

"Yes. Basic day to day. But the important things? I'm not so sure."

Stella took a deep breath to ease the trembling taking over her body. Her dad appeared to be gaining strength. Stella smiled inwardly because this time she believed he did want to hear what she said. He studied her while listening without condemnation.

Fortified by this knowledge, Stella said, "It wasn't as I thought. Maybe nothing is. Things were so much harder than I anticipated. I thought love solved everything, but instead everything I ever hoped for fell apart. What did I do wrong?"

"You must not blame yourself. Your husband, what's his name?"

"Richard."

"Yes, him. Where is he? He should be with you now. When is he going to find a proper job and take some responsibilities?" her father said, exasperated.

"So, Ma told you?"

"Yes. I know that you moved several times. His days as an actor didn't work out very well, I heard."

"No, but we are settled in San Jose now."

"Is he working?"

"As an insurance agent. He says he hates it. I think he would hate anything that didn't include acting."

"I see. Now you have two children."

"Yes. Rosie and Donna. They are the best part of my life!"

"Rosie, yes, that makes sense, but the other one? Why, she's an imbecile. You should put her away before you become too attached to her." Stella's father looked at her sadly, "That would be better for everyone."

Stella couldn't breathe. She stared at her father for what seemed like an eternity. She had thought they were connecting emotionally for the first time in her entire life, yet he said the one thing that could tear her apart.

In a slow and steady low voice, Stella replied, "How dare you! What a horrible, horrible thing to say! She is your granddaughter. You haven't even seen her. You don't want to, do you? Be honest. Do you?" Stella clenched her jaw. She had completely ignored the gravity of her father's illness. All she thought about was her baby and this man's disinterest in his own granddaughter. How could he be so uncaring?

Stella dropped his hand hard, curled her fists tightly, and flew to the doorway. Once there, she turned around abruptly and yelled, "You talk about regret and remorse. Where do you get your own personal moral compass from, Father?"

"Stella, wait," her dad begged.

"Why, so I can watch you die and, for the rest of my life, not know if I was hurting because we parted on hateful terms or if I hated you for dying without loving the daughter that I love?"

"Stella, please understand. In my day, that's how a child like Donna would be identified. I think people use the terms moron or idiot," her father said in a shaky voice. "I've never even seen a mentally retarded child."

Stella turned back to him and, clutching the doorway, said in a lifeless tone, "The doctor called her a Mongoloid child. He said they were given that title because of the eyes. It's funny. Rosie says she has pumpkin doodle eyes. She says she loves Donna's pumpkin doodle eyes and wants some just like hers."

"Where was Richard when Donna was born?"

"Across the street at the bar. He did come over afterwards. He took one look at the baby and bawled like a baby himself. Richard was in my hospital room when the doctor walked in. The doctor said I should let her go. I didn't understand. Let her go? Let her go where? She was going home with me."

Stanley sat up straighter with enhanced vigor. In a steady, almost strong voice, he said, "What did Richard say?"

"He said, he said," Stella choked on the tears now running freely down her face, "he said Donna needed to be put away and forgotten. We'd have a normal baby another time."

"Come here, child," Dad said without hesitation.

Stella came to his bed and stood by his side, shaking. He reached out to her as she collapsed into his arms.

Her father held her as tightly as he was able and lightly rubbed her back. "It's all right now. Don't cry. You will always be my sweet baby girl. There is no way in God's green earth I would ever let you go either."

"Oh, Daddy. Please don't die. Please God, don't let him die."

The sounds of Stella's quiet sobs echoed throughout the chilly room, then only silence. Summoning up the courage he never knew he possessed, Stanley ran his fingers through Stella's hair and said, "My mistakes would be impossible to count. I'm ashamed of myself. I don't know what to say other than I am sorry. Can you forgive an old, stupid man? Oh, my sweet girl, instead of you getting your strong, stubborn, and determined demeanor from me, I suspect I get it from you."

Stella knew immediately that, despite everything, her dad loved her unconditionally, and she loved him. That's the way it had always been and always would be.

Stanley closed his eyes for a full minute. He heard words scrambling inside his head. "In the end, you are the one who must face the consequences of your actions when it pertains to those you love." He took a deep breath, opened his eyes, and stated simply, "I absolutely refuse to go to my maker without meeting my granddaughter. Stella, if you could forgive this fool for his cowardliness, can I see her?"

Stella left the room without a word. She returned only a few minutes later with the two-year-old baby wrapped in the puffy pink baby blanket her friend Veronica had given her. "Donna, meet your grandpa."

Grandpa held the child gently in his arms and didn't speak. There were no more tears. He stroked her cheek while kissing the top of her head. "You are the most wonderful, special baby girl I have ever seen. Don't tell your mama, but that includes her!

"Stella, look at me. Sometimes I think God has some interesting or maybe just odd ways of twisting fate. He gave me a beautiful daughter and an exceptionally beautiful granddaughter. Yet, look at me. I'm no Cary Grant!" They both tried to laugh. "I believe that God has truly sent you an angel."

Chapter 4

1946 – OAKLAND, CALIFORNIA

*A*FEW MORE MINUTES, AND THEY WOULD ALL ESCAPE THIS STEEL contraption Stella felt imprisoned in for the last two days. Oh, the beginning of the journey hadn't been so bad. Getting to know Veronica and some other passengers was pleasant enough. Like so many of the others confined in this rumbling tin can, though, she thought she would explode if she didn't reach fresh air and open spaces soon. Stella couldn't help but notice how the various people on board reacted in anticipation of finally being able to step foot onto solid, unmoving ground, even if they still needed to take the ferry from the terminus in Oakland to San Francisco. Stella sighed to herself while thinking that nerves were raw and everyone around her was exceptionally irritable. Everyone except Veronica, that is. Veronica somehow got to know everyone in the carriage. They had warmed to her over the past couple of days, undoubtedly due to her kind heart and gentle composure. Veronica was often shy as well as unusually friendly. She was the kind of person who could talk to anyone about anything. She listened intently and never monopolized any conversation by talking about herself. Stella envied those traits in her, as did many others, but no one would ever say so. Stella assumed most people just examined the outside definition of a person without considering the whole person. Maybe she was wrong, she thought to herself.

The conductor stumbled down the narrow passageway. Veronica was standing by her seat trying to get her suitcase down from the luggage rack above her.

"Here, let me help you," the man from across the aisle said. He easily leaned over her and grabbed the bag.

"Thank you, Mr. Smith."

"Oh, please! Call me Brian."

"Well, thank you again kind sir...Brian," she said.

Stella looked at her when Veronica sat back down. "Brian? I didn't even know his name was Mr. Smith," Stella said, amused.

The conductor grasped seats on each side of the aisle as the whistle blew and the train screeched toward a final stop. Everyone clapped and cheered.

"Ladies and gentlemen, please remain in your seats until the train has come to a full and complete stop." The conductor strolled straight to Veronica, cleared his throat and said, "Miss, I'm aware that we turned a blind eye and allowed you to sit in this particular carriage car due to the unexpected situation that the colored car was full. However, you must now abide by the rules and wait until everyone departs before you. Then you may gather your things and get on the ferry." He walked quickly toward the back-exit door.

The train was now at a complete stop. Stella jumped up and squeezed past Veronica.

"What are you doing?" Veronica said in a state of bewilderment.

Ignoring her, she turned to the man across the aisle and asked pleasantly, "Please reach my suitcase for me, Mr. Smith."

Mr. Smith looked at her oddly but offered his assistance. As he brought the case down, she grabbed it immediately from his grasp and surreptitiously unhooked the clasp. All her clothes and various other odds and ends came flying out. She gestured to Veronica to move past her without haste.

"Oh, my goodness! How did that happen? I am so embarrassed and so very sorry. Oops, Mr. Smith, please don't look, but

1946 – Oakland, California | 23

an unmentionable garment appears to be on your head. Would you be so kind as to hand those items to me?"

As the other passengers tried to push past the suitcase mishap, each person slowed to a standstill as one by one they became aware of the commotion now ensuing at the exit doorway. The conductor was blocking Veronica's path, but Veronica stood firm. She was now blocking his way as well.

"Okay, lady," the conductor said exasperated. "What's the hold-up? Let these people out." He turned toward Veronica and pointed to a seat. "You sit here."

"Excuse me, Mr. Conductor. Is it possible you might not be aware of the new law recently enacted?" Stella raised her voice to be heard over the confused rumblings of the passengers.

"What law are you talking about?"

"Why, Public Law 69-132, of course."

The conductor rubbed his closed eyelids and yawned as if he were uninterested. "And, pray tell, what exactly is that?"

Stella looked around and noticed all eyes were on her including Veronica, who appeared dumbfounded. She continued, "Public Law 69-132 is called the Passengers on the Train Act. Surely you must know about this important legal requirement. It would be incomprehensible that this train company would hire an employee who wasn't aware of the current railway laws. My goodness."

He stared at her and everyone else but did not give her a yes or no response.

Stella was not finished, "This new law states that when two young ladies of opposite color are on the same train, they may exit at the same time and with everyone else and in no particular order."

The conductor looked skeptical and guffawed, "That is ridiculous."

Mr. Smith broke in, "I've heard of it."

The knitting lady said, "I have as well."

The man who had been sitting in the front row added emphatically, "Doesn't this train company give you any training? This is common knowledge now for anyone who keeps up with the times."

All the other passengers nodded and added their agreement.

The conductor turned abruptly and exited the train while saying flatly, "Fine. Have it your way."

Stella grinned and moved aside. Veronica and the others left the train. Being the last to exit, Stella finally jumped down the last step of the train compartment. Veronica was standing a short distance away waiting for her. Veronica waved and smiled.

"A new law?" Veronica asked.

"Well, if there isn't one, there should be," Stella answered with a twinkle in her eye.

Chapter 5

1946 – SAN FRANCISCO, CALIFORNIA

STELLA FIGURED IF IT WORKED ONCE, IT WOULD WORK AGAIN.

"Come on, Veronica. Let's go find that boardinghouse." She hooked her arm through Veronica's, and they strolled contently amongst the crowd. "I wrote down the address from the advertisement I saw in the *San Francisco Chronicle*."

"We will need to catch a taxicab, but I really don't think…" she hesitated and didn't finish her thought. She was pretty sure no taxi would take them together.

Ignoring the comment, Stella focused on her new friend with a gleam in her eyes. "I have always wanted to try something I saw in a movie once," she said. "Wait by the wall. I'll go to the roadside curb."

Stella lifted her skirt slightly and reached down to straighten the lined hem on her hose at the back of her calf. Three taxi cabs screeched to a stop. One pulled in front of the others and stopped right next to Stella. A middle-aged man wearing a cap, with a plaid shirt loosely tucked into baggy trousers, jumped out, licked two fingers, and smoothed the tiny mustache on his thin upper lip. Grinning he said, "Where are you headed, Miss? I'll be happy to assist you."

"You are awfully kind, sir, thank you."

"Let me put your suitcase in the trunk."

As he was doing so, Stella motioned Veronica to come over.

"This one, too, please," motioning to Veronica's case.

"Wait a minute, here. What's this all about then?" the driver squinted his eyes in anger. "I don't drive the likes of her around."

The driver went back around to the trunk and reached in with the obvious intention of removing the case.

Stella put a hand on his arm and said in a low voice, while surreptitiously glancing back and forth toward her friend, "You see, it's like this. That young woman and I were on the same train. We made a bet. I won. I tried to collect my wager, but she told me she had no money. If I truly wanted to receive my winnings, I'd have to obtain it from her brother when we got to San Francisco. So now I need to take her to her brother's house to keep her honest. Have you ever been in a position of possibly being cheated out of your earnings?"

Before he could answer, she handed him a scrap of paper with the address on it.

Without even looking at it, he exclaimed, "Hey, I ain't going into that kind of neighborhood."

Stella thought she might lose the battle, so she broke through his thoughts and blurted out, "I suppose you listen to the radio a lot? Read the newspaper? You look like you're a well-informed person."

The man wrinkled his brow in confusion. "Well, yes, I suppose you could say that, but..."

"Then obviously you're aware of the recent law called Public Law 76-176?"

"Huh?"

"Public Law 76-176 is The Taxi Passenger Act." Her face brightened as if it was the most obvious statement ever mentioned.

The cabby tilted his head somewhat while asking, "Remind me again about that one. We're told so many news items it's hard to keep track."

"Well, yes, of course. How can anyone take it all in, I say."

During this interchange, she motioned Veronica to put her luggage in the trunk.

"Public Law 76-176 simply states that when two young

ladies of opposite color are headed to the same location, it is permissible to allow them to ride together in the same taxicab."

"Now, wait a minute here. No one told me about…"

He stopped abruptly as Stella waved to a policeman, "Oh, Mr. Policeman, sir, could you come and tell this man about the new law?" Stella was pretty sure the officer couldn't hear her. The taxi driver wasn't so sure, however.

"Never mind," the man whined, "I don't need no trouble. Just get in already. But, no talking and no touching anything. Got it?"

Stella pushed Veronica in first and jumped in rapidly while closing the door at the same time. The car took off in a flash.

The women looked at each other. "Well, if there isn't one, there should be," they both mouthed in hushed tones and laughed again.

While forty-five minutes crept by, the fog had rolled in and around their car. It nearly blinded them and quite possibly the driver too. It felt strangely cold and eerie. No one said a word for the entire trip. The driver inched his way down what the women hoped was the correct street. They did not notice any other cars or houses or people. They couldn't see much of anything. A tunnel of murky gray nothingness appeared before them. The cab driver seemed oblivious to the situation, but the women were almost in a state of panic.

"How much longer, sir? Can you actually see anything?" Stella inquired.

"Shush! Can't you tell I'm driving? Noisy females!" he growled.

"I can't see anything," Veronica whispered to Stella.

"We're just about there," the driver said, tightening his grip on the steering wheel. "It's just around the corner."

"Oh, thank heavens."

The car came to a complete stop.

"You can get out now," the cabby instructed them as he opened his door and got out of his seat.

The ladies opened their own doors and stepped onto the

sidewalk. They walked around to the back of the taxi to retrieve their luggage when the driver opened the trunk.

"Are you sure this is the right place? This is a pretty swanky neighborhood," the cab driver said as he looked around suspiciously.

Veronica tried to speak to him this time instead of Stella. "Well, let me explain, um…"

Stella jumped in, asserting, "Her brother is what we call in Chicago a mobster."

Veronica gave a shocked intake of breath and hissed dramatically, "Stella, that wasn't to be revealed! Bugsy will be so upset."

She turned to the man for further discussion, but he had grabbed the five-dollar bill Stella had been holding in her hand. He raced back into the driver's seat and took off like a speeding bullet.

Stella put her arm through Veronica's and grinned, "Hey, you are getting pretty good at this!"

"I have an unusual teacher," she replied.

Chapter 6

1946 – SAN FRANCISCO, CALIFORNIA

THE FOG DIDN'T SEEM SO DENSE ONCE THEY STARTED WALKING down the sidewalk. It appeared to be clearing somewhat as they searched the neighboring houses to find the address they were looking for. They knew they were on the correct street, but it was difficult to detect the house numbers.

"That's it!" Stella shrieked.

"Mercy me," Veronica gasped, her eyes wide open.

Ahead of them stood the must unusually beautiful house that either of them had ever seen.

"Is that a house or Sleeping Beauty's castle?" Stella suggested in a state of bewilderment.

"I wondered the exact same thing," Veronica said. "This can't be it."

The house dated from another time period. Stella thought it could very well have been built by an eccentric back in the last century. It was an unapologetic pink three-story Victorian-style mansion. There were turrets and balconies and flowers galore. The ladies were stunned.

Veronica was close to tears. "Now what?" she asked. "No one will let me stay here. Even if you try one of your tricks, I can't afford this!"

Stella was unconvinced, "A new law?"

"I guess it can't hurt to try. What do we have to lose?" Veronica acquiesced.

"That's the spirit. Let's go check it out!"

Stella was excited, but she could tell that Veronica was not as confident. Both women walked up the steps with newfound determination. The huge wooden door had carved etchings with an oversized door knocker that looked like a lion's head. Together they put their hands on the lion and knocked once, twice, three times. Silence. Just when they turned to leave, feeling discouraged, the door slowly creaked open.

"Yes, may I help you?"

Both young women stood transfixed. It was Sleeping Beauty's castle all right and this was the wicked old witch.

The lady was even tinier than Stella or Veronica. She leaned on a cane carved with a cat's head in one hand and held a knitted shawl around her shoulders with her other hand. The darkness made it difficult to discern her facial features and her age. She had totally white hair tightly bound in a French twist at the back of her head. Odder still was the fact that her skin was even whiter than her hair. It was as if she had never seen the light of day. The sun had never tanned any part of her. On the bridge of her nose rested a pair of tiny wire-rimmed glasses. She appeared to squint as she repeated, "Yes?"

Stella smiled widely and calmly said, "We are inquiring about rooms to rent. Is this the boarding house that we saw in a newspaper advertisement?"

"Why yes it is. I had completely forgotten. You see, dearies, my memory isn't quite what it used to be. What is it you want?" she laughed.

"Rooms to rent?"

"Yes, I was having my little joke. Please, please do come in," the lady said as she pushed the door fully open.

"Oh, good gracious, what a beautifully charming home," Veronica said as she gazed with wonder at the elaborately furnished house.

In Stella's mind, however, she could only think that this old lady was perhaps from another century as well. Yet both girls would soon discover that appearances can be deceiving.

"I'm so sorry. Forgive my manners. I didn't introduce myself. My name is Elsie Starr. And you are?"

"So very nice to make your acquaintance, Mrs. Starr. My name is Veronica Boyd, and this is my friend, Stella Kluskowski."

"Oh, please. I insist you call me Elsie. I'm very happy to meet two such lovely ladies. Why are you here?" she laughed again.

"Dorothy, Dorothy dear," Elsie called out. "Please bring our guests some tea."

Within seconds Dorothy appeared through the French doors. Dorothy was as dark skinned as Veronica and a good ten years her senior. It was immediately apparent that Dorothy was confident and friendly, showing no airs or feelings of mistrust. She greeted the newcomers with kindness. She offered to hang up their coats while asking if they liked milk, sugar, or lemon with their tea. Veronica and Stella watched her leave. Stella said to no one in particular, "She is awfully sweet and quite lovely."

"Yes, and very helpful to me as well," Elsie said, smiling. "I'm assuming you were talking about Dorothy, or maybe my ears were stinging with compliments for me alone."

The young women looked at each other very embarrassed but laughed as well. "It was meant for both."

"I have lived here my entire life. A few years ago, I convinced Dorothy to come live here. She helps me out now and then."

"Very kind of her," Stella said.

Veronica looked a bit shy, but took another quick breath and said bluntly, "We would love to rent rooms from you, Mrs. Starr, but we don't have a lot of money."

"Now, now, I told you to call me Elsie. Let me think..."

Elsie Starr didn't have a moment to complete her thought as Stella quickly jumped in, "We will both be looking for jobs. We could share a room and the rent if that would be agreeable to you."

Both girls waited quietly for her response or maybe her reaction. At that moment, Dorothy walked in with a tray of tea items. It was an exquisite set of matching china unlike anything either girl had ever seen. Veronica was hesitant about reaching for the tea pot and cup for fear she would drop and shatter it.

The elderly woman poured out the tea while saying, "Here, do let me help. Lemon or milk?"

"Lemon, please."

"Milk for me. Thank you." Veronica hesitated, then added, "Thank you, Elsie."

"Well, I just so happen to have a nice large room with two twin beds in it," Elsie said, "It's called the Peacock Room. It's just right for best friends. Would you be able to split $8.00 a week for rent?"

Stella almost spilled her tea. Veronica's mouth fell open. Both girls were stunned. Stella almost shouted out, but at the last moment she contained herself and said, "Yes, please!"

"Then it's all settled. Dorothy, will you show them to the Peacock Room, please?"

To the newcomers, she said, "Come back to finish your tea and have a bit of a chat with me after you take your things up. You can settle in later."

Dorothy led the way up the grand freshly polished stairway. Stella said conversationally, "Do you like working here?"

"Oh, I don't really work here. I'm a teacher actually," Dorothy said. "You see, that lovely lady downstairs is my grandmother."

Chapter 7

1957 – CHICAGO, ILLINOIS

The morning after Stella's emotional turmoil with her father, stillness filled the house. The morning sunlight squeezed through the open blinds from the upstairs hallway window. Stella quietly descended the stairway with Donna in her arms. Rosie flew past her jumping down each step, deliberately awakening the atmosphere with her gleeful exuberance.

"Ma, where are you?" Stella called out.

"What's all the racket?" Stella's sister said, putting down her crocheting and glaring up toward the stairs.

"Oh, Kathy, there you are."

"It's Kathleen, not Kathy," she responded to no one in particular.

"Hi, Auntie Katie," Rosie interrupted with a slight smirk pasted to her face.

"Oh, you are a little monster!" Kathleen winced.

"I am *not* little!" Rosie protested vehemently as she stood quite erect with her little fists firmly planted on her hips. "Mommy says I'm a big girl now!"

"When are you going to teach that child some manners?" Kathleen preached to Stella.

"I can teach myself," Rosie said stoically as she continued to protest.

"Kathy, I mean Kathleen, would you please watch Rosie and Donna for me, so I can go visit Veronica?" Stella asked.

"Why in heaven's name would you ever want to go to that filthy, flea-bitten rat's nest tenement house in the Negro district?" Kathleen sneered.

"Can I go, Mommy?" Rosie grinned at her aunt Katie.

"I'm absolutely sure that Veronica must keep her apartment sparkling clean. I know she was adamant about cleanliness when we shared a room together in San Francisco all those years ago."

"And that's another thing," Kathleen persisted. "Living with a colored person. What were you thinking?"

"Well, unlike you, I didn't need to think about it. At least Veronica has a place of her own. She doesn't live with her parents still," Stella argued.

"You are wretched! No wonder Rosie is a pill!" Kathleen almost shouted.

Stella glared at her and was just about to retaliate when Ma walked into the middle of their confrontation. "That's enough, girls. Go ahead, Stella. I'll watch the children."

"I can show Auntie Katie how to take care of Donna," said Rosie. "I'll give her lessons. Then she'll be ready when she has a Donna, too."

"Heaven help me," Kathleen moaned as she returned to her crocheting.

"Stella?" Ma continued just as Stella was going to the door, "Please invite Veronica and her family for Sunday dinner with us."

"Dinner?" Kathy gasped, "You can't be serious! It's bad enough Stella takes the entire day to cross over into the bad side of town, now she's bringing it back with her!"

"Kathy! Do not talk like that. I won't have it. I can invite whomever I like, and I happen to like Veronica and her family," Ma said. "They have visited a few times over the years when you were at work. Now you'll be able to get to know them. This will be nice."

"Don't I have any say in this? I live here, too," Kathy said angrily, wondering why her family couldn't just stay with their own kind.

"Of course you do," Ma answered, "Please invite your friends over for dinner Sunday, too. We'll have a small party. Your dad could use a little excitement."

"You can't be serious," Kathy said, "His heart will stop from the shock!"

"It would be better than starving from stomach cancer," Stella said irritably as she gave her mother a quick hug and walked out the front door.

Chapter 8

1957 – CHICAGO, ILLINOIS

It would take three bus transfers before Stella reached the south side of Chicago where Veronica now lived with her husband Bill, their twin boys, and her mother Barbara. Stella didn't really mind the journey. The day was clear and bright, which finally matched her mood to perfection. Just being able to escape her parents' house, even for a short time, felt like a long-awaited freedom. She had time to reflect on times past and purposely ignore times to come. She'd been in Chicago for only a few days, yet in many ways it felt like she had never left. She marveled at all the changes while wondering when and why they had happened. The bus jostled to a stop. Stella looked around anxiously. She took a deep breath and told herself that the best thing about this side of town was that she would see Veronica again. She jumped down the steps of the bus, smiling at everyone she saw. The sea of colorful faces turned away and let her pass by. Stella shrugged without comment and strolled the three blocks to reach Veronica's apartment. As she rounded the corner, she saw Veronica sitting on the steps of a group of apartment buildings that appeared all stuck together like cereal boxes lined up evenly on a grocery shelf. Veronica was wearing a black and white polka-dotted dress with a thin red belt cinched tightly around her middle. Her hair was pulled back with a bright red scarf wrapped around her head and tied with a big bow at the side. Her hands were folded neatly on her lap. She looked up.

Stella cried, "Veronica!"

Veronica jumped up and raced down the steps as Stella ran the last few yards to reach her. They embraced with a friendship filled with unforgotten memories.

"Mercy me. How long has it been?" Veronica said as she wiped the tears from her eyes.

"Seems like yesterday. You haven't changed a bit. How are Bill and the twins?" Stella asked while blinking back tears as they gradually released their hold on each other.

"I guess we shouldn't stand in the middle of the street in such close proximity or people will talk," Veronica said, laughing slightly.

"Talk? Not likely!" Stella continued, "Have you noticed? No one is even looking. Every time we have ever been together in the past, no matter where we are, no one says a word. Absolute silence."

"Just until they get to know us. I don't think it's silence, really. We just don't hear them. I'm sure people turn away, undoubtedly talking behind our backs," Veronica said.

"How do you know that?"

"When someone stops talking as we go past, their thoughts seem to scream in my head. I wonder how long it will be before those thoughts explode into actions."

"I think it may be happening more than we know. We just need to pay attention. In fact, I'd like someone to pay attention to me sometimes," Stella was on a roll now.

"Do you have a bee in your bonnet again? Before we know it, you'll start a new law." Veronica looked at her through blurry eyes.

"Not a bad idea, if I do say so myself." They both laughed.

Veronica took Stella's arm and sat down on the stairs.

"Speaking of bonnets, what is that on your head?" Stella asked inquisitively. Maybe you should design scarves now."

"That's a good idea, since I can't find anyone even remotely interested in my hats. I think the hat craze has ended. I just don't see a lot of women wearing them anymore and certainly not in this neighborhood."

After only a short silence, Veronica changed the subject, "How is your dad?"

"The cancer is eating away at him. No one really knows how long he has. We walk around and talk as if our grief is stuck in our throats trying in vain to hide. I did talk to him yesterday," Stella stared through the mist in her eyes, lost in her thoughts, "It was about Donna. At first, he refused to meet her. Do you believe it? His own granddaughter and he didn't even want to see her. He said that he didn't understand about handicapped children."

"But, did he?"

"Yes. It was good in the end. I truly believe that he looked at her with love in his eyes. How could you not see her without an overwhelming love pouring out of you? If he had more time, he would be able to watch her grow up and discover a love beyond expectations. Sometimes I think that people just don't understand. If they could just gaze into another's soul, they would understand and accept one's differences."

"Maybe then we wouldn't have so much silence. Or, maybe there would be too much noise," Veronica added. "Mercy me, we have become quite the philosophers."

"I'd love some lemonade. Do you have any?" Stella asked.

"You read my mind," Veronica grinned and went inside. Stella waited on the steps and let her thoughts float away.

Veronica returned with three empty glasses and her mother, Barbara Boyd, close on her heels carrying a pitcher of freshly made lemonade. Stella stood up as the screen door clanged shut.

Barbara looked at Stella, opened her arms wide, and cried, "Glory be to God. My, oh my, you haven't changed a bit. Just about seven years ago, I'd judge. We've surely missed you, child." Barbara filled all three glasses with the lemonade. She gave one to Stella, then handed another to Veronica while keeping the last for herself. Veronica raised her glass, followed by the other two, and toasted, "Friendship always and unconditionally, no matter how long we've been apart." They clinked glasses.

"I came back for Veronica's wedding in 1950 and a few months later, it was my turn."

"Do you remember how horrified my father was when he discovered that you were standing up for me at my wedding? It was just at the Justice of the Peace, but you would have thought I was getting married in St. Paul's Cathedral," Veronica sighed. "Oh, he ranted and raved and declared all sorts of misfortune would befall us!"

"I remember it well."

"In the end, it wasn't your downfall, it was his," Veronica's mother said without a tone of regret in her voice.

"Oh, Barbara, surely you do not believe that Veronica's marriage caused his death? That's not fair," Stella scolded her.

"Well, no, not exactly. But it wasn't too long after the wedding that he stayed out all night drinking at the local tavern. We were told that he passed out just down the road. At approximately four in the morning, he managed to get himself up and sauntered across the street. A milk truck came around the corner and hit him. It was fast. It was sudden. The police said that he was dead before he even knew what happened." Veronica put her arm around her mother but did not say a word.

Stella looked at Barbara sincerely, "My wedding was only a month later. I told you that I would postpone it, but you absolutely refused. I tried and tried to convince you that we could wait, but you just wouldn't have it."

Barbara continued with undeniable strength, "Veronica's father had caused enough problems in our lifetime and this time I absolutely refused to allow him to cause any more after his death. I never completely understood why I didn't have the courage to defy him years ago but was able to after his death."

"You know something, Mama," Veronica sighed, "you sometimes say the oddest things. I don't think I ever gave you much credit for the inner strength that you truly have."

Stella looked at Barbara but spoke to Veronica, "Your mother is certainly amazing. She came unapologetically to my wedding wearing not black but that beautiful lilac gown."

"I was so very proud that my daughter was your Matron of Honor as you were hers," Barbara added.

"It was strange, though. Mama and I were the only black people there. Oh, and Dorothy. No one talked to any of us," Veronica added with a shrug.

"I did."

"Well, of course you did. You wouldn't have been able to find your way down the aisle if you hadn't asked me!" Veronica smiled.

"If I would have known others, there would have been many more interesting colors in the church, just like flavors in an ice cream store," Stella grinned.

"As I remember, you only like vanilla and chocolate!"

"Maybe if I just tried something else, I might have liked it," Stella chuckled.

Veronica shook her head and laughed, "Oh, my. I'll never forget your days of selling ice cream"

"I had to push that horrible cart and ring a bell while at the same time yell, 'Ice cream, ice cream, we all scream for ice cream.' And they all came screaming!"

"That might have been one of your longest jobs," Veronica added.

"Unfortunately, long enough for me to gain ten pounds. I doubt that I made any money because my boss wasn't happy that there wasn't any chocolate or vanilla when he came by for an inspection. I told him that I was only tasting it for freshness. He made me pay for the product. And that was that!"

Stella and Veronica sat quietly enjoying their time together. Nothing felt strained or hurried. Although it had been seven years since they had last seen each other, it could have been yesterday. They knew about each other's lives from their frequent letters, but nothing could really replace just sitting silently next to each other and knowing without any doubt that their unconditional friendship would last a lifetime.

Lost in her thoughts, Veronica laughed, "We were so young."

"Too young or too impulsive?" Barbara queried.

Laughing harder now, Veronica ignored her and went on, "I will never, ever forget how Stella and I met our future husbands."

"That was a little embarrassing."

"A little?" Veronica shook her head while continuing to laugh. "It was all because you couldn't keep a job."

"I tried. I really did. I have never been one to give up, but work doesn't like me," Stella moaned.

"You and your job skills leave something to be desired. My goodness, you sure had a unique string of bizarre opportunities."

Now Stella laughed, too.

Chapter 9

1947 – SAN FRANCISCO, CALIFORNIA

*I*T HAD BEEN ONE YEAR SINCE STELLA AND VERONICA HAD DISCOVered the comfortable boarding house that they were now proud to call home. Stella sat up in her bed and absentmindedly removed the bobby pins she had used to set her hair the night before. She stared at the morning sunlight pushing its way through the half-opened blinds casting geometric designs on the floor and opposite wall. Stella was lost in her confused reflections of how one's moods might possibly correspond to the weather. Two weeks ago, the days were cloudy and gray; nevertheless she had remained hopeful and excited about her new job. Today, however, she felt despondent and discouraged since she had lost another employment opportunity. Still, the sun burst through the dimness of yesterday ready to start again. She wasn't so sure.

"Stella, why aren't you up and ready to go?" Veronica admonished while sitting at the vanity adjusting her hat.

Stella jumped out of her meditative state and looked at Veronica. "That's another nice hat. I'm surprised you haven't tried to sell any yet."

"Oh, I tried, but failed miserably."

"You didn't tell me about this. What happened?"

"I brought my entire box of hat creations to school one day. I opened them up in the teachers' lounge. Just as I was pulling one out to show some of the staff, the principal walked in. He walked over to me, glanced inside the box, and asked what I was doing. I told him I hoped someone might be interested in buying one of my handcrafted hats. He glared at me. He told me his school was not a department store and if I wanted to sell hats, I should work at a ladies' apparel counter, not as a teacher's aide in his school!"

"Ouch!"

Veronica sighed, "I absolutely love my job at Lincoln Elementary School. I'm still overwhelmed at my unbelievably good luck when Dorothy suggested that I apply for the job only a week after we moved in here. I would never jeopardize that. So, I guess I will put my hats in the back of the closet."

Stella raised herself out of bed, walked over to the vanity, and stood behind Veronica, "I could sell them."

"You have enough to worry about. Don't you have another interview today?"

"Yes, I'm going to be a nurse!"

"A nurse? I'm pretty sure you need some training for that. I think you need a college degree."

"Well, maybe not quite a nurse. The ad said an assistant."

"A nurse's aide?"

"An assistant to the nurse's aide, actually. Or maybe it was an assistant to an assistant to an assistant," Stella smiled.

"You have to start somewhere," Veronica laughed. "I'll meet you downstairs at breakfast. Don't be too long."

Sunlight flooded the room as Stella pushed open the kitchen door. Elsie, Dorothy, and Veronica were sitting at the oblong Formica table idly chatting while drinking tea and munching on homemade apple muffins.

Elsie looked up cheerfully when she saw Stella, "Come in, my dear girl."

Stella pulled out the remaining chair and sat down. Her

despondency must have been obvious as all three women were looking at her with concern in their eyes.

"I'm okay, really," she said.

Elsie sat up as straight as she was physically able and looked at the ladies with venom in her eyes, "It's the horrible Mr. Sleazy situation, I would wager!"

Stella sighed as if her world had collapsed, "I wasn't a real secretary. I tried to bluff my way through it, but in the end, I didn't really know what I was doing."

"Since when has that ever stopped you?" Veronica inquired.

Dorothy jumped in, "What did happen at that job, by the way?"

Stella knew she wouldn't be able to leave for her next interview any time soon if she didn't confide in her friends.

"When Mr. Measly interviewed me to be his personal secretary, he asked me if I knew shorthand. Of course, I said yes. I had never heard of shorthand before. I expected that I would have to take notes and write very fast. I would leave out the ifs, ands, and buts and put it all back in when I typed up whatever he wanted me to type. I didn't know how to type, either. How hard could it be, I asked myself? I would find the letters on the typewriter and push down on the keys. I would learn."

"You managed to get the job, though," Dorothy said.

"Yes, but I don't think he truly cared about my skills for the job. He seemed to be looking at my legs the entire time. Maybe I just imagined that. I'm not sure."

"What happened next?" Elsie asked.

"Mr. Measly sat at his chair behind his desk and tapped his fingers together as if he was playing a musical rhythm in his head. He was probably around fifty years old. It was difficult to determine his height and weight as his desk blocked my view. His hair was loosely combed over his head until it reached his eyebrows. His tiny round eyes stared at me for a long time until I felt slightly uncomfortable sitting in the tall chair in front of him. I looked around nervously and focused on a framed photo of a horse-faced woman.

"'That's a very nice photo of your mother,' I said and

immediately realized my mistake when I saw the look of annoyance on his face. I don't know why the word mother came out of my mouth instead of wife. I was so embarrassed; I couldn't say anything except 'sorry' as I got up to leave.

"'Where are you going?' Mr. Measly asked me.

"I told him again I was sorry to have wasted his time and thanked him for the opportunity. Abruptly he stood up and told me I could start right away. With a peculiar smirk he led me to my desk and said he would dictate a letter right after he called his mother."

"You worked for him for about two weeks, I remember," Veronica said.

"Yes, but it got more and more uncomfortable."

"I remember your last day there when you came home crying," Elsie added. "From what little information we were able to ascertain from you, there is good reason to call him Mr. Sleazy."

"I had told you some issues prior to that. He would touch my back often or try to stroke my hair, but I'd move away quickly and ignore him. But, yesterday, my last day, was the worst."

Dorothy got up from her chair and went to the stove. She filled the teapot with more hot water and tea. As she was pouring the steaming liquid into Stella's cup, she said, "What did Mr. Sleaze do?"

Stella rubbed her brow while she continued the story. "I was trying in vain to type one of his prolific letters when a cold chill went down my back. Mr. Measly was standing right behind me with his face on my neck. The first thing I noticed was his foul cigarette-laced breath blowing in my ear. As he put one hand through my hair and the other one down my blouse, I jumped up. I inadvertently hit the bottom of his chin causing him to bite down hard on his tongue. He yelled out as I turned around sharply. My elbow accidentally hit his nose. Droplets of blood cascaded downwards, causing dark reddish ringlets to form on the white paper like pebbles falling from a hillside to meet a calm clear pond below. He choked on some swear words while twisting the sleeve of his shirt up toward his bleeding nose. I grabbed my handbag from under my desk, backed out toward the door, and took my hat and coat off the hall tree."

Veronica clenched her teeth, "Did you confront him or say anything?"

"Without looking back, I walked briskly down the hallway and shouted, 'If you had any intentions of firing me, don't bother, I already quit!' I heard applause from the secretarial pool as I slammed the exit door."

Dorothy looked aghast, "There needs to be some agency or someone that you can report him to!"

"That would be nice, but in the end, he holds all the cards. Nothing would happen," Stella sighed.

Elsie put down her cup and said, "Girls, you need to know one thing. Foul men like him might hold all the cards, but you hold the chips. Grab all the chips, cash in, and get out. If you see anyone going in, warn them to stay out of the game!"

Chapter 10

1957 – CHICAGO, ILLINOIS

"What you girls laughing about?"

"Hello, Mad Molly. I'd like to introduce you to my friend, Stella," Veronica said with a smile.

Stella fell silent as she gazed up in astonishment at a rotund woman who was stuffed into what looked like a paisley tablecloth woven around her and tied with a section of a frayed clothesline. Stella tried not to stare at her elongated bosom that she was sure had never been captured in a brassiere. She was black as the night sky with two star-like eyes that blazed straight through Stella, seemingly able to detect her every thought. Stella felt hot with embarrassment and at the same time mortified when she opened her mouth and unwanted words dropped out, "Do they call you Mad Molly because you are angry or just crazy?" Stella slapped a hand over her mouth. *Had she just said that? How could she be so rude? When would she ever learn to hold her tongue? Why were there no screens to her thoughts, only outbursts? Veronica must be so disappointed in her.*

As Stella was wordlessly beating herself up with hidden emotions, she was unaware that Veronica, Barbara, and Mad Molly were laughing hard.

"Hey, Harold, get your bottom over here!" Mad Molly shouted to a tall, lanky middle-aged man across the street. He sauntered over without regard to any possible traffic. His gruff, dirty face focused directly at Stella as he drawled, "Now who this white lady?"

"This here is Veronica's famous Stella."

"You don't say. Well, well, this is a good day!" Harold turned his head back from where he came from and yelled, "Dixie, Dixie! Grab some beers and get yourself over here. Bring Big Tommy. We got ourselves a celebrity!"

"What?" Stella stuttered as she focused her attention on Veronica.

"I may have told one or two friends and neighbors a little bit about your escapades."

"Oh, Veronica. You didn't? I'm not that interesting." She noticed the growing crowd smiling with anticipation at her. "How much did you tell them?"

"Oh, I don't know. Maybe one or two or three little stories," she answered.

"Is that Veronica with her unusual white friend?" another woman strolled up to them, firmly gripping the hands of identical twin girls. The girls were eagerly trying to pull away as their mother scolded, "Take care and just stay close. Do not scare that stray dog down the road again. You hear me?"

"Yes, Mama," they replied sweetly in unison. Just as quickly, they both escaped and ran in the opposite direction.

"My, my, Gladys, those sweet baby girls of yours are getting so big!" Mad Molly said.

"Too big for their britches, I'd say," Gladys added.

Before Veronica had time to finish greeting and introducing everyone who came by, a small group had gathered around demanding to hear about one of her exploits, as Veronica called them.

Stella sighed. "I don't think my tales are exactly exciting," she tried to explain to the neighbors.

"Oh, honey child," cried Mad Molly, "No one here has one of those new-fangled television boxes and the radio can be downright dull. You are the next best thing to liven up a boring, gray day!"

1957 – CHICAGO, ILLINOIS | 49

Harold leaned against the stone wall next to the steps and beamed broadly, "My favorite is Stella as a ballpark vendor selling my favorite beverage."

"No, no," Mad Molly nudged Harold, "Never you mind. We will get to that, but I want to hear the one where you took over the hospital."

Everyone laughed as Stella took a deep breath and closed her eyes.

Chapter 11
1948 – SAN FRANCISCO, CALIFORNIA

STELLA STOOD TRANSFIXED AS SHE GAZED WITH TREPIDATION AT the ominous building just a block away. The tall frightening building stretched over an entire city block. The Notre Dame Catholic Hospital had been opened recently by the Sisters of Mercy as a haven for the sick and weary, but in Stella's mind, it was a place where her demons lived. How could something be considered a place occupied by future saints when it looked like the devil's habitat? She knew that wasn't fair, but hospitals had always scared her. Many years ago, when she was only a small child, her older sister, Sylvia, had to have her tonsils out. For some unknown reason that was never explained by anyone, her parents and the doctor felt it would be a good idea to remove Stella's at the same time. Stella had never had a sore throat, let alone tonsil problems that would necessitate surgery. But she was put in a bed next to Sylvia. The next thing she remembered she was sucking on a root beer Popsicle. It might not have been a horrible experience, except that her other sister, Kathy, had told her to say the Act of Contrition because she was doomed to die. She never ate a Popsicle again.

Now she didn't know how she was going to enter what her subconscious deemed a dreaded haunted house, and even more worrisome, how could she possibly work there? Still, she was running very short on money. Veronica told her that she would take care of the rent for them both, but Stella was not going to allow her to do that. She was determined to find employment that she could do. Hospitals did good deeds. She could do good deeds. With a deep breath, Stella crossed the street and entered the building.

Directly in front of Stella, as she pushed hard to open the door, stood an elderly woman behind an information counter. The woman had to be in her seventies or eighties as evidenced by her tightly curled gray hair and abundant wrinkles. Her brightly colored flower-patterned dress was buttoned from the bodice down to just inches above her sturdy flat shoes.

"May I help you?" the woman looked at her with a smile pasted on her face.

Stella jumped. Her immediate thought was to turn around and ask for her ice cream job back, but with newfound determination and a bit of tenacity, she walked straight to the woman and opened her mouth. Nothing came out.

"Yes, miss? Are you here to visit someone?"

"No, I'm..." she stopped and looked around before saying directly, "I have an appointment with Mrs. Witty. For a job. I hope she is Witty. I mean, is she amusing?" Now she knew she was rambling.

"Names can be deceptive," the lady answered mysteriously.

"Oh? I am sorry. I don't know why I said that. I am terribly nervous. Witty is a very respectable name I am sure."

"She expects to be addressed as Head Nurse Witty, by the way."

"Oh?"

"Do you know where her office is?"

"No."

"You sure you want to work here?"

"No. I mean, yes."

"Just go up the stairs to the fourth floor. The elevator isn't working. Turn right and walk all the way to the end of the corridor. Turn left. Her office is the third door on the right," she instructed. Noticing Stella hadn't left yet, she continued as if she were talking to a small child, "Do you think you can do that?"

"Yes, thank you," Stella responded. She turned around and headed toward the elevator.

"The elevator is not working, my dear. Use the stairs," the lady instructed again, shaking her head.

Stella walked up the stairs. She felt very foolish because now she couldn't remember anything that woman had told her. Was it the third or fourth floor? Turn left or right? She just didn't know. Luckily when she was on the fourth-floor landing, a young nun was skipping down the stairs.

"Excuse me. I'm sorry to bother you, but I'm having difficulty finding Mrs. Witty's office," Stella asked the nun.

Did Stella imagine it or did the nun chuckle? The nun told Stella to follow her. She led the way to the office door that Stella had been searching for. "This is it. Good luck."

How did this nun know she was going to be interviewed for a job? Well, she is a nun. Maybe she gets her orders from a higher being, Stella chuckled to herself. Stella put her hand on the doorknob and froze. How was she supposed to address Mrs. Witty? Was she to be called Mrs. or Nurse or Mother Superior or Your Honor? *No,* not that. This was not a court of law. She just couldn't remember. But her name was Witty, so it shouldn't be so difficult. Mrs. Witty would probably have a great sense of humor if she heard how confused she was.

"Who by God's good name is standing outside my door muttering? Come in, come in already," a heavy deep female voice commanded.

Stella opened the door a crack and peered inside, "Hello, I'm looking for Mrs. Witty, Nurse Witty."

"I am Head Nurse Witty. What is it you want? I don't have all day," she snapped.

"My name is Stella Kluskowski. I have an appointment for a position at this hospital."

The large expressionless woman behind the desk squinted at her, "Oh, dear. Look what the cat brought in now. A position, you say?"

Stella felt herself shaking as she barely got the words out, "Yes, to assist the nurses."

"This position, as you call it, is just an assistant's assistant. A do anything and everything girl. But *only* do what you are told," she dramatically emphasized the word *only*. "Is that completely understood?"

"Umm, yes. I think so."

"What is there possibly to think about? You do exactly as you are told and absolutely nothing else!"

"Yes."

"I guess beggars can't be choosers. We are very short handed. Just this morning a patient asked *me* to get her a magazine. *Me*, can you believe it? I knew I had to hire someone right away. And, now you walk in. Timing is everything. You are hired."

"Oh, yes, please. Thank you, Mrs. Witty."

"First of all, my name is Head Nurse Witty. Practice it!"

"Thank you, Head Nurse Witty."

"There are uniforms in the supply room. Find one that fits you and put it on. Report back to me in five minutes."

Stella ran out of the room and immediately dashed back in.

"Are you daft, girl? What do you want?"

"I'm so sorry, but I don't know where the supply room is."

"It is across the hall. Please be more observant. Now go. I'm very busy." Head Nurse Witty dismissed her with an abrupt wave of her hand.

Stella found a dress, quickly put it on, and crammed her old clothes into her purse. She raced back across the hallway to her new boss's office.

"Oh, my lord. What were you thinking?" Head Nurse Witty gasped.

"I found a uniform and put it on as you said," Stella squeaked.

"Not an RN nurse's uniform. You are not a nurse. And, don't put on the LPN uniform, either. Nor the candy striper," she shook her head in disbelief. "Three minutes!"

Stella had no idea what the initials stood for, nor what uniform she should put on, but she immediately backed out of the office and opened the door to the supply room to try to figure it out. The nun who helped her before was just inside the room.

"I figured that you might need a little assistance." She handed Stella a gray cleaning staff uniform.

She looked forlornly at the nun and said, "I am to be an assistant to the cleaning woman?"

"Possibly. You will do a little of everything, but not much of anything."

Stella had no idea what that meant, but hurriedly thanked her and raced back to the office.

"Will this do?" she asked her new employer.

"Yes, that will do fine. Now remember, it is very important that you don't do anything unless you are instructed to by someone who knows what you are to do."

"Yes, but..."

"Do not give out any information to anyone, especially to patients. Do not talk to the doctors. Do not talk to the patients. They need rest and don't need you to be pestering them. Do not give your opinions about anything to anyone. *No* talking to visitors except to tell them to leave if the on-duty nurse wants them to leave. Do not touch anything. Stay away from anything that looks even remotely medical. I think I've covered everything. You can start now. Goodbye." With that, Stella was unceremoniously dismissed.

Stella walked out of the office and almost jumped for joy when she saw her new nurse friend and confidant. Stella smiled at her and said, "I'm ready to do whatever you want me to."

"I'm so sorry, but I'm only a novice. I can't tell you what to do. But a word of warning, just make sure you stay busy or Head Nurse Witty can become very unpleasant. Confidentially, I've never seen her laugh. Names can be deceiving."

The novice nun walked away. Stella was left to figure it out on her on. She walked over to the nurses' station and spoke to the first person she saw. "What would you like me to do?"

"Did Witty tell you to come to me?" the non-nun nurse growled.

Stella paused half a second before saying, "Why, yes. Yes, she did."

"Why me? I swear she has it out for me!"

"Oh, I'm sorry. I didn't..."

"Don't worry. Here, take these magazines to Mrs. Wooster," non-nun turned swiftly and left.

"Mrs. Wooster," Stella repeated, hoping by some Catholic miracle that Mrs. Wooster would just materialize.

At that moment, she got her wish. "I'm over here, young lady. I'm in room 404. Turn your head toward my voice. Here I am. Come in, come in."

Stella did exactly as she was told and walked into room 404. Mrs. Wooster was a kindly-looking woman of an unknown age. Her white hair fell over the crisply starched white pillowcase. She had bright blue eyes that opened wide when Stella entered the room. Mrs. Wooster had an IV in her arm and only a thin white sheet over what seemed to be a very slim body. She beamed at Stella and said, "It's okay, young lady. Come closer. I won't bite."

Stella walked toward Mrs. Wooster and put the magazines on the table next to the bed, then turned to leave.

"Whoa. Where are you going? Sit a spell and chat with me," Mrs. Wooster suggested sweetly. But Stella stood transfixed.

"Are you deaf and dumb, child?"

"Oh, no. I can hear, and I can talk. I'm not supposed to, though."

"Why ever not?"

"It's my job."

"Your job is to not listen or talk?"

"I don't know. Maybe. I guess so."

"Well, isn't that the most foolish thing I ever heard," Mrs. Wooster sighed. "Is this a new job for you?"

"Yes. I'm sorry, but I'm not allowed to talk to the patients," Stella apologized.

"Do you know the reason for that?"

Stella shook her head no.

"Then why do it?"

Stella shrugged her shoulders.

"Hmmm," Mrs. Wooster groused. "I think if you talked to the patients, they might enjoy your conversation, get a happy positive attitude, laugh a bit, and get well! We wouldn't want that now, would we? If a patient gets well, she goes home and there are no more patients to pay for this new hospital. How's that for an optimist deduction?"

Laughter filled the room. Stella couldn't help it. She pulled up a chair and sat down.

For the next half hour, they talked about anything and everything. Stella told her about the strange interview that she just had. Mrs. Wooster told her about how she had fallen and was discovered two days later lying on the floor. It was the first time Stella truly missed her mother. She thought she saw her mother's reflection in Mrs. Wooster's eyes.

"Can I give you some advice, Stella?" Mrs. Wooster asked.

"Of course."

"I know you are young and eager to start your adult life but be very mindful how you go. It can be difficult out in the real world. Question everything and don't settle for just anything. Know what you want and go after it zealously."

"How do I do that, Mrs. Wooster? I don't know what I want, and I don't think I'm very good at anything. I'm not sure what to do. My girlfriend, Veronica, found a job she absolutely loves. I seem to fail at everything. Maybe I should look for a husband like my dad says."

"My dear girl, don't be ridiculous. You will know what is right for you when it comes. Keep looking, keep exploring, and don't you dare give up. There are good opportunities out there. You will find that perfect opportunity in which you will be able to use your hidden talents. You have a kind of power that can change lives. I can feel it!"

Just as Stella was going to question a seemingly mystical Mrs. Wooster about her confusing prophecy, a shout rang out through the halls. "Where is that new girl? Why is she not where she should be?" Witty was on a rampage.

Stella hurried out to the hallway. Standing directly behind Head Nurse Witty, she cheerily replied, "Yes, what can I help you with?"

Head Nurse Witty squawked, "If you had a nose, you'd be able to smell the problem and do something about it!"

"I'm so sorry, but I didn't want to do anything until I was instructed to."

"Do not be impertinent," Mrs. Witty spat out. "Clean up the vomit in Mr. Field's room."

"Where is his room?"

"Use your nose!" Mrs. Witty exclaimed and left.

Stella poked her head back into Mrs. Wooster's room and whispered, "See you again very soon." She walked across the hallway to the supply cabinet to fetch a mop and bucket, returning minutes later to what could only be Mr. Field's room.

"Hello, Mr. Field. I guess you're not feeling very well today."

"You're a clever girl," he grumbled. "Why doesn't someone give me something for nausea? Will you get something for me?"

"I'm very sorry, but I don't know anything about medicine. I will ask the nurse, however."

"Go on then. What are you waiting for?"

"I'll finish up here and find the nurse." She speedily mopped up the remnants of Mr. Field's illness and fled the room.

At the nurses' station Stella inquired about medicine to help Mr. Field with his nausea. She was told he had been given his cancer treatments and nausea was a common aftereffect. Overwhelmingly saddened to hear about Mr. Field, she didn't have time to reflect further when non-nun called out to her from another room.

"Hello, new girl? Hello? Can you come help me, please?"

"Yes, yes, of course. I will just put away the bucket and mop, wash my hands, and be right over," Stella hastened to answer.

In only a few moments, Stella was in the room. She immediately averted her eyes as she glanced in astonishment to see non-nun washing a naked man. "Take over here, please. I have to check on another patient," non-nun directed, leaving Stella all alone with this man.

The man was a surprisingly good-looking young man in his late twenties or early thirties. It looked as though he might have been in an accident because he had numerous cuts on his face and the parts of his body she wasn't afraid to scan. He was hooked up to a needle lodged directly into a vein in his neck. Some machines were making a lot of noise. They showed numbers and line charts she didn't understand. He was breathing hard and perspiring profusely. As Stella put the sponge into the pan of soapy warm water and wrung it out, the man gradually opened his eyes. He stared at her for only a moment before he moaned loudly and grabbed the wires attached to him. Stella backed away with a start. She took a long look at his body and the blood now rushing out of his neck and screamed. Doctors and nurses rushed into the room and shouted orders. Stella fainted over the washing tub and onto the floor.

The first thing Stella noticed when she awoke was the smell of antiseptic and soap. She looked around but had difficulty focusing because strong lights blinded her. She realized immediately that she was in a bed on top of the sheets. A doctor was opening her eyes and shining a light into them. "How are you feeling?" he inquired.

"I don't know what happened," she responded.

"We don't know yet, either. But this next question is very, very important," the doctor said.

Many people were gathered around her bed staring at her. Some, however, were pulling money out of their wallets or pockets. She was very confused. Head Nurse Witty was there along with non-nun, the nurses from the nurses' station, the cleaning crew she had met earlier, a candy striper, and a variety of doctors she had never seen before.

"We are trying to deduce why you fainted," the doctor continued.

"I'm so sorry. I honestly don't know."

The doctor looked her over one more time and very directly said, "Could you have fainted because of all the blood or the fact that you've never seen a naked man before?"

The audience gathered around her, leaning in a bit closer but still standing transfixed.

Stella wrinkled her brow and almost cried, "I think it was because he waved at me!"

Money changed hands rapidly.

Chapter 12
1957 – CHICAGO, ILLINOIS

The steps to Veronica's home and the street in front of it were quite crowded now. Some neighbors had brought over lawn chairs and set them up in the street. Others were lounging against the brick wall or parked cars. They were not bothered by any traffic because no car would be able to make its way down this street. There were just too many people lingering about.

Mad Molly broke a stunned silence when she said loudly, "Oh glory be, that's a good one! But, sweet child, I don't understand one thing." Everyone waited hesitantly. "If that man's hands were struggling to get the needles and wires out of his neck, how could he wave to you?"

Other people around them nodded their heads as if they were also puzzled. Stella replied nonchalantly, "I didn't say he waved with his hands."

Harold's beer sprayed out of his mouth as wild laughter erupted along the whole street in waves as one group told another.

Bill strolled over to both women out of nowhere and put his arms around both, "There you have it, ladies and gentlemen, Stella's brilliant nursing career ended with a bang on the same day that she began. Good thing, though, I say. If it hadn't, I would not have met my precious girls!"

"Oh, Bill, you are sweet," Veronica kissed him on the cheek. "Did you pick the boys up from kindergarten?"

"Speaking of doctors and such, our little rascals are out back looking for frogs. They asked if we could dissect one to see how it works," Bill said proudly.

"They are only six years old," Veronica whined. "Where do they get such ideas?"

"You've got two smart baby boys, that's for sure," Mad Molly said.

Stella stood up pressing down her dress. "Oh, Veronica, Bill, I can't wait to meet the twins. I have their photos in frames at my house and you've told me about them so often."

"Probably too often," Bill chuckled as he gave his wife a hug.

"Don't be silly," Veronica said nudging her husband. "Let's go to the backyard and see what the boys are up to."

Bill said, "You go ahead. I'll stay out here awhile and chat with our neighbors a spell."

The crowd of people that had been enjoying Stella's stories was now gathering their belongings and mingling with friends and neighbors. Gradually many of the people dispersed, leaving only a small group chatting amiably on the steps.

"I'm so sorry, but this will have to be a quick hello and goodbye. I have to go soon. I can't believe the time went by so fast."

"Do you have to go already? It seems like you just got here."

"Oh, my goodness," Stella continued, "I almost forgot. Ma said you are supposed to come for Sunday dinner. She said to bring the whole family."

"Stella, that is too much for her to do. We can't impose like that."

"Ma also said not to listen to any excuses. She is expecting you after church this Sunday and that's that." Stella added with a whisper, "I want to warn you that Kathy will be there."

"I don't have a problem with Kathy, but I'm afraid she is a bit standoffish with me. I think it's my height!"

"Absolutely, what else could it be? I don't think she realizes yet that you and I are the same height. But she isn't too fond of me, either. So, I guess you're right. Kathy is prejudiced against short people!" Stella laughed.

Veronica observed Stella closely. A few seconds of silence ensued. Stella took a deep breath as she grabbed her purse and got up.

Out of the blue, Veronica jumped up, grabbed Stella's arm, and said, "What is going on, Stella? Something is wrong."

"I'm just joking around. Nothing to worry about," Stella countered.

"Not that. I can tell something is bothering you."

"Oh, Veronica, you are too suspicious. I'm just worried about my dad."

"I understand that, but there's more. You hide it well, but I can read you like a book."

"A dull one?"

"Hardly that. Plan on telling me everything when we come for dinner," Veronica was adamant.

After her brief visit with the twins, Veronica and Bill walked Stella to the bus stop. Harold and a few of the others followed along. As Stella stepped up onto the bus, Harold shouted out, "Should we wave?"

"Don't you dare," Stella shouted back.

Chapter 13

1957 – SAN JOSE, CALIFORNIA

The alarming noise of the ringing telephone sliced through the silent atmosphere of the early evening household calmness, like the sounds of cathedral bells on an early Sunday morning awakening its parishioners to attend mass. Stella had just finished washing, drying, and putting away the dinner dishes. Rosie was looking at picture books in her room while Donna lay quietly in her playpen. Richard put down his newspaper and reached for the telephone on the end table next to the couch. "Hello, yes, she is here. Hang on a moment. I'll fetch her."

Holding his hand over the receiver, he called out, "Stella, it's your mother. She's calling long distance."

Stella untied her apron and raced into the front room. As she reached the telephone, Richard added, "At least she isn't calling collect."

A quick look of annoyance crossed Stella's face as she took the receiver. "Hello, Ma, how are…" She was not able to finish her thoughts. "Yes, yes. I understand. I'll make arrangements. Yes, tomorrow. I'll be there. No, I don't know yet. Expect me tomorrow. I will talk to Richard right now. Ma, I'm, I'm…" She couldn't finish. Holding back a sob, she added, "I will see you tomorrow, I promise." She gently hung up the phone.

Richard stared at her for a long time. Stella's eyes watered with tears.

"What is wrong?"

"My dad is dying. He has stomach cancer. He doesn't have much time left. I must go to him."

"Yes, of course. I think you should take an airplane with the girls. I know it will be expensive, but we'll work it out."

"The girls?" Stella queried. "Can't you take care of them? This may be difficult, not to mention expensive."

"I have to work. I can't be babysitting and working at the same time. You must take them with you."

It didn't take long for Stella to acquiesce when Richard pulled her down next to him on the couch and wrapped his arms around her. "I'm so sorry, sweetheart."

Stella sobbed unashamed tears onto his shirt. They comforted each other for what seemed like a very long time with only the sounds of Stella's soft crying. Richard lifted her head and wiped a tear or two off her face with his finger. "Put the children to bed and come to bed yourself. I'd like to hold you in my arms one last time," Richard soothed.

"Last time?" Stella asked, confused.

"I meant before you go."

"Oh, yes. Of course." She got up and walked directly to lift Donna out of the playpen. She carried her gently to the bedroom she shared with Rosie while kissing her forehead.

An hour later, Stella got into bed wearing the negligée that her husband had given her for her last birthday. Richard pulled her into his arms while cooing, "You look absolutely beautiful."

"I'm not sure that is possible with my tear-soaked eyes and red face."

"I didn't even notice."

They made love softly, swiftly, and without ardor. Stella fell asleep in her husband's arms without noticing Richard's own private tears.

Richard woke Stella very early the next morning. They dressed hurriedly and prepared for the journey Stella and the girls would take that same day. After Stella got the girls up and dressed, she made breakfast for everyone. They had a quick meal of bacon and eggs. Stella washed, dried, and put away the dishes. Richard came behind Stella and untied her apron. "I can't do this," he said simply.

"You can't do what? Get the airplane tickets? Are they sold out?" Stella inquired.

"No, it's not that. Rosie, take Donna and go play in your room. I want to talk to your mother."

Rosie picked up Donna and frowned at her parents, "Why do I always have to go to another room so you can talk? I promise I won't even listen."

"Go," her father demanded.

Stella looked at him with shining eyes. It was as if she knew what he wanted to say. "I don't have time for this. I need to get ready."

"No, we must talk. Stella, I can't do this anymore."

"Richard, I can't. My father is dying. This isn't the time."

"There is no other time. You need to understand. I've tried. I really tried."

Stella looked at her husband with fear and regret in her wet eyes. "I know it's been hard for you, but we will work it out. You'll see. When I come back from Chicago, we'll figure it out."

He looked at her for a long time before saying, "I can't be the husband and father you want. I don't want this life. I've tried. Really, I have. This isn't for me."

"Well, it's too late now. You are a husband and father with responsibilities. That's the way it is."

"I want to be an actor. The limelight has always been my dream. Why should I have to give up those exciting, carefree days? I feel stifled here."

"We tried the acting thing. I was your best and only fan, remember? We lived in Hollywood. But you were only able to get bit parts. You spent more time hobnobbing with the famous people, going to cocktail parties, drinking, and flirting with any pretty face you saw. The worst was when you openly dallied with various models. You didn't even try to keep it from me!" Stella's face was red with anger and frustration remembering actions that she had worked diligently to forget and forgive.

"Don't you understand, Stella, that is who I am! I love the thrill of the chase, the excitement of the rich and famous. I want that again!"

"You're a fool," Stella almost screamed. "You're just an extroverted egomaniac who wants it all but has no resources to back it up."

"I'm the fool?" Richard chided. "You're the fool trying to make a family out of nothing. And, what's worse is that now you have a feeble-minded baby to add to the mess."

"She is your child, too!" Stella shot back.

"I don't want her," Richard said almost under his breath.

"What?" Stella was incredulous.

"I told you, Stella. I can't do this. I look at Donna and feel such remorse. I hate myself for it. What kind of man fathers a child with no hope of any kind of life?"

"Of course she has a life."

"She is retarded, Stella. Try to get that through your head. Retarded!" he yelled.

"Quiet, the children will hear you."

"So? Donna won't understand. She will never understand! I can't take this anymore!" Richard finished.

Stella stood in the middle of the kitchen and tried to breathe. "What are you saying, then?"

"I don't really know. I think you and the girls should go to Chicago. It'll give us both time to figure this all out," Richard said calmly as he walked toward Stella and put his arms around her, cradling her neck on his shoulder.

"Why did you marry me, Richard, if you didn't really want a wife, family, and a home?"

Richard sighed while gently running his fingers through his wife's hair, "The first time my eyes met yours, I was lost. My heart pounded erratically, and I couldn't think about anything except you belonging to me. I'm certain that I gave my heart to you that day. I loved you then and you may not truly believe it, but I will love you forever."

Stella looked up into Richard's eyes and nodded. "I love you, too. Do you know that the only thing I knew I wanted was to travel and explore places I had never been to before? I wanted to search for adventure. When I met you, I thought I found the dream my heart had been longing for. I always believed that a woman was supposed to marry and start a family. The rest of my adventure would come eventually. It's all I knew or truly expected. Oh, Richard, I know we can make this work. We are worth it. Our children are worth it. I must go to Chicago now, but my focus will be entirely on our marriage when the children and I return. I know we can figure out how to make our marriage work. We can start fresh when I get back. Our family is too important to give up on."

Chapter 14

1957 – CHICAGO, ILLINOIS

TWO WEEKS LATER

Veronica and Stella sat next to each other on the top step of Stella's parents' house. Her mother had told them dinner would be ready in about half an hour and there was nothing they could do to help, that they should go have some private girl time. Bill quickly agreed while picking up one of Rosie's books to read the children a story. Veronica's mother, Barbara, was in her element in the kitchen chatting with Frances while helping with dinner preparations.

Stella had just finished telling Veronica about the confrontation with Richard when Kathy threw open the door to tell them dinner was ready. She made a very undignified grunting noise while glaring at them. Stella cursorily wiped an escaping tear from her eye and leaned over toward her sister to say, "It's quite all right. You see, we just discovered that Veronica is actually my youngest sister."

Veronica jumped in, "We think there may have been some mistake at the maternity hospital."

Stella finished, "But we're not really sure."

Veronica turned back without another thought about Stella's infuriating and interfering real sister and said directly to Stella, "It'll be okay. You will see. Richard and you can work this out."

Kathy left abruptly without another word.

"I hope so. I just don't know what I'll do if we can't work it out. I don't know what I'll do if we can work it out. I'm so confused that I don't even know if I want to go back."

"You don't mean that," Veronica sighed. "It's hard enough having to accept your father's untimely disease. You shouldn't have to be upset about Richard, too."

"It's been going on a long time. I didn't want to tell you."

"Why not?" Veronica clearly was not happy about that. "We're best friends and now sisters, I might add. We should be able to confide in each other about anything and everything. No matter what. I mean that!"

"I know, but I was just so embarrassed. Bill and you have the perfect marriage and family. I do not."

"I don't believe everything is the way it seems on the outside. People tend to hide what hurts them the most," Veronica said.

"You always said that you wish you had had a better education, but you are without a doubt the wisest person I've ever known," Stella squeezed and released Veronica's hand. "Let's go see what Ma has experimented with this time."

"Good heavens. Let's just hope it's not another version of her famous chicken and dumplings. I don't think I could cope with any more surprises," Veronica laughed.

They stood up and opened the front door. Veronica swiftly took in the scene with loving eyes as her husband, Bill, read to the children. He was dressed in his best blue suit with the striped tie she had made for him last Christmas. He was tall and extremely handsome. To her, he seemed like a gleaming bronzed statue everyone should gaze at with wonder and admiration. How foolish, but she knew how very lucky she was. She didn't want to say that to Stella. It would be unfair to flaunt her happiness in the face of Stella's misery. Yet, paradise had its problems, too. They had very little money. Bill was going to lose his job as a milkman. His company recently told employees that their job was a dying art. She wasn't even sure what that meant. She only knew Bill had been looking for another source of income.

An hour later, everyone was finishing their meal while chatting comfortably.

"Mrs. Kluskowski, this is the best chicken and dumplings I have ever had the pleasure of eating," said Bill. "I've never enjoyed a meal more."

"Really?" Veronica said with a wicked smirk.

"Except for my wonderful wife's exceptional cooking, that is."

"To be honest, I truly doubt Bill married me for my cooking," Veronica said, laughing.

"Why *did* you marry her?" Kathy demanded.

"Kathy!" her mother admonished.

"It's Kathleen!"

"I know perfectly well what your name is. I named you," her mother scolded.

"Daddy said that he did!"

"Never you mind. There is no reason to be rude to our guests."

"Your guests, not mine," Kathy argued. She turned to Stella and immediately added, "And why did you marry that bum, Dick or Rich or whatever his name is? Where is he anyway?"

"I'll tell you if you tell me why you never married. Wouldn't you be considered an old maid now?" Stella was quick to respond.

"Girls!" their mother said irritably. "We have guests. Mind your manners or you two will be doing the dishes – together!"

Bill immediately broke the ice, "Would you like to hear how we all met?"

"We've all heard Stella's outlandish version, but I'm sure she exaggerated the whole thing," Kathy sneered.

"Don't be so sure," Veronica answered. "I'll never forget when she came home after losing yet another job."

Chapter 15

1948 – SAN FRANCISCO, CALIFORNIA

STELLA STOOD OUTSIDE THE FRONT DOOR AND PUT HER HAND ON the lion knocker. She hoped that no one would answer. She didn't have the faintest idea where her keys were. She didn't know how she would explain why she was so wet from head to foot, especially since it wasn't raining.

The door to the boarding house flew open before Stella could even attempt to use the knocker. Veronica took one look at her and burst into uncontrollable laughter.

"It's not funny."

"Dorothy, Elsie, come here. You have to see this."

"Oh, please. Don't tell..." Stella couldn't get a complete sentence in before all three of her closest friends stood on the doorstep in hysterics.

"I never liked sports, anyway," Stella mused. "I thought this job would be easy. I would go to the ballpark and sell popcorn or something simple. That's what vendors do."

"You don't smell like popcorn," Dorothy giggled.

"I might be mistaken," Elsie added, "But I seem to remember that is how beer smells."

"This could very well be your shortest employment," Veronica laughed again.

"It's not funny," Stella said as she tried to squeeze past them and enter the house.

"Wait a minute," Dorothy said, "You are not going inside to smell up the house. You need to dry off first. I'll bring some towels, but not until I hear about this escapade."

"I asked my new boss what I would be selling as the newest vendor. He just grunted and put a large tray bounded by thick suspender-type straps around my neck and shoulders. That was heavy enough, but next he loaded every square inch he could fill with cups of beer. I was stooped over, but he pushed me ahead of him and suggested that I climb up the stairs to the highest stands. The only thing I could do was keep moving with the darn things encased around me or I'd tumble over. So, I did what I was told."

"So, you tripped and spilled the beer?" Elsie asked.

"Well, yes and no," Stella continued. "I was walking toward the top row of bench seats when a young man shouted out, 'Hey, sweetheart, over here. I wanna beer.' That sounded wonderful to me. It would ease my load and I'd finally make some money. I was right next to him ready to turn carefully around when he grabbed my behind and squeezed. All his friends thought this was the most amusing thing they had ever witnessed. I heard one of them say, 'Hey, sweetie. Can I have a bite, too?'"

"Stupid boys!" Elsie said.

"Before I had time to think, I turned abruptly around and accidentally spilled my entire load of beers over his head. Some spilled on his annoying friends as well."

"That was lucky," Dorothy said.

"Yes and no. The creatures started screaming that I cheated them out of their beer. My boss sprinted up the stairs and fired me before I had a chance to explain."

Less than a week later, Stella again stood next to the lion door knocker contemplating how to explain why she was so wet once again. At least she didn't smell like beer this time. She smelled and even tasted a bit like a chocolate malt mixed with cherry soda. Before announcing her arrival home, Stella put her forehead directly on the lion. She wondered if she could magically gain courage from its presence. She lifted her face and laughed. It was a silly thought, but could that lion be smiling back at her?

The door opened abruptly, revealing her three closest friends. They stood transfixed like tin soldiers at attention. No one said a word as if they might be worried about Stella's mental status. This time it was Stella who broke into laughter. After a few seconds, her friends laughed with her.

"I can't wait to hear this one!" Elsie said. "Waiting for you to come home and anticipating the story of your latest 'employment opportunity' has become the best part of my day."

"Don't you dare say a word until I get back with a towel," Dorothy said.

"No need," said Veronica as she handed Stella a towel, "I'm one step ahead of you."

"I'm in love!" Stella exclaimed.

"Oh, lordy. Get in here and don't leave out a thing!" Veronica ordered.

Stella couldn't wipe the wistful smile off her shiny face. Her friends watched her intently as she told them the story of meeting the man of her dreams.

"Early in the morning when I awoke, I knew this day would be unlike any other. I could feel it. I sensed it. The sun had broken through the clouds, shining its way through my bedroom window. The beam of light seemed to tell me to get up and find my way to my destiny.

"I had no idea where I should go or what I was going to do. The most reasonable idea was to look for help-wanted signs on storefront windows. I walked down close to the waterfront. A drive-in café was directly in front of me. Curiosity gripped me as I had never been to one of those before. Cars were parked next to short poles with speakers on them. Customers rolled down their windows and gave their order to a box. Since I was hungry, I thought it sensible to have lunch there. I hoped there would be some seating inside as I don't own a car. I walked eagerly toward the café and was surprised to find a sign on the window asking for waitresses to apply inside. *I could be a waitress,*

I thought. Someone would call me from one of those little boxes and I would write down their order to give to the cook. What could be easier than that? Finally, something I could do.

"When I opened the door, a bell rang out proclaiming my entrance. The memory of my dad's shop stunned me for a moment but left as soon as I entered the pleasant café. The first thing I noticed was a jukebox that stood in the corner. A young man was putting a coin in the slot while scanning the list of songs. He hit some number combinations and a sweet love song filled the air. A few tables were scattered about the room dressed in red and white–checked tablecloths. On each table sat a silver napkin holder, a cylinder glass sugar container, salt and pepper shakers, as well as ketchup and mustard. A tall, thin-faced woman with a pencil stuck securely in her French roll–styled hairdo stood behind a counter. She had a pad in her hand and a white frilly apron tied around a red and white–checked dress with a name tag attached in the upper left-hand corner that read, 'Hi, my name is Ruby.' She looked up expectantly at me and said, 'May I take your order?'

"I gazed at her with the excitement of a schoolgirl, 'Hi, Ruby, I saw your sign in the window. I'd like to apply for a position here,' I said excitedly.

"'Why?' was all she said but directed me with a nod of her head to a door with the word 'Manager' posted prominently.

"I knocked on the door and waited briefly before a gruff voice yelled out the words, 'Come in already. I don't have all day!'

"I hesitated somewhat but plucked up my courage, opened the door, and walked in.

"'Hello, my name is Stella and I'm here to apply for a job as a waitress,' I said before he even had time to look up from the newspaper he had been reading.

"The first thing I noticed about this middle-aged man was that he appeared to be composed of all rounded shapes. He reminded me of a red rubber ball. His head was stuck onto his torso without an exposed neck. He was completely bald, which accentuated the wire-rimmed glasses that were tilted on his pushed-in nose. His facial features looked squashed as if someone had shoved a hand into his unfortunate face.

"'Well, well, what do we have here?' the man said when he looked up from his newspaper and examined me with his deep-set eyes.

"My first thought was to turn around and run as fast as I could, but I refused to be intimidated yet again. I looked directly at him and said, 'I'd like to work here.'

"'Why?' the man echoed exactly what that woman had said.

"I was curious and a bit confused. 'I'd like to be a waitress.'

"'You got some experience?'

"'Experience?' I muttered.

"'Yes, experience,' he growled, 'Oh, who cares. You look appetizing. That's all that matters. I need customers. Can you be good to the customers?'

"'Yes, yes, of course. I'm very friendly,' I smiled.

"'I don't want you to be friendly. I want you to give good service to the customers. Just give them what they want. Understand?'

"'Yes, I can do that,' I reassured him.

"'Ruby will give you a uniform. You can start right now,' he said and dismissed me.

"I headed immediately to Ruby and told her the manager hired me.

"'Oh, swell,' Ruby said without enthusiasm.

"I was thrilled to put on my new uniform. Well, I wasn't an assistant to a nurse's aide, but I could still help people. I would be helping them get food to eat. I could do this! In less than five minutes, I rushed out and almost bumped into Ruby.

"'I'm ready,' I practically squealed. I had on my crisp red and white uniform with the starched white apron. I eagerly put on the name tag Ruby handed to me. She had my name already written on it. I attached it with pride. I could do this. I was basking in my newfound enthusiasm when my breath caught in my throat. I saw Ruby pick up a pair of roller skates while gleefully saying, 'Put these on and report back to me. I'll tell you what to do next.'

"Without thinking I felt for the counter stool and plopped down completely stunned. Never in my life had I gone roller skating. I took off my own shoes with great trepidation and slipped on the heavy skate boots that laced up above my ankles. They were probably one size too big, but that was the least of my worries. As I tried to stand up, I swayed back and forth until Ruby grabbed my arm.

"'Steady there,' she said. 'Just take a moment or two to get used to it.'

"I slipped forward and backward a few times but somehow managed to get the hang of it. I had succeeded in steadying myself for a few seconds when Ruby handed me a tray consisting of two chocolate malted milkshakes, a cherry Coke, and a strawberry soda as well as four hamburgers and French fries. My mind immediately raced back to my career as a sports vendor and I grimaced nervously. Ruby gave my back a bit of a shove and I slid out the swinging door she quickly opened. 'Car number five,' she shouted behind me.

"I'm not sure how, but I managed to skate out the door while desperately trying to balance the loaded tray of food and drinks. I shot a glance toward the convertible in the number five spot. Two incredibly gorgeous young men in sailor uniforms were sitting with women who were apparently glued to the men. One couple (who happened to be white) was in the front seat and the other couple (who happened to be black) was nestled in the back. Just as I got to the convertible, the incredibly handsome young man in the front untangled himself from the blonde and jumped up and over the closed door as he said, 'Here, let me help you with that.'

"The backseat man also simultaneously flipped out of his confinement while absentmindedly pushing the first man out of the way. I tried to steady myself, but the skates had a mind of their own. As I locked eyes with the first man and glanced expectantly at the second, the tray somehow flew out of my outstretched hand. The contents went every which way like crisp leaves on a windy autumn day. The two average-looking women squealed as if they had been attacked. Everyone, including me, was drenched in drive-up café food and drink.

"'Well, hello there. My name is Dick Ensign,' the first man said as he licked the chocolate shake around his lips. He didn't seem bothered whatsoever.

"'Dick? You don't seem like a Dick to me,' I blubbered, completely embarrassed.

"'That's what people call me, but my mother calls me Rich, short for Richard, which is my given name. I sometimes think she harbors hopes that I'll be rich someday. I'm not rich now by any means. Does that bother you?' Rich was also jabbering.

"'I'll call you Richard then. I like Richard. It suits you,' I mumbled as he continued to stare at me while I did the same. The women were not so hypnotized, however. They continued to complain loudly. I don't really remember what they were saying.

"'My name is Bill. Don't you worry about a thing,' the second and equally gorgeous man said. 'It must be impossible to handle such a load. Please let me sort this out for you.'

"'No, no. I'm so sorry. I can do it,' I protested as I tried to pick up the pieces of empty containers. I even took a napkin and tried in vain to wipe the face of the girl who was sitting in the middle of the front seat. Unfortunately, a false eyelash fell into the upside-down plate. She screamed louder, which brought out what I thought must be the entire staff, including the manager and Ruby.

"Richard held out a hand, pushing Bill back a few steps, 'This one's mine, buddy,' he laughed with a grin that practically encircled his face.

"'Hey!' Blondie screeched as she wiped the chocolate shake off her face with the sleeve of her blouse.

"Bill gallantly turned toward the now extremely irritated girls, saying, 'Don't worry, ladies, we'll have this sorted out in no time.'

"'Take me home this minute,' the backseat girl shouted.

"'Please say you will go on a date with me. I won't be able to breathe until I see you again,' Richard crooned.

"'Oh, please, Dick, you are blowing this. Listen, miss, we would both enjoy a nice evening out with you. I mean, that is, if you have a friend that looks like me, we could double date,' Bill stammered.

"'Tall, dark, and handsome?' I smiled at both men.

"'I was thinking dark,' Bill added.

"'Would it matter to you what color she was?'

"All the commotion seemed to settle into a surprising calmness as everyone listened intently with their eyes wide open ready to gasp or relax.

"Bill looked at me strangely, 'No, I guess not.'

"'Then you shall be very pleasantly surprised.'

"Bill couldn't let this go, 'The world may not look kindly on it if my date looked like you.'

"'Short and wet with dripping soda?' I laughed.

"'White.'

"'So maybe the world needs to change. I think a new law is in order,' I said, thinking of course about you, Veronica.

"Bill grinned back and knocked Richard on the shoulder, 'Tell Richard your address before he collapses. I'll look forward to my surprise.'

"I hastily gave him my address while we all continued to try to make amends by cleaning things up. While doing so, I overheard Ruby say to the manager, 'I told you she wouldn't last the day, George. You owe me $5.00!'

"'You're fired!' the manager yelled."

Chapter 16

1957 – CHICAGO, ILLINOIS

"I'M NOT SURPRISED THE ONLY WAY YOU COULD ATTRACT THE attention of a man, a military man at that, was to drop a plate of food on his head," Kathy mused while shaking her head.

"Kathleen!" her dad admonished. Kathleen went directly to her father and tucked the blanket more securely around him, then gave him a quick soft hug. Stanley Kluskowski seemed to shrink into his armchair. His eyes glassy, full of love and hopes for all of them, he watched his family engage with their guests. Knowing these were his final days, he didn't fight his ongoing anxiety partly because he truly believed that everlasting life would indeed follow this life. His sadness came from knowing his family would grieve because of him. Although he was weary with pain, today held a flickering light like a candle steadfastly burning down to its final glow. The family saw a shrunken man with sallow skin taking slow, gasping breaths. He barely talked anymore but could hear and understand everything said around him. He watched the lively activity around him and could only smile. Stanley knew beyond a shadow of a doubt that they would be okay and for that he would be eternally happy and proud.

Bill was still laughing when he said, "Oh, it was quite a sight all right. Stella looked dazed like someone had hypnotized her. Dick looked the same. I wasn't given a second glance and would not have, even if I had been white!"

"That is not true," Stella argued. "I noticed you. I noticed you would be a perfect match for my best friend!"

Bill put his arm around Veronica and kissed her cheek, "I'll always be grateful for your clumsiness."

Rosie popped up with excitement, "What happened next, Mommy?"

"Well, your dad asked me for a date almost immediately. His so-called girlfriend wasn't happy. She said some words that were not nice," Stella said.

"What words?" Rosie clapped her hands with glee.

"Words that little girls should not hear," Kathleen glared at Stella.

"Oh, Aunt Kathy. Please," Rosie pressed.

"No, this time I agree with your Aunt Kathy," Stella said.

"Kathleen! Why can't anyone here except my dad remember what my name is?"

No one appeared to be listening to her as they continued to probe Stella for more information.

Stella looked at her best friends and sighed, "Oh, if only I wasn't white. It could have been Bill and me."

"Well, I gave it a good college try," Bill laughed.

Veronica looked at Bill, interjecting, "What was that all about, Bill?"

Stella jumped in to respond, "Bill asked if I had a friend for him. He also requested a double date but said he had to escort the ladies home that they were currently entertaining first. I suggested they both help the ladies back to where they belonged. Richard agreed, but only if I gave him my address. He said Bill and he would be over later that evening."

Veronica broke in, "It wasn't long after Stella came home, told us the story of being in love, and finally got cleaned up that two young sailors came to our front door. Their white uniforms were as spic and span as their ship must be during inspection. I'll never forget how shy but confident both men appeared to be. Each held a small bouquet of flowers. Elsie answered the door. As Stella and I watched intently by the staircase, the men graciously handed her the flowers. Elsie was very impressed and immediately invited the men in while introducing herself.

"You should have seen Veronica," Stella continued. "She looked like a lovesick puppy."

"Oh, for heaven's sake," Kathy scowled, "Who ever heard of such a thing as a lovesick puppy? It makes no sense. You hadn't even met the man yet. This is getting more and more bizarre. You are making it up!"

Bill ignored Kathy. "I took one look at Veronica and I was smitten before I even knew her name. Without a doubt, it was the greatest surprise of my life. How can anyone look at her and not see how she was, and still is the most amazing and beautiful creature on earth?"

"I think I'm getting a headache from this nonsense," Kathy exclaimed.

"Maybe you should take an aspirin and lie down," her mother suggested.

Kathy didn't move, but she did notice that her dad appeared to be smiling.

Veronica continued the story. "Bill seemed to illuminate the entire room with his warmth and immediate charm. He looked like he could be the star in a hit movie, if a dark person could get a role of anything other than a servant."

"Dick was the actor, not me," Bill said. "I'm just a working stiff."

"To me he wasn't an answer to my dreams, he *was* the dream," Veronica gushed.

"Now I know I'm going to be sick," Kathy rolled her eyes.

"I think it's so swell that Aunt Veronica and Uncle Bill found each other because my mom can't do anything," Rosie said.

Kathy looked up, "Wait, my headache is going away. Rosie, you are a smart little monster!"

"Thank you, Aunt Kathy."

"My name is Kathleen, you little monkey. Maybe you're not so smart after all," Aunt Kathy glared.

"Tell us what happened next," Ma directed.

"I suppose the rest is history, as they say," Stella said. "We dated and double-dated for over a year. Things were looking better and better. A week after my disastrous waitress job, Dorothy was able to secure a position for me as a library assistant at her school."

"A Negro elementary school?" Kathy asked with a look of astonishment.

"Yes, of course. I thought you knew that."

"I knew you worked in a school, but not that kind of school."

"It was the best job I ever had. I absolutely loved it. I knew without a shadow of a doubt I had found my calling in life," Stella said with a grin.

As the group had been chatting, they didn't realize Stanley's breathing had gotten worse. Nonetheless, they all knew immediately when it had stopped. No one moved. No one said a word. Silence spread throughout the room like the calm after a winter storm. Ma walked over to her husband, kissed him on the top of his forehead, and said goodbye.

Chapter 17

1957 – SAN JOSE, CALIFORNIA

A MONTH LATER, STELLA AND HER TWO DAUGHTERS BOARDED the Pan Am airplane that would leave Chicago and head straight to what she now considered her home state of California. Flying was a brand-new experience for all of them. Although this was the return flight, Stella felt as excited as she had when they had left San Jose almost two months earlier. Since very few people at that time had the opportunity to travel by air, the thrill of adventure almost overwhelmed all of them. Rosie was wild with anticipation and couldn't wait for the flight to begin. The fact there were no other children going aboard the plane made her feel very privileged and incredibly important. Donna was nestled in her pink blanket asleep on Stella's lap. Frequently a stewardess or various passengers would ask if they could see or hold the baby, but when Stella lifted the blanket away from Donna's face, the reaction was not what Stella expected. Some people just walked away without comment while others expressed their sorrow or confusion. One middle-aged woman looked at Stella, shook her head, and said mournfully, "You must be horrified." Stella wasn't sure if she should be horrified by the remark, angered, or relieved the person wouldn't be sitting next to them. So her reaction was to totally ignore it.

Rosie, on the other hand, received more attention than she really deserved, and she reveled in it. Rosie was in her element playing a character totally at ease with the situation at hand while delighted by being in the limelight. The stewardess attached a pin shaped like the wings of the airplane to the child's dress. She also gave her a box of gum squares to pass out to the other passengers. Suddenly, a gleeful Rosie pointed toward the window and shouted, "Inka and Knocka are on the wings. Look, everyone!" The noise in the cabin went up dramatically. The cockpit door opened, and the captain came down the aisle.

"Good afternoon, young lady," he said as he bent down close to her level.

"Hello, Mr. Airplane man," she replied. "I think we may have an issue. Inka and Knocka are on the wings."

"Well, we better tell them that it is safer to be inside the plane. Would you like to come to the cockpit and see how we fly the plane? I can speak to them on my radio phone."

Rosie turned to her mother excitedly, "Can I, Mom? Please, please, please?"

Stella just nodded, but Rosie had already skipped toward the open cockpit door. Stella peered down the pathway and shook her head as she watched Rosie laugh while being bounced on the captain's knee. His co-pilot was pointing toward the wings. A few minutes later, Rosie was back and announced to anyone who would listen to her that Inka and Knocka flew off and all was well now. Stella was proud of her daughter's vivid imagination but wondered if she might need to be seen by a psychologist. Could persisting in making up stories about imaginary characters be normal? She decided to worry about that later. Right now, Rosie was having too much fun.

Many hours later, Stella and the children arrived home by taxi. Rosie and Donna were both asleep. Stella was confused because she couldn't understand why Richard wasn't at the airport to pick them up. They had waited more than two hours for him. Stella had telephoned many times when they were in Chicago as well as when they arrived at the airport. He never answered. She also had written frequently when she was at her parents' home, but never received a reply. Richard never liked writing, so she thought he was probably just busy with work. Before they had left Chicago, Stella sent a telegram to say when the flight would arrive. She was positive that he would be there. She had never doubted it for a moment.

The house was eerily dark as they drove up. The taxi driver took the suitcases out of the trunk and set them on the driveway. He was eager to be on his way once Stella had paid him. She held a sleepy Rosie by the hand and carried Donna to the front porch. She knocked first, but there was no answer, so she dug her keys out of her handbag and struggled to unlock the door in the dark. *Maybe Richard was sleeping,* she thought. *After all, it was a work night.* She opened the door to a cold and dark room. The house was as still as a tomb. She reached over to switch on the light, but nothing went on. She stumbled her way to the kitchen's light switch. Still no light went on. She tried every lamp she could find but to no avail. She came to the unnerving conclusion that the electricity wasn't working, but she just couldn't figure out why. Rosie started to cry. It was obvious that she was scared. Stella felt her way toward the kitchen cabinet drawer where they kept a flashlight as well as matches and candles in case of a power outage or emergency. Luckily the flashlight glowed bright enough to lead Rosie to her bed and Donna to her crib. She tucked them in and kissed them both goodnight. Fortunately, both girls were so tired that they immediately fell asleep. Stella, on the other hand, knew she wouldn't be able to sleep anytime soon.

Stella walked with trepidation to the bedroom that she shared with her husband. By this time, it was no surprise to her that he wasn't there. The bed had not been made, nor had it been slept in for quite some time, she surmised as she looked urgently around for a note of explanation. She wandered around the house with the flashlight illuminating the way. She wasn't quite sure then, but it felt like things were missing. Now, however, she only thought she must be imagining it. She went next outside to the mailbox and gasped. Holding a hand over her mouth so she wouldn't scream and wake the children, she found the mailbox full to overflowing. The letters she had written were unopened. Bills fell out onto the ground. They were also unopened and obviously unpaid. Stella ran back inside the house and straight to her bedroom, throwing open the closet door. Richard's clothes were gone. Next, she went into the bathroom. The medicine cabinet was empty of all his belongings. Stella looked around frantically. Reluctantly she forced herself to check her jewelry box in the dressing table drawer. Her jewelry as well as the hidden emergency fund cash was gone. Stella sat on their bed and shut the flashlight off. She stared at nothing while she whispered to the ghosts of her marital bedroom, "I've been keeping a secret, Richard. Remember how you said we would have another child after Donna? Well, you got your wish."

Stella smothered her face into the pillow as she tried in vain to silently swallow the sobs escaping from deep within her.

Chapter 18

1949 – SAN FRANCISCO, CALIFORNIA

If it hadn't been entirely inconceivable, Stella would have sworn that old lion smiled at her when she grabbed both sides of its door knocker face and kissed its cold metal nose. Maybe the lion even winked at her with a glint in its eye as she jumped up the stairs with giddy excitement counting each step, reminiscing about the time she bounced down the steps of her parents' home three years before. So much had transpired since that fretful time after the war. She didn't know what she was going to do or where she was headed. Stella only wanted to go experience the adventure of life.

Opening the large door in one exuberant movement, Stella shouted out in glee, "Elsie, Dorothy, Veronica? I'm home. Where is everyone? I have exciting news!"

Her summons worked as all three women rapidly materialized from every direction. "Oh, my goodness, please don't tell us you lost the school library job!" Elsie inquired with a worried expression.

Dorothy looked equally nervous, "Or found another 'employment opportunity,' as you are so fond of saying?"

"Wait, wait. I know," Veronica jumped in, "I know. I can see it written all over her face." She turned to Stella and began to speak, "Stella, are you…?"

"I'm in love! Richard asked me to marry him!"

"Goodness gracious," Elsie said as Stella raced to her closest companions and embraced each one while accepting their heartfelt congratulations.

"Oh, isn't it wonderful? All my troubles and worries are over. I will no longer have to find a job, try to figure out what I'm doing, and then manage to lose it a few days or weeks later," Stella sighed.

"You have a good job now. No, it's actually a career you absolutely love. Why would you jeopardize that?" Dorothy protested.

Stella raced to Dorothy and squeezed her once again. "I will always, always be grateful for your help getting me that employment opportunity. Don't worry so much, I'm not leaving yet," Stella laughed. "I can finally see my wonderful future written in the night sky."

"It's only 3:00 on a Saturday afternoon," Veronica tried to say in a deadpan manner, but no one was listening to her. They stood transfixed, marveling at Stella's obvious joy.

"I'm going to marry the most handsome man alive!"

"Bill?" Veronica mused.

"Don't be silly. Of course, he is certainly handsome in a dark sort of way."

"Whatever do you mean by that?" Veronica reacted swiftly but was undisturbed as she knew Stella had not meant anything derogatory. Stella didn't often think before she spoke.

"Richard is fun and funny, too. He's so charming. Everyone loves him, but he only wants me. Can you imagine? Just me! He loves *me*! Oh, I can't believe how lucky I am. Do you know that Richard is the life of any party? He swings me around the dance floor and the whole room is envious." Stella was lost in her own daydreams as she continued, "We're going to be married! I think two children will be a nice family. We'll get a nice house in a nice neighborhood. I'll become the best housewife and mother in the whole wide world. I may do a little gardening in our backyard – herbs for cooking, I think."

Veronica interrupted, "You told me you never gardened in

your life. And we've seen your cooking attempts. Have you forgotten that you're not even allowed in the kitchen anymore?"

"Very funny," Stella chuckled. "I'll learn. I'll get a cookbook and a gardening book. Do you think the school library would have one?"

"A children's version maybe, but you would know more about that than I do. You work there," Dorothy said.

"I'll look Monday. I absolutely love my work at your school, Dorothy. How did you ever talk them into hiring me? I'm the only white person there. Do you think anyone has noticed?" Stella asked without a trace of sarcasm.

"Well, you see," Dorothy began, a little embarrassed, "Everyone in the teachers' lounge used to erupt into laughter when I told them stories about you. One day, the principal walked in while we were in hysterics. Mr. Brown asked if he could get in on the joke. Everyone told him bits and pieces while still chuckling. He looked around with a bit of a superior type of frown but broke into a massive grin. I overheard him say that this might be just what we all need. He called Veronica and me into his office later in the day. I can tell you that we were never more nervous. We thought we were going to be fired."

"Why?" Elsie interjected.

"I don't know really. I had never been called into the principal's office before," Veronica pointed out. "Even as a young girl. I was the straight arrow type."

Dorothy continued, "Mr. Brown asked how soon Stella might be losing her current job. We were both confused, but I told him honestly that your days as a garbage collection clerk were numbered when you told a customer that their bill wouldn't be so high if they reused a few things and didn't waste so much by throwing it all away."

"Well, I believe there's too much garbage in the world," Stella grimaced.

Dorothy continued, "Mr. Brown and the librarian, Mrs. Peacock, were both in the office when we arrived."

In a stern male tone of voice Veronica took over, "Girls,

there is no need to look so troubled. We are considering hiring your friend, Stella. You see, Mrs. Banner had to resign due to the fact that...um... well..."

Dorothy took over, "Oh, he looked like there was just no way he could actually say the words. So, Mrs. Peacock whispered that Mrs. Banner was in the family way."

Everyone let out expressions showing understated comprehension.

Veronica decided that she sounded pretty good imitating Mr. Brown so she continued expertly, "So girls, I believe this school could use someone like your Stella. She'll be the challenge we need to keep all of us on our toes."

"Both Veronica and I were bewildered," Dorothy interjected, "so I mentioned to Mr. Brown that we didn't quite understand."

Veronica continued repeating Mr. Brown's words. "I'm going to tell you a true story. When I was a child, I had trouble learning how to read. I was teased a lot. Other children and even some adults called me slow witted and a dummy."

At this point Veronica said in her own voice, "All three of us stood dumbfounded. Probably not a good choice of words, but true, nonetheless. This is what he told us."

Back to her Mr. Brown persona, Veronica continued, "You see, I had a hard time reading. I looked at the word 'saw' and read it as 'was.' My parents didn't understand, but always told me that I was smart. I should always work hard, never give up, and mind my P's and Q's. I remember that P's and Q's seemed to be my downfall. Yet, my parents and a few extraordinary teachers took me on as their personal challenge. I was told that it may take a little longer for me to learn, but I would get there in the end. They were right. Math and many other subjects were quite easy for me once I mastered the more difficult task of reading."

Dorothy took over the story. "Mr. Brown went on to explain that when he had graduated from high school, the Great War had begun. He enlisted and served his country for three years. Afterwards, he was accepted into Southern Oregon Normal School. He became a teacher. He told us he always wanted to know how to teach children like himself, but he had difficulty finding any kind of information specific to his dilemma. He was pretty sure this kind of problem was not only in Negro children. But he never taught any others. Children with severe educational difficulties did not go to school. Maybe that would change someday."

"I told Mr. Brown that Stella could read just fine. I wasn't quite sure where the challenge was because she wasn't a child, nor was she qualified to teach," Veronica said. "Mr. Brown just looked at us and said that we would see."

Stella grinned, "I never told you this, but when Mr. Brown and Mrs. Peacock interviewed me, I was asked if I was familiar with the Dewey Decimal System. I told them quite confidently that Dewey was my favorite subject in Math. Mr. Brown told me right then and there that I was hired!"

Chapter 19
1949 – SAN FRANCISCO, CALIFORNIA

"Don't worry, Elsie," Stella said while she hugged her, "I'm not going to quit. Richard and I are not going to get married until 1950 at the earliest. He has to finish his stint in the Navy first."

"What kind of work will he do afterwards?" Elsie asked.

"He wants to be an actor."

Elsie gasped, Dorothy smirked, and Veronica turned her head away while lifting her eyes upwards. Stella knew that it wasn't the career her friends were expecting.

"He's really good. I watched a community theatre production in which he had the leading role. It was some courtroom drama thing. I couldn't really follow the action. I only know that he was terrific. He got a standing ovation," Stella said with infectious enthusiasm.

"I'm sure he will be a fine actor, Stella dear, but will he be able to make a living at it?" Elsie asked.

"Yes, I'm certain his good looks and charisma will help him be successful, but in the meantime, I would love to stay at our school and continue as a librarian assistant. I love it! The kids are wonderful. They love it when I read to them or tell stories. Mrs. Peacock gets a kick out of my attempts to try new things. Remember, Veronica, when I had some fourth graders help me build a cardboard spaceship that they could crawl into to read?

They loved to talk about Buck Rogers. I suggested when they could show me that they had read an entire book, they could go into the spaceship."

Dorothy added, "I'll never forget. My students were so excited they could talk about nothing else. We had to have a waiting list sign-up sheet because so many children were reading."

"What really stuck with me was a question a little girl asked when I had only been working there a week," Stella said. "She asked me where the white children were. She asked if it would be okay if white children could come to our school. She wanted to know if she would be allowed to play with a white girl because she thought she'd like that. I told her I didn't know. She answered that if I could be there, why not little white girls and maybe even little white boys, but she would have to really think about the boys, though. She wasn't so sure about them. I was at a loss for words. I put my hand on her soft cheek and said to her and all the other children around her, 'If not now, maybe someday. Maybe you will be the ones who will make it happen.'"

Unbeknownst to the others, Elsie had tears in her eyes. She fiddled with some items on the tea tray, wiped her eyes with a napkin, then turned back to the young ladies she had grown to treasure. "Stella," Elsie continued, "I'm still concerned about how Richard and you will earn a living. I must be honest."

"Do you think Richard will let me keep my job? I can try to talk him into it."

Veronica put her hands on her hips, "Mercy me. Now that is something I never expected to come out of your mouth!"

"Me, neither," Dorothy erupted, "We're almost in a new decade. Maybe the 1950s will be a little more open minded. Tell your future husband that you'll be working and that's that."

"Oh, good heavens, I couldn't do that," Stella looked almost frightened. Then, before she realized what she had said, Stella added pensively, "Wait, maybe I could. There could be a new law!"

They all laughed.

Chapter 20

1958 – SAN JOSE, CALIFORNIA

The shrill familiar noise of the telephone blasted Stella out of her reverie. She gazed at the contraption as if she had never heard it before. After five rings, she closed her eyes while slowly lifting the receiver to her ear.

"Hello," Stella answered.

"Stella? Kathleen here," came the brisk reply.

"Hello, Kathy," Stella said simply with newfound confidence. She wasn't quite sure if she was ready for what was undoubtedly coming, but she knew there would be no way to avoid it. How can one ever stop a moving train that is barreling out of control? "I was just going to call you," Stella tried to say but was immediately cut off.

"So, you got it? I was pretty sure you would undoubtedly take your sweet time to acknowledge the incredibly generous act of kindness I bestowed upon you."

Stella took a deep breath and wondered why she put up with her annoying sister. She didn't need to ponder this question, however. She knew. She was her sister and that was that. It was just Kathy's own strange way of dealing with her world. Still, Kathy frustrated her beyond measure. With a sigh she said, "I only got the mail a half hour ago."

"I knew you would find some excuse not to thank me. I worked so hard for that kind of money and now I have to give it to you!"

"Thank you, but you didn't have…"

"It is *not* a gift. Make no mistake."

"No, I'm sure it's not…"

"It's a loan until that useless excuse of a husband figures out he has a wife and children to take care of."

"I'm not sure that is going to happen, but thank…"

"Or, you figure out how to work. I doubt that will ever happen. You don't know how to do anything. Nor can you keep a job for more than a few minutes."

"I do try. I worked at the school for…"

Kathy didn't let her finish. "You really should be more like me. As you know, I have a very prestigious position in the Sears Building."

"You are a receptionist, which seems incredibly odd to me," Stella snapped.

"Whatever do you mean by that? I am the first person customers and clients and of course important people see. I'm the one who directs everyone to where they need to go," Kathleen maintained.

"Yes," Stella cleared her throat, "Well, your gift was very unexpected."

"It's not a gift. I told you that already. Weren't you listening? It's a loan," Kathleen hissed.

"Yes, okay, I understand."

"It's a lot of money, but I couldn't let my nieces starve. I had visions of Rosie begging on the street corner. That monkey isn't doing that, is she? I wouldn't put it past her."

"Good heavens, no!"

"Two thousand dollars is a great deal of money!"

"Yes, I know, and I thought that I should refuse, but I guess I can't be too proud. I have to admit that right now we could use it."

"I figured one year at ten percent interest would be fair. By then, you should be able to find a somewhat decent man to support you."

"Well, I don't know about that."

"You don't know much, but with a new baby on the way

and that rascal Rosie, not to mention your obstinate refusal to put Donna in an institution where she belongs, well it's pretty obvious someone had to do something!"

Stella gripped the telephone so tightly that she thought it would break – or she would. With more tension in her voice than she expected she calmly said, "Goodbye, Kathy."

"It's Kathleen, I've told you a million times. One would think you would be a bit more considerate. That is entirely impossible for you, I suspect."

"Kathy," Stella wanted to yell but controlled her voice, "the check will be returned today. I cannot and will not accept it. Thank you for your overwhelming generosity, but I'll figure something out. I don't need your charity!"

"You're unbelievably stubborn, not to mention rude and ungrateful. Fine, send it back. I don't care. I better not hear that Rosie, the scamp, had to take a job at the Five & Dime."

"I wonder if there is an opening at the cheese factory. I think she would like that better," Stella growled.

"Now you're just being facetious. Never mind; have it your own stubborn way. I'll tell Ma that I tried and tried to help, but you refused. You'll break her heart. She worries so much about you that she'll probably have a heart attack. Well, at least she never has to worry about me because I do have a very promising career."

"No, she just has to live with you. Send my love to Ma. Thank you anyway, Kathy," Stella insisted. She hung up the phone.

As soon as Stella ended the call, she picked up the receiver again and immediately dialed Veronica's number. It was answered on the first ring.

"Hello?"

"Veronica? Oh, thank goodness you're home. I'm dialing long distance, so I have to make this quick."

"What's wrong, Stella? Are you all right? How are the girls?"

"We're fine. The baby is coming soon and..."

"Now? It's premature? Oh, no. I'm on my way," Veronica was beginning to panic.

"No, no," Stella calmed down somewhat, "It's Kathy."

"Oh, Kathy. Well, that's a relief," Veronica exclaimed.

"No, it's not. She sent me a check for $2,000!"

"Good heavens! Has Kathy lost her mind?"

"She told me that she was being generous when she called to admonish me about not bowing down and kissing her feet the second I received the check!"

"Oh, Stella, surely she wasn't that difficult!"

"It was Kathy's usual way of making me crazy. I couldn't help myself. I told her I didn't want her precious money and would send it back."

"She does have a tendency to get your goat."

"Whatever that means," Stella continued. "She just annoyed me in the usual predictable way. What she did was very generous and would be very helpful if I could only keep it. But I wanted to yell at her to jump off that Sears building from the window of her prestigious career!"

"She's a receptionist," Veronica pointed out.

"Or she owns the building and everyone in it. I can't figure out which," Stella added with an edge to her voice.

"Mommy, Mommy!"

"Rosie, I'm on the phone to your aunt Veronica."

"Mommy, it's Donna. You have to look at Donna now!" Rosie shouted.

"Veronica, I have to go," Stella apologized. "Rosie said it's about Donna."

"I heard. Don't hang up. I want to know what is going on. Besides, you have two thousand dollars. You can afford to pay for the call," Veronica teased, but she knew Stella wasn't paying attention to her.

Without thinking, Stella carried the phone with its long extension cord around the corner to the living room. Donna was jumping up and down in the swing chair laughing excitedly. Her face was full of such glee that she seemed to glow.

"Look, Mommy, there is a rainbow around Donna. See, see? She is shining!" Rosie pointed enthusiastically.

Donna's back was to the sliding glass door. As the rays of

sunshine pushed through the glass and touched the chrome of the dancing chair, Donna appeared to be illuminated with magical wings of light.

"Mommy, Mommy, Donna is an angel! Look!" Rosie's smile and exuberance were infectious.

Stella stared at her two exceptional girls. At that very moment, she felt a love so strong and so tender that she thought she just might burst. These two precious girls were her very own miracle. And, now she was to have another. How did she get to be so lucky?

"Veronica, are you still there?" Stella said with a small catch in her voice.

"Yes, what in heaven's name is going on?" Veronica asked confused.

"Rosie and I think Donna is an angel. She's so very beautiful without a care in the world. She can't walk, and she still hasn't uttered one word, but you know something, Veronica, I don't care. I love her unconditionally and I will forever."

Veronica broke through Stella's musings, "Can Rosie hear me?"

"Yes, I think so. Come here, Rosie. Your aunt Veronica wants to talk to you."

"Hi, Auntie Veronica. Donna is an angel!" Rosie shouted with glee.

"I believe you may just be right," Veronica said from thousands of miles away, but they knew without a doubt that she had a big grin on her face. "Maybe things happen for a reason. I'm certainly no expert on this, but somehow, I truly believe that Donna was sent here for a purpose. Even more importantly, Donna may teach us more than we can teach her."

"I'm trying to teach her things, Aunt Veronica."

Finally, Stella added to the three-way conversation by just saying slowly but with conviction, "Empathy, understanding, confidence, respect, but more than that – no regrets. Why didn't I see that before? I know what I need to do."

Veronica added quickly, "You're going to keep the money.

It's the right thing to do. Would you like me to go over to the house and chat with Kathy and your mother?"

"Of course, but not about this. This I need to do on my own."

"Bye, Aunt Veronica. I'm going back to play with my sister, the angel," Rosie shouted as she ran off.

"Rosie, don't let that go to your head. Oh, never mind," Stella chided no one in particular.

"Okay, Stella," Veronica said, "I better go now. This call will cost a fortune. Good thing you can afford it now!"

"Very funny. I will call Kathy back and thank her with my sincere appreciation this time. Well, maybe."

Veronica laughed, "Just don't call person to person collect."

Stella was still laughing as she hung up the phone and picked up the still unopened letters that were awaiting her attention on the table. She had been so stunned when she opened Kathy's gift – no, loan – that she completely forgot about the other letters. Stella shuffled through an electric bill and the water and sewage bill, grimaced as she glanced at a notice for life insurance, and threw away an unwanted advertisement. At the bottom of the stack was an envelope from her mother. She picked up that one piece of mail and opened it while walking slowly to the living room to keep an eye on her girls.

> My dearest Stella,
>
> I hope you and my sweet granddaughters are doing well. I know things have been rough for you. I worry about you every day. It would be so easy for me to tell you to just come home, but I also know how determined you are to do what you feel is right. You're still in love with Richard and probably will be for a long, long time. I understand your reluctance to leave the home the two of you started. I'm sure you're hoping he will find his way back and you can be a family again. Right now, he doesn't even know you are about to have another child. It has been said before that hope springs eternal. Maybe those dreams will become a reality or maybe there will

be another dream. Wherever your life leads you, I will forever support and love you. I asked Kathy to send you a check for $2000 to help in any way it can. Sylvia, Kathy, and I all chipped in. This is a gift. There are no conditions and no strings attached. Please let us do this for you.

Love always no matter what.
Mom

The pages of the letter slipped through her fingers and slapped their way to the carpeted floor like the lost feathers of a solitary bird in a soft wind. Stella picked up the phone once again and dialed.

Chapter 21

1960 – SAN JOSE, CALIFORNIA

The heat of the lazy summer ended abruptly as autumn arrived to give it a swift kick, tossing away the warmth of the days. A gentle cool breeze blew the crisp multi-colored fallen leaves around Stella's feet as she sat in a lawn chair on her front lawn. Madeline slept soundly in her arms as Stella wrapped the blanket a bit more snugly around her small tired toddler. Rosie called her Maddie because she said Madeline looked mad when she was a newborn two years earlier. That was reasonable enough, she supposed, as how else might a child feel who had come into the world upside down, or a breech birth as it was called. Still, Maddie certainly wasn't cognizant of the worries continually swirling through Stella's mind. Donna certainly wasn't aware of anything other than the joy of her world. She was five years old now but could not walk, nor did she speak any recognizable words. This wasn't what bothered Stella, however. In her mind, Donna was perfect. She was serene and happy without a care in the world. When she laughed or smiled, the world seemed to light up. Stella was engulfed in love for her, as she was with her other two girls. Yet she knew that Donna would always hold a very, very special place in her heart.

No, it was Rosie that Stella could not stop worrying about. Sitting quietly with her two babies, Stella watched her oldest daughter ride the English Racer bicycle her grandma Ensign had given her for Christmas. She was almost nine years old but still could not sit on the bicycle seat and reach the pedals at the same time. This didn't seem to bother her in the least. Rosie flew past her mother waving excitedly as she pedaled as hard as she could. Stella's concern focused on the fact that nothing apparently got past Rosie. It was as though she could sense all the anxiety around her. She masked the feelings of loneliness and heartache she surely must be feeling since her father left. They still hadn't heard one tiny word from him. There had been no phone calls or letters or even a short visit to see the children. Stella was grieving silently as well but knew she needed to keep a happy demeanor so Rosie wouldn't be affected. Stella had come to grips with her disappointments. What she did not truly understand was why others appeared to be ignoring them. Rosie had no friends. She tried very hard to find the other children in the neighborhood and asked if she could play with them. Often, they would start to chat or chase each other, but within a few minutes a mother or father would come out and tell the child it was time to come in. Rosie was never allowed to visit or convince someone to stay overnight with her. No one asked her to play.

Stella also tried to make friends in the neighborhood. One sunny August day, she sent out invitations to each house she could see in her immediate area to come to her backyard for a barbecue. She was overjoyed to make potato salad, hamburgers, and corn on the cob. The four of them waited and waited. No one came. They had a quiet evening on their own and leftovers for the whole week. Rosie didn't complain. She only said that everyone must be very busy with their lives.

Stella had managed a full two years on the money that her family loaned her. She had no doubt in her mind that she would someday pay them back. She knew that her mother didn't expect that and probably wouldn't even accept it, but Stella knew she would do it. Right now, she wasn't sure when or how it would happen. As she continued to watch Rosie circle around and around the street, Stella decided she had to find employment but in order to do that, she must find childcare. A few weeks previously, she had gone to the Catholic church, which had a school and daycare. She asked the Mother Superior if she could work there as a library assistant for reduced wages while her girls enrolled in their school and daycare. Although very pleasant, the Mother Superior explained that even though Donna was old enough for kindergarten, they did not have anyone with the experience to teach her. She felt that it would be unwise to put Donna in school because others would tease her and tease Rosie. Would she really want to subject her children to that? Stella was stunned and at a loss for words. She quietly stood up and apologized for wasting her time. Mother Superior hurriedly came to her side and said that she could take a position at their school. Unfortunately, they could not accept Donna as a kindergarten student or in their daycare. Stella left without a word.

Now, Stella needed to figure out another strategy. She went to various other daycares over the next few days after her failed attempt at the Catholic school. Each facility turned her down once she explained that Donna had Down's syndrome. She thought for a moment of not telling them but realized quickly that would be a hurtful lie – to Donna, not to them.

The neighborhood that Stella lived in was a new development of single-story ranch-style tract homes. There were four or five similar designs, with each house containing a small front and backyard. Inside was a nice kitchen with a breakfast bar and an alcove eating area, a door that opened into the living room, and a long hallway that contained two or three bedrooms with one bathroom. Richard and Stella had bought their house when it was just out of construction about five years earlier for $9,000. It was a lot of money, but they were able to acquire a VA loan once Richard had gotten employment as an insurance agent. Now, the difficulty making those payments worried her. Stella liked the neighborhood but was frustrated that she was unable to make friends and truly feel at home here. Yet, as her mother had explained in her letter, Stella felt compelled to remain until Richard found his way back home. It was just a matter of time.

At the very moment when she was deep in thought, another woman approximately Stella's age was sitting on the steps of an identical home four houses down the road. When Stella looked up, the woman waved to her, so she waved back. The woman stood up and went into her house without another glance. Stella was perplexed but shrugged her shoulders and continued to observe Rosie weaving from one side of the road to the next. It could not have been more than five minutes later when that same woman strolled down the sidewalk toward Stella carrying two beverage glasses.

"Hello, Mrs. Surly. Do you live there?" Rosie exclaimed as she rode her bike next to the woman. "That's my house," she continued, pointing toward her mother and sisters.

"Is that so? Why, I never knew. That just happens to be where I'm heading," Mrs. Surly replied. "Would you like to introduce me to your family?"

"Mommy, Mommy," Rosie shouted while skidding her bike to a stop next to the sidewalk in front of her house, "This is Mrs. Surly. She's a second-grade teacher at my school." Rosie was back on her bike and off again before anyone noticed.

Stella stood up smiling as she put Maddie into the playpen next to Donna, "Hello, Mrs. Surly, I'm very happy to meet you. I am Stella Ensign."

"Call me Shirley, please. Oh, I know, Shirley Surly, who would want such a name? But I'm afraid I got stuck with it when I married my Sam. Why is it we girls never think to ask a fellow's last name before we agree to date them? Next thing you know, we are stuck with their horrible last name. I brought you some lemonade. I hope you like lemonade?"

Stella looked stunned before she shook some words out of her mouth. "Why, yes. That would be very nice."

Shirley was tall and slender with an easy outgoing manner. Her hair was cut short and held back out of her eyes with several black bobby pins. She had a very pretty, soft face with not a drop of make-up or even lipstick. She wore red and blue plaid trousers with a matching short-sleeved top. On her feet were very loosely tied white sneakers.

"It's starting to get a bit chilly out. Would you like me to run inside and grab a sweater for you?" Stella said.

"Oh no, I'm always hot. I love the fall, don't you?" she replied.

"I guess I do. I never thought about it before, but yes, I do very much," Stella added.

"I wanted to come by to apologize for not going to your party."

"Oh, no, that is perfectly fine..." Stella tried to say but was rapidly interrupted.

"You see, I just got the invitation yesterday when we got back from Oregon. My husband, Sam, and I were visiting family during the time of your party, so I'm very sorry we missed it."

"You didn't miss much. No one came."

"Why ever not?" Shirley asked confused.

"I'm not entirely sure, but if I had to venture a guess it would be because I have a handicapped daughter," Stella explained while looking lovingly at Donna.

"Can I pick her up?" Shirley asked. "She is beautiful!"

"Yes, yes, of course. Do you really think so? Her name is Donna."

"Hello, Donna," Shirley cooed as she lifted Donna out of the playpen, "My name is Shirley. I'm very happy to meet you."

"She doesn't talk," Stella said.

"Sometimes children talk too much," Shirley responded as they both laughed.

Rosie jumped off her bike and came running over, "Mrs. Surly, I'm going to get the other lawn chair. Don't move; I'll be right back."

"I wouldn't dream of it," she answered lightly, watching Rosie race around to the backyard. "Since Rosie will be gone for a couple of minutes, I thought you might like to know what Rosie has been saying at school, that's if you want to know. I don't mean to be intrusive."

"Oh, yes please. Tell me what the little rascal has been up to," Stella insisted, wrinkling her forehead.

Shirley grinned as she recounted the tale, "When Rosie is asked by anyone where her father is, she tells them that he's a war hero on a top-secret mission. He's currently on a journey to rescue survivors that were left stranded on an enemy-occupied island in the South Pacific. She claims solemnly that it is highly doubtful that he'll be able to survive this harrowing adventure!"

"Well, she has quite a vivid imagination, I must say," Stella sighed, "but the truth is far less exciting, I'm afraid. The only war going on is the one inside Richard's head, while I have been left alone to pick up the shattered pieces of our lives here at home."

"Rosie also has quite an extensive vocabulary well beyond her eight years."

"Yes, she's almost nine. I used to wonder about that, but she does read a lot and she loves to imitate people as well as try out new words and even voices," Stella shook her head as they both laughed companionably.

"It must be tough for you to raise three children on your own," Shirley consoled her.

"I can't deny it. I have to admit I'm a bit anxious. I know I need to get a job, but I have to find childcare first."

"I wish I could help, but I teach every day," Shirley said.

Both women drank a bit of their lemonade and seemed to be lost in thought when a teenage girl walked out the front door from the house next to hers. Stella jumped up, "Hello, I'm Mrs. Ensign. I don't believe we've had a chance to meet. What is your name?"

"How ya doing? I'm Patty. I live here."

Rosie returned, hauling another lawn chair, and set it down next to Shirley. "Mommy, that's Patty. She lives next door to us."

"Hello, Patty," Shirley said.

"Hi, Mrs. Surly," Patty answered without really noticing her.

"Do you go to school, Patty?" Stella inquired.

"I just graduated a few months ago," Patty said without interest.

"Are you going to college soon?"

"I don't know. My parents are pressuring me, but I dunno

what I wanna do. I'm thinking about travel or taking a break maybe. High school was hard work. I need time to think about things," Patty said with a noncommittal shrug.

Stella had an impulsive thought, "Do you ever do any babysitting?"

"Some."

"Would you be interested in babysitting my three very well-behaved girls?" Stella asked.

"I don't need any babysitter!" Rosie exclaimed. "I can take care of Donna and Maddie!"

"I know you could, Rosie, but you are still a little young," her mother consoled. "And you're in school most of the day. Right now, it would really be a help to me if you let an older girl help you with your two sisters while I find a job. Once Patty goes to college or maybe even sooner, I'll see if I can find someone like your grandmother to come stay with us."

"Yes. I want Grandma Ensign. She gives me Hershey candy bars and we sit under the weeping willow tree in her backyard and feed the birds rice. Let's go live with her!" Rosie gushed.

"Well, I was thinking that maybe we invite her to live with us. What do you think about that idea?"

"I love it. Today?"

"No, not today. Let's do one thing at a time, okay?" her mother added.

"Patty," Shirley cut in, "babysitting would be a nice idea. You could earn a bit of money and use it for college or travel or whatever you decide to do."

"Hmmm," Patty said while chewing a large piece of bubble gum. "How much you gonna pay?"

"Unfortunately, I can't pay much. I can pay 50 cents an hour and all the food you want to eat. It'll only be for a few hours while I look for work and if I do get a job, there will be more hours. Do you think you can do that?"

Pointing at Donna, Patty said, "What about her?"

"What about her?" Stella retorted.

"What am I supposed to do with her?"

"The same as you would with this one," she said while showing her Maddie, who was still sleeping.

Rosie jumped in, "Donna is easy. I'll teach you what to do."

"Okay, fine. When d'ya want me?" she asked as she blew out a big bubble that popped, sticking to her face. She scraped it off with her tongue and fingertips.

"How about nine o'clock tomorrow morning?"

"Okay, fine. I don't know what my mom is gonna say, but I could use some dough to hang out with my friends," Patty said and just as quickly walked away, still peeling off the gum and reinserting it into her mouth.

"One thing crossed off the list and one item to go," Shirley looked pensive.

"What do you mean?"

"You still need to find a job that will support the four of you."

"Yes, I need a good employment opportunity, but to be honest, I don't have a very good track record when it comes to work," Stella sighed.

"Well, I might just have an idea. My brother works at IBM in San Jose. He says their receptionist left, and he got stuck trying to fill in. I'm afraid he doesn't know what he's doing and is eager for them to hire someone who does."

"A receptionist? Well, why not? I'll go apply first thing tomorrow morning," Stella said as she stood up and hugged Rosie hard. "It's going to be okay now. I just know it. Tomorrow, I will get a job!"

"And tell Grandma Ensign to come live with us," Rosie almost jumped for joy.

"Yes."

Chapter 22

1960 – SAN JOSE, CALIFORNIA

No one seemed particularly surprised Stella was offered employment the same day she went on her quest to find work. No one except Stella, that is. She still couldn't believe her good fortune. Maybe the winds of good fate were blowing her way, she thought, as she left the huge IBM building and walked back to the bus stop. Earlier in the morning, she had walked toward the company with a rolled-up newspaper under one arm while tightly grasping the handles of her handbag with both hands. She had circled every advertisement in the help-wanted classifieds she felt she might be able to do just in case this IBM position didn't work out. However, she didn't even know what IBM stood for. Why did people always use initials?

Stella stood on the sidewalk for a short while gathering her courage and preparing an inner monologue for her interview. She was dressed for success, as Veronica used to say. Today, she was wearing a slimming navy-blue skirt that hugged her legs down to mid-calf. She unconsciously pulled down her fluffy pink sweater with tiny pearl buttons and readjusted the pink and blue scarf around her neck. The hat was her pride and joy. She felt if anything would impress an employer, it would be one of Veronica's original hat creations. It perched snugly on the side of her head with one edge pulled up and accentuated with a silver clasp.

She gave herself a mental voice of encouragement and walked into the building. The first thing she tried to avoid doing was letting out a gasp, but she couldn't help herself. She was overwhelmed. Doors were open to other rooms where she could easily spy large unusual machines that had a lot of gadgets and levers of some kind. Still, the most unusually curious thing was the slender man at the front desk. He was probably a little younger than middle-aged with a dark crew cut and black-rimmed thick glasses, and had quite possibly forgotten to shave this morning. Stella wanted to laugh as she observed him for a few moments, too embarrassed to speak to him. The man was struggling with three phones. He had gotten himself tangled in the cords while trying to speak to all three conversations at once. As he put one receiver under his chin, he dropped another. He reached over to grab a notepad and was searching in vain for a pen that was right in front of him. The man was sweating profusely, undoubtedly why he was also trying to loosen his wide-striped tie and take off his jacket, when he inadvertently managed to lodge one of the phone receivers in his sleeve.

Stella was on the verge of hysterics when she decided that she had to help the poor man before he collapsed. She walked calmly over to the reception area, put down her purse and the newspaper, and said, "Here, please let me help."

The man looked at her as if she were his very own guardian angel. He stuttered something even he didn't understand while Stella untangled each phone. She put the receivers of each phone back into their correct positions, picked up the papers as well as the various items on the floor, then quickly straightened up the desk. At that moment, three men came into the lobby. They were identically dressed in black suits with nondescript ties. All three sported black-rimmed glasses like the man at the desk. If she didn't know better, she would have thought they were speaking another language. She couldn't figure out what they were saying until one man addressed the man she was trying to help.

"Oh, there you are. What have you been doing? We need you to get busy on the tape reels. What are you doing out here? Where is Lory, the receptionist?"

The man stood transfixed and nodded. He squealed a quick thank-you to Stella and raced around the desk to the back room. As he did so, the three men spotted Stella. If deer needed to be taught how to stare into headlights, these men would be the professors. Stella was surprised pale white skin could redden so swiftly. Since they were frozen where they were, Stella walked over to the men. She held out her hand and said, "Hello, my name is Stella Ensign. I'm looking for employment."

No one moved. It was as if the men forgot how to breathe yet alone talk. Finally, they all started stuttering at once.

"The girl that belongs at this desk appears to be missing," the shorter man said.

"Frank," one of the other men gulped, "Lory got married and left. I believe yesterday was her last day."

"That must be why a congratulations and goodbye cake is in the staff room," said the third man.

"Are you getting married or going to have a baby, or whatever women do?" Frank asked, blushing further.

"No, no. I'm free to work," Stella rushed her response.

"Are you a receptionist?"

"Yes," Stella simply replied.

The three men looked at each other, looked at her, and said almost simultaneously, "You're hired. You can start now. That's your desk."

She turned around to look, but when she looked back, they were rushing back to the room with the odd machines.

Stella went to her workstation and sat down. She shook her head and giggled while thinking to herself, "What in heaven's name am I supposed to do? Well, if Kathy can be a receptionist, then so can I. I might not own the building, but I can figure this out."

Chapter 23

1960 – SAN JOSE, CALIFORNIA

A MONTH HAD GONE BY QUITE SWIFTLY SINCE SHE WALKED INTO an employment opportunity that she hadn't really understood before. Stella enjoyed her new job although she still wasn't entirely sure what she was doing. Still, no one seemed to really mind. For that reason, she managed to answer the phones, take notes, and deliver messages. The men were a bit awkward around her as they often continued to stare and stutter when in her presence. Most of them simply ignored her and spoke amongst themselves in their odd communicative mode. The first man she had encountered when she started her job was very attentive toward her. The other men in the office called him Rollins. He often stopped by her desk offering his assistance in any way. She secretly hoped that he wouldn't help her. She couldn't afford to lose this job, too.

It was a long distance from the bus stop to her simple ranch style home on Branham Lane in San Jose. Stella had time to think about what she wanted to do and what would ultimately be in her three girls' best interests.

Although she appeared to be doing well at work, she constantly worried about leaving her children at home so long with Patty, the teenage babysitter. Stella had not been able to go see Grandma Ensign yet due to lack of funds. After receiving her first paycheck, she was eager to visit Grandma Ensign this weekend and do everything in her power to convince her to come live with them. Grandma Ensign was a widow who had been living alone for many, many years. Her isolated loneliness was apparent as she was so undeniably thrilled whenever Stella and the girls came for a visit. Stella had wanted to ask her own mother to move in with them, but she was afraid of the uproar such a request would undoubtedly set off with her sister, Kathy. Grandma Ensign seemed like the perfect solution.

Stella also envisioned a time that she might be able to buy an inexpensive used car and teach herself how to drive. She was just contemplating how she would be able to find a driver's manual when she stepped up to her front door.

Rosie flung the door wide open while shouting, "Mommy, Mommy. I saw you coming up the sidewalk. I've been watching since I got home from school!"

Stella gave Rosie a big hug. "That must have been exhausting!"

"No, not as much as watching Donna and Maddie all the time. Donna keeps trying to get up and walk! I've been helping her," Rosie grinned.

"You're a wonderful big sister."

Patty glanced over while turning off the small black-and-white television set. "It's about time you got home," Patty whined. "There's nothing good on the tube right now, just some dumb cowboys and Indians thing. Gotta go. Gotta date."

Stella tried to ask how things had gone today, but Patty ran out the door ignoring her.

"Mommy," Rosie said, "I think something is wrong with Maddie."

"What do you mean?" Stella asked as she raced over to Maddie and picked her up over the wall of the playpen.

"She won't walk," Rosie said while shrugging her shoulders.

"Oh, Rosie. Maddie walks. Maybe not a lot but she walks back and forth in the playpen."

"When I take Maddie out of the playpen and tell her to walk, she falls flat on her bottom and gives me that awful Maddie wrinkled look on her face just like the clothes on the clothesline. She just watches Donna. Sometimes she scoots around on her bottom and sometimes she stands, but she won't walk even when I tell her to. She won't talk, either."

"Rosie," her mother gently scolded, "She's just a baby."

"She's a big old baby. Big old babies are supposed to walk and talk and go potty on their own. Maddie doesn't listen to me," Rosie said with real concern in her voice.

"Oh, Rosie, give her time. She does crawl when she wants to. Not all babies develop those skills at the same time. Sometimes it takes longer. Just like Donna."

"Maddie must be just like Donna without pumpkin doodle eyes!"

Stella set Maddie down on the shag carpet next to Donna. She reached over the playpen to grab some toys, then sat down close to all three girls. The four of them were laughing and playing when Donna grabbed her mother's arm and stood up.

"Mommy, Mommy. Look what Donna is doing!" Rosie exclaimed.

"Oh, my goodness. Easy, Donna, easy," Stella coached as Donna let go of her mother's arm.

"Come to me, Donna, come," Rosie cheered. Rosie's excitement was infectious. Donna took two steps toward Rosie.

With tears in her eyes, Stella stood up and took a step backwards. "Donna, come to mommy."

Rosie helped Donna turn around and let her go. Donna walked six steps without assistance. Rosie and her mom clapped and gave Donna many hugs and kisses. They practiced more and more until Donna walked twenty steps. Rosie was counting each step while their mom excitedly cheered her on when both stopped and stared at Maddie. She stood up without any assistance and eagerly walked over to Donna.

"I told you Maddie was just like Donna," Rosie grinned.

"Looks like I have three big girls now!"

Chapter 24

1960 – SAN JOSE, CALIFORNIA

The next day, Stella left for work happier than she had been in years. She was full of wonderful hope and positive anticipation for the future. Maybe Richard would come home soon or maybe he wouldn't, but Stella wasn't going to agonize over it any longer. She had things to do and she would do them confidently.

When she arrived at her desk, the shy man that everyone called Rollins was there. It appeared he had been waiting for her. For some odd reason he acted extremely nervous, even for him. He was shuffling his feet while tightening and loosening his tie.

"Hello," Stella said smiling.

"You seem in a happy mood this morning," he said shyly.

"I am, Rollins," Stella added with a grin.

"Ummm," he was obviously struggling with his words.

"Yes?"

"Can you call me something other than Rollins? I mean, if you don't mind. That is my last name you see. I never understood why anyone would want to call me by my last name. But at work and even when I was in the service, I was always called by my last name." He knew he must sound like a babbling idiot.

"Why, of course. Why don't you like your last name? It sounds like a perfectly nice name to me, although I'm sure you must have a very nice first name," Stella responded.

"My family call me Willie. It's short for Wilbur. But that

just makes some people laugh. They think it's funny. Maybe they're not really laughing. Maybe I'm just ridiculously sensitive. I'm not really a funny person, more the down-to-earth type, I suppose. This may sound odd, but I guess when I was born there was a name mix-up with a calf and me. The newborn calf was supposed to be named Wilbur and my name was to be William after some ancestor, but we were born at the same time and confusion occurred. It's ridiculous, but my sister loves to tell the story. I usually leave the room. I hope that doesn't make you see me differently. I mean, I hope you won't look at me and think of a cow. I hope you'll still like me. Do you like me?" Wilbur could feel himself rambling and started regretting his self-doubting words.

Stella answered with some confusion and nervousness, "Of course it doesn't bother me."

She wondered what this was leading up to. "Well, let's see," she continued, "Wilbur seems like a perfectly fine name to me. I don't see you as a Willie, though. Your last name has an 's' at the end. So, how about Wills?"

"Wills?" he queried as if rolling it around his tongue to taste it. "Yes, Wills. I like it. My family and friends might not even know it's me. This will be our own private identity, just between the two of us. I mean, if you think that I'm not being too forward."

"Of course not. Wills it is!"

"Stella?" Wills began slowly and blushed as Stella shuffled some papers on her desk, "Stella, you never mentioned if you had a beau or worse, a husband. You don't, do you, because..."

The phone rang, interrupting Wills. He watched silently as Stella picked up the phone with a pleasant expression on her lovely face, "Good morning, IBM. May I..." Stella abruptly stopped talking, the color draining from her face.

Wills stared as Stella dropped the phone and ran to the door without regard to anyone or anything.

Part Two

Chapter 25

1961 – SAN JOSE, CALIFORNIA

Rosie

Mommy is crying again. She cries all the time when we're home. She never cries when we're not home. Mommy laughs around other people. She tells funny stories that make them all laugh. She even told the nuns who take care of my sister, Maddie, and me something that made them all laugh, which is funny itself because I never see the nuns laugh.

The neighbors talk to us now. I don't know why. They never used to before. A lady came by with a casserole dish the other day. Mommy invited her in for a cup of coffee, but she had more important things to do.

At first, I wasn't so sure I liked all this new attention. I never really liked Mr. Schultz. He was always yelling at the gigantic dog that often roamed our neighborhood. Mr. Schultz said the dog would dig up his carrots on purpose. Mommy had read Beatrix Potter's Peter Rabbit book to me. Mr. Schultz reminds me of the adventures of Peter Rabbit to outfox Mr. McGregor, the farmer. So now, I call him Mr. Farmer. I call him that a lot when I'm with Mommy. It makes her laugh.

One day, Mr. Farmer was chasing the gigantic dog down the street, yelling at him. He screamed, "Let go of my carrots! I know you were in my garden. You can't fool me, you horrible creature!"

I ambled over to Mr. Farmer and with my cutest curtsey that often makes grownups smile, I said, "Why don't you like your dog?"

"He's not my dog!" Mr. Farmer growled, "He's nobody's dog. He's an escape artist!"

"Oh" was all I said.

"He just magically appears and gets into the worst kind of mischief. I'm calling the dog pound right this minute. They need to send out a dog catcher immediately!"

"No!"

"No?" Mr. Farmer looked at me strangely.

"No," I continued quickly. I had to think of something fast. "No, I'm sorry. He's my dog. He accidentally escaped from my backyard. I'll be more careful about letting him get out, I promise."

"He's your dog?"

"Yes."

"Where is his collar and license?"

"He buried them in the backyard. He does that sometimes. That's why we have so many holes back there. We used to think it was gophers."

"You listen to me, missy," Mr. Farmer screamed. He puffed up and seemed to be about ready to explode as his face was now brighter than his garden beets. "Don't let that dangerous hound escape again, you hear me?"

I tilted my head and gave one of my famous smiles that my dad used to say could melt the frown off a snowman. "Yes, Mr. Farm...I mean Mr. Schultz."

"See that you do. Okay, then." He started to walk away, but turned around and asked me one more question, "By the way, what's his name?"

I held my breath for a few seconds, then blurted out, "Merlin!"

"Merlin?"

"Yes, after Merlin the magician."

"It should be Houdini."

"Who?"

"Houdini, after the escape artist." Mr. Farmer walked away shaking his head. His color returned to that pasty gray it usually is.

Once Mr. Farmer was out of sight, Merlin stepped around from behind a bush. He gradually sauntered over to my side. He put his head on my shoulder. I put my arms around him. Merlin followed me home.

I was so nervous when we reached the front door. I told Merlin to get behind me and try to blend in, so Mommy wouldn't notice him. I didn't really think that would work, especially when Merlin barked twice. Mommy immediately opened the door.

"Well, well. Now who do we have here?" Mommy simply said.

"It's me, Mommy. Your Rosie."

Before I could stop him, Merlin jumped up and put his two big, fluffy paws on Mommy's shoulders. She almost fell over, but quickly grabbed the door and held on. For a moment, I don't think that any of us breathed.

Mommy said, "I was watching you from the open window."

I wasn't sure if she was talking about Merlin or me until she hugged me and said through those moist eyes of hers, "Rosie, never ever doubt how much I love you. Maybe it's your destiny to rescue others. I hope it is. I wish that..." she stopped. "Oh never mind."

Merlin pushed between us and grinned with his long pinkish tongue hanging loosely from his mouth.

"Come on, you two. Let's have dinner."

That night, Mommy made the worst food in the whole wide world – liver! Merlin already had his dinner, so he settled under the kitchen table with us. Every time I noticed Mommy not looking at me, I hid a piece of that horrid substance in my hand and gave it to Merlin.

"I think both of you are a bit sneaky," she said while pushing her food around the plate. She wasn't eating it, either.

"Mommy, you don't like liver either."

"No, I guess I don't, but it is supposed to be good for us, so that's why I make it."

I looked straight at her and said, "Why are things that are supposed to be good for us so terrible?"

"I don't know, sweetheart. Just eat."

"I think Donna going away is terrible and not good for us."

Mommy made a sound that I can't describe. I stared into her eyes for a long, long time before she said something to me in a shaken voice, "Why are you looking at me like that?"

"I'm trying to see the words in your eyes."

Mommy's eyes flooded with water. She picked up her napkin from the table and patted the escaping tears. "What do you mean?"

"My teacher, Mrs. Nun," I tried to say before Mommy interrupted me.

"Polite girls should use a teacher's proper name."

"Okay, Sister Agnes said that if you look long enough, you can read a person's thoughts by looking in their eyes. I thought maybe I could find the words to read in your pretty blue eyes, except they always seem to be clouded over ready to erupt into a rainstorm."

Mommy didn't say anything. She picked up both plates and walked slowly to the garbage can. She opened the lid and tossed our dinner inside. She took the plates to the kitchen sink but forgot to turn on the water. I think she may have been washing the dishes with her tears.

I knew now what I had to do.

Merlin and I left the table. Without Mommy knowing, I went directly to her small desk in the hallway. I opened the drawer and found an old box where she keeps her letters from Veronica, plus a few stamps, stationery, and pens. I took out a piece of paper and an envelope. First, I addressed the envelope with Veronica's address. I know it by heart, but I looked at it again from one of her letters. I copied it exactly as Veronica had written it. I put a stamp on the upper right-hand corner. Next, I held the pen in my left hand and wrote one word on the stationery paper – HELP. I folded the paper and put it in the envelope. I licked it closed and stuffed it in my pocket. Tomorrow, I would put it in the mailbox down the street.

Chapter 26

1961 – SAN JOSE, CALIFORNIA

When the doorbell rang, Stella wasn't especially surprised since an increasing number of visitors had been briefly coming over during the last couple of months now. Nevertheless, Stella stood transfixed as if rooted to the spot. Rosie glanced her way but swiftly ran past, skirting her mother to reach the front door. The bell sounded again, echoing throughout the entire room. Rosie grabbed the knob but looked back at her mother to get permission to open the door. Why would her mother's eyes be so watery now, Rosie wondered, but shrugged it off since it appeared to be a regular occurrence these days. Rosie opened the door hastily. In front of her stood Veronica. Within seconds, Rosie squealed, jumped up, and folded her arms around her.

"My, my, how big you have grown! I don't think I can lift you anymore!"

"Oh, Aunt Veronica. I know you are joking with me. I'm still the runt of fourth grade, as Pete the Creep tells anyone stupid enough to listen to him," Rosie said.

"Rosie, calling someone a name is not a nice thing to do," Veronica admonished.

"He calls me names and teases me all the time."

"Two wrongs do not make a right."

"Did you hear that from my mom? That's what she says."

"We will continue this conversation later. Right now, please go get Donna so I can give her a big hug!"

"No," Rosie said.

"No?" Veronica was incredulous.

"I can't."

"You can't?" Repeating her words would get her nowhere so Veronica asked a specific question. "Is Donna visiting her dad?"

"No," Rosie said emphatically as she ran down the hall into her room and slammed the door.

"Good heavens, what is going on?" Veronica walked straight to Stella, who was huddled in a corner, put her arms around her, and repeated her name over and over as Stella wailed.

"Come on, Stella. Let's sit down. I'm going to put the kettle on for some tea. I have a feeling this is going to be a long night."

Stella shook her head yes and automatically went to the kitchen. As Veronica occupied herself with the task of tea making, Stella sat at the kitchen table and pulled a handkerchief out of her pocket. She wiped her eyes and blew her nose. Veronica found a dish towel. She drenched it in cold water, wrung it out, and handed it to Stella to wipe her face.

"I never knew hurt and despair could have so many layers," Stella sniffed. "I don't know where to begin. I don't know what will happen. I don't know what to do."

Veronica walked over with two cups of tea made especially the way they both liked it – lemon for Stella, milk for her. She set the cups down before settling herself on the chair across the table from Stella.

"I suppose it'll be a little difficult to know what we are going to do until I know what exactly happened," Veronica said.

"We?" Stella asked.

"Yes, of course," Veronica continued. "Gather your thoughts together as I go check on Rosie and baby Maddie. Is Maddie here?"

"Yes" was all Stella replied.

"I'm very excited to meet Maddie. If she is asleep, I will let her sleep. But if she is awake, I will bring her out here with us. I do need to have a little chat with Rosie, too, but that may have to wait until I hear the entire story from you."

Veronica got up and walked down the hallway. Stella stayed frozen in place, only her eyes following her best friend's steps. Stella wanted to tell Veronica everything. She wanted Veronica to make it all right. She wanted her to fix it because she couldn't. She wanted to change the past and make the future bearable. Nevertheless, she realized that this burden should not be placed on Veronica's shoulders. Veronica wasn't the one responsible; she was. Veronica hadn't made bad, horrible choices; she had. Stella didn't know how she could live with the consequences of her own foolish actions. The fault was hers alone. She knew that Veronica wanted to help her, but she could not. Stella felt like such a failure and now the worst mother in the world. She was just too embarrassed to reveal her soul to her friend. She didn't deserve a good friend like Veronica.

"Are you done beating yourself up?" Veronica scolded as she reentered the kitchen and sat down. She sensed Stella's despair almost as if she could read her mind.

"You can't help me," Stella wailed.

"I'll be the judge of that."

"Oh, Veronica. I made such a mess of everything and I just don't know what to do," Stella started crying again. "I feel like such a failure that I'm even afraid to confide in my best friend."

Veronica waited a few moments for Stella to catch her breath before she jumped in. "Who are you?" Veronica asked. "This is not the formidable Stella who can and does stand up to any and all authority. This is not the Stella who never backs down under any circumstance. This is not the relentless Stella who finds a way out of all obstacles for anyone around her and for herself. This is not the obstinate Stella who refused to give up when she failed at something. This is not the Stella who stood up unashamedly around those who would gladly cut her down."

Stella looked at her as if she had hit a nerve. Veronica wasn't going to let her wallow in her sorrow or self-pity.

Veronica was almost angry now as she went on, "This is not

the Stella who allowed, no, expected and wanted a black woman to sit next to her on the train when no one else would. In fact, I'm not so sure that you even realize that I am a Negro!"

"You're a Negro?"

"I am not done, so just hold your sassy tongue! This is the Stella who is my best friend – unconditionally. You stood by me; now it is my turn to stand by you. No matter what!" Veronica finished, wagging a finger at Stella's face.

Stella smiled and shook her head, "Okay, I refuse to let it defeat me. I'm done crying. Are you ready to hear the whole sordid affair?"

"You had an affair?" Veronica grinned.

"Now who is being sassy?" Stella teased. "I'll tell you the whole story; then let's figure out a plan."

Chapter 27

1961 – SAN JOSE, CALIFORNIA

STELLA'S STORY – 1960

"*I* WAS AT WORK WHEN THE PHONE CALL CAME FROM HOME. ROSIE was crying. A policeman or the ambulance driver, I don't know which, took the phone from her. I remember running out the door and hearing Wills yell in the background. 'Stella, wait, what's wrong?' 'Accident at home. I have to hurry,' I told him.

"Wills grabbed my purse off the desk and raced out of the door with me. I barely noticed what was going on, but I followed Wills as he said, 'Follow me. My car is in the parking lot. I'll drive you home. It'll be faster than the bus.' He was right. I couldn't wait for the bus. I didn't answer him; I just ran with him. As we got into the car, I directed him where to go. I kept urging him to drive faster and faster. Wills could sense my fear and anxiety, so he did just that. He drove as fast as he could while gripping the steering wheel. I stared out the window at the blurry objects as we sped by.

"As soon as he drove up in front of the house, I was out of the door before he even shut off the engine. I raced inside. Funny, I don't even recall if he shut off the ignition or opened his door, yet Wills was on my heels.

"When I entered the house, I did a quick survey of the area around me. Rosie stood trembling in the corner, tears running freely down her face. She was gripping Maddie's hand tightly.

Maddie was silently standing very close to her looking frightened. 'Patty, what is going on here? What happened?'

"Patty didn't even look at me. She acted like nothing in the world was amiss. 'It's okay now. Don't worry about me,' she said to no one. She just sat back on the couch and let the sounds of *American Bandstand* soothe her.'

"I really wanted to scream at her. Maybe I did. 'Where is Donna?' No answer. If I were a violent person, I'm pretty sure I would have struck her right then. I had never been so angry and scared in my life. 'Where is Donna?'

"Wills put a hand on my shoulder to calm me I suppose, but I didn't care about that. I brushed it off angrily. I flew toward Patty as I continued to yell one word at a time, 'I SAID, WHERE IS DONNA?' Patty stood up and shrugged her shoulders as if nothing happened. 'They took her,' she said. 'I gotta go home. You owe me five dollars.' I raced to the door before Patty could get there. I jerked it open and shrieked like a lost owl in the dark woods, 'Get out of my house and never – I mean NEVER EVER RETURN!'

"Wills told me later that he watched me transform with a tenderness that shocked him to his core as I went directly to Rosie and said, 'I know this is hard, sweetheart, but I need you to tell me what happened and where Donna is. You are a big girl now. It's all right. You can tell me. I'm sorry that I yelled. Please, please tell me.'

"Wills handed Rosie a big white handkerchief he retrieved from his jacket pocket. She took it without looking at him. She wiped the tears off her small face and blew her nose as she sniffed a few times. In a slow, choked voice, Rosie said, 'Donna was walking. I was so excited. I clapped and cheered. Patty told me to shut up because she couldn't hear her boyfriend over the phone. Donna turned around. Mommy, it seemed like slow motion. I tried to get to her. She, she...' Rosie started crying even harder. 'I'm here, Rosie,' I cried while I put my arms around her. 'Just tell me what happened.'

"'Donna fell. She fell hard on the edge of the table in front of the couch,' Rosie continued. 'Donna started jerking and shaking. She seemed to be choking. Oh, Mommy, she wasn't breathing. Patty started screaming. I grabbed the phone out of her hand. I hung up her call and dialed zero. The operator answered. I told her that my sister was dying. She asked me if my mother was there. I told her no, but the babysitter was. The operator asked to speak to the babysitter, but Patty screamed no. The operator asked if I knew my address. I gave it to her, Mommy. I remembered my address and phone number because you made me memorize it.'

"'You are a very smart and brave girl,' I told her in the most tender voice that I could summon up under the circumstances. 'What happened next?'

"'An ambulance came and men in white coats put Donna on a flat bed and carried her to the ambulance. One white coat man told Patty that she needed to control herself and take care of us. I told him that I was going with Donna. I ran outside, but he grabbed me and carried me back inside. I kicked and screamed. I think I may have bit him because he yelled and put me right down. He told me the best thing that I could do for Donna was to wait for you. He asked if I knew your phone number. That's when I called you, but the man took the phone from me.' Rosie's tears flooded her eyes once again and she said no more.

"Wills immediately took charge of the situation. 'Stella,' he said, 'take the girls. I will drive all of us to the hospital right now, then I'll return here and ask my sister to stay with the girls until you call for us to pick you up or when your husband gets home.'

"I don't even know if I told Wills that the chances of a husband coming home were slim to none, but I do remember accepting his generous offer and telling him that it could be a long time. He only said, 'It doesn't matter. I will wait.' Later, though, he told me that he wondered at the time why I never mentioned that I had three children or a husband, and where he was. Little did I realize at the time that I would soon be able to answer that question.

"When we arrived at the emergency entrance, Wills dropped

me off. I pulled open the door handle while turning my head toward the girls in the backseat. I shook my head no to Rosie as she tried to escape the vehicle. Wills told her that she could not go with me to see Donna. Rosie flew into a rage unlike any I had ever seen before. Wills came around to the side of the car as I physically tried to put Rosie back inside. I said to her, 'Rosie, please be my big girl now. Children are not allowed at this time. I promise to come get you when they say you can visit. Let Mommy find out what is going on and I will immediately call you. Please, go with Mr. Rollins now. He is my good friend and a very nice man. Remember, I told you about him. He is Mrs. Surly's brother. She will come over and take care of you.' Rosie sobbed, 'I want to go with you, Mommy. Please!' The only thing I could say before I shut the car door again and ran into the hospital was a choked no."

Chapter 28

1961 – SAN JOSE, CALIFORNIA

The once pristine white tablecloth was now a wadded-up mass of damp material in Stella's tight fists. She lifted her head from the table and watched Veronica in astonishment. "What are you doing?"

Veronica had every cabinet door open. She was on her hands and knees with her head under the kitchen sink counter. "This is not a one box of tissues story, I can tell. Where are your sobbing supplies?"

"We may have to get the tea towels and rolls of toilet paper out."

"And a bottle of wine. I have a feeling that you have one hidden somewhere."

"The garage."

"I'm on it," Veronica said as she opened the kitchen door leading into the garage. She came back moments later and took the teacups from Stella to deposit them into the sink. "There's a car in the garage."

"Yes. Stay tuned and all will be revealed. The corkscrew is in the second drawer next to the fridge. The wine glasses are on the top shelf. I'm going to check on the girls."

"I'll meet you in the front room shortly," Veronica said.

STELLA'S STORY – 1955

"Six years ago, when my second-born was tenderly placed in my arms for the first time, I was overcome with a sense of serenity that I had never known before. The heightened feeling of pure ecstatic joy and absolute love was overwhelming. I could almost see the unbreakable cord tethering our souls. I knew then and I know now that nothing in this world could tear us apart. I would protect her; I would care for her; I would do anything for her. Maybe I cried out loud or maybe only in my private thoughts, but I looked toward the heavens asking Mother Mary to watch over us. Richard walked in at that moment. He had apparently been in the bar across the street since he reeked of alcohol and was slightly tipsy. He looked at me and smiled. 'Another girl?' he asked, slurring his words. 'Oh, sweetheart. I'm so proud of you. Can I hold our new baby?' I shook my head slowly while saying, 'She's my Donna.' I have no idea why I said that, but Richard didn't question it. 'Why, hello, Donna,' he cooed as he picked her up.

"His expression changed as he turned back to me and said, 'Where is the doctor?' I was confused and asked him why he wanted to know. He said that it was nothing. He told me that Donna looked a bit odd, but he was sure it was just a newborn look and that she'd become as beautiful as her mother in no time. I just laughed at him. 'Give her to me,' I said, 'You don't know what you are talking about.'"

THE PRESENT – 1961

Veronica topped up their glasses with more wine. "What happened after Wills dropped you off at the hospital? What happened to Donna?"

Stella drained her glass and held it out for another refill before continuing her story.

STELLA AT THE HOSPITAL – 1960

'My impatience, waiting to talk to someone after I had run through the emergency room door, must have been obvious. I had to stop abruptly behind another woman who came in with a man on a stretcher. I couldn't see his face, nor could I hear what the woman was saying to the nurse at the desk. I could feel my irritation growing as I bit every one of my nails and childishly stomped my feet on the floor. I was feeling lost in a tunnel of emotions. I wasn't paying attention to any sights or sounds around me. My only thoughts were of Donna and my self-imposed guilt. Blame and fear engulfed my entire being. If something didn't happen soon, I didn't know what I would do. Vivid images in my head were spiraling out of control when a stout, middle-aged woman dressed from head to foot in a bleached white uniform rushed toward me. I noticed her rigid thick-soled white shoes first as my eyes traveled from the floor to her stiff white hat. It is funny how the mind can readjust one's thinking or maybe I was going crazy, but the only thing that I could think of at that instant was that Veronica needed to redesign that headgear.

"'Miss, miss, are you feeling all right? Can I help you?' the nurse questioned me. 'My daughter, where is she? How is she? I want to see her?' I babbled almost incoherently. 'Let's take a look at my list,' she replied calmly while looking closely at the clipboard held in her hands. 'She came by ambulance about 40, maybe 45 minutes ago. I think.' 'She's only five years old. Her name is Donna,' I said to the nurse, who was smiling sweetly. 'Oh, yes, of course. I remember now. The little Mongoloid girl,' she replied. 'Her name is Donna. Take me to her, please,' I begged.

"'Doctor Weissman instructed that when you arrived someone should take you to the waiting room and he would be with you shortly.'

"'I want to see Donna now. How is she?' But the frustrating, evasive nurse wouldn't tell me what I needed to know. She kept repeating that she didn't know. 'I do know that they are taking very good care of her and that Doctor Weissman will be out as soon as he can. You can't go back there now. You would just be in the way. You do not want to scare the poor little thing now, would you?' the nurse said. 'No, no. I guess not,' I managed to respond.

"'Very good. I will show you to the waiting room. Please

wait there until the doctor comes to talk to you,' the nurse said as she directed me to a nice quiet room. 'There is a pot of coffee on the table in the corner,' she said, pointing in that direction, then speedily turned to leave.

"For the first time since arriving at the hospital, I looked at my surroundings. The room was sparkling clean with uncomfortable looking couches and matching chairs. They had a sleek look with wooden arm rests and green vinyl upholstery. I remember thinking that my dad would have been horrified. The side table had an acrylic top and slender legs. On the table was a small lamp and some magazines. The woman that had been in the line in front of me took a last drag of her cigarette and smashed it in the ashtray that was also positioned on the table. She was around my age, I surmised, but looked weathered somehow. She wore very tight yellow pedal pushers that molded completely to her legs. Her blouse was probably two sizes too small for her. Maybe that was why she had the top two buttons unfastened, which exposed parts of her that I had no desire to look at. Her hair was teased and piled high atop her head. Her spiky high heels gave the impression that she was ready to topple over.

"'Hey,' she said to me as she lowered her orange-rimmed eyeglasses, which pointed outward toward her ears. 'Hello,' I replied without meeting her gaze.

"'What you in here for? I was in a car accident with my husband,' she said without waiting for a response from me. I'm sure I must have said that I was sorry. 'It was the other guy's fault. You see, that fool in the car in front of us put his brakes on and my guy stomped on the brakes so as not to hit him. Well, he got lucky, you see, cuz he sped off. My guy wasn't so lucky, though. He wasn't wearing one of those new-fangled seatbelts that tighten down by your hips. I was wearing mine. I don't like how they can wrinkle a nice dress, but since I just had on my casual wear, I didn't care one way or the other. My guy, however, went flying into the dashboard. He hit his head. He ain't bad, but the ambulance came, and a man said that his thick skull should be looked at for a concussion or something like that.'

"'Oh' was all I could get out, but I wasn't really listening. After a short while, she shrugged her shoulders, sat on the couch, and picked up the *Look* magazine. I continued to pace the floor.

"'Mrs. Ensign?' a nice-looking young man said. He had to be the doctor as he had on a physician's outfit with a stethoscope wrapped around his neck.

"I turned around while the woman reading the magazine stood up. 'Yes?' we said simultaneously.

"'I'm Mrs. Ensign,' I said quickly. 'How is Donna?'

"'Wait a minute, dearie. I'm Mrs. Ensign, not you,' the woman said as she charged in front of me. The woman was either crazy or maybe she had hearing problems. 'He said Mrs. *Ensign*,' I emphasized for her. 'I know what he said, sweetie,' she scoffed.

"'Wait, wait a minute. I'm looking for a Mrs. Dick Ensign,' the doctor added.

"'Yes,' we both said again, but sharply this time.

"'There can't be two Mrs. Dick Ensigns,' the doctor scolded. 'That is the name written on this form.' I ignored the crazy woman and just spoke to the doctor, 'Is it about Donna?'

"'Who is Donna?' the annoying woman interrupted.

"'No,' the doctor continued. 'It's about Dick.'

"'Richard is here?' I asked confused. 'He knows about Donna's accident. He must be here to see her. Of course, that's it.'

"'Who's Donna? And who are you, by the by. Dickie isn't here to see no Donna. My Dickie is here because he has a bump on his head,' the woman seethed.

"'He is *not* your Dick,' I wanted to scream. 'You must be talking about someone else.'

"'Well, this is an odd situation,' the doctor said as he rubbed his chin. 'One of you must be married to a Dick Ensign, but which one?'

"'I am. Take me to the weasel!' I said and left the room, taking the doctor's arm and ignoring that other creature.

1961 – San Jose, California | 137

"As we rounded the corner and headed down the hallway, I looked into every room with an open door. We reached room 25B. The doctor stopped and said nervously, 'This is your husband's room. Well, I guess he is your husband.'

"I turned sharply toward him and said directly, 'Are you Doctor Weissman?' He almost laughed as he replied, 'Oh, no. I'm just an intern.'

"'Well, you go find Doctor Weissman and tell him to meet me in room 25B. Now!'

"'Yes, right away, Mrs. Ensign,' he said, rushing away without a backward glance.

"I stood outside the closed door for a moment before summoning up the courage to walk in and confront my once-missing husband. I gradually opened the door a crack and peered in. For a moment, I thought to myself that maybe, just maybe, it could be another or different Richard Ensign. I shook my head in disgust as three years of pain swept over me while I reluctantly faced the stark truth. An assistant's assistant, I knew this position quite well, was standing close to Richard's bedside with a tin washing bowl full of sudsy water. She held a wet washcloth to his forehead as he stroked her hand and arm. Her forced giggling stopped rapidly when she noticed me watching her.

"'Oh, Mr. Ensign, sir, there is someone here to see you,' she squeaked while jumping away from the wounded man.

"'Tracy?' Richard chirped while slowly removing the washcloth from his face.

"'No, it's your real wife, not the fake version!' I hissed. Richard jerked up into a sitting position while at the same time overturning the basin of water all over himself and the assistant's assistant. 'Stella!' he shouted, confused. I glared at Richard while saying sharply, 'What's wrong with you?'

"'There's something wrong with my head,' he answered weakly. 'Well, that's a significant grasp of the obvious,' I countered.

"'Why can't you ever speak normally? Who says things like that?'

"'Maybe your Ph.D. geriatric bimbo could give you terminology lessons!'

"'She's not old,' he replied. But I growled back, 'And not exactly the smartest bimbo in the bar!'

"'Now, now, Stella. What are you doing here? Did the hospital call you?' Richard questioned me.

"Tracy bounced into the room as a chagrined intern followed in her wake. She took one look at the frozen people in the room and said frantically, 'Dick, who is this woman and what is she doing here?'

"'Funny,' I said to no one in particular, 'I just asked the same question.'

"'Stella,' Richard said, ignoring Tracy, the fake wife, 'Why are you here?'

"'Your daughter is in emergency right now. She had an accident,' I said with a heart full of anger this time, not grief or self-reproach. 'Oh my God, Rosie,' he cried while throwing off the sheet and trying to get out of the bed.

"'You have a daughter?' Tracy queried.

"'Not Rosie, it's Donna.'

"'Oh' was all he said.

"As if I had a thought bubble emanating from my cartoon head, I thought I could easily take that wash basin and hit him over his idiotic head. I truly wanted to, but instead I just glared at him without speaking.

"'You have *two* children?' came the question after a few seconds of stunned silence.

"'No, he has *three* children,' I emphasized for the brilliant Tracy.

"'Three?' Richard asked as if he really had been struck by a basin of icy water.

"'Three,' I answered easily.

"'Three?' the assistant's assistant responded as if anyone cared that she was there.

"'Yes, three,' I said again.

"'Three?' Tracy added as if just figuring out how to count.

"The intern decided at that time to break the ice by adding, 'I think it is pretty clear that Mr. and Mrs. Ensign have three children. How nice.'

"'It is *not* nice!' Tracy exploded.

"'A boy or a girl? When, how?' Richard stuttered.

"'I'd certainly like to know the same thing,' Tracy said to the room, but no one paid attention to her. All eyes were on Richard and me.

"'Her name is Madeline,' I answered simply. 'I don't like that name,' Richard pressed. 'I don't care!' I shot back. 'Rosie calls her Maddie.'

"'Now Rosie knows what she is doing. That's a great name.' Richard was on a roll. 'You must meet my Rosie, Tracy. She is the smartest and cutest little elf this side of heaven. And, wow, can she perform! She'll be an actress and her brilliant stage presence will astound everyone lucky enough to buy a ticket. You mark my words.'

"I turned on Richard once again and with controlled anger clearly announced, 'You may visit all three of your children anytime, Richard, but don't you dare bring that floozy or I might just kill the both of you!'

"'Hey, wait a minute. My Dickie and me are married,' Tracy purred.

"'Well, actually Tracy, sweetheart, we are not exactly married,' Richard said with a sheepish glint in his eyes.

"'Now this is getting good,' the intern said while pulling up a chair.

"'What do you mean?' Tracy asked.

"'Yes, Dickie, sweetheart,' I said sarcastically, 'What *do* you mean?'

"'We sorta got married in Las Vegas so I could, well...' he couldn't finish.

"'So you could what?' she asked.

"'Get you to go to bed with him would be my best guess!' I jumped in quickly.

"'Oh, Dick. Well, you got your wish,' Tracy cried.

"The room froze until I couldn't help myself. The words flew out of my mouth before I had time to think, 'My goodness, Tracy, dear, that must have been a shock to the system when you realized that you got the wrong end of a very limp-minded Dick stick!'

"The door opened again and a tall, very distinguished looking man with graying thick hair and a slight graying moustache entered the room. 'Is Mrs. Ensign in here?'

"The intern shot up and everyone appeared to stand at attention, except Richard and me. We continued to glare at each other. 'Dr. Weissman,' the intern said in a small choked voice. 'I was just bringing Mrs. Ensign into the child's room. I also found Mr. Ensign.'

"'Come with me,' Dr. Weissman said without further delay.

"I pushed past everyone and hissed to the intern, 'Why didn't you tell me immediately that I could go see Donna?' I got no answer, only a groan from Richard. 'I'm staying here,' he said. I dashed around and in words that left no room for interpretation or debate, I said, 'You are coming this instant to see your daughter, or I will knock some sense into that fat head of yours and believe me it won't look like that measly scratch when I'm done with you!'

"'Oh, I get it,' the invisible assistant's assistant said, 'You are the dad of the poor, little retarded girl down the hall.'

"'What?' squealed Tracy, holding tightly to her stomach. 'Do you mean *our* baby could be an imbecile?'

"'Why, who knew? Fake wife does have a vocabulary,' I said as I grabbed Richard's arm and pushed him ahead of me with herculean strength.

"The wash basin screamed past Richard's head and slammed into the door jamb. He rapidly rushed out the door with the words, 'This is all your fault!' echoing in the background. I'm still not sure who said it.

"Following Dr. Weissman down the hallway toward Donna's room filled me with extreme trepidation. No one had told me anything yet about her condition or the prognosis.

"I had never been so scared in my life. As we got to the room and the doctor opened the door, I turned to look at Richard. He had the look of fear in his eyes. But I didn't know if he was frightened for Donna or for himself. I gave it no more than a fleeting thought as I turned back and stepped into the room. Everything at that moment blurred out of my vision except for the angelic child reclining at a forty-five-degree angle in a crisp white hospital bed. In three steps I was at her side. She was so deathly pale. Her eyes were open but totally unresponsive and completely devoid of the usual high-spirited joy she often exhibited.

"'Donna,' I called to her, 'Donna?' There was no recognition; no sound; no movement at all. I took her in my arms and put her head on my shoulder. 'Donna, it's Mommy,' I called to her again, trying with all my fortitude not to cry.

"'You shouldn't do that,' the doctor said.

"'What? Why not?' I questioned without looking at him.

"'It is best to leave her be. Don't allow yourself to get too attached,' the doctor added.

"Physicians are important people. I have always known and respected that. They know things. They know more than other people. They know about life and death, sickness and health. They know how to save lives. They are valued everywhere. We should always do what they say because they know what is best. That is what I was taught. That is what I always assumed without question. It is the same way with teachers, clergy, our leaders, and our parents. Well, I am still not so sure about the leaders or politicians, but Dad always said, 'You don't have to agree with them, but you do need to respect and listen. These people know more than you do. They are the pillars of any society.'

"I put Donna gently back to rest against the pillows. 'Will it hurt her if I hold her like that? If so, I will stop immediately.' I could tell that my voice was strained.

"'No, no, it's not that,' he answered.

"Suddenly and with no warning, Donna started shaking and gasping. She seemed to be choking and unable to breathe. I was pretty sure I lost the ability to breathe myself as I, too, started shaking and gasping. But my reaction was not the same as Donna's.

"Richard came out of his stupor and said out loud, 'My God, doctor, what's wrong with the child? What is happening?'

"Dr. Weissman was at Donna's side in an instant, pushing me aside.

"'Nurse,' he directed, 'hold her down and make sure she does not fall out of the bed.'

"'She's having a seizure,' the doctor spoke to us in a loud authoritative voice, 'Do not be alarmed.'

"It was over within seconds, but for me it could have been hours. I looked at the doctor and said with a shaky voice, 'Is this what happened that brought the ambulance to my home? This must be what my oldest daughter tried to explain to me.'

"'Yes. When she fell, she probably went into a grand mal seizure. She has been having a number of these convulsions since she's been admitted. It is unclear if the accident caused it or if she had always been prone to the condition and the accident somehow set it off. We are doing some tests and will be giving her medication to control the intensity of the seizures.'

"'Will she be back to her normal self once she is on the medication?'

"'Mrs. Ensign, I am afraid you do not understand the gravity of the situation or you might possibly be under a false assumption about Donna's condition and abilities,' the doctor said flatly.

"'My wife has always been in denial when it comes to Donna,' Richard explained.

"'Oh, so I am your wife now, am I?' I seethed. 'Well, maybe I do think there is more ability in her than anyone gives her credit for, but at least I don't blame myself and everyone else on heaven and earth like you do!'

"'Mr. and Mrs. Ensign, please,' the doctor interrupted, 'that won't help matters. We need to talk seriously about this child.'

"'Yes, of course. I am so sorry, doctor. When can I take her home? When will she get better?' I asked sheepishly.

"'You don't understand,' the doctor said with no emotion. 'She's not going to get better.'

"'What? What are you saying? I don't believe you!' I choked.

"'I'm sorry to tell you this, but Donna will probably only be in a vegetative state for the rest of her life. It is unlikely she will live past her teen years.'

"'Is it because she is a mongoloid?' Richard asked.

"The doctor continued, 'No, no, although individuals with that syndrome typically don't live a long life. They often have heart ailments or other health problems. Donna has other complications now. There is a distinct possibility that she lost oxygen to the brain due to the rapid continuous convulsions she's been having. Medications will calm it down, but not eliminate it entirely.'

"My eyes were so full of tears and my throat was so dry that I was unable to choke out any words. Richard did the talking, but I could tell that he was shaken as well.

"'What does this mean, doctor?' Richard asked.

"'My advice is to put her in an institution and try to forget about her. The staff will know what to do and how to take care of her. There are other children there just like Donna. Sometimes they have music or other activities for the handicapped individuals that live there. It is the best place for her to be, I assure you,' Dr. Weissman concluded.

"I finally found my voice and said with suppressed depression verging on anger, 'The best place for her to be is with her mother and a family that loves her!'

"'Mrs. Ensign, you must come to the realization that you cannot take proper care of her,' Dr. Weissman sighed.

"'No!' was all I could say.

"Dr. Weissman seemed to have gotten tired of this conversation, 'I'm so sorry for your loss. Please accept my condolences. I am a very busy man and I must leave now. I have other patients to attend to.'

"'How long does she need to remain in the hospital, or rather how long do we have to make this decision?' I hastily added before he was able to exit the doorway.

"'One week,' he said, then turned and left the room.

"Richard held me tightly as we both cried an ocean of tears."

Chapter 29

1961 – SAN JOSE, CALIFORNIA

Stella

I was surprised that my eyes could create even more tears. I laughed quietly to myself thinking I was just like a water well that would never dry up. Turning my head toward Veronica to tell her my little joke, I sighed, noticing that she was dead to the world. Even my story couldn't keep her awake. Moving around the coffee table, I made my way down the hallway to check on the girls. They were also sleeping soundly. I wiped my eyes with my sleeve once again while realizing that there must be more tissues in the linen closet. I found a couple rolls of toilet paper and quietly tiptoed back to the couch. Images continued to invade my consciousness. Veronica wasn't aware of the whole ordeal yet. I knew I would tell her tomorrow, or was it today already? I didn't know. I just knew that I couldn't get the thoughts out of my mind.

STELLA'S RECOLLECTION – 1960

Richard left me alone in Donna's room a short time later as silently as he had entered. I sat frozen in a metal folding chair watching my daughter for any little movement to justify my obstinate belief that the doctor was wrong. The only sounds came from an insistent beeping from one of the machines. When I saw Donna gradually close her eyes, I did not panic because it was easy to tell that she had just fallen asleep. The colorful lights and graphics on the machines indicated simply that, but I remained fearful all the same. Although the room was spotlessly clean and organized, there was nothing in this little unwelcoming, sterile environment to evoke hope or compassion. I stood up to press the call button. A few moments later, a nurse entered, looked at the various tubes and needles Donna was hooked up to as well as the machines and charts, then asked if I needed anything. I told her that I needed to call the friend who was watching my other children. She nodded her assent and left.

I walked down the hall to Richard's room. The room was completely empty with a freshly made bed. I asked at the nurse's station where Mr. Ensign was. I was told that he had been released a couple of hours earlier.

The pay phone was in the lobby close to the waiting room. I dug out a couple of dimes from my change purse and inserted one into the slot at the top of the telephone and dialed my number.

"Hello," Shirley answered on the first ring.

"Hi, Shirley. First, I can't thank you enough for helping me last night. How are the girls?"

"Everything is fine here. Rosie is quite an independent child. She refused any help from Willie and me. She demanded that we stay in the living room while she got Maddie and herself ready for bed," Shirley said with a bit of a chuckle in her tone.

"That doesn't surprise me," I tried to laugh back.

"An hour later, I tiptoed down the hall to their room and opened the door slightly just to check on them. They were fine," Shirley added.

"Oh, good. I'm so glad something is going well. It is not good news here," I said knowing that I needed to check my grief, so I wouldn't start crying again.

"Do you want to talk about it, Stella? I'm here. I won't leave until you tell me to," Shirley said in a calm tone of voice.

"You are very kind. I know you must be very tired and I'm sure you must want to be on your way, but I wonder if I can impose on you for just a while longer," I asked, biting my lower lip.

"I'm at your beck and call," Shirley laughed. "No, really. I know this is a terrible time for you. I want to help. Please believe me."

"Would you be so kind as to call Wills and ask..." she wasn't able to finish as Wills was immediately on the phone.

"Stella?" he said, "Are you okay? How is your daughter?"

"Wills, I didn't know you were there. Thank you so much for everything. You've gone above and beyond. I truly appreciate it."

"It's my privilege. No problem at all. Is there anything else I can do to help?"

"Well, actually, there is if you don't mind. I need a couple of favors. I know I'm asking your sister and you for a great deal, but right now I need to figure out what my next steps should be, and I really do need your help," I said, swallowing the lump in my throat.

"Yes, of course. We are both more than happy to help in any way we can. But, please, tell me about your daughter. Will she be all right? I've been very worried."

I couldn't talk. Finally, after taking some small breaths and blinking my eyes a few times, I said, "No, I don't think she will be all right. I do not know what is going to happen or what I should do. Today is Saturday. I would like to stay at the hospital with Donna right now. Tomorrow, I'd like to take the girls and go visit their grandmother. I'm hoping to talk her into coming to live with us. Would you be so kind as to drive us to Palo Alto where she lives?"

"Yes, of course. Shirley and I will take care of the girls today and tonight. Please don't worry about that. I'll pick you up at the hospital with Rosie and Maddie as soon as you call."

"When you come tomorrow, I will tell you everything. You deserve to hear the whole story."

"Thank you, Stella. And your husband? What about him?" Wills asked.

"I have no husband."

༄

Sunday morning, I called Wills again. We agreed to meet outside the hospital entrance door in an hour. I was waiting there when he drove up with both girls. I opened the front passenger door and quickly jumped in. Turning around, I looked at both girls while giving them my best courageous smile. Rosie was sitting in the backseat stubbornly folding her arms in a crisscross fashion, staring out the window and refusing to talk.

"Rosie, I know you are upset, but we are going to see Grandma Ensign now."

"No" was all she said.

"Talk to me nicely, please," I urged her softly.

"Let's go see Donna now."

"It's not visiting hours yet. No one can see her right now."

"Is Donna going to be all right?" Rosie cried, brushing tears off her cheeks.

"I don't know, Rosie," I answered her honestly. "She is very ill right now. She had a seizure."

Rosie's whole body shook as tears flooded over her face.

"Wait, Wills, please," I said as I opened my door and immediately got out. I promptly made my way to the backseat door, opening it and enveloping my first-born in my arms while stroking her back. "Donna told me to tell you something."

"She only says a few words. Donna is still learning how to talk. She can't do sentences yet, but I'll teach her. I will, I promise." Rosie sobbed uncontrollably.

"Do you remember how Donna and I sometimes communicate without talking? She tells me something and I tell you in Donna's voice?"

"Yes, you are so funny when you do that. Donna laughs, too." Rosie's sobs lessened.

"Well, she said to tell Rosie that she is lucky that she can go to school. She wants you to learn a lot, so you can come home and teach it to her."

Rosie sat up straight, wiped the tears from her face with her shirt sleeve, then immediately turned to Wills and spoke in a very adult tone, "I'm sorry to have caused you any trouble, Mr. Rollins. I'm ready to go to my grandma's house now. I need to work on my lesson plan. Grandma can help me."

"I'm happy to oblige," Wills answered.

"There are a few things I need to do if you don't mind being our chauffeur for a little while, Mr. Rollins," I turned my face and smiled weakly. "The nurse suggested that I come back this afternoon. They need to run a few tests and Donna needs to rest right now."

"I am happy to oblige you as well, Mrs. Ensign," Wills answered. "Also, I wanted to let you know that I called work and told them that you would be absent for a couple of weeks due to a family emergency. I'm supposed to go back to work tomorrow, but they told me that if you needed help, they would allow me to assist you for a few days until you could get back on your feet. They were happy to oblige."

"Thank you, Wills" was all I said, but I wanted to hug him.

Chapter 30

1961 – SAN JOSE, CALIFORNIA

"Your eyes are drooping." Veronica sat up and arched her back.

Stella blinked a few times before she reached toward the end table to turn on the lamp. "I thought you were sound asleep."

"Not even close. I might have nodded off for a few seconds. Keep going, I'm on the edge of my seat."

"You certainly are. It looks like you're ready to fall off."

"Very funny. Fill me in and don't leave out a thing."

Stella put her head in her hands for a few moments. She stood up and paced in front of the coffee table. Veronica remained silent but watched her intently. She knew Stella would tell her the entire story. She also knew how difficult it would be.

STELLA'S STORY – 1960 – PALO ALTO, CALIFORNIA

"The drive to Palo Alto was uneventful. No one spoke. Since the children were in hearing distance, I did not want to tell Wills what had happened at the hospital. Small talk seemed inappropriate and unnecessary, so our entire journey remained silent.

"Marie Ensign's small cottage was directly behind her sister Laura's larger house. When we drove up, Aunt Laura was sitting on her porch in her rocker. She looked up and noticed us immediately. I got out and raced over to give her a gentle hug. Rosie jumped out of the backseat and ran toward her great aunt.

"'We're going to see Grandma,' Rosie announced.

"'Not right now, child,' Aunt Laura said solemnly as she took my arm and walked me slightly away from Rosie. 'Marie has been drinking again.'

"'Oh, no, I was worried this might happen,' I nodded.

"'It's worse than that,' Laura continued. 'Richard and his chit are over there.'

"I immediately took Rosie's hand and walked her back to the car. 'I need you to stay here. I will be right back,' I said with a tone more forceful than I intended. Rosie knew that arguing would be useless.

"There have been times in my life that I willingly confronted difficult obstacles with a fierce determination and courage. This wasn't one of those times. It may have been cowardly or maybe I just didn't want to acknowledge the whole sordid situation all over again, but I chose to hide myself behind a dense bush close to Marie's cottage. I was able to see and hear everything, for better or worse.

"Marie Ensign was sitting at her large wooden dining room table. There were two long benches on both sides of the long table. It looked as though she had been playing solitaire, as a deck of cards was spread across the area in front of her. She had a tumbler glass in one hand and an almost empty bottle of whiskey sitting on the bench next to her. I watched as she took a swallow, then wiped her mouth with her hand.

"Marie growled at Richard, 'What do you want, Rich? Come to play cards with me, have you? Well, forget it. I don't need you.'

"'No, Ma, I came to introduce you to my wife, Tracy,' Richard said calmly.

"'You have a wife. Go back to her. Get rid of that floozy! She ain't no good for you!' Marie snarled.

"'How dare she?' Tracy whined. 'What did I ever do to her? Your family is not very nice to me, Dickie.'

"'He has a family, you trollop!'

"'Ma, please listen.'

"'*No!*" she shouted. 'You listen to me, you ungrateful bum. You have three beautiful children and you are shirking your responsibilities.'

"'I couldn't do it, Ma. Really. I had a talk with Stella. She understands.'

"'Understands? Understands? Are you crazy or what? Do your sweet children understand?'

"Richard put his arm around Tracy and said in a forceful tone, 'You are going to have another grandchild!'

"'What? A bastard!' Marie tilted her head back and laughed hysterically.

"Hiding behind the bush offered me the opportunity to see and hear everything that was happening. I hoped that I wouldn't be noticed when I inadvertently let out a small gasp. I was shocked and totally confused.

"'A bastard?' she laughed harder to the point of hysteria.

"Why would Marie laugh at this whole horrible situation? I was completely stunned.

"Tracy looked frightened, but Richard walked closer to his mother. I thought that he might be trying to put his arms around her as he said, 'This child won't be a bastard, Ma. Stella and I will get a divorce and I will finally do the right thing by marrying Tracy, so I can raise my child as I should.'

"'Bastard! *You* are a bastard!'

"'I deserve that, I know, but I'm trying to do the right thing.' Richard went on, 'I will live close by and see my other children on a regular basis. I promise.'

"'No, you won't. You say that, but I know you. I know you. I know how it works. I knew your father. He said he would stay. He didn't.' She was dazed as she continued muttering unintelligible words that were slurred and laced with sobs. 'You are a bastard!' she screamed again. '*You!* Do you hear me? You!'

"'What?' Richard looked stunned. Tracy tried to touch him, but he flung her hand away without regard to her feelings. He stared at his mother and uttered the same words one last time, 'What are you saying?'

"'You are a bastard. Your father never married me. I just pretended so you would grow up without the stigma of being fatherless. He drank himself to death. His brother sent me a letter a few years after your birth saying that he died under the Palo Alto tree. History continues to repeat itself,' Marie said finally before collapsing on the bench.

"Richard watched her hopelessly before tenderly picking his mother up and placing her on the bed next to the wall in her tiny living room. He kissed her on the cheek, then sat down on the bench and wept.

"While trying to quietly escape from my hiding place, I turned quickly, almost running into Rosie. In every fiber of her being, Rosie resembled an alabaster statue. Laura was watching us solemnly. Oddly, I wanted to ask her who looked more frightened, but I said nothing as I took Rosie by the arm and went straight to the car. 'I'll call you later,' I said to Laura as I got in.

"'What about Grandma?' Rosie squeaked.

"'She isn't feeling well, but she will be all right. She will not be able to move in with us. I'm sorry. Let's go home,' I said to no one in particular.

"Rosie appeared to understand without further questioning. Again, the stillness in the car was unnerving as we drove back home.

Wills pulled into my driveway and turned off the car.

"'Would you like me to come in or wait for you?'

"'I want to chat with Shirley for a few minutes, then go to church,' I said, exiting the car, 'Will you take me there?'

"'Of course.'

"Rosie continued to stare out the window until I opened the car door and helped her out."

Chapter 31

1961 – SAN JOSE, CALIFORNIA

Stella continued relating her story to Veronica.

STELLA'S RECOLLECTION – 1960

"The grand front steps of the massive Catholic church were completely deserted when we arrived. During the drive, I gave Wills an abbreviated detailing of the events that had taken place during the last few days. He was genuinely empathic without unwanted sympathy. He listened intently without comment or opinion. Once he parked the car and shut off the ignition, he turned to me and said, 'Would you like me to go in with you?'

"'No. This I must do on my own. Please don't wait for me. I know you must have many things to do besides dealing with my horror story. I will take the bus home.'

"'No.'

"I smiled at him warmly as I exited the car."

"The church still retained a sense of power. I felt tranquil somehow, reminded of my days going to mass with my mother. I put my fingers in the holy water and genuflected while performing an automatic sign of the cross. The church filled me with an unexpected awe as I entered a middle pew and fell to my knees, breathing in the pungent scents of incense and candles. Lights were flickering from an alcove of votives. The sun filtered through the stained-glass windows casting a myriad of soft colors fanning the altar. I folded my hands together and tried to pray. I called out to the Madonna statue, sensing that it was casting eerie doubts toward me. I started crying and couldn't stop. Without knowing how long I knelt there, I eventually realized that someone was beside me. I remember silently laughing, thinking a spirit was visiting me. I was surprised to see Sister Agnes sitting on the pew bench with her hands folded and head down. Without turning my head around, I got up from a kneeling position and sat down next to her.

"'I am sorry to interrupt your praying. I felt a need to be here to comfort you. Can I help in any way?' Sister Agnes asked softly.

"'No,' I said but then immediately changed my mind, 'yes.' I was overwhelmed with the knowledge I had to do something and I absolutely did indeed need help. But I just didn't know how anyone could help me. Still, feeling as though I was frozen in my own grief, I poured out my pain of Donna's accident and the doctor's suggestion that Donna be institutionalized.

"Sister Agnes listened without judgment and said the only thing that she could, 'God works in mysterious ways.'

"I gave her a look of horror, wanting to scream at this naive nun and the world.

"Before I could respond, Sister Agnes spoke up quickly, 'I know it is an old platitude, but...'

"I regained my angry muffled voice, 'God clearly does not know what He is doing! How dare He do this to Donna, to Rosie?' I stopped and took a deep breath, 'To *me?*'

"Sister Agnes did not flinch. She continued to sit quite still. After a few moments of silence, she added softly, 'I truly believe there is a reason for everything. We just don't know what it is.'

"Shaking my head back and forth, I sighed, 'What should I do? What can I do? I am utterly lost.'

"'Stella,' Sister Agnes said, 'You asked our Mother Superior for guidance once before. She discussed it with me and a few of our order as well as Father MacGregor.'

"I looked at her, stunned. 'Is there a possibility I could bring the children here while I work in the school library? Will you take Donna now?' I couldn't breathe.

"'We were considering just that, but the situation, as you know, has changed. We don't have the skills to help Donna. She needs more care than any of us can realistically provide. Please understand that. We do want to help. We would like to offer Rosie a place in our fourth-grade classroom tuition free. Your youngest child can attend our daycare. You could help in the library as often as possible before and after your current job and some weekends.'

"'I don't know what to say,' I replied. 'You might not accept us now because my husband wants a divorce. My mother thought that I might be excommunicated from the Catholic Church. Is that right?'

"'That would be a question for Father MacGregor. I don't know, but it was our priest that offered this suggestion.'

"'And Donna?'

"'Only you can answer that. I believe you know what must be done. Always do what is in her best interests as well as yours. We will pray.'

"When I opened my eyes sometime later, Sister Agnes had gone."

Chapter 32

1961 – SAN JOSE, CALIFORNIA

The gradual awakening of dawn squeezed its light through the window blinds, abolishing the house's dark chill. Merlin pushed the children's bedroom door open with his nose and sauntered out to the hall with Rosie following closely behind as she rubbed the sleep out of her eyes with her small fists. She stretched her arms up, then down to her head to comb her hair with her fingers. At the end of the hallway, Merlin stopped and sat down, blocking Rosie's entrance into the front room. They both surveyed the room with curiosity. Stella was soundly sleeping slumped on the floor, barely being supported by the armchair. Her fingers were woven crookedly around an empty wine glass that looked like it had been trying to escape her grasp. Veronica was lying oddly on the couch with one leg on and one leg off. A cushion was snugly sitting on top of her face secured in place by her left arm. Her right arm dangled toward the floor barely touching a wine glass that appeared to have a few drops remaining. A couple of empty wine bottles remained upright on the coffee table. Still more unusual to Rosie, and possibly even the dog, was the appearance of the room itself. The entire room looked as if there had been a snowstorm of tissues and other white debris covering every visible surface. Tissues, kitchen towels, paper towels, bathroom towels, and even the sofa doilies littered the area as soft, damp, rounded balls. Rosie leaned over and put her arms around Merlin's neck, hugging him softly. She kissed the top of his head and whispered, "Grown-ups are confusing sometimes." The dog gave her a huge grin and jumped over to the unrolled tube of toilet paper. Rosie laughed as it reminded her of an airplane skywriter that she had seen not long ago. A long strip of white was left behind in the sky as the plane flew away. Her teacher told her that they were clouds of messages that only lasted for a few moments, then disappeared. Rosie thought that all this mess should disappear, too; then no one would remember what happened.

An hour or two later, Rosie had gone back to bed. The sun was fully illuminating the room. Merlin was getting a bit restless as the door was closed and he wanted to go out. He plopped down onto Stella while nuzzling her neck. She tried to sleepily push him away, but he gave a little bark, waking her up. Stella put his face in her hands and kissed the top of his head. "I guess you'd like to go out and dig a hole somewhere, Merlin? Come on, boy, I'll open the door for you."

Stella pulled up the blinds and opened the sliding glass door to a warm day with a strikingly blue sky. Merlin bounded out rapidly.

"Veronica, are you awake?"

Veronica sat up slowly and looked around dazed. "Did I just have a nightmare?"

Stella also gazed at the immaculate scene around them. "It might have been a dream for you, but I'm afraid my dreams are recurring nightmares."

"Did we clean up last night?" Veronica asked confused.

"I am not sure. I only know that I was a tad bit tipsy."

"A tad? I don't think we have ever drunk so much in our combined lives!" Veronica said and they both laughed.

"Oh, my head hurts, but I need to get the girls up."

"I will help, then we have things to do and places to go," Veronica said. "Does that old car in your garage belong to you? Can you drive it?"

Stella answered with a bit of pride and some embarrassment,

'Yes, after the hospital incident, I guess I might have gone a little crazy. I bought an old used car for $100 and taught myself how to drive."

"I might just have to agree on that crazy bit, but why a car?"

"I knew I had to be able to see Donna and provide transportation for the girls as well as be able to get to work and back quickly. I had a lot of planning to do."

"You still do, but this time, we will do it together. Let's get the girls ready."

Chapter 33

1961 – SAN FRANCISCO, CALIFORNIA

The Ensign sisters were squeezed tightly together on one half of the backseat of their mother's car. Part of Merlin's hundred-pound bulk occupied the other half while his head and front paws provided ample warmth as a favorite furry blanket.

"Mommy, are we almost there?" Rosie moaned as she tried to readjust Maddie to make more room, "Maddie's pushing me. She's taking up all the room!"

"No, I'm not," Maddie squealed. "That dog is!"

"No, he is not! Mommy, let's throw Maddie out to make more room for Merlin." Rosie pushed back at her sister.

Veronica turned her head around to check on the girls just as Rosie opened the window. Merlin jumped up swiftly from his quiet slumber and tiptoed over Maddie. He planted two paws on Rosie while putting his head out the window.

"Mommy, Mommy," Maddie wailed, "Merlin is heavy. He is squishing all the air out of me!"

"He is not," Rosie grumbled, "you are a big baby!"

Veronica held out her hands toward Maddie, "Come here, sweet baby. Let's have you sit between your mommy and me in the front seat."

Maddie's smile was almost as wide as Merlin's. Rosie's tongue seemed even longer than Merlin's as she stuck it out toward Maddie.

The adults ignored the confrontation, but Merlin brought his head in for only a fraction of a second – just long enough to give Rosie a quick lick on her cheek. She put her arms around his neck, cuddling him closely for the rest of the journey to San Francisco.

The pink Victorian mansion always put Stella and Veronica in a state of unspoken awe every time they saw it. The other passengers were oblivious to its charms; they just wanted to get out of the car as Stella glided to the curb in front of the huge stone stairway leading to the massive front door.

Merlin escaped through the car door as soon as Rosie opened it. "Rosie, wait," Stella cried in an exasperated mood. "Don't let Merlin out!" But it was too late. He was having none of it. He bolted up the steps eager to see what awaited him behind the huge door. Merlin stopped dead in his tracks and glared in astonishment at the brass lion door knocker.

"Merlin, wait," Rosie shouted as she raced past everyone to reach the door first. Merlin's growl came from deep within his throat. When Rosie reached his side, he barked and pushed her away, leaning his body toward her and blocking the doorway.

"No, Merlin. It's okay. Look," Rosie was secretly proud that he wanted to protect her. "Watch me. It knocks, and the lion will tell Auntie Elsie and Auntie Dorothy that we are here. It's a special lion." She put her two small hands on the large brass handle and pulled, eliciting an immediate solid clang.

Merlin tilted his head, jumped up on his hind legs, and put his two front paws on both sides of the lion's shiny face. His nose touched the lion's face as the door opened.

"My, my, what do we have here?" Elsie greeted the group but looked directly at Merlin.

"It's a big doggie," Maddie said as she hugged Elsie's knees.

"She knows that Merlin is a dog!" Rosie huffed, wondering to herself why no one would believe her that Maddie was dumb as a box of rocks. When she mentioned it very nicely to her mommy a few weeks earlier, she was sent to her room without dinner and wasn't allowed to ride her bike for a week. That certainly wasn't fair!

"Hello, big dog Merlin. Welcome to my home," Elsie patted him on the forehead as he simultaneously made sure this elderly lady's scent matched his meticulous standards.

Dorothy opened the door wider and squealed with delight as she greeted everyone with hugs. "It is so good to see all of you. We missed you more than I can say."

Veronica and Stella wiped tears away as Rosie stared, confused. "What's wrong now? I can say the words for Auntie Dorothy if she can't think of any."

"You little monkey," Dorothy hugged her fiercely.

Maddie beamed, "Rosie is a monkey; Rosie is a monkey!"

Everyone laughed except Rosie, who just pouted, "Why won't anyone believe me? There is something wrong with that big baby!"

"Rosie!" Stella scolded. "That is enough! Go show Merlin and Maddie the backyard. Go play."

Stella turned to Elsie, "Is that all right with you, Elsie?"

"Yes, yes, of course."

"Come on, girls and big dog Merlin," Dorothy shooed them outside, "I have lemonade outside on the patio and a big bowl of ice water for Merlin. Lunch will follow shortly."

"Let's all go out," Elsie added, "Stella has some explaining to do."

Veronica gave Elsie a long hug. "How do you stay so vibrantly young? I dare say you don't look one day older than the first time we met you."

"My goodness, child. You two thought I was an old lady then and that was fifteen years ago."

"We were only nineteen. Everyone looked old to us then," Stella said as the companions walked to the back courtyard.

Bountiful flowers and foliage cascaded profusely from hanging baskets, washing the backyard patio with color. Comfortable lawn chairs and loungers took full visual advantage of the lush green lawn dotted with a variety of trees. The deep pink magnolia blossoms were fully in bloom as summer was ready to make its yearly debut. The weeping willow tree spread its branches toward the enclosed terrace as it entangled its leaves through the crisscross diamond shapes. The apple tree was gradually losing its many flowers preparing for the abundance of fruit to come.

The four women chatted amicably as the children and their dog romped around the yard. The story that Stella had told Veronica was unveiled in dribs and drabs to Elsie and Dorothy. They listened intently as if watching a stage play, except for a few questions and conversational comments intertwined in the dialogue. Stella felt a bit more at ease with the abbreviated version this time. They laughed and cried, but Stella had never felt such comfort and true camaraderie.

Elsie wiped her face with a linen napkin and asked Stella, "From what you have said so far, I'm assuming it has been around eight months since Donna's accident. What has transpired since that time?"

Stella didn't waver. She was with her closest confidants. She felt composed and secure in the absolute belief of their unconditional support. "I went to church."

"What?" Dorothy and Elsie gasped in unison.

Elsie looked at Stella with a glint in her eyes and a smirk on her lips, "I don't recall you being particularly religious."

The women listened intently as Stella brought everyone up to date on the current situation. The divorce from Richard was almost finalized. Rosie had just finished the fourth grade at the Catholic school. Maddie went to the daycare there. Stella helped the nuns set up a school library after her work at IBM. She continued seeing Wills every now and then on a friendship basis. Donna had been placed at the Porterville State Hospital, a treatment center for the mentally retarded – an institution.

Dorothy poured the lemonade from a daisy-patterned pitcher into matching tumblers. When she sat down, she chuckled, "Maddie thinks Merlin is a horse."

Stella jumped up suddenly, knocking over the bistro table. Frightened, she yelled, "Rosie, get Maddie off that dog immediately! What do you think you are doing? She could fall!"

Rosie pulled Maddie off easily without a word, then erupted into hysterical sobs never before heard by her mother.

Stella was glued to the spot. Her sapphire blue eyes were lost in a haze of mist, like fog rolling in from the bay.

Dorothy and Veronica were at Rosie's side in three strides comforting her.

Elsie stood next to Stella still as an ancient oak providing refuge for those who gather close during a storm. "It was not Rosie's fault."

Stella said nothing. She nodded, slowly understanding.

"Stella, look at me," Elsie demanded. "It was not your fault either!"

Elsie might have looked frail but at that moment she was as strong as a lion. She took Stella by the arm and forcibly moved with her toward the children. When Stella reached Rosie, she fell to her knees, taking Rosie and Maddie into her arms simultaneously.

"I am sorry" was all she could say.

Maddie was bewildered but full of untapped energy, "Merlin is a horsey. I love to ride my horsey."

"Leave Merlin alone, you big baby!" Rosie said, her tears drying up.

"Let the children play," Veronica suggested. "I would like some more of that lemonade."

"Don't forget about dessert," Dorothy said.

"Oh no, please tell me it is not your famous no-sugar apple pie," Stella joked as she stood up, briefly wiping her eyes with her blouse's sleeve.

All four women linked arms and headed back to the patio where they spent the rest of the afternoon chatting comfortably. The children fell asleep under the oak tree nestled in the furry comforting embrace of Merlin, the dog.

Chapter 34

1961 – PORTERVILLE, CALIFORNIA

Early the next morning after a wonderful overnight visit with Elsie and Dorothy, Stella announced that she was going to drive down to Porterville to visit Donna.

"Oh, I would love to see Donna again. Do you mind if I go with you?" Veronica asked.

"Of course," Stella said, "But I warn you, a four-hour drive can be long and boring. I suppose we could stop along the way to ease the monotony."

"It will give us more time to chat before I have to go back to Chicago in a few days."

"Do you have to go so soon? You just got here."

"I have been gone almost two weeks. Bill keeps reminding me."

"I think your entire family should move out here," Stella said with determination in her voice.

Veronica shrugged her shoulders without responding.

"Elsie, Dorothy?" Stella called out from the living room doorway. "I'm just about ready to leave. Are you sure you don't mind taking care of these little characters today?"

Elsie came around the corner steadying herself with a cane. "I told you not to worry about a thing. We're thrilled to have them stay. Even that monster dog. Maybe you should stay in a motel overnight due to the length of the journey. Take your time. We'll be fine."

"I'm going, too," Rosie announced as she raced down the stairs.

"Wait, I don't…" Stella was not able to finish her sentence before Rosie jumped in with heated determination.

"Mom, I'm going into the fifth grade this fall. It's about time you let me go visit Donna."

"Yes…" Stella tried again.

"I'm not a baby anymore."

"Yes."

"I can handle it."

"Yes."

"Donna wants to see me, and I want to see her."

"I said yes."

"I need to remind Donna how to use a spoon and reteach her how to walk and…" Rosie couldn't finish this time. "Yes? I can go?"

"Oh, for heaven's sake, Rosie. I said yes," Stella almost laughed.

Rosie kissed Merlin on the nose, opened the door, and rushed down the stairs, "Hurry up!"

"I guess we should go," Veronica said as Stella gazed at her daughter.

"Yes," Stella replied.

Although the journey was long, it wasn't unpleasant. The undercurrent was one of excitement. They sang silly songs, told jokes, made up car games, and talked about anything they could think of, except Donna. They weren't sure what to expect. No one claimed to be nervous, but their combined anxiety was evident. After four hours of steady driving, Stella asked if they wanted to stop for lunch since they had reached Porterville a full ninety minutes before their arranged appointment time with the supervisor of Donna's cottage.

Veronica and Rosie cried in unison, "No!"

Stella grinned, "Let's go see Donna first. Maybe we can have lunch with her."

"Yes," they both shouted in good spirits.

As soon as Stella drove the car into a parking space and shut off the ignition, Rosie eagerly opened the back door and jumped out of the car. "I'm going to search for Donna's cottage. I don't see it here. Maybe it's around the corner."

"No, Rosie, wait for us," her mother shouted as she rapidly rolled down the window.

Veronica picked up her handbag from the floor next to her feet and took her hat off the dashboard. "Don't worry about her. She'll be back in a heartbeat if I know that little monkey."

Stella reached around to grab her handbag from the backseat. She unfastened the clasp and dropped the keys inside. Taking a quick glance at herself in the rearview mirror, she ran her fingers through her hair. "I guess this will have to do. My hair goes flat no matter what I try to do with it."

Veronica grimaced, "And mine curls up or turns frizzy. What's a girl to do?"

The women opened their car doors and adjusted their clothing as they got out of the car.

"Rosie?" Stella yelled. She was quite confident that Rosie wouldn't go very far, but she worried all the same. Looking around, she stretched her back and put her hands behind her neck, rubbing the tension away.

Veronica took her hat off, waving it in front of her face only minutes after putting it on. "I don't think I'll need the sweater I brought. My goodness it's hot."

Stella reached into her purse and pulled out a linen handkerchief. She wiped the sweat off her brow just as Rosie careened around the corner.

"Mommy, Mommy," Rosie yelled. "You came to the wrong place. Donna's cottage isn't here. Even if it's not identical to Snow White's cottage, there are no woods around here and the grass is brown. So this can't be it. All the buildings seem like a gigantic giant stomped around to flatten them out. I think we better check the map again. Can I take my shoes and socks off?"

"No to the shoes and socks. Yes, this is the place. That big building to your right is Donna's cottage."

"Doesn't look like a cottage to me," Rosie mumbled under her breath.

"Let's hurry inside. A little air conditioning would sure feel fine right now," Veronica laughed as she took Rosie's hand in hers.

The glares the women received when together never ceased to amaze them. Frequently, they would hear comments, or what they considered rude remarks, aimed at them, but ignoring them seemed the most logical response. Rosie, on the other hand, missed nothing. As the three of them ambled their way toward the building, a middle-aged man and woman cut off their path on the sidewalk by stopping dead in front of them, blocking their way. The woman gave a huff, but before either of them could say anything, Rosie interjected in her typical animated fashion, "Hello there. I'm Rosie. We're going to visit my sister, Donna. Do you know her? Oh, sorry, I forgot to introduce my mother, Mrs. Ensign, and my aunt Veronica." When no one said a word, Rosie pulled Veronica's hand and walked right between the couple. Stella shrugged and followed as she beamed with great pride.

"Why I never..." the woman gasped.

"I'm sure she hasn't," Rosie said confidently craning her neck backwards to spy on the couple now hurrying away.

The expansive glass doors of Donna's cottage loomed ahead as the three slowed to a stop.

"This is it."

"This is not a cottage, Mommy. This is a dull gray and boring stone building."

"Rosie!" her mother scolded. "Let's go inside and find Donna. I will go to Mrs. Rogers's office to let her know we have arrived. She is the supervisor."

Stella and Veronica opened the doors together and led Rosie inside. Directly in front of them was a medium-sized room with an artificial palm tree in the corner, a green vinyl sofa with two matching chairs, and a simple coffee table completely devoid of any items. Long wide hallways extended to the left and right of them. The abrupt change from the outside brightness of the sun to the inside dimness of the room had them squinting to refocus their vision.

Rosie rubbed her eyes then her nose. "It smells like Maddie in here! I have to hold my nose around Maddie sometimes when she stinks."

"Rosie! That is enough. Behave yourself," Stella admonished, thinking she had made a mistake bringing Rosie along.

Veronica imagined the fumes exploding as tension around Stella, but she only wanted to stifle a laugh. In a soft calm voice, she murmured, "I will stay here with Rosie while you go find Mrs. Rogers."

"Thank you. Her office is down this corridor on the right. The area we're in right now is the visiting room where they bring Donna to spend time with me. And Rosie, do what Aunt Veronica says and be good. I'll be back shortly."

As soon as her mother was out of sight down the hallway, Rosie turned her face to Veronica and said, "Well, she does! Mommy doesn't want Maddie in diapers anymore, but Maddie is still a big baby sometimes and doesn't always do what Mommy wants."

"My twin boys used to be a little stubborn like that, too," Veronica said. "Children have their own timetable. Boys and girls learn at different rates and different speeds. It's important to understand why and not show your frustration; only then can we help teach them in their own way and in their own time."

Rosie nodded, "I'm getting used to it. Can we open the doors or a window?"

Veronica and Rosie got up and walked to the entrance. Each of them opened a door fanning it in and out. "I'm not so sure if we are letting the hot air in or out," Rosie said as they both chuckled.

"Well, it looks like I have two mischief-makers," Stella said as she stood watching them. "Mrs. Rogers wasn't there. She must be at lunch. I guess we'll just have to wait."

"I think we should go find Donna." Rosie raced past her mother and down the opposite hallway.

"I think she is right." Veronica put her arm around Stella and squeezed.

The two women followed Rosie a bit more slowly, observing her and the surrounding area. Rosie stopped as she met and introduced herself to everyone she saw. A young girl with trousers too long on her was walking sideways with her hands flat against the wall. A young boy of about Rosie's age was on the floor across the hallway rocking back and forth and gnawing on his wrist. His other fist hit his head repeatedly. He had a mop of red curly hair and a sprinkle of freckles across his small nose. Rosie walked over to him and squatted down. She tried to calm him with soothing words and by touching his arm, but he didn't react. Another young child with a runny nose and short dishwater blond hair scooted down the hallway on his bottom.

"Hi, my name is Rosie. What's your name?" She did not receive a response.

Rosie turned back to Stella and Veronica. "We're pretty close to the cafeteria. It's a little noisy in there but at least it smells better. Maybe Donna is in there."

As they were turning left toward the open room, a young lady in her early twenties sped around the opposite corner pushing a wheelchair. She wore a blue and white shapeless shift dress, flat white shoes, and a polka-dotted hair band that held back her light brown bangs while her ponytail swung from side to side. Her face shone with a pale translucence as she wore no makeup including lipstick. She spoke to the teenaged girl in the wheelchair with a genuine smile, "We are almost in the dining hall, Cindy. I hope you are hungry because it's your favorite today – macaroni and cheese."

Cindy grinned and nodded as the girl pushed her chair and wiped the drool escaping from Cindy's mouth. She was incapable of doing that task herself as her hands appeared permanently stuck at right angles to her wrists. Her head was equally bent toward one side of her body and her toes pointed inward. Every part of Cindy appeared rigid. Stella observed Rosie survey the scene without embarrassment, fear, or concern. The girl reminded Stella somewhat of the branches of a gnarled old-growth oak tree. The limbs should be spread far and wide, but instead had grown into their own unique shape quite different from others in the forest but no less beautiful.

Rosie rushed over to both girls and said, "Hi, I'm Rosie, Donna's sister. Do you know Donna?"

"Oh, I'm sorry," the girl said with surprise as she stopped pushing the wheelchair and stared at the new people around her. "I wasn't aware we had visitors. My name is Marilyn Maris. May I help you?"

Stella walked up to them and held out her hand. "Hello, Miss Maris. It's a pleasure to meet you. I'm Mrs. Stella Ensign, and this is my good friend, Mrs. Veronica Donaldson. You've already met my daughter, Rosie. We're looking for Donna Ensign."

"Yes, yes. I remember now. I'm supposed to have Donna ready by 1:30 this afternoon. I'm sorry, but I haven't been able to do that yet. It's only 12:15 now. Let me take Cindy to the dining hall and I'll get Donna ready."

"No, no," Veronica jumped in. "We can do that. You must be awfully busy. Please let us help."

"Thank you. That is very kind of you. She's down that hall in the first ward on the right," Miss Maris said, pointing in the direction behind her. "I'm sorry that she's not ready yet. I'm the only one working this ward today, so I have been extremely busy."

"We understand. Don't worry. We'll find Donna and bring her into the lunchroom."

Miss Maris nodded and continued in the direction of the dining hall while Stella, Veronica, and Rosie turned in the opposite direction. They walked down the corridor until they found the first open door on the right. The three of them stood frozen in the doorway as they gazed inside with apprehension. Twenty beds lined each side of the walls in a large room. Some beds were flat and almost touched the ground. Twin-sized beds with rusted metal railings apparently attached as a barrier against falling out crowded amongst the other sleeping structures. A dozen paint-chipped cribs took over the middle of the space. Many of the mattresses had no sheets or blankets to cover the stains or absorb the aromas emanating from them. Items of clothing and linens littered the floor. Several female children of various ages and sizes and descriptions occupied the room. Bewildered, Stella and Veronica scanned the room wondering what to do or how to help.

Rosie searched urgently before pointing at a crib halfway into the room and shouting, "There she is. Donna, Donna!"

Stella and Veronica turned their heads in the direction Rosie had pointed. Inside the crib were Donna and two other little girls around her age. They had the same cast to their eyes and were similar in structure. One girl wore a simple short-sleeved dress while the second child only had on wet diapers. Donna turned her head toward Rosie's voice. She put her hands on the bars of the crib and lifted herself up from a sitting position. Her face blossomed into a ray of sunshine when she stood up as her bright smile and laughter engulfed the entire area. Stella thought her heart would explode as she watched Rosie hug Donna. Stella's first impression was of solid steel bars in a jail cell that Donna could look through but never escape. Veronica put her arm around Stella once again and said, "It'll be all right."

"Mommy, Mommy, Aunt Veronica, I found her!" Rosie cried with great glee while Donna babbled unrecognizable noises. "I think she is talking to us. She wants us to get her dressed."

Stella was frozen. She saw her little girl and she didn't see her at the same time. This child had the heart and soul of her Donna but didn't resemble her. This Donna was so unbelievably thin. Her face was sallow, and her eyes lacked her usual joyful expressions. Donna's short thin hair was styled as if a bowl had been placed on her head, so that her hair could be cut around the contours. Her belly extended out like a small balloon. Stella was absolutely determined not to cry. This would be a wonderful visit. It had to be.

Veronica helped Rosie pull off Donna's flannel nightgown. "Donna has a smelly diaper, too. Is this just like Maddie, Rosie?"

Rosie smirked and said, "No, Donna couldn't help it because she is trapped in a cage."

"Rosie!"

"I'm sorry."

Ten minutes later, Stella was carrying Donna, Veronica held one of the other little girls, and Rosie walked with the third child holding her hand. They all headed to the dining hall for lunch. Once inside the enormous room, the little girl pulled Rosie toward a large rectangular table and plopped down on the bench that matched it. The cafeteria was like the one at Rosie's first elementary school. The tables were long and narrow with wheels on the legs to allow them to be easily moved when necessary. The long identical benches were attached to many but not all the tables. Some tables did not have benches. Instead they allowed room for wheelchairs or even a space for those that wanted or needed to stand instead of sit. Away from the tables and closer to the walls stood huge, dark fans that swiftly moved the air around, providing a respite from the stifling heat. The unadorned cement walls were painted a light gray. Stella had expected a collection of artwork or crafts made by the children, but there was no evidence of such.

As she surveyed the room, she thought this could be like any other cafeteria, only the children were unique. Some appeared broken or hurt, some were laughing, some crying, some children were playing or misbehaving, some were silent, some were scared, some seemed confused, some were probably just hungry. All the children were visibly different from any she had ever known or seen before, but no less beautiful. A cacophony of noises filled the air. It was impossible to detect any conversations as the sounds consisted mostly of guttural babbling or excited jabbering. Trying to command attention, but not quite gaining an advantage, a tank of a woman with plump, rosy cheeks and wispy graying hair held together in a tight black hairnet picked up a huge metal spoon and pounded it against a metal pot. Without waiting for quiet or even a lull in the noise, she shouted, "Boys and girls, please take your seats. Lunch is about to be served. Dolores and Midge will bring your trays to you and set them on top of your towel. Remember to tuck the other end of the towel into your shirt top, so it forms a secure bib to keep you clean."

No one appeared to be listening except the visitors. Veronica and Stella sensed that the children didn't understand what the cook had said. After waiting a few moments for the cook to finish her directions, Veronica walked briskly to the open table where Marilyn Maris was sitting next to two young girls. "May we please join you, Miss Maris?"

"Yes, yes, of course. Oh, please, call me Marilyn."

"Mare Mare. Me want eat now," the teenaged girl, Cindy, said with a huge smile that tugged at their hearts.

"It's coming. Please wait nicely. Cindy, these people are Donna's family. They came to visit her," Marilyn said.

"She called you Mare Mare," Rosie pointed out, confusion showing on her face.

"Yes, many of the children who can talk call me Mare Mare because my name is Marilyn Maris. I'm not sure if it's easier to say or if it has become a habit. Mrs. Rogers, who is in charge, told me to teach the children how to say Miss Maris. I always laugh at the irony because Mrs. Rogers doesn't think any of these children will ever be able to learn anything. Oh, I'm sorry. I shouldn't have spoken." Marilyn reddened as she closed her mouth and took the tray from Dolores, setting it in front of Cindy.

Stella's eyes darted around the room before focusing on Donna when a tray slid down the table. Rosie snatched it before the food flew off and immediately put a spoon into Donna's hand to help her start the meal. Donna's hand grasped the spoon tightly, but it appeared to stay frozen in the air until Rosie guided it to her sister's mouth.

Stella gazed at Marilyn somewhat befuddled. "I was overwhelmed by how you managed to bring all these children out here for their lunch. We were struggling to get three little girls ready and you did everyone else all by yourself!"

Veronica added, "You amazed me as you walked in and out of the ward until you took care of each and every child."

"When we arrived in the cafeteria, you had all of them

sitting in their place ready for lunch," Stella said. "How do you do it?"

Veronica wrinkled her forehead in curiosity. "Well, today is Sunday. I suppose that during the week with school and lessons and activities, it's probably a bit easier as most of the children would be involved in that sort of thing."

Marilyn looked stunned, "There's no such thing as that here. There's no school, not at this cottage anyway. I can't really say about the other buildings, but I doubt it."

"Why ever not?"

"No one truly believes any of these children can learn, so they figure what's the point. I've heard some say that it's not cost effective."

Without looking up, Rosie broke into the conversation, "What's that supposed to mean? I don't understand."

"Some people believe that it's not worth spending money on a future that cannot possibly happen," Marilyn said as she continued to feed Cindy and direct the other children to eat their lunch.

"Do you believe that?" Stella asked.

Marilyn surreptitiously glanced around and whispered, "Well, if I'm to be completely honest, I'd say that it is a load of chicken feathers!"

The two women only stared, but Rosie laughed, "Or a load of cow manure!"

"Rosie!" her mother scolded her once again, "Where do you hear these things?"

"My classroom."

Veronica grinned, "So how is that fancy Catholic school working out for you?"

Marilyn leaned in, "I hope I don't get fired for saying this, but those so-called experts are wrong. These children learn all sorts of things, every day. I see it."

In a voice more forceful than she expected, Stella said, "I wish more people like you worked here!"

"Oh, well now. We have some good folks here," Marilyn stated unapologetically.

"I'm sure you do," Veronica said, feeling a bit embarrassed.

"Well, look at our cook. Her name is Mrs. Baker. Yes, it is a coincidence and we all think it's hilarious, even Mrs. Baker. She says she can't bake a thing and hates to cook. But, she does it every day all day long and everyone seems to like her food. When she thinks no one is looking, she will give extra helpings. She's always trying to figure out what each individual might like and give them their own special treat."

"Look at that silly man over there," Rosie interrupted, "he's giving a little boy a piggyback ride. He's waving at us."

Marilyn turned around swiftly and blushed, "Oh, isn't he swell? He's a blond Elvis. I bet you've never seen such a dreamboat before."

"Bernie. He is a funny boy in my class. Bernie is round. Sometimes he reminds me of what Merlin must have looked like as a puppy."

"His name is Peter," Marilyn continued without acknowledging Rosie's musings. "He does what I do, only in the boys' ward. The boys love him. He plays with them and tries to teach them things, but he thinks no one knows."

"Sounds like a nice young man," Stella sighed, noticing Marilyn's obvious infatuation with Peter.

"Do you know that he goes to college, too? He says he intends to become a teacher for children in this population. That's what he calls it. He told me that there are no specific classes at his college for Special Education, but he wants to get an advanced degree in education so he can do research that would allow others to learn how to help these children."

"I bet he was the one who taught the kids to say Mare Mare," Rosie said.

"Mrs. Rogers told him and all the staff we were not to be experimenting with these children. He got angry with her and almost lost his job. He told her in no uncertain terms that no one was experimenting. He only wants to teach them. She told him to mind his own business and that if he wasn't busy enough taking care of the children's daily needs, then she would find other tasks for him."

"So, did he stop?" Stella asked.

"Oh, no. He just tries new things when he thinks no one is looking," Marilyn responded as she turned back to watch Rosie, 'Just like how your daughter is trying to teach Donna how to eat by herself."

All of a sudden, surprising everyone, Donna threw her spoon as far away as she was capable. It clanged on the floor a few times before skidding to a stop. Donna took both of her hands and hit her food and tray as if she were playing a bass drum set. She laughed and laughed. Other children did as well, but the adults and Rosie did not.

"Donna!" Rosie screeched, "You're being naughty!"

Stella looked at her children and admonished Rosie without thinking, "Donna doesn't know any better. Don't be upset with her, Rosie. She doesn't understand what she's doing and I'm not sure she ever will."

The air around Stella froze. She didn't know why she said that. She didn't know if she even believed it. Stella's head was whirling, lost in a tangle of thoughts and emotions. Could she be falling into a trap of confusion, unable to rescue herself or her children? She stood up abruptly, holding onto the table.

Veronica reached over and took her arm, "Stella?"

"I can't breathe," Stella whispered in a voice so small only Veronica could discern what she said. Only Veronica knew what she meant.

Rosie, however, was angry. Her mother said things that didn't make sense sometimes and it really bothered her. Rosie's tone was almost bitter, "Donna should be punished. I would get into a ton of trouble if I did what she did!"

"No," Stella said.

Marilyn diverted the commotion by pointing to a man coming around the corner. She lifted her head excitedly toward Veronica and said in a proud voice, "Why, we even have a Negro like you who works here. His name is Frank Davis. He is our custodian."

Neither Veronica nor Stella knew quite how to respond. Rosie thought they must be tongue tied, so she jumped in, "That's swell. Is Mr. Davis the man you're pointing at?"

The striking black man was very tall and thin with curly black hair escaping from a small cap on his head. He wore bright blue overalls and solid black shoes. He strode into the room with obvious confidence but did not acknowledge or speak to anyone.

"Well, not exactly like me. He is a man after all," Veronica said with a chuckle.

"Oh, I'm sorry," Marilyn cringed, "I meant no offense."

Veronica started to say something but became still as her curiosity overcame her. The man was rushing toward the enormous fans and pulling the plugs out of the wall, shutting them off.

"Mrs. Rogers must be coming."

"I don't understand," Veronica said.

"You will" was all Marilyn could say as she continued to help her charges finish their lunch.

A quick succession of tapping heels could be heard coming down the hallway to the dining room. Maybe Stella and Veronica both imagined it, but the atmosphere seemed to change dramatically when Mrs. Rogers entered the room. The noise level plummeted but Mrs. Rogers didn't take heed of that. She headed straight to Frank.

Mrs. Rogers looked to be in her early forties. She had sharp features that may have hidden a beautiful face at one time. Her hair was pinned into a French roll at the back of her head. Her posture was erect, and her clothes fit her expertly. Mrs. Rogers was clearly a no-nonsense type of woman determined to make her way up the ladder in a man's world.

"Mr. Davis, are you trying to turn those fans on?" Mrs. Rogers questioned in a stern voice.

"No, ma'am."

"I should hope not. Money doesn't grow on trees, you know. The temperature is just fine to me."

"I certainly wouldn't want it to get too cool in here by any means," he mumbled.

"Do not get impertinent with me, Mr. Davis."

"No, ma'am." Looking beyond her shoulder he added, "Looks like we've got visitors."

Mrs. Rogers spun around and walked directly to Stella's table as she burst into a surprisingly pleasant manner. Stella noticed the supervisor's smile was dazzling but showed no warmth and could not lighten up the room as Donna's happy grins could. The tension was like a dense fog on a dreary, cold day. Mrs. Rogers was the first to break the stillness as she directed her comments specifically and smoothly to Stella, "Why, Mrs. Ensign, I do believe that you are early for your appointment. Visiting hours start at 1:30 in the visitors' room – not in the cafeteria."

"I am sorry. We arrived a full ninety minutes early. I did knock on your office door, but you must have been at lunch. So we decided to find Donna on our own. I was sure you would understand," Stella said with a determined grin pasted on her own face.

"I was undoubtedly at an important meeting," she scolded. "Next time, I would expect you to wait."

Before Stella could respond, Mrs. Rogers's face turned a pale red as she turned her attention to Donna, then to Marilyn, "Miss Maris, what is this mess? Clean this up forthwith and see that the children go back to their quarters."

"Yes, Mrs. Rogers," Marilyn answered without looking up.

"I can tell you're not helping matters here, Mrs. Ensign. Donna's tray and food is in complete disarray." Mrs. Rogers sounded exasperated, "Mr. Davis, bring some cleaning supplies at once."

"We would be happy to help clean it up," Stella said.

"You've done quite enough for one day. Please take your entourage and go to the visiting room. Donna's nap time is one half hour from now. That should give you enough time to visit your daughter. Good day to you." Mrs. Rogers whirled around and walked briskly down the corridor, leaving only the echoes of her clicking heels to follow in her wake.

In a state of disbelief, Stella said nothing but stood up and walked around the table to Donna. She picked her up and walked out of the cafeteria. Veronica and Rosie followed her while saying goodbye and expressing their thanks. Stella, however, did not speak. They spent the next half hour walking Donna up and down the hallway until Marilyn came in.

"I'm sorry to interrupt, but it's Donna's nap time," Marilyn spoke in a low hesitant voice.

"We understand," Stella said with a catch in her throat.

"I don't," Rosie mumbled.

Marilyn picked Donna up as if she were a big puppy. Donna squirmed around but did not whine or cry.

"I guess it is time to leave." Veronica put her arm around Stella.

Stella's eyes stung with fresh tears threatening to escape. She quietly nodded and walked to the exit. When she noticed Rosie was not with them, she stopped and turned around, facing her eldest daughter, "Let's go."

Rosie did not move. For a long, tense moment, no one spoke. Stella was surprised as Rosie had never shown such stubbornness. She focused her attention frantically at her mother and suddenly shouted, "No!"

Stella was just as determined, "Rosie, let's go..." but she couldn't finish.

"I am going to live with Donna," Rosie declared without a tremor in her voice.

The jumbled combination of words from both her dad and Elsie echoed into Stella's mind as they had all day long. "You have to be able to look at your reflection in the mirror and see no regrets. You must be able to live with your choices. Think about what is most important for you and make that decision. Be certain whatever that decision is, you will know you did all that you were capable of doing. You can look at yourself in the mirror and feel relief and comfort knowing that without a shadow of a doubt it was the only thing you could do, and it was ultimately the right thing to do!"

Stella looked at Rosie and saw her child's reflection of despair and hopelessness. She knew what she had to do.

Every muscle in Stella's body shivered as she drew closer to her nine-year-old child, who was shaking her head and sobbing uncontrollably. Stella wrapped her arms around her beloved first-born. "Rosie, let's take Donna home!"

Part Three

Chapter 35

1961 – SAN JOSE, CALIFORNIA

Wills

THE WALLS MARCHED TOWARD HIM, BUT HE WAS NOT IN AN enclosure. Sweat dribbled down his face and neck, but he shivered from the cold. He could not escape the cloth that bound him, yet he wore nothing except his shorts. The light hit his face, but it was dark still. Was it a flashlight or a flaming torch? Were they coming finally? The quiet was unnerving and he did not sense any smells, but he was only a few yards from the ocean. A loud blast shattered the stillness. They were coming. Now he was sure. Would he be rescued or destroyed?

Wills's eyes shot wide open as he sat up with a jolt. He shaded his eyes quickly and blinked from the sun that blazed through the thin window curtains. His other hand automatically reached over to pound the top of the alarm clock, which brought quiet back to his realm. Wills struggled out of the tangled sheet while wiping his face and neck with the pillowcase. He took a few calming breaths as he gazed around his studio apartment. Wills hated this yellow box he called his temporary abode. *Why would anyone paint all the walls yellow?* he thought to himself. He hated yellow. He hated that dream which continually invaded his lackluster sleep.

Today, his life would change. Maybe it already had. Fate had started working her magic when he first gazed into Stella's wondrous blue eyes, which took him back to the crystal, sapphire water of the South Seas. Wills became lost in her vision. She somehow took over his senses, although Stella was unaware of her impact on him. She was only being kind.

Wills wondered if Stella had been playing with his fragile state of mind last night, too? Did she truly want him? Or did she only need him? Would that be enough? It had to be. With Stella close beside him, the nightmares would vanish. His demons could stay hidden deep inside him and no one would ever need to know, not even Stella. He saw no reason to concern her about his lost soul. She needed his support, not his despair. Yes, today everything would change. He would start a new life.

Chapter 36

1961 – SAN JOSE, CALIFORNIA

THE PREVIOUS EVENING

Shirley sat at the Formica countertop breakfast bar drinking a cup of coffee. Stella paced back and forth in her small kitchen wiping her dry hands repeatedly on her clean apron.

"Are you sure?" Stella asked one more time.

"I have never been more confident about anything in my lifetime," Shirley said, thinking that her idea was in everyone's best interest. She had discussed it the night before with her husband, Sam, and he agreed with her. Those two needed each other. This would be a wonderful match. This would be the solution neither Stella nor Willie had anticipated.

Stella was in emotional turmoil. This would certainly solve her problems, but would she be creating new ones? No, she couldn't think that way. She had no other choices. Wills was a good man and a kind man. She was certain that he was smitten with her. Would that be enough? She didn't know. Stella stopped suddenly and turned toward Shirley. She sat down next to her on a bar stool that was a bit too high and had always frustrated her. "But marriage?" was all she could say.

"Why not?" Shirley answered. "It's the perfect solution."

"I tried absolutely everything I could think of after we got back with Donna. Veronica wanted to stay and help, but I knew she needed to be with her family and secretly wanted to be. I talked her into leaving the next day," Stella said, remembering that tearful goodbye.

Shirley got up and brought the coffee pot over. She poured both another cup. Stella reached over and added more sugar than necessary. She sipped it and cringed. "I prefer tea," she said; "at least with tea it can be as sweet as you want."

"What happened after Veronica left?"

"I went back to the church and practically begged Father MacGregor to take Donna in the daycare. He was adamant that it was not in God's plan. I guess I should not have run out yelling, 'Oh, why don't you just excommunicate me for Christ's sake!'"

Shirley couldn't help but smile, "Probably not one of your best moments."

"Oh, I know. Father MacGregor called later that day. He said that he had a slight change of heart. He told me that he had prayed. He decided that Rosie and Maddie could come back. So, I took them to the summer daycare and took Donna to work with me. I was able to stretch that misguided solution to a whole week with Wills's help in my subterfuge, but it wasn't long until my boss had a private conversation with me."

"Did he try to fire you?"

"No, he actually said that he was sympathetic, but this was a place of work, not a daycare facility for impaired children! He gave me until the end of the week, but if I brought Donna in again, he would have to let me go."

"I need to go back to my teaching position in a few weeks as you know, so unfortunately I won't be able to watch the girls while you work."

"Yes, I understand." Stella took Shirley's hand and squeezed it, "You're a good friend."

Shirley jumped up, "Okay, this is the plan. Here is what we are going to do!"

Later that evening, Wills stood on Stella's front porch step cradling a bottle of wine under one arm, an assorted bouquet of non-yellow flowers in his hand and a tightly gripped note in the other hand. Just as he considered turning around to leave without being noticed, the porch light blinked on and off several times. The moths appeared to be mesmerized, flitting around the light as if they were in a conga dancing contest. He wanted to laugh at the absurdity of his thoughts, but the door flew open and an impossible vision exploded in his brain as if he were in a dream.

"I suppose you are laughing at that note?" she winced, embarrassed at her inability to express herself. Usually it was Wills who stammered in her presence. But now, she was clearly the one who was on the defensive.

Still, Wills just stared at her. He focused on her entire being all without words. She was beyond words. Her sandy-colored hair fell gently in waves that seemed to splash calmly around her bare shoulders. Those expressive sapphire-blue eyes twinkled in the glow of the tiny porch light. Her beautiful eyes perfectly complemented a dress unlike any he had ever seen before. She was elegant in a chiffon strapless dress. A light wrap draped softly around her shoulders as the dress continued snugly toward her slender waist. He was sure he could easily wrap his two hands around her waist and touch his fingers. Just thinking about that made him turn all shades of red, he was sure. The skirt of the dress swung out widely from her waist to her knees with the help of numerous petticoats hidden from view. As he tried to catch his breath again, he noticed that she was not wearing shoes.

"I can fix that light for you," was all he could manage to say as he stared at her feet.

Stella smiled, "That would be very nice."

Both stood in the doorway, neither knowing what to say next.

Finally, it was Wills who broke the tension. "I was supposed to go to dinner at my sister's house this evening. But when I got to the front door there was this note taped to it. Do you want to read it? I can read it." Wills was clearly getting frustrated,

"It says that I went to the wrong house. I was to go to Stella's house. That's why I'm standing on your porch like a lost puppy."

"I'm very fond of lost puppies," Stella said, easing his discomfort.

Wills didn't know how to respond to that. He continued to gaze into those eyes. He was sure to drown in her gaze if he didn't say something promptly. "I prefer cats."

As if on cue, Merlin jolted into the room from behind a closed door that was now swinging wildly open. He dashed around the furniture like a race car driver determined to hit the finish line before any others. Merlin must have decided that the finish line was the open door to the porch. He zoomed toward Wills with a wild but not unfriendly leap. Flowers, note, and the bottle of wine cascaded over Wills's head as he tumbled backwards to the grassy ground next to the porch. Merlin jumped on top of him, simultaneously lapping the escaping wine with his enormous tongue.

Wills wondered if he could talk Stella into trading this monster in for a cat.

"Oh, no. Merlin, bad dog! I am so sorry. Merlin, leave Mr. Rollins alone," Stella stammered as she tried in vain not to laugh. Instead, Stella dropped to the ground next to Wills, trying to pry Merlin off him. Merlin gave Stella a sloppy lick of his tongue and raced off the porch toward Shirley's house. Wills and Stella sat on the grass while they gathered the fallen flowers.

"These are for you" was all Wills could say.

"Thank you. I love flowers," she answered with a wide grin and an unexpected laugh.

Wills gathered his wits about him and jumped up, "Let me help you up." He reached for her and as he took her hands, he slipped once again and tumbled down toward her reclined body. They both dissolved into uncontrollable laughter.

"I certainly hope you will have this much good grace when you taste my dinner. I'm not a very good cook. I have been working on this meal for hours and..." Stella wanted to explain but could not finish. Wills leaned over and quickly gave her a tiny kiss on the lips. She was not afraid, nor was she embarrassed. She felt comforted by his kindness. Instead of throwing her arms around him or kissing him back passionately like she had seen on the big screen, though, she displayed girlish shyness. Wills continued to gaze into her eyes. Stella was feeling a bit unnerved, so she struggled to stand. He immediately helped her up and they walked into the house hand in hand.

Stella was deliberating whether she should turn his head around toward hers and kiss him again when the sound of the telephone sliced through the tension like a thunderbolt. Stella raced to the phone as if escaping her dilemma.

"Hello," Stella answered immediately.

"Mom, you let Merlin escape," Rosie squealed.

"No, he got out. He was full of Merlin mischief again. You would have laughed. Merlin ran around and around the furniture, then he saw Mr. Rollins and me at the front door. He tumbled over Mr. Rollins as he flew out the door. I'm assuming he went directly to find you at Mrs. Surly's house. Am I right?"

"He was scratching at the door, so Mrs. Surly let him in," Rosie said but her words were almost unintelligible as she could not quite be heard over the commotion at her end of the conversation. "Merlin, *no*, no, Merlin, get off Mr. Surly. Mom, Mom, Merlin is going to get in trouble!"

"What is happening, Rosie? Let me speak to Mrs. Surly." Stella was shocked and concerned. She knew Merlin's unbounded energy. He could be a terror, but they knew that Merlin was an adorable, sweet giant with a rascal streak.

"Hang on, Mom," Rosie shouted over the noise of what Stella assumed was falling furniture and possibly various knickknacks on tabletops. "Bad dog. Mom, do you know that lounge chair that Mr. Surly often falls asleep in? Well, he had it all the way back. Merlin just wanted to say hello to him. Merlin jumped on top of him and the chair sort of fell over backwards."

"Get that monster moose off of me!" came a male scream from somewhere close to Rosie.

"He is not a moose. He is a dog."

1961 – SAN JOSE, CALIFORNIA | 191

Between gasps of breath, Stella could hear Sam Surly coughing and shouting, "I am allergic to dogs and mooses. Get him out of here!"

Shirley Surly took the phone from Rosie, "Hello, Stella. No need to worry. Continue with your romantic dinner. I can handle everything on this end. Sam is crawling out of his now broken chair. I always hated that lounger anyway. Maybe we can finally get something a bit more modern chic. We will need to replace the standing lamp and a few vases and ashtrays and the wet *TV Guide* that was soaked by the broken beer bottle. Don't you worry about a thing. It is all taken care of now."

"I'm so sorry. I will come get the dog and the girls and I will make it up to you somehow, I promise," Stella said.

"Don't you dare. You might just end up being Sam's sister-in-law. He would never dare be inhospitable to a sister. Sam? Sam? What are you doing?"

"What now? Oh dear, now what?" Stella winced. "Never mind. I figured it out. There is a monster dog bounding down the road toward me as we speak. Tell Sam that I'm sorry. I better get back to my date."

"Yes, you do that!" Shirley laughed but hung up the phone swiftly, hoping that Sam wouldn't make a scene in front of the children.

As Stella gently hung up the phone, she closed her eyes and took a deep breath before turning around to face Wills. But when she was ready to explain the situation or apologize, she noticed that Wills had poured each of them a glass of water from the pitcher that was on the table and was now pouring two glasses of wine. He had also put the remains of the flowers he brought in a tall vase that she assumed he found on the display shelf by the table.

"The table looks very nice," Will offered without looking around toward her surprised face.

"Thank you," Stella responded automatically with a wide grin.

Wills wanted to say something – anything – but he couldn't

get words out of his mouth. He only smiled until the undisciplined monster bounded through the slightly ajar front door. Merlin stopped, surveyed the situation, and leaped for the sliced Wonder Bread that he had noticed on the table. Stella put her hands over her mouth and stood shell-shocked. Wills backed away slightly stunned. Merlin put his two front paws on the table, grabbed the bread in his mouth, then hurriedly ducked under the tablecloth with the bread firmly between his teeth.

"Merlin, *no!*" Stella shouted as she tried to crawl under the table to retrieve the dog.

Wills crouched down with a misguided vision to help. He knelt on one knee next to Stella with one hand on top of the table and the other toward Merlin. "Come here, nice doggy?"

"Nice doggy?" Stella laughed.

"Come here, you annoying beast!" he substituted.

Merlin tilted his head with the bread still clutched tightly in his mouth. Maybe he was afraid they would take it away from him. He had no intention of moving until he eyed that man reaching toward him with a devious plan to snatch his food. Merlin jumped up, rapidly toppling the table. He dashed straight between the two people and ran with all his might out from under the table and down the hallway. The table was still shaking slightly as Wills held tightly to Stella's arm. As he tried to help her stand up, he inadvertently grabbed the tablecloth. In a flash, the entire contents of the table came tumbling down on top of them with the tablecloth. Wills and Stella were immediately drenched with water and wine while they sat in a heap of flowers, butter, peas, mashed potatoes, and broken dishes.

After a beat of a few seconds Wills sighed, "Well, I really did think you had the table set very nicely."

"Thank you." She looked at him and beamed.

They both laughed.

Stella was nervous and convinced that she was incapable of enticing a man. She inwardly berated herself for buying an expensive cut of meat just to impress him even though she had no idea how to cook it. Her family never got more than a steady diet of home-cooked casseroles she had learned from her mother. "I hope you will still stay for dinner. The roast is in the oven. I've been cooking it all day. I really don't know how to cook. I have some canned corn I can open. And there is water. I'm afraid I don't have any more wine. Oh, I am sorry. I'm just so embarrassed. I don't know how to date a man, I..."

Before she could finish, Wills reached over and tugged her into his arms. He ran his fingers through her hair and looked at her fondly, then kissed her.

It didn't take long for Wills to pick up the various pieces of the disaster. He wanted to recreate what Stella had so easily displayed earlier. When he had first noticed the beautifully arranged table setting, he immediately felt a sense of awe mixed with confusion. Now he thought that Stella would think he was ridiculous if she knew how intimidated he had truly felt. Luckily that foolish dog became the catalyst for the magic that had ensued. Merlin really was a magician. Wills was laughing quietly when Stella came in from the kitchen. She had a small bowl of corn in one hand and a large serving plate in the other.

"Let me help you with that." Wills blew out the match he had used to light the candles.

"Thank you," Stella answered. "The table looks amazing. I'm glad you were able to recover most of the flowers."

"The vase didn't break, but I'm afraid only four flower stems survived," Wills said.

"I think it looks very pretty. Thank you for cleaning up the broken dishes and glasses, and the wine, and..."

Wills stopped her with a finger to her lips after he put down the food. "It's perfectly fine," he said, "but I am afraid the tablecloth is a bit too wet and stained to put back on the table right now."

"I don't mind if you don't."

Wills pulled out Stella's chair and easily helped her sit down. He glided his chair closer toward hers and seated himself.

"I hope you like roast beef," Stella offered, not looking at him.

There was a small black, rounded, rock-like substance on the serving platter. Wills hadn't been sure what it was. Now he knew.

"Yes, yes, of course," he said, wondering how to start this meal.

Stella watched him with trepidation. She also was wondering how to begin.

Finally, Wills stood up. "Do you have a knife? I will cut the roast and serve it."

Stella jumped up and ran to the kitchen. "Oh, yes. I forgot. Just a moment."

She raced back into the room within seconds. Wills again held out her chair, so she could sit down, when she pointed the knife at him.

"Oh, I am sorry. I didn't mean to..." Stella's complexion turned a crimson red and her voice seemed overly hoarse. She was clearly flustered and couldn't continue.

"No, no. It's perfectly fine. Here, I'm pretty good at cutting meat, or so my family says. I think it comes from growing up on a farm," Wills felt himself rambling but couldn't stop.

Stella put the knife gently down on the table. Wills immediately picked it up and stood poised to slice the tiny mass of what he assumed must be the roast beef, although it resembled a single lump of coal. He grabbed a fork to place in the meat, so he would be able to use his other hand to cut with the knife. Wills was mesmerized by Stella, certain he was captured in her spell. He was lost in his thoughts, staring at Stella, when she touched him lightly on the arm.

Biting her lip, "Do you think you can slice the meat?"

"Yes, yes, of course," he replied with great confidence. He tried to put the fork in the meat, but it would not budge. Since he refused to give up, he tried once again, but this time with a bit more force to stab the meat. The fork bent with a groan – or maybe that sound came from him. Wills was determined to make a grand impression in front of Stella; instead he was sure he looked like a fool. Next, he grabbed another fork and the knife to forcibly attack the stone lump in front of him. Just as the knife touched the meat, it slipped. The dark blob bounced off the plate and cascaded in a tumbling escape to the floor, where it rolled toward the slumbering dog. Merlin swiftly jumped up, eyeing the morsel as if he were the star forward in a championship hockey game. Using his paws as hockey sticks, he lunged toward the puck, batting it back and forth between the walls while he raced fiercely toward the end of the hallway, the goal post. Retrieving his prey, Merlin walked purposely back to the table. He leaped up between the two humans, put his paws on the table, and dropped the object as though presenting them with a prize. He turned abruptly away and marched back down the hall with his head and ears and tail held high. Stella imagined that Merlin was hearing the screams of "Goal!" echoing off the walls.

A heartbeat later, Stella and Wills focused on each other, frozen in time. If it wasn't for the ticking of the wall clock signaling an obtrusive warning, they might have been forever lost in their own private confusion.

"Will you marry me?"

"Yes."

Chapter 37

1961 – SAN JOSE, CALIFORNIA

THREE WEEKS LATER

The warmth of the day and the sapphire glaze of the sky seemed like a good omen for the beginning of their journey to a new life. Shirley stood close to her brother while cradling one arm securely around his waist. "Stella wanted me to remind you to use extra care packing the antiques into the moving van."

"What antiques?" Wills exclaimed with a look of horror in his eyes. "I didn't notice any antiques."

"For someone who has nothing, she sure has a lot of stuff," Shirley's husband, Sam, said as he pushed a few more boxes into the trailer.

"Sam, Sam, don't close that yet," Stella hollered from the kitchen window. "I have a couple more boxes."

Wills put his arm around Shirley's shoulder, "Maybe you could bring the rest when you come up for Thanksgiving?"

"Thanksgiving?" Sam cried, "You didn't mention Thanksgiving. That's my day of rest. I don't do anything on that day."

"That's for sure," Shirley sighed.

"I'm so busy doing nothing that I don't have time to do anything!" Sam thought everyone would appreciate his wit.

"Try to latch the door, will you?" Wills asked as he walked toward the back of the car.

"I suppose that moose will be at your place for Thanksgiving?" Sam whined, "Do we *have* to go?"

"Yes!" Shirley glared at her husband.

"Well, I suppose, as long as that mutt doesn't stay here with us. We are *not* keeping that dog! Where is he? Where is that insufferable moose? I bet he is hiding at my house ready to attack me!"

Wills grinned mischievously at his sister and brother-in-law, "You know Merlin would never leave Rosie's side, but I'm sure that he'll be very happy to give you a nice moose kiss send-off as soon as Rosie jumps into the car."

"Are you sure this car can handle the moving trailer *and* that five-hundred-pound mutt?" Sam smirked. "I'm worried the trailer hitch might scratch the road. Look how low it is now."

Shirley waved her hand at him, "Oh, you worry too much. They will take it slow and easy, won't you, Willie?"

"Yes, yes, of course," Wills answered, but he wasn't really paying attention to his sister. He looked up at the kitchen window where Stella had been moments earlier. He was still in a state of shock that a woman as gorgeous and brilliant as Stella would marry him. Was it only three weeks ago that they were married in Las Vegas? Wills knew beyond a shadow of a doubt that it would remain the highlight of his life. He would cherish every moment, every day of his life. Stella's house sold almost immediately after she put it on the market. They were both quite surprised at the unusual bidding war that occurred during the selling process. Stella walked away with ten thousand dollars in equity, which she immediately put into the bank. Wills was surprised that Stella's only comment was that she wished she had sold it sooner. Still, he was "over the moon," as his mother used to say. He went to the bank with her and transferred his small hard-earned savings into a joint account. Stella suggested that she should get hold of Richard to give him half of the sale. Wills convinced her that the money should be used in lieu of child support since she had never received any. She agreed reluctantly but said no more about it. Wills couldn't wait to show Stella the surprise he had for her. He was daydreaming about the anticipated excitement it would bring when Stella rushed out of the house almost invisible behind the two large boxes she was carrying.

Stella gasped for breath, "That's it!"

Sam took the heavy load from her and opened his mouth to make a wry comment, but shut it again quickly when Shirley shook her head in warning.

"I think I did a pretty good job packing. I bet you have plenty of room in the trailer for these last two boxes. I used every space I could find. Oh, Shirley, you should have seen how ingeniously I packed. I even put candles, candlesticks, and linens in shoes to make every space count. Sam, why did you close and lock the trailer door already? What about these two boxes?"

"I'm happy to say that we wanted to have a good excuse to come see you this Thanksgiving. We'll bring them with us," Sam grinned, not looking at Shirley's confused expression.

"Oh Sam, Shirley. I think I might cry." Stella went to each and hugged them tightly.

"Enough of that," Shirley murmured, wiping a tear from her eye. "I put Maddie in the middle of the front seat between Willie and you. Donna is in the back. I couldn't find Rosie and Merlin, though. Do you know where they are hiding?"

"I have a hunch," Stella said. "Sam and Wills, please finish the last-minute safety checks while I go get them."

Sam watched her head toward the house and disappear around a corner before answering, "Safety checks? You will be lucky to make it out of the driveway, let alone to Hidden Lake, Oregon."

"Sam!" Shirley scolded. She turned toward Willie and added, "Now, Willie, you have the keys to our house in Hidden Lake. It hasn't been occupied since you left there two years ago, as you know. It's going to need a little clean-up."

"Stella and I can handle it. Don't you worry. We can do all the fixing up that it needs."

"What will you do for work if the mill isn't hiring?" Sam asked.

"Don't worry about a thing. I have a backup plan. It's a surprise."

Chapter 38

1961 – SAN JOSE, CALIFORNIA

The door seemed to creak open into an empty shell of a vacant house, no longer a home. Stella gasped at her own sadness. She stood very still as the ghosts of a lost dream invaded her thoughts, a dull emptiness deep within her chest. The emergence of tears was very close, but she was absolutely determined not to cry. The only thing she could do was shake her head and allow a new life to begin. That ancient memory would fade in time as she filled her new home and her new life with new memories. Now, she was excited.

Stella had no difficulties finding Rosie. She knew where she would be. Many years ago, Rosie and her father had worked together to build a small brick enclosure for the backyard flower garden. The flowers were long dead. Stella hadn't had the heart to continue planting. They used to laugh that Mommy had such a black thumb, as Rosie called it. Richard had said he didn't marry her because of any hopes of a green thumb, but only because of her blue eyes.

Rosie was sitting very still on that small brick wall. Merlin had his head and big paws on her lap. Rosie stroked his head over and over, ignoring the tears flowing down her face.

Stella was very calm. In a soft voice she said, "It's time to go, Rosie."

"I'm not going, Mommy. Merlin and I are staying here," Rosie insisted without looking at her mother.

Stella walked slowly toward her daughter and sat down next to her. She stroked Merlin's silky fur, saying softly, "I'm afraid it won't work this time, Rosie."

"Are you scared, Mommy?"

"A little. What about you? Are you afraid?"

Rosie continued to stare into the distance. She wiped her cheeks with the back of her hands. Merlin looked up at her. "I'm a whole lot afraid," she said.

Stella nodded, "That's very easy to do."

"What's easy to do?" Rosie didn't understand what her mother was talking about. How could going to a strange place with a strange man be easy to do?

"Being afraid," her mother said, "Being afraid is easy. Do you know what is very hard to do?"

"No."

"Being brave. It takes courage to do something that is hard. It takes courage to do something you have never done before. Few people have that kind of courage," Stella said. "Merlin does, though."

"Merlin?" Rosie questioned as she tilted her head toward her mom. Merlin also tilted his head as if he, too, were listening and understanding every word.

"Merlin has a kind of magic. Can you feel it? Remember how he just moved in with us? That must have been scary for him, but he loves us now and we love him," Stella explained, taking a handkerchief out of her sleeve and wiping Rosie's face.

Rosie beamed and put her arms around Merlin's neck, "Merlin knew he belonged with us. But how do we know that we belong with Mr. Rollins?"

"How do we know that we don't? We won't know until we try."

"Why did you marry him, Mommy?" Rosie sniffed again.

"It's hard to explain."

"It was hard? You were being brave?" Rosie again ran her fingers through Merlin's fur. Her eyes were getting moist once more.

"I wish I could tell you that I'm the bravest mommy in the world, but that would be a lie. Sometimes people do things for a lot of different reasons. I believe being a family is very important. I wanted you girls and our dog to have a father and a good home where we can all be happy."

Rosie stuck out her stubborn chin. "I have a daddy. I want him, not this other father."

"I know, and your daddy will always be your daddy. He just can't live with us now. He chose to start a new family. Please, Rosie, I want you to know that your father does love you very much. He just chose a different path, a different life. We all make choices in life. The hard part is living with the consequences of those decisions."

Looking baffled, Rosie asked, "What are con-se-quences?"

"Well," her mother began, "Let's say you have three Popsicles – orange, cherry, and root beer."

"Orange is my favorite flavor."

"I know but remember that you are allergic to orange. What happens when you eat oranges?"

"I get hives. It's not fair because orange is my favorite."

"That's a consequence. You might like orange the best, but if you eat it you'll get hives. You would have to live with those consequences. So maybe you might want to choose a different flavor."

Rosie thought for a moment and said, "I do like cherry. It's okay."

"That would be an easy choice then, but what about root beer?"

"I've never had root beer."

"That would be the hard choice. Now, think about it. Root beer would be something brand new for you. It may be horrible, and you might decide to go back to what you are used to – the just-okay cherry or the it-gives-me-hives orange. Or, and this is important, you might find that root beer is the best thing you have ever had in your whole life!"

"That would be courageous!" Rosie grinned widely at her mom.

"Yes!"

Rosie turned back to stare straight ahead again, "What if

Daddy comes here looking for us? Maybe he will realize that he ate an orange Popsicle or that he hates root beer?"

"You are a clever girl," her mother said as she put her arm around Rosie's shoulder, "but I'm one step ahead of you. I gave Grandma Ensign our new address and I made sure that your father has it, too."

Rosie gave her dog a big hug, "Come on, Merlin. Time to get up. We have a journey to go on."

Merlin jumped up almost immediately as Rosie also stood. They turned toward the front of the house. Stella took a deep breath as she looked around the yard quietly. Without looking at her mom, Rosie said, "Mommy, can we stop for a root beer Popsicle on our journey northward?"

Without a second thought, Stella jumped up and quickly took two giant steps toward her daughter and their massive dog. She dropped to one knee and hugged them both, "I think we are going to have a grand adventure!"

"What if Mr. Rollins hates root beer?"

"I'll tell you a little secret." Stella turned her head and whispered into Rosie's ear, "He thinks Merlin is magical!"

Rosie and her dog smiled.

Chapter 39

1961 – EN ROUTE TO HIDDEN LAKE, OREGON

Rosie raced around to the side of the car where Shirley and Sam were standing next to Wills. Merlin was right on her heels. Sam's eyes went wide as he moved behind Shirley, holding her shoulders and pushing her playfully side to side. "Watch out, a monster is on the loose!"

"Goodness gracious, Sam. Stop your silliness. Come here, Rosie, and give me a big hug," Shirley directed, looking straight at Rosie but ignoring Sam.

"Goodbye, Aunt Shirley. I guess it's legal for me to call you that now," Rosie said, wrapping her arms around Shirley's middle and tucking her head close to her.

"It's not only legal, it's the best gift you can give me." Shirley leaned down closer to Rosie and whispered in her ear, "I want to you know something that's very important. Please always remember it's okay to be a little girl. Now, go teach Maddie and Donna how to play and have fun. I know you can do that. We love you."

"Yes, I promise. I love you, too, Aunt Shirley. Don't tell that goofy husband of yours, but Merlin and I love him, too," Rosie sniffed before swiftly escaping into the backseat of the station wagon. Once inside she leaned over to push down the button and lock the door next to Donna.

"Go ahead and get into the car, you big mutt," Sam said to

204 | Uniquely Stella

Merlin as he came around Shirley to shake Wills's hand and give him last-minute driving instructions.

Shirley led Merlin to the car but before he could jump in, she put her two hands on his face and kissed the top of his head. She was rewarded with big smiles from Merlin and all the girls. Merlin jumped into the car next to Rosie. Shirley opened the window, so he could get some air when she closed the door.

At that very moment Stella raced to the front seat of the car with a shopping bag hanging on her arm. "I almost forgot the sandwiches I made for our lunch. Now, I'm ready. Goodbye, Shirley, Sam. We will see you this Thanksgiving. I can hardly wait. Okay, Wills, I think we're all ready."

Sam stood next to Shirley and closed the backseat door for her. Seeing that Sam hadn't moved away yet, Merlin stuck his head out the window and gave Sam a gigantic lick from his chin to his forehead. "Shirley!" Sam screamed, "Get the anti-moose-dog germ disinfectant out before I come down with some terrifying disease that will prevent me from going up to Hidden Lake in a few months."

"Maybe you'll finally grow a few hairs on your chest," Wills laughed as he stuck his hand out his window to wave. He put the car in reverse to ease the station wagon and trailer out of the driveway. The sound was deafening. All stayed very quiet wondering if they were truly going anywhere. Even Donna stopped jabbering and rocking back and forth.

Stella said, "Good gracious. This squealing reminds me of the train when the cars were being added or taken off. Are you sure the hitch is on correctly, Wills?"

"Yes, yes. We just need to take it easy. Here we go. Hang on, everyone!" Wills held his breath and put his foot gingerly on the accelerator. The car bucked backwards. He switched gears into first and they jerked forward. Little by little the car eased down the road at a turtle's pace. Sam and Shirley were waving as they moved out of sight.

Wills's grin was as broad as he could manage, "There, all is well now. We are off!"

Rosie, however, was not ready to be pleasant. She was determined to keep a scowl on her face for the entire trip. "How long will it take us to get there, Mr. Rollins?"

"You can call me Dad now if you'd like. I'm your new father after all," Wills said without turning his head around. Both hands were gripped tightly on the steering wheel with his eyes intently following the road ahead of them.

"I have a dad, thank you," Rosie said without emotion.

Stella turned her head around to the backseat and gave her daughter a stern warning, "Rosie!"

"That's fine, Stella. I understand. It will take time. So, Rosie, what would you like to call me? Your mother calls me Wills. Would you like to use that? I think that would be less formal than Mr. Rollins."

"No, that's for her. I'm thinking I like Wilbur. It reminds me of Wilbur the pig in *Charlotte's Web*. Although it also sounds like a cow's name."

"Rosie!" her mother scolded her again, "Behave and be polite. I mean it!"

Wills shook his head and winked at Stella, "If Wilbur is good enough for a pig or a cow, then I must assume that it is good enough for me, too." Turning to Stella he said, "My sister has a lot to answer for."

"So how long, Wilbur?" Rosie asked again.

"Probably two days. We will stay at a motel tonight," Wills answered as he slowly maneuvered the large car and even larger trailer down the road.

"I thought it might take a couple of years," Rosie mumbled under her breath.

Stella closed her eyes and repeated, "Rosie, I said that's enough."

"Do you like root beer Popsicles, Wilbur?" Rosie asked, ignoring her mother's warning.

"I don't know that I've ever had one," he responded, turning his head toward Stella. "I think I'm more of a beer kind of fellow."

Stella felt a tiny shiver head down her spine, but it immediately evaporated when Wills reached for her hand and squeezed it. He lifted her hand to his mouth for a quick kiss before he released his hold to pay strict attention to the road. Her sudden fear disappeared.

THREE DAYS LATER

Rosie woke from a deep slumber. "Mom, Mom, wake up," she implored, leaning toward the front seat and shaking her mother's shoulder. "Are you awake, too, Wilbur?"

Wills sat up straight and squeezed all the exhaustion he could from his shoulders, "Yes, of course I am. You will be happy to know that we're almost there."

Stella opened her eyes and looked around as though lost, "Are we there? Oh, my. Look to your left, everyone. Oh, Wills, it's unbelievably beautiful."

The sky was bathed in a brilliant glow of orange and yellows with thin strips of pink. The sun was melting into the horizon of the Pacific Ocean, casting thin streaks of light in all directions as if opening a fan of shooting stars. The others gazed with wonder as the swirling colors intertwined and changed into a kaleidoscope of artistic designs.

"The sunset is pretty dramatic here, but as it comes on suddenly, so does it vanish into darkness. I need to find the sign to Hidden Lake before it gets too dark and we end up going too far north to Bridgewater Harbor," Wills said, searching the right side of the road closely while still clutching the steering wheel.

"I'm happy to help look. What am I looking for? Is there a street sign?" Stella asked.

"Well, not exactly a street sign. Unless it has changed in the last year or two, it's more like a direction sign. Look for a piece of wood shaped like an arrow with the words Hidden Lake painted in block letters. It'll be posted on a big tree to the right. That will tell us which road to turn off onto."

Another hour went by. Wills had slowed to a crawl. Luckily there were very few cars on the road, but darkness was encroaching.

"There it is!" Rosie shouted, "I found it!"

"You sure did," Wills turned right onto the road toward Hidden Lake. "Nice job, Rosie. Thanks! I would have missed it and I've been here many times over the years."

"Wills, I can't really see much of the town or the houses. It's so dark," Stella said, turning her head side to side eager to visualize her new environment.

"I know, and I'm sorry. I promise to take everyone out for a grand tour of the entire town of Hidden Lake tomorrow when the day will bloom bright and sunny. You should know, however, that it won't take very long to see it all. Main Street is only a couple of blocks with just a few shops. Not much to look at, I'm afraid."

Stella was confused and queried, "I thought there was a lake."

"Mommy, it's hidden," Rosie interrupted.

"No, no. There's a lake all right and it's a beauty. In fact, there are two lakes connected by a channel. You will love it. Tomorrow, I'll take everyone on a grand tour by boat," Wills said as he maneuvered the car around the corner.

"Oh, how exciting! I can't wait," Stella exclaimed. "See, Rosie. This will be quite an adventure." She could sense Rosie's excitement as well.

Wills pulled into a driveway and announced, "We have arrived!"

"It's so dark, Wills," Stella said.

"Stay here for just a few more minutes. Let me grab the flashlight out of the glove compartment. I'll open the house and get some lights on. Shirley mentioned that she had the electric company reconnect the power last week."

"What about unpacking?" Stella asked.

"Let's wait on that for now. I think we should get settled first. Besides, I have a big surprise for everyone later. Right now, the box of linens and bedding is in the back of the station wagon. I'll fetch that once everyone is inside."

"Mommy," Rosie whispered once Wills was out of the car, "this is scary."

"Remember, Rosie, what I told you. Scary is tough, but this

could very well be the adventure of a lifetime. How do you want to look at it?" her mother answered with excitement in her voice. To her, a new life was beginning, and she was determined to make it a grand adventure.

Chapter 40

1961 – CHICAGO, ILLINOIS

Veronica

WHILE STELLA AND HER FAMILY WERE PREPARING FOR THEIR upcoming journey to a new life in Hidden Lake, Veronica was pacing the floor of her tiny living room in Chicago. Veronica was frustrated and upset with everything and everyone. She had sent her twin boys up to bed early due to their horrible attitudes and surly behavior. The boys were barely ten years old but thought they owned the world as they held giant chips on their collective shoulders. Veronica's thoughts exploded in her brain, leaving her with an enormous headache that made her anger rise to the surface. She could not understand what was happening to her children. When they were babies and later toddlers, she was convinced that they were the most beautiful and brilliant children on the face of the earth. Now, they were acting like little thugs.

An hour earlier, she had been sitting at the dining room table. The table was set, and the food was ready. Her mother had finished her dinner in silence and left to sit in her favorite rocking chair on the front porch. Veronica pulled a fork through her food but couldn't eat a thing. She had been getting increasingly angry that her boys were late for dinner once again. Bill, her husband, should have been home from work hours before.

The twins were supposed to be down the road at a friend's house. When they didn't come home on time, she went looking for them. They were not there. Where were they and why weren't they home? Now she knew, and she was livid as she recalled the confrontation with her children:

The screen door flew open and Veronica heard the boys trot up the front steps. She glared at them from the doorway.

"Hey, Granny, what's happening?" Anton shouted toward his grandmother, who was rocking steadily but not looking at the children.

"Do you two realize what time it is? Where have you been, anyway?" Veronica scolded them.

"Don't have a cow, Ma," Leon answered, "It's all cool."

Anton jumped in, "Yeah, we had a blast at Leroy's bash. It was crazy cool!"

"You were not at Leroy's. Do not lie to me. I went over there. They had not seen you," Veronica's voice was starting to shake. She needed to settle down. Where was Bill? She needed his authority right now.

Leon and Anton, or the Lion and the Ant as everyone called them now, were a mess. Veronica and Bill certainly didn't anticipate those nicknames when the twins were born, but they accepted it now. The boys looked like they had been rolling around in mud puddles. Their faces were covered in grime and even their clothes were ripped in various places. She had spent a lot of time taking out hems and sewing patches over the past year. Their clothes seemed to be shrinking daily. "I will not ask you again. Tell me now where you were and what you've been doing, or we'll wait until your father gets home. I'm sure you will not like those consequences."

"What are consequences?" Anton asked.

"We only went to the park to mess around with the guys. We had a bit of a tumble with some white boys. It's no biggie, Ma. We're stronger and took care of them easy enough," Leon added with a huff.

"Nothing to flip your wig about," Anton laughed.

"Go to your room, both of you! Now!" their mother was beside herself. It was unlike her to get so mad. Right now, she wanted time to think.

The boys scurried up the stairs without another word. Veronica's mother, Barbara, looked at her with concern in her eyes. "Boys will be boys. Don't fret so, Veronica."

Veronica slammed the screen door shut as she went back inside without answering her mother. Another hour had passed. Barbara came back inside. She reached around to turn on the front porch light and close the door. Before she turned back to go up the stairs to her room, she walked over to Veronica and touched her arm, "He'll be home soon. I'll give you some private time. Good night, sweetheart."

"Thank you, Mama. We'll be fine now. I've made up my mind. I have a plan," Veronica replied calmly.

"I was pretty sure you would figure it out. This may come as a surprise, but I think I know what it is, and it's a good one. We'll work this out and I promise to help," her mother added as she turned to take her time ascending the stairs.

Veronica felt a little like a boomerang pacing back and forth from one wall to the other. The house was deadly still. The only sound that could be heard was the ticking of the wall clock. Just when she finally sat down on the couch, she heard Bill come up the front steps. She didn't move.

The door opened, and Bill swayed into the room. He had clearly been drinking and looked as ruffled as the children had. His face was dirty and his clothes disheveled. Still worse was the smell of beer and cigarettes. She had a vehement hatred of both. Bill knew that.

"Hey, Babe. Sorry I'm late," Bill said as he tried to smile.

Veronica thought he only looked smug and answered him with venom in her voice, "Do not Babe me!"

"Oh, Veronica, come on. Hey, I'm sorry. It's not my fault. Really."

Veronica glared at him. Bill took his hat off and flung it to a nearby table before walking slowly to the couch to sit next to his wife. She immediately jumped up and moved to the other side of the room.

"Are you going to have a wonderful excuse this time or have you made up a truly forgettable story?" she demanded, ignoring the lump in her throat.

Bill put his elbows on his knees and his hands on his face. He looked down at the floor as he tried to collect his thoughts before he said, "The truth this time."

Veronica could feel his sincerity. She knew without a shadow of a doubt that he was in distress and only she could help him. "Tell me."

"You know that I clean up people's crap..."

"Bill," Veronica interrupted, "You work as a janitor at Union Station. There's nothing wrong with that."

"I suppose, but it certainly isn't a lifelong ambition. That's not the problem, though."

"Go on."

"I was just coming out of one of the men's stalls with the mop and bucket. Some squirrely, pock-faced white boy stood right smack in front of me and wouldn't budge. I was polite and asked him to please move aside so I could finish the clean-up. He said this was a white man's retreat, not for Negros. Retreat? Retreat? Was he joking? I looked him straight in the eye and said that this was Chicago, not the South. He kept poking me in the chest. Another pal of his came into the joint and grabbed my arm. He growled that I was undoubtedly one of those southern migration boys. I told them both I was from California, but I doubt they even knew where California was. The pockmarked boy swung his fist into my stomach, but I grabbed my broom and swung it toward his friend, then directed my attention toward my attacker and kicked my foot into a part of his scrawny anatomy where I knew would hurt him the most."

"Oh, Bill. Did they attack you?" Veronica cried, moving toward the couch to sit next to him.

"I hightailed it out of there fast. I jumped right over that rolled-up squealing weasel and took off running. I didn't stop until I had navigated in and out of numerous streets and alleyways. Once I realized I wasn't followed, I got on the bus to head home. Walking from the bus stop, I saw a buddy of mine who convinced me to stop in for a quick drink at the corner tavern. Several of the fellas were there. Once they heard the story told and retold a dozen times, I had so many free drinks on the bar that I didn't count."

Veronica just glared at him but didn't say a word.

"I'm not drunk. Not really. Please understand, Veronica. I'm so sorry. Forgive me," Bill's eyes were welling up.

She put her head on his shoulder and sighed, "Oh, Bill, I..." but she couldn't finish.

Bill stopped her and said, "I've heard about things going on all over. They're calling it a civil rights movement. I'm ready to move in that direction. I'm ready to fight and stand up for our rights. I've been in a war and this is war. I'm so sick of this dilapidated apartment we're forced to live in. I'm sick of feeling like we must stay behind invisible bars in this segregated neighborhood. I'm so sick and tired of various clashes whenever one of our own kind tries to go to any neighborhood park or beach. I'm sick of unequal opportunities, or I should say *no* opportunities in mixed employment, or housing, or even political representation. It's a world of white folks' power and I'm sick of it!"

"Don't forget the lousy schooling our children are exposed to. Even though it's a law now that education segregation is unconstitutional and illegal, I cannot get my children in a good school and believe me I have tried and tried. And now, the twins are acting like little hoodlums."

"That may be the worst of all because their future and the future of all of us depend on education."

"Why is it some people see only color and others seem oblivious to it?"

"Your best friend is one of those oblivious types, I know. I'm not so sure Stella even knows that you are black," Bill said.

Veronica just shook her head, "It doesn't make any difference to her."

"My close buddy from the service, Dick, was the same. Stella and Dick seemed to be such a good match. I don't understand what happened to them."

"For some people, it's not color that bothers them but the inability to adjust to their own guilt and fears. Dick couldn't accept the fact that his own daughter has a handicap. His prejudice went deep into his soul," Veronica sighed, "yet Stella sees her child as only her child, not a disability."

"When I was in the Navy, we managed to get along. Well, I was put on the kitchen staff as a steward and had to wait on the higher-ups. I'm not saying there weren't the odd skirmishes now and then, but our captain told us in no uncertain terms that we had a bigger enemy to fight and he would not tolerate fighting amongst his men. Besides, I came away with best buddies that were just your average joes – black and white."

Veronica nodded her head in assent. She had lost her anger while she resolved to carry out her plan. Her voice returned to the quiet, soft tenor it typically exhibited as she said, "That's why we need to move."

"Move?" Bill was incredulous. "Where would we be able to move in Chicago? It's difficult enough just keeping this dump!"

"Hidden Lake, Oregon," Veronica replied.

"What?" Bill exclaimed. "The Oregon Territory. It's full of Indians!"

"Now you're just being facetious as well as prejudiced," Veronica declared.

"Where do you get these words? From your white friends in California?" Bill said as he stood up and paced the floor.

"Dorothy, actually. I do read a lot, Bill. I also worked at a very fine school in San Francisco. The kind of school that our children should be going to. Besides, you know very well what I'm talking about. You went to Stanford, or did you forget that?"

"No, I hadn't forgotten. It was only for a couple of years, though. My parents worked so diligently to send me to college. Sadly, Pearl Harbor happened the same week that they died in a car accident. I enlisted the day after their funeral," Bill said in a tone that was so sullen that Veronica's heart ached for him.

"Bill, now is the time for us to do something to change people's attitudes and to change our very own lifestyle. Don't you see that?"

"How could moving to some backwoods country where the natives probably have never even seen someone with a darker complexion than their own be helping this 'civil rights movement'?" Bill demanded.

"You may be right about that. They don't tan there, they rust, you know."

"Now who is being facetious?"

"I don't believe fighting with angry words or physical actions is the best way to change attitudes. The way I see it, this leads to more anger and resentment from both sides. Instead, when we gradually assimilate into each other's lives, we get to know each other on a personal level. We may or may not like each other, but this way we find out not by hurtful actions, but by everyday friendly encounters," Veronica said, watching Bill intently.

Bill continued to pace back and forth as he responded, "I can feel something in the air. The tension is thick with rage. The world is changing, Veronica. We, or maybe just I, should be on the front lines, being part of a movement that will determine what kind of future our children and their children will have. I can't hide while others fight for a necessary cause."

"I am sick of war. I don't want another war and I certainly don't want my children involved in any war! There are other ways to fight without being on the front lines. I fought, but in a completely different way. I did my part. Obviously, it wasn't dangerous like what you were exposed to, but I did work for the war effort in numerous ways. What I am suggesting is a risk and it's frightening. Bill, I must do this. I love you with all my heart, but I cannot and will not allow my children to be in a war, any kind of war, even if it is for civil rights, not in the streets, in the parks, or in the schools. We are going with or without you," Veronica concluded, tears ready to escape her eyes.

A few minutes went by before Bill stopped directly in front of Veronica. He knelt on one knee and took her hands. "There are some things ultimately more important in life. I don't know if you're right or if I am. I'm not even sure if one of us needs to be right. I only know that you and my children and even that stubborn mother of yours are my entire life. Without you, I would be in my own private war. I could not and will not live without you. If you want to go to Oregon to face bears, moose, Indians, and the almighty unknown, then so be it. I was never a coward. We will face this together."

Veronica put her arms around Bill's neck as he lifted her to stand. She hugged him with all her strength. He gently pulled away and put his hands on her face. "I love you so," Veronica said as Bill gave her a tender kiss. They walked hand in hand toward their room.

"Let's move to Oregon."

Chapter 41

1961 – HIDDEN LAKE, OREGON

Stella

HIDDEN LAKE ELEMENTARY SCHOOL WAS CERTAINLY NOT HIDDEN. The stark, unimpressive single-story brick building serving grades 1–6 was situated in the middle of a most unimpressive, tiny town. For a young woman who had been born and raised in the metropolis of Chicago and later moved to the fast-paced city of San Francisco, Stella was in a state of shock. She expected a small town, but she was totally overwhelmed by the emptiness of her new surroundings. Wills, however, was on the opposite end of the spectrum. He could not have been more excited to show them around. The morning following their arrival, Stella stepped out of the house and stood very still on the front porch. She glanced around nervously as she watched the rain pellet huge droplets in what appeared to be connecting lakes, not merely puddles. Maybe this was why it was called Hidden Lake – except they were quite visible everywhere one looked.

"Wills, should we unpack first before our tour of the town?" Stella suggested, still feeling anxiously hopeful and determined that a little downpour would not dampen her spirits.

Stella's new husband put his arm around her and grinned. "No, no. We can do that later. I have a big surprise for you, but it can wait until this afternoon. I'm sure you'll want to register

Rosie for school first. Today is Friday. The new school year starts Tuesday, the day after Labor Day."

"Donna, too," Stella added as she picked up Donna and gathered the children close to her to lead them toward the car.

Wills stopped her and said, "Wait on the porch while I go to the car to get an umbrella and Donna's stroller. We're going to walk."

"Walk? In the rain?" Stella questioned. "Won't it be too far for the children?"

Wills only shook his head and smiled.

༺࿐༻

Now as Stella headed down the bleak outside corridor of the school, she had to giggle. "Too far?" she laughed to herself. The main street surprisingly enough was called Main Street. The only cross street she noticed was called Hidden Lake Road. It was on this road the school managed to take up a full block. There was no way she could have missed it. She shook her head thinking how nervous she had been when Wills sent her off to find the school on her own while he went to do a little grocery shopping. She laughed out loud remembering the way Wills pointed out every store and feature of the town.

"See that green corner building?" Wills gestured.

Stella just nodded.

"That's Hidden Hazel's Soda Fountain Café."

"Is Hazel the owner?" Stella asked.

"No, no. No one knows why it's called Hazel's. I guess Elmer just liked the name. His wife has owned the business ever since Elmer died in the war. It's a small café with a few tables. She also sells some knick-knacks, candy, ice cream, and what Shirley calls crafts. That sort of thing."

"I wonder if I could ask her to display Veronica's hats. I could have Veronica send some and see if they would sell."

"I'm not so sure about that. Maybe Ross and Lynn Armstead's General Mercantile might be better. See that big building at the end of the road? That is our main grocery store. The townspeople call it the Mercantile. I know it doesn't look like much, but it has just about anything anyone could want, like cigars and fishing tackle for the men, kitchen items and linens for the women, and comic books and gumdrops for the kids." Wills grinned when Rosie clapped her hands in glee.

"What if *I* want to buy a cigar?" Stella teased.

Wills had a moment of hesitation that instantaneously vanished into a wide grin, "Stella, you are a laugh a minute. You know that?" He kissed the top of her head as his arms touched her shoulders to turn her around.

"On the other side of the street is the Hidden Lake post office. The woman who runs it believes she runs the entire town. She has been the postmistress for so long no one in living memory can remember a time before her. Be careful what you say around her because she knows everyone and everything and will make sure everyone else knows it, too."

Rosie tugged on her mother's skirt, "Mommy, look. Some man just fell out of that doorway."

"Rosie, quiet. Try not to embarrass the man. He is probably ill. Is that the doctor's office, Wills?" Stella asked.

"Well, afraid not. That is the Wander Inn Tavern." Wills was the one embarrassed now, but he promptly jumped in to identify other establishments.

"I'm surprised it isn't called the Hidden Tavern," Stella joked.

"Well, to tell you the truth, some people claim they try to hide in there sometimes, but Ted, the bartender, says he wants people to wander in and out, not play hide and seek. Ted tells tales about the men hiding while their wives seek them out."

Stella and Wills laughed but Rosie and Merlin tilted their heads sideways as if thinking adults were a bit odd.

"Next to the tavern is the Hidden Lake Barber Shop. Joe even does ladies' hair, too, but don't let him touch yours! Now, around the corner on Hidden Lake Road, you will discover one of the most beautiful lakes anywhere!"

"Yes, I can see an old pier. Wills, I think it's swaying slightly in the water. Are you sure it's safe?" Stella thought this pier seemed more of an afterthought than a solid feature for docking boats. "There are two young boys sitting on the edge of the dock with their feet swinging wildly. Oh, look. They each have a long branch with a string tied to it. I bet they are trying to fish."

"Yes, of course. You'll also notice a boat ramp, a dock, lots of moored boats, and even a small beach where the children like to swim."

"Can we go swimming?" Rosie squealed.

"No!" Stella answered quickly. "We have to get Donna and you registered for school."

"Please?" Rosie wasn't giving up.

"I'll think about it. But why would you want to swim in the rain?" Stella asked.

"I'm just going to get wet anyway."

"Me, too," Maddie squealed as Donna clapped her hands and made what Rosie called her happy noises.

Wills put his arm around Stella, "Looks like it's going to be a busy day. Listen, how about I go to the Mercantile and get a few items while you take Rosie and Donna to the school. I'll keep Maddie with me and introduce her to the old gents at the store."

"I can see them from here on the store's front entryway landing. Three elderly men are sitting on a bench chatting and two others seem to be playing chess at a large wooden barrel," Stella said. "I think they're all looking this way."

"Yes, I'm pretty sure the entire town knows we've arrived. I noticed earlier that Emily, the postmistress, was looking out the window watching us intently," Wills laughed.

"Shouldn't you show me where the school is before you go to the Mercantile?"

"That won't be necessary. Just head down Hidden Lake Road," Wills said as he turned her around toward the direction of the school.

"All right, but I probably should go back to the house first and get cleaned up. My shoes are wet through and through. And I'll need to change my clothes before we head to the school."

"Why?"

"I certainly can't go in my traveling outfit. I'll wear my interview ensemble that I put in my carry bag," Stella thought aloud. "Rosie and Donna need to be in their best clothes, too. They might meet their teachers today."

"I really don't think…" but Wills wasn't able to finish.

"I'll need a house key."

"No need," Wills replied. "It's not locked."

Stella stared at him, "Not locked?"

"No one locks their doors here. There's no need."

"Okay," Stella answered but was not convinced. "Please pick up some Wonder bread, bologna, a couple tins of Campbell's tomato soup, and milk. I'll make lunch when we get back."

It didn't take long for Stella to get herself and her two older children ready. Everyone was excited and eager to go. This was quite an adventure for all of them. As they walked the easy two blocks to the school, Stella mused about the town itself. She wondered why every establishment had to be called "Hidden." She thought the whole place lacked imagination and interest. She supposed it could be a quaint little town with a little work. Now she berated herself for being too pompous. She would change this. She would change her attitude. She was determined to take up the challenge.

The rain pounded the tin roof of the school's outdoor breezeway. Stella, her two school-age girls, and their dog slowed their steps and explored their surroundings. The noise of the rain couldn't drown out the apparent arguing that emanated from a doorway at the end of the hallway. It sounded very one-sided, as if a woman was arguing with herself.

Stella paused and wondered if it might be better to come back later in the day.

"Well, well, what do we got here?" a grizzly voice demanded from behind them.

Stella jumped and flew around as Merlin growled.

"My goodness, you gave me a start!" Stella scolded.

"Oh, very sorry, ma'am. I meant no disrespect," the man said.

Although initially taken aback, Stella realized this man was more confused than she was. She believed he had to be around 60 years old, maybe even older. His lined face was prominently covered with a gray beard that matched perfectly with simple wisps of graying hair that escaped from a snugly fitted gray cap. He had on identically colored dusty overalls with a plaid woolen shirt. His boots were also completely covered in dust. Stella feared that she might laugh out loud if he told her that his name was Mr. Gray.

"You are obviously new around here. Can I help you?" the man stuttered.

"Yes, we arrived last night. My husband gave us the tour of the town a short while ago."

"Oh, well, that must have taken a good five minutes," he said brushing more dust off his arms.

"No, no," Stella said, but the man looked forlorn as if he was worried what she might say, so she promptly added, "no, I'd say eight minutes."

The tension was broken. Everyone laughed, and Merlin gave his approval with a quick one-syllable bark.

"My name is Bernard Boiler, but all the kids and everyone around these parts call me BB," he said, holding out his hand.

Holding out both of her hands to shake his, she said, "So very, very nice to meet you, Mr. BB. My name is Mrs. Stella Rollins, and these are my daughters, Rosie and Donna."

Rosie gave a quick curtsey. Donna clapped her hands and made her happy noise. Merlin marched straight to Mr. BB, sat down within inches of his leg, and raised his paw. Mr. BB shook his paw and said to all assembled close to him, "I am happy to make your acquaintance."

"This is Merlin," Rosie said as Merlin's tail shook rapidly while he grinned from ear to ear.

"You have quite an attractive family here, Mrs. Rollins," Mr. BB said as he continued to scratch behind Merlin's ears. "Wait a minute now. I seem to remember someone by the name of Rollins who lived here after the war for a spell. He stayed with the Surly family, but they moved south a couple years ago. Heard tell that Sam Surly got some fancy teaching job in California."

"Yes, Sam and Shirley Surly are now my brother- and sister-in-law. I'm married to Shirley's brother, Wilbur Rollins," Stella said.

"My oh my. So, the young soldier found himself a beauty," Mr. BB said, blushing.

"You are quite the charmer, Mr. BB," Stella beamed at him.

The noise emitted from the far end of the corridor was getting louder, causing everyone to glance in that direction.

"Goodness gracious. I don't mean to be nosy, but what is that commotion down there?" Stella asked.

"That's Mrs. Lillian Fox, the school secretary. She's complaining about one thing or another. Who knows what it is about this time? It's always something. I think poor Mr. Silver should toss her out, but no one gives a hoot what I think."

"Mr. Silver?"

"Oh, yes, the principal. His name is Simon Silver. I told him that everyone should call him SS since they call me BB. But heaven help me. You should have seen the look he gave me. I tell you I was chilled to the very bone. He could've drilled a hole right into my skull with that horrific stare he gave me. I'll have nightmares, I will. And, you know what? He didn't say one word, not one word. He just walked away, he did. I tell you, I never suggested it again. No sirree. I say nothing, nothing. I keep my thoughts to myself, if I do say so myself."

"Maybe it's a bad time to register the girls for school. I could come back later," Stella suggested, looking toward the noise.

"This is the perfect time. I'll introduce you. Mr. Silver will be happy to escape Mrs. Fox's wrath for a few minutes at least."

Mr. BB led the group toward the office. Stella stopped a few feet before the wide-opened door. She couldn't see inside yet since Mr. BB was blocking the entrance.

"What do you want, BB?" Mrs. Fox growled. "Can't you see we're busy?"

"Oh, BB, please come in. I want to chat with you about, uh, something," Mr. Silver interjected.

"Well, that's all well and good, but I'm not done!" Mrs. Fox continued her increasingly loud tirade while at the same time ignoring them. "How you expect one person to do the work of dozens is beyond me! I won't stand for it. Do you hear me? I won't do it! Bad enough I must cater to every whim for every single man, woman, and child in this forsaken lousy town. I come here every day out of the goodness of my heart to help our thankless community while that useless dimwitted fool of a brother-in-law of mine destroys my shop. Does anyone even care? No!"

Mrs. Fox appeared to be on a never-ending roll, but she froze when she saw Mr. BB take off his hat and direct an unknown attractive woman into the office. Stella gently pushed her girls in front of her. Merlin jumped immediately in front of them and snarled at everyone else in the room. Stella did a quick survey around the room before introducing herself. The expansive room had two little offices with good-sized windows that enabled one to easily see in and out. A small desk extended in front of the offices as if symbolically protecting the leader. Half a dozen tiny chairs lined the front wall, waiting for children to occupy them.

"Hello, I'm Mr. Silver, Simon Silver, the principal. May I be of assistance?" Mr. Silver said with welcomed self-assurance.

Slender and soft-spoken, Mr. Silver seemed undisturbed by his secretary's antics. He wore a threadbare suit with a striped bow tie, and his clothes hung loosely on his small frame. He wasn't much taller than Stella, which was extremely short for a man, and he was about her age as well. Nonetheless, he exuded a confidence that demanded respect, and Stella had to admit that she liked the man immediately.

Mrs. Fox, on the other hand, intimidated everyone. She was overbearing, loud, and abrasive. She was solidly built and strikingly tall, which allowed her to tower over the others. Her steely gray hair was tightly coiled into a bun at the base of her neck, while her penetrating gray eyes missed nothing.

"Why, I never," Mrs. Fox growled louder. "I am talking here!"

"I came to register my children for school. We just moved to your tiny town yesterday. I'm Mrs. Stella Rollins, and these are my children, Rosie and Donna," Stella said to both the principal and the secretary.

"Tiny town?" BB laughed, "Well, it certainly is that. Do you know it took her all of eight minutes to see it?"

"I would have thought you could have accomplished that task in five minutes," Mr. Silver grinned.

"Well, I for one am not amused!" Mrs. Fox tried to turn the attention toward herself once again.

"I'm so sorry for the commotion here," Mr. Silver said. "I'm afraid it has been somewhat hectic today. We just found out that our first-grade teacher left."

"Miss Brandt thinks she can up and get married and take off without a by your leave," Mrs. Fox complained. "No notice. Nothing! Now we've got no one to take her place. Mr. Silver here thinks I should step in. Can you imagine?"

"Just for a day or two. You have an old teaching certificate," Mr. Silver interrupted.

"It must be *really* old," BB said under his breath.

"You say something, you old coot?" Mrs. Fox glared at BB. "I certainly have enough to do around here without dealing with the help as well!"

"The help? I'm the custodian!" BB snarled.

"Then short stuff over there wants me to start some sort of library, too. As if these foolish kids would ever pick up a book!" Mrs. Fox glared at Mr. Silver.

The tension was getting thicker. Stella jumped in, "Excuse me, please. Can I register my daughters?"

"Yes, yes, of course," Mr. Silver said. "Mrs. Fox, the registration papers are on your desk."

"You want *me* to get them?" she sneered.

"I would be happy to find them," Stella suggested.

"No, no. You will just mess up my organization," Mrs. Fox responded with a haughty tilt to her head.

"Organization?" BB said, "That's a laugh."

Mrs. Fox took two quick steps toward BB. No one was quite sure what she would do, but BB wasn't about to wait around to find out. He left the office before anyone told him what to do next.

"So, who are our new students? I'm hoping you don't have a first grader," Mrs. Fox said, shuffling through the papers piled high on her desk but ignoring the children in front of her.

"This is Rosie," she said grabbing Rosie's hand as she tried to escape with BB. "She will be in fifth grade. My other daughter, Donna, will be in the first grade."

Mrs. Fox stretched her fingers across her forehead and rubbed her temples. "Why am I not surprised? So, where is she?"

"This is Donna," Stella said pointing to the quiet child in the stroller.

Mrs. Fox frowned as she looked closely at Donna.

Mr. Silver jumped in, "Mrs. Rollins, do you happen to have an Oregon teaching certificate?"

"No, unfortunately, no," Stella said. "I did work in an elementary school in San Francisco. I was an aide for the teachers. I also worked in the library and the office. I loved those days. Best job I ever had, and I've had plenty."

Mr. Silver looked regretful as he sighed, "I wish I could hire you here."

"Wait a minute," Mrs. Fox interjected. "This girl can't go to school here. Or anywhere for that matter. Why, she is mentally retarded!"

Mr. Silver clearly was not pleased with his secretary, "Mrs. Fox, that is quite enough!"

"No, look at her. She's a mongoloid!" Mrs. Fox scolded, getting closer to Donna.

Stella stepped closer to the stroller and said, "They're starting to use the term Down's syndrome now. Yes, she has Down's syndrome. But she is a child and should go to school."

"She can't. She can't learn anything. No one wants her," Mrs. Fox said.

"Mrs. Fox, that's enough. Go on your break!" Mr. Silver was getting angry now.

"You can't register this child!" Mrs. Fox spat, ignoring her boss.

Mr. Silver turned to Stella, who looked ready to cry but had the determination of a fierce mother lion. He said, "Mrs. Rollins, as much as I would like to have your daughter come to our school, I'm afraid that we don't have anyone qualified to teach her."

"But you will hire a first-grade teacher very soon, won't you?" Stella asked.

"Yes, but that's not the issue I'm afraid," Mr. Silver said. "Even if we had a new teacher today, I sincerely doubt that she would be qualified to teach a child with disabilities. I could make some enquiries but if there were any Special Education classes available for your daughter, they would most likely be in Eugene or Portland."

"I live here. Those cities are many hours away. Surely, Donna could be in a class with the other children. She would learn just by being around them. She may learn more slowly, but I know she can learn."

A familiar woman's voice behind her said, "I am sure there is a law!"

Chapter 42
1961 – HIDDEN LAKE, OREGON

STELLA SPUN AROUND AND SQUEALED. ROSIE SPRINTED AROUND the corner into the room shouting incoherently. Merlin started barking as he raced around everyone, jumping up and down. Papers flew off Mrs. Fox's desk. Mrs. Fox screamed. BB sauntered into the room without seeming to realize there was anything out of the ordinary going on. He grabbed his wide broom and swept Mrs. Fox's papers while purposely pushing at her feet. She jumped away and yelled at Mr. Silver, who was calmly viewing the entire scene as if he was leaning against his living room wall watching the television.

"Veronica!" Stella shrieked. "What are you doing here? Oh, goodness gracious. I'm so excited, I can't think." She hugged Veronica hard as Veronica hugged her back. They disengaged their embrace, grabbed hands, and danced around and around. Everyone talked at once.

Stella saw Bill and the twins and even Barbara, Veronica's mother. She raced over and gave them quick hugs.

"We are taller than you are now, Aunt Stella," the twins said in unison.

"Aunt Stella?" Mrs. Fox winced as she tried to get Mr. Silver's attention by announcing very loudly above the ruckus, "They're not the same color!"

Ignoring the others, Stella hugged both boys and laughed, "When did that happen?"

As all the friends cried and had a joyous reunion, Stella noticed Wills in the background. She immediately walked over and put her arms around him while crying real tears, "Oh, Wills, so this was your surprise! This is the best surprise in the whole wide world. Nothing could make me happier!"

"No, wait, this isn't..." Wills tried to explain but no one was listening.

Stella quickly took Wills's hand and led him toward Veronica's family. "Wills, please meet my dearest friends in the whole world." Wills shook hands with everyone as Stella introduced him to each person one at a time before racing back over to Veronica.

"When did you get here? How did you get here? How long can you stay? We were just going to unpack today. There is a separate dwelling you can stay in. Wills said that Sam and he built it out of the garage, so he could live there after the war. So now we have a guest room." Stella kept asking questions, but everyone seemed to be talking at once and not really paying attention.

Veronica pushed forward and walked completely into the now crowded office. "I came to register my two boys!" she said with authority.

Stella put her hands over her mouth and gasped as tears ran down her face.

Mrs. Fox's face had turned crimson. She looked around in panic as she screamed, "I want to work in some normal school, not some darned carnival! I'm done. Do you hear me? Done! I quit!" She reached over and swept the papers off her desk that BB had just replaced there, then fled the office and the school for what she was convinced would be for all time.

Mr. Silver grinned very slowly. "Mrs. Rollins, would you like a job?"

"Yes!"

"Please register our new students," he continued.

"Donna, too?" Stella asked.

"I wish I could tell you yes, but I cannot," he sighed.

"There is a law. Public Law 89-231..." Stella started.

Veronica stood next to Stella and added, "Yes, it is the Education for All Act."

"Thank you for your enthusiasm, but I actually do know about education law. There is a law that states schools cannot discriminate against minority children because of their color. That law came from a recent lawsuit called Brown vs The Board of Education. But I'm afraid that there is no law regarding the handicapped. If we have no one to teach them or if it is determined that the child cannot or will not learn, then the school is not obligated to provide an education for them. I wish there was an Education for All Children Act. But there is not," Mr. Silver said.

Stella and Veronica knew that they would not be able to bluff their way with this man. Stella stood her ground and said, "Well, if there isn't a law, there should be. I think it is time we made one!"

"I would support you, as well," Mr. Silver said. "Still, you also need to make sure there are programs that will instruct teachers how to teach these children. They will need to be qualified and that is not easy."

"It will happen, but what about my Donna? Who will teach her?"

Veronica put her arm around Stella, "We will figure this out."

"Yes, yes, I will. I mean *we* will." Stella smiled knowing that everything would be all right now that Veronica and her family were here.

Stella gazed lovingly at her family and best friends and marveled at her own joyfulness. She couldn't remember a time she had truly been this excited. She knew it would be a huge challenge to find appropriate schooling and care for Donna, but now she also knew it would happen one way or another. She felt the strength that she had hidden inside herself earlier. She knew she could do it no matter what occurred next because now she wouldn't feel so alone. Maybe Hidden Lake would prove to be a blessing in disguise. She didn't know, but she did know that against all odds, she would do whatever was necessary to keep her family together.

"Well," Bill broke in, "It looks like you need to start your new job and we need to find housing and work ourselves, so we best be on our way."

"Wills?" Stella broke in, "Can you please take everyone over to the house and make some lunch? Since I seem to have a new job, I guess I do need to stay here until the bell rings."

"What? Cooking? I don't know, I...I thought that you..." Wills was lost for words.

Stella went to his side, put her arm around his waist, and joked, "I suppose you wouldn't want the fellas at the Mercantile to have a field day with that information. Don't worry, your secret is safe with me."

Veronica immediately noticed Wills's discomfort. "I have an idea," she said. "How about if Ma and I make some sandwiches for everyone. Afterwards, I think I better come back here and help Stella figure all this out. It seems that the previous secretary left things in a bit of a disarray."

"Truer words were never spoken," Mr. Silver said under his breath.

Wills tried to hide his overwhelming relief as he said, "That's a wonderful idea. Thank you, Veronica. If the children can come back with you and play on the playground, Bill and I could check out the Hidden Moose Mill to see if they are hiring."

Mr. Silver nodded, adding, "Yes, we can see the playground from the office so that won't be a problem."

"Merlin will take care of us," Rosie pointed out, stroking her dog's thick fur.

"We don't need anyone to watch us. Ant and I will take charge. *No* one will bother us," Leon said with an air of righteousness.

"Boys, Mr. Silver is in charge and you will be respectful to him. Do you understand me?" Bill directed with absolute authority. He turned toward Mr. Silver and added, "I'm sorry, Mr. Silver, I forgot to introduce my boys to you. The determined one here is Leon and the identical smart one next to him is Anton."

"Dad, we are called Lion and Ant back home," Leon protested.

"This is your new home, so get used to it. We expect you both to behave and you *will* do what you are told. Do *not* cause any trouble. You hear me?" Bill ordered.

"Yes, sir," the boys said in unison as Rosie smirked.

Stella noticed Rosie's attitude but decided to have a quiet chat with her later.

"So, you're the Lion and the Ant?" Mr. Silver said to the boys. "I like that. It would be a good story to tell on the first day of school. You look like big boys so I'm guessing fifth grade?"

"Yes," the boys said in unison.

"I will be your teacher then," Mr. Silver grinned.

The children stared, not knowing if this would be a good thing or the worst thing that could ever happen to them. They remained silent.

"By the way," Mr. Silver continued, "I know the mill is hiring. I'm not sure what jobs are available, but you tell Edgar that Simon said to hire you. He may grumble a little, but just ignore the old goat. He'll do the right thing.

"Is Edgar the foreman?" Bill asked.

"He runs the entire operation. We go way back. Edgar is one of the good guys, you might say," Mr. Silver commented as he walked over to the men and shook hands. "Welcome to our community. I'm very happy you are here."

"Well, I certainly hope the rest of the town will accept us. I suppose anything can happen once they notice that my family and I are black," Bill said.

"You're black?"

Chapter 43

1961 – HIDDEN LAKE, OREGON

Bill

"ARE YOU READY FOR THIS?" WILLS ASKED, LOOKING AT BILL. They had just walked the four blocks to the Hidden Moose Lumber Mill and were now standing in front of the wide-opened gate entrance.

Bill was more surprised than Wills that he was truly shaking in his boots. He always thought the expression was odd. Now he knew better. "No. Are you ready? This is a tiny town. I haven't noticed a lot of people of my color around these parts."

"I would be surprised if you saw any. You, my man, are the first," Wills chuckled.

Bill wasn't so sure that was funny, but he laughed all the same. He would never admit how anxious he was at this very moment. His undeniable fear stemmed not from being frightened of those around him or his new environment, but of the unknown destiny awaiting him. Unfortunately, the historical truth remained that those who did not match society's expectations in appearance or identity often had an unjust or sometimes just a difficult time assimilating. He had told his boys to be brave; now he had to do the same. He had to adjust to a new way of life without conflict or demands. He would do it for Veronica. He would do what he needed to do for his family.

"Let's go find this Edgar," Wills said.

As the men walked closer to the main entrance to the mill, the noise was deafening. Men were talking and yelling and swearing as saws screeched and logs were undoubtedly dropping against each other.

"I am not so sure this is a good idea. I really don't have any experience with mill work. I wouldn't know what to do," Bill said as he stopped in his tracks before the doorway.

"Who does? You'll learn quickly enough. We teach one another. That's the way of things here." Wills slapped Bill on the back.

Wills stepped in first as Bill stood behind him in the shadows. Bill told himself that he wasn't afraid. He doubted they would gang up on him but was nervous whether these lumbermen would accept him.

"Hey guys, would you look at this? If it isn't Wilbur Rollins!" one of the men shouted above the machine noise.

"It's been an age, Rollins. Hey, you back to stay or visit or what?" another man stopped the saw and yelled out.

"Heard that you got yourself hitched to a big city model!" another said with a loud guffaw.

"What's a gorgeous woman see in a runt like you?" the first guy who noticed him said.

At that very moment, Bill stepped into the building and stood next to Wills. As if in slow motion, the entire shop seemed to put on its emergency brake and screeched to a stop. No one moved or said a word. Machines were silenced. Even the air stood still. Dust floated to the floor and still no one moved.

"What in blazes is going on in here? Why aren't you men working? Has someone declared a national disaster day or what?" a gigantic mountain man yelled as he came stalking into the room in two or three long strides. Bill would later describe this man as resembling a huge grizzly bear even more ferocious than the one in the Chicago zoo.

"Edgar," Wills said holding out his hand. "It's been a long time."

"Who you got with you there?" Edgar demanded, squinting.

"This is my friend, Bill. We've come to apply for work."

Edgar surveyed the new man as the men gathered around. "Don't you have something to do?" he growled just like the bear Bill envisioned. "I'm not paying you to stand around gawking, that's for sure!"

"Hey, Edgar, you gonna put this black man to work here in our shop? I'm not so sure we want the likes of his kind around here," complained a rugged man as he broke through the gathering crowd and walked directly toward his boss.

"Don't you be telling me what I can and cannot do, Warren! You might be the labor union leader here, but I am still the boss. You get that through your thick skull, you hear!" Edgar shouted.

"I don't want any trouble, Mr. Edgar, sir. I just want to work and earn a living for my family," Bill said with solid confidence.

"Does that mean a black family has come to invade Hidden Lake?" another man asked no one in particular.

"What's it to you?" Wills yelled back.

"Hey, I want no problem here. You understand?" Edgar turned toward the workers, making it crystal clear that he was in charge.

"No, sir," Bill said holding his hands up with palms out, then swiftly put them down.

At that very moment, a pipe exploded from the ceiling. Water gushed in every direction, thoroughly drenching everyone and everything in its reach.

"Dammit anyway, Warren. I told you to get that thing fixed!" Edgar hollered above the forceful spray.

"I have been trying. We've used up a dozen rolls of duct tape to hold it together. We need a new pipe. I've been telling you that for ages, but you won't requisition it," Warren shouted back.

"How can I when you all are demanding yet another pay raise?" Edgar yelled over the increasing noise.

"I can fix it," Bill suggested, examining the pipe and the layout of the building.

"You?" Edgar squinted once again at Bill. "How?"

"By rerouting the water flow pipe design. I would need to

look at the building plans, but I am sure I could do it without excessive cost," Bill declared with confidence.

"How would the likes of you know how to do that?" one of the workers shouted above the others.

"I studied engineering in college for a few years before I enlisted in the Navy," Bill said.

"You see any action in the war?" another called out.

"Yes," Bill said.

"One dollar an hour," Edgar said rapidly as he stared at Bill.

"What?" Wills protested. "The entry level workers make twice as much, maybe more now."

"That's true enough," Warren added.

Edgar looked around at the now very wet faces, "Yes, but he is black. He can't make as much as the white men."

Warren didn't really care how much this new man would make but he wasn't about to let the boss upstage him. "He should make the same pay. That's what the union says and that's what you will do!"

"Since when does the union tell me what to do? There are no guidelines in your contracts for Negros. We've never even seen one around these parts, so don't you be telling me what to do!" Edgar had been shouting so much that he now sounded hoarse.

"You might be drowning in this flood in about two or three hours I would say," Bill pointed out, rubbing his chin.

Wills, on the other hand, put his hand on Edgar's shoulder and said with urgency, "Simon said to hire us."

Edgar looked around and loudly sighed, "All right already, I give in but this time only. Now, get back to work, *all* of you. You, too. Get this mess cleaned up." He turned around and swiftly made his way back to his office and slammed the door.

Warren came over and shook hands with the new employees. "Welcome, both of you," he said. "Hey fellows, come over and give a hearty hello to our new members, Black Bill and White Will."

Others gathered around greeting one another. The usual activity of the mill returned to life. In the chaos of work, Bill shouted, "Where's the water shut-off valve?"

"Around the corner outside the main door," someone shouted back.

Just as Bill returned from shutting off the water flow, a loud whistle blew. "That's the end of the shift. It's Labor Day weekend, so everyone shut down. We'll see you back Tuesday morning bright and early!" Warren declared.

Edgar put his head out of his office door ready to shout at everyone, but his throat seemed to fail him. He shook his head and slammed the door.

One of the guys looked over at the newcomers and shouted, "Hey, Black Bill and White Will, a bunch of us guys are going to the Wander Inn Tavern for a few beers. Want to join us?"

Bill was taken by surprise and wanted to accept the offer immediately, but Wills shook his head no, "Thanks, guys, but I have a surprise for my wife. Next time."

Their fellow workers filed out of the mill laughing, jeering, and making silly comments that were ignored by all.

"I've got an idea," Bill said to Wills. "Let's make our wives and the kids dinner tonight."

"And I thought *I* had a big surprise for everyone. *Us* making dinner might just be the biggest surprise of the day!"

"There's no doubt that this has been one surprising day!"

Chapter 44

1961 – HIDDEN LAKE, OREGON

The incessant downpour ceased its thunderous roar, giving way to a quietly decreasing array of tiny raindrops. As it so often did in the Pacific Northwest, the late afternoon sun pushed its way through the gray clouds on its descent toward the horizon. The colors of the sky were changing in preparation for the waiting darkness. Mr. Silver walked out of his office and stood at the window, forming visions in his mind. He watched the day end as he thought to himself how the beginning of a school year was more like the beginning of a new year than the New Year itself. He smiled to himself, almost rejoicing that the vibrating negativity of Mrs. Fox's madness was dramatically being replaced by the calm, positive energy that Mrs. Rollins and her family and friends brought with them. He turned his head and watched the twin boys play a game of marbles while Rosie read a story to her younger sisters. He knew without a doubt that Rosie would be a firecracker. Their massive dog was positioned in the doorway, preventing anyone from going in or out. The women had totally transformed the office area already. There was even a vase of flowers on the front desk in the open area. Yes, his world was changing. No more looking backwards toward those days of confusion and fear. The war had been over for sixteen years, but he continued to live in a vacuum of darkened memories. He was determined that the time was ripe for a new outlook. Change was coming with the assurance of a bright new day. It would take time, but he was ready.

"Mr. Silver?" Mrs. Rollins asked as she and her friend quietly stared at him. "Is everything all right? We were wondering if we could leave for the day. It is a little after five and we thought we should probably go home to make dinner. You are welcome to join us if you would like."

Mr. Silver was jolted into the present reality, "Oh, yes. Of course. I am so sorry. I had completely forgotten the time. Please forgive me. Yes, yes, quitting time. That's for sure. Thank you, but no. I cannot intrude on your family festivities tonight. I will see you bright and early Tuesday morning. A new year will begin."

The women realized that Mr. Silver was completely flummoxed by all the changes around him. Veronica went to the coatrack and got everyone in their jackets. Stella walked over to Mr. Silver and looked out the window. "Thank you, Mr. Silver, for everything. I think we are going to be very happy here. I, too, am looking forward to the new year and the adventures ahead. We will see you Tuesday morning."

"It looks like the rain has stopped and the sun is peeking through the clouds. It will be light for a few more hours, I'm sure. Good day, everyone," Mr. Silver directed, walking back into his office.

Stella and Veronica herded the children out of the office as Veronica observed, "I would love to see the town. Do we have time?"

"Yes, absolutely. I think we need to visit the grocery store anyway to get some food for dinner tonight as well as breakfast tomorrow. Later this weekend, we will figure out what we need to do and get."

"Good idea," Veronica said.

"Wills told me that the store is called the Hidden Lake General Mercantile but everyone calls it the Mercantile. I will give everyone the ten-minute grand tour!"

"That's even longer than Wilbur's tour," Rosie said as she clapped her hands in glee. "Can I show the twins the beach instead? We can take Maddie and Donna with us if they do as I tell them since I am in charge."

"Since when do you need to be in charge? I'm taller than you are. I have decided that I am in charge!" Leon spoke in his most authoritative voice.

"One's height does not determine superiority!" Rosie yelled back.

"Good heavens!" Stella and Veronica said almost in unison.

"Let's see if we can solve this rationally," Stella said simply. "Now, who is the oldest?"

"I am the oldest by two minutes," Anton replied, smiling.

"So, there you have it," Veronica added. "Anton, you are in charge, but you are not allowed to boss anyone around. Do you understand?"

Anton looked around as if he was the king of the hill. "Of course I do, but does everyone else?"

"Just go already. Take especially good care of Maddie and Donna. Watch them closely, Merlin. We won't be long. And no swimming!" Stella said.

"Meet us at the beach, Mom. I know how to get there," Rosie said. "Follow me," she added to everyone else.

Stella and Veronica watched their children race toward the beach. Once they were out of sight, Stella showed Veronica around while identifying the shops that Wills had initially described. Veronica had the same immediate reaction as Stella upon seeing the town for the first time, yet she gave no indication of how she felt and never said a sarcastic word. Stella knew that she would not. Veronica always tried to make the best of any situation or find a way to make it better. Stella had always wished she were more like Veronica.

"This could be a sweet little town," Veronica said. "I'm up for the task. How about you?"

"Our project?" Stella chuckled. "Now for the Mercantile."

"I can hardly wait." Veronica laughed too.

The three elderly gentlemen were still on the same bench as earlier in the day. The chess game was still going on as well.

"Hello, gentlemen," Stella said as she walked up the three steps to the store's landing, "My name is Stella Rollins and this is my friend, Veronica Donaldson. We just moved here."

"We've been wondering when you would come around. Never saw such excitement in years, I tell ya. My name's Joe and this here is Tommy and Johnny. Over at the game table are Lester and Ralph."

"Where you ladies from?" Lester asked without looking up from the chess match.

"How long you staying?" Ralph added, also intent on the game.

"Hey, you boys leave my customers alone," Ross, the grocery store owner, said as he opened the door wide for the ladies to enter. "About time I had some real paying customers here, not some good-for-nothings that scare away people with money."

"Oh, Ross boy, we've been here longer than you. We know everyone hereabouts and believe you me, no one has any money," Joe retorted as they all laughed.

"Besides," Tommy said with eyes wide open, "We never seen any dark, beautiful young lady here before. This is quite a treat!"

"Ignore them, ladies. Please come in, come in," Ross held out his hand, escorting them through the door. "Now, what can I get you? Anything at all. We can get whatever your heart desires."

A middle-aged woman with ultra-thin sharp features came from behind a curtain and strode next to the shop owner. "I will take over from here, Mr. Armstead. You have some tasks to do in the storage room," the woman commanded. Her demeanor was one of complete power and control. She wiped her hands on an off-white apron that she wore over a faded flower-printed yellow dress.

"No, I don't," Mr. Armstead protested, still smiling at his new customers.

"Yes, you do," the woman insisted in a sharp tone directed straight to him.

Mr. Armstead walked away as he mumbled under his breath, "Yes, dear. Anything you want, dear."

"That man is Mr. Ross Armstead. He is my husband and half owner of this establishment. I am Mrs. Lynn Armstead. I own the other half. Who are you?"

"So very pleased to meet you," Stella said as she held out her hand to shake hers, but Mrs. Armstead did not stop wiping her hands on her apron. "I am Mrs. Stella Rollins."

"And I am Mrs. Veronica Donaldson," Veronica added.

"We just moved to Hidden Lake with our families," Stella said.

"Why would you ever choose to come to this useless backwater town anyway?" Mrs. Armstead asked, glaring at them both.

"Well, my husband loves it here and thought that we would as well. He lived here after the war. You might know him, Wilbur Rollins," Stella said.

"I came with my husband, Bill, and our twin boys to escape Chicago and live a quiet life close to my best friend, Stella," Veronica said.

"Hmmm?" After an awkward minute or so, Mrs. Armstead continued, "We've never had black people here before."

Stella said, "Won't it be a nice change then?"

"You have any money?" Mrs. Armstead inquired.

Stella and Veronica looked at each other in complete confusion. No one had ever asked such a question before.

"Not a lot, no," Stella finally responded.

"Got enough to pay for your groceries or you gonna want it on account like most folks do here?" Mrs. Armstead said. "I'm no charity. I want to get that straight."

"We intend to pay for any items we buy. You won't need to worry," Stella smiled, adding, "I just started working at the Hidden Lake Elementary School."

"Yes, I heard from Lillian Fox that you stole that job from her," Mrs. Armstead said.

"She did no such thing!" Veronica snapped.

"Mrs. Fox quit," Stella answered calmly.

"I expected as much," Mrs. Armstead said.

"We will just look around if you don't mind and get a few items for now," Stella said.

Mrs. Armstead shrugged her shoulders and walked into the back room as she yelled, "Mr. Armstead, get out here and take care of these paying customers. I've got work to do."

Fifteen minutes later, the two friends left the store and bade a quick farewell to the men on the porch landing. They each held a bag of groceries and their purses as they walked to the beach. The children were romping in and out of the shoreline getting their bare feet and the bottoms of their play clothes wet. Donna was sitting in the sand and throwing it up in the air laughing as it came down. Merlin was sitting close by her side scratching his ear with his back leg. Stella couldn't remember when she had seen Donna happier. Her heart swelled and instant tears came to her eyes. She blinked them away as she hollered, "Time to go, kids. We have a lot to do. We still need to unpack as well as make dinner. Let's go, everyone."

"Coming," they all seemed to say at once while gathering their shoes and socks to put them on.

Stella put Donna back in the stroller as Veronica held Maddie's hand. It didn't take them long to walk the few blocks to the Surly house.

"Wills hates the color of this house," Stella remarked as they opened the white picket fence gate into the yard.

"Why? What's wrong with yellow?" Veronica asked.

"I have no idea, but I do know that he wants to paint it right away. He probably has paint brushes in his hand right now."

Stella opened the front door to an expansive living room. The children squeezed through the door ahead of her and raced to the suitcases lining the far wall. Directly in front of the doorway was a tired-looking, battered couch with an end table next to it. On the other side was an easy chair with a small table and standing lamp. A mismatched coffee table full of various items from partially unpacked boxes stood directly in front of the couch.

Still holding the groceries, Stella looked around as if seeing it for the first time and said, "Shirley did tell me they left some old furniture in the house in hopes of advertising a furnished rental. Shirley said she had an odd feeling that they shouldn't rent it right away and now she knew why."

"I think it will be just fine. You will make it look like home in no time," Veronica said. "By the way, what is that noise and where is my mother?"

"I think Dad and Wilbur are arguing," Anton said.

"Wilbur?" Veronica looked at her boys sternly. "Did Mr. Rollins indicate that you may address him as such?"

"Rosie calls him Wilbur and *she* said it was okay," Leon answered.

Rosie smirked as she continued to look through the luggage. Stella stared at her daughter ready to say something but decided against it for the time being.

"You are to ask him later this evening what name he would like you to call him," the twins' mother said.

"I think the boys are right," Stella interrupted her. "I can hear the men arguing. I guess we better find out what is going on. Boys, that back bedroom will be yours tonight."

The boys ran into the room and almost immediately out again. "Grandma is resting in there. She said Daddy and that other man who we shall not name yet were giving her a headache."

"Fine," Veronica said, "stay here and find something to wear. I want you to change into dry, clean clothes."

"Girls, you will be in the first bedroom on the left when you enter the hallway. You also need to find dry, clean clothes," Stella instructed.

"I can help Donna and Rosie, Mommy," Maddie said.

"That'll be the day," Rosie glowered at her.

Both women hid their thoughts and started down the long hallway. They passed two bedrooms and a bathroom when Stella held out her arm and stopped abruptly. "Listen," she said. Hidden from view, the two women put down their grocery bags and hugged the hallway wall while they paid rapt attention.

"How would I know that you didn't know how to cook?" Wills complained.

"I never told you that I knew anything about cooking. Don't hang this on me. This was your idea, I might remind you," Bill hit back.

"No, it wasn't. This was your brilliant idea," Wills argued.

"I would have been perfectly fine going to that tavern."

"So now we are stuck trying to figure out how to cook this stuff Mrs. Armstead forced on us."

"How are we supposed to cook a chicken?" Bill said.

"How am I supposed to know? Maybe we should just wait for the girls."

"No way. We are going to surprise our wives and the kids with a magnificent dinner!"

"Well, I hope so, but I really wish you would have gotten something a bit easier to cook," Wills said.

"That crazy woman scared the bejesus out of me."

"How difficult can chicken be anyway?"

"Do you know how to cook a whole chicken?" Bill crossed his arms.

"Let's see now. Maybe we fry it. Fried chicken. That's it. Let's make fried chicken," Wills said as he pulled out a frying pan from the bottom cabinet.

"Right. You oversee the chicken and I will make the potatoes. How do you cook potatoes?"

"Peel them and cook them until done."

"With what? Veronica uses a potato peeler, but I can't find one here," Bill complained, looking around.

"Stella probably hid it in a shoe or something," Wills replied as he plopped the chicken in a big pan.

"Hid a peeler? Did she hide the knives, too? I can only find what Veronica calls a butter knife. It doesn't cut anything. I doubt it could even cut butter."

"That's fine," Wills said as he poured half a bottle of cooking oil over the whole chicken.

"You're not listening to me."

"Just toss the potatoes in the oven. You got the easy job." Wills turned on the stove and watched as the chicken sizzled in the pan. He watched it for a short time and decided the chicken needed the rest of the oil. He rapidly emptied the bottle.

"The potatoes are in the oven. What temperature do you think?"

"Put it on the highest number so they will cook faster."

"Here is a can of corn, but I can't find a can opener."

"Well, can't you use your imagination?" Wills said, moving the chicken back and forth. He turned the heat up to high.

"What are you doing?"

"I'm looking in the closet in this outer room. Where's the light? Come here and help me find something that will work."

Wills joined Bill to rummage in the closet. "Look, I found a hammer," Wills said. "You should be able to knock it around a bit until it comes open."

As the men turned back into the kitchen, they gasped. The kitchen was filling with smoke. "The chicken. I think it is burning! Shut the burner off!"

The women immediately ran into the kitchen and took charge. "Wills, open the back door," Stella demanded.

"I've got the stove and oven," Veronica said.

"What were you two trying to do – burn down the house?" Stella said.

"We wanted to make you a nice dinner." Wills looked around trying to figure out what to do next without looking too foolish.

"I've got an idea," Veronica said. "How about if we help? Don't be upset, Wills. Stella doesn't know how to cook, either."

"That's the truth!" Wills said.

"Hey," Stella laughed.

"Someone go get my mother. The two of us will host a cooking demonstration for everyone," Veronica said as small popping noises emanated from the oven. "I think the potatoes just exploded."

Chapter 45

1961 – HIDDEN LAKE, OREGON

Early the next morning, the aroma of coffee floated throughout the house. Barbara hummed while frying bacon and scrambling eggs. Little by little everyone came into the kitchen, the adults pouring themselves cups of coffee or helping the children with orange juice. A large oval dining room table formed the centerpiece of a spacious room in front of the kitchen. Rosie and the twin boys watched Barbara cook as they sat on the tall stools at the breakfast bar that stood between the table and the kitchen. The adults sat at the table with Maddie and Donna. Everyone chatted at once. As Barbara dished out the eggs and bacon, Bill leaned over and set the window ajar. The soft, warm breeze played with the silk curtains that hung loosely from a simple rod a few feet above the opening. It was a rare sunny day in the beginning of September on the coast and everyone appeared in exceptionally good spirits, especially Wills.

Wills's elation, though, seemed to be mixed with anxiety. He tapped the table and moved his chair back and forth before he stood up like a jack-in-the-box being released for the first time. Excitement beamed throughout his entire body. He looked joyfully around the table as well as acknowledging the children at the breakfast bar before he spoke, "Good morning, everyone. Gather around."

"Wills? We are all here. What is this all about?" Stella asked, seeing the others were also clearly baffled.

"Yes, yes. I know. I'm just so excited. I know you will all be as well," Wills started. "Remember I have been saying that I have a big surprise for everyone?"

"Yes, pretty much every other sentence you say," Rosie said with a scowl. The boys snickered.

Stella and Veronica glared at their children and were just about to scold them, but Wills jumped in. "That's right. But here is the even bigger surprise: I am going to tell all of you at once right now!"

Everyone exchanged quizzical glances, and even some murmuring ensued. Ignoring their responses, Wills continued, "I am so thrilled that I don't even know how to start, but here goes. This will solve all our problems. The Donaldsons will have their own place to live and we will also have our own place."

Stella started taking slow deliberate breaths. She wasn't sure what was coming, but she could feel a tension that she couldn't explain. Now, she was nervous.

"About twenty minutes from here by boat is the most beautiful forty acres on God's green earth. There is an old log house, a couple of outbuildings, a fenced area for chickens, a ramp that leads down to a dock, a boathouse, and there is even a grape arbor! Do you believe it? A grape arbor. Well, there are no grapes planted there yet, but there could be. And two large pastures for cattle. I know it'll take a bit of work, but..."

Stella froze. Veronica asked for her, "What are you saying, Wills?"

"I bought it!"

"How?" was all Stella could say.

"With our money, Stella. Yours and mine. It will be our home," Wills said.

Stella put her napkin on her plate of uneaten food. She pushed out her chair, stood up, and purposely left the room, walking rapidly down the long hall. Two minutes later the sound of the front door slamming reverberated throughout the house.

"I'll go talk to her," Veronica said.

"No," Wills said. "I did this." Without another word, he got up and went down the hallway. The front door did not slam this time.

"Will we be able to fish off the dock?" Leon said to no one in particular.

Rosie ran to the window, followed by the boys. Bill stood up next to them peering outside, trying to see the couple.

"Hey," Veronica scolded, "spying on them is so wrong. What do you think you are doing?"

"Yes," Bill said, but before he could say that he was sorry, Veronica jumped up.

"Move over and give me some room," she said.

─────

Stella was at the front gate pushing it forcibly back and forth as if she couldn't remember how to work the latch.

"Stella?" Wills said from the front porch.

Stella spun around and yelled, "How could you?" She started pacing rapidly.

"I thought you would be happy. We have a home now." Wills was obviously confused.

"You bought some property without my knowledge or consent? You didn't even think that maybe, just maybe I should see what I was buying first?" Stella was practically screaming.

"It was supposed to be a surprise. I thought you'd be happy."

"Happy? Happy? You spend *my* money without telling me and think I would be happy? Are you crazy?" Stella was furious and couldn't control her anger. In fact, she thought to herself that she had never known such rage, even with Richard. With him, it was disappointment and sadness. Now, she felt like a fool, as if she had been duped. How could she have made such a mistake? What had she done? He wanted to control her, to take her money. To take her life. She was beyond anger, she was livid! She wanted to hit something, to run, to get away. She didn't know what she wanted to do. She just screamed!

Wills went directly to her and tried to put his arm around her shoulders. She pushed his arm away frantically. "Don't you dare touch me!" she shouted loud enough that the entire neighborhood would be talking about this for weeks.

"Stella, please. Calm down. I don't understand why you are so upset." Wills was clearly baffled. This didn't make sense. He was sure that she would be happy, no, thrilled about his surprise.

"You don't, do you? Well, that about says it all! You think you can tell me what to do and control me, take charge, take my money. You didn't even bother telling me or at least asking me what I might want. We should discuss things like this first."

"Wait a minute, Miss Hypocrite!"

"How dare you! I am not the one who stole your money!" Stella yelled, sobbing in great gulps.

"You took a job without asking for my permission or even mentioning it to me first," Wills snapped, angry now.

"Ask for permission? Are you serious? If I am working, then we would have money to pay the bills. Instead of being happy that I got a job so quickly, you go and take my money and buy some stupid property without a by your leave. Well, it is *not* your money and I don't want your stupid house. I am not so sure I want you anymore! I had so many hopes, I..." Stella cried hysterically.

Now Wills abandoned his typical serenity and yelled back, "You had hopes? *You* had hopes? Well, so did I! I hoped that you might want to marry me. I hoped that maybe someday you might even love me a little bit. I hoped that we could be a family and have a nice home. I hoped..." He couldn't finish. Stella fell silent.

Wills turned around and wiped his eyes with the sleeves of his shirt before he turned back to face the woman he truly desired. He was shaken to the core, but knew he needed to carry on somehow. "Stella, when I look at you, I am dazzled. I am so madly in love with you that sometimes I can't speak. You are my very hope for today and the future. Don't you realize that?"

Stella couldn't speak. She only looked him straight in the eyes without flinching.

"When I am with you, I know without a shadow of a doubt that I am happier than I have ever been in my lifetime. My soul is healing, all because of you. I love your tenacity, your wit, your strength, and yes, even your stubborn attitude at times. I love those children. I want to be their father. Maddie is as cute as a bug's ear. Donna is the sweetest thing this side of heaven. Rosie is, well Rosie is a rascal, but I get a kick out of her shenanigans."

Stella shook her head as anger started to drain away, "But you said that I needed your permission to work. And yet, you didn't get my permission to use my money or to buy a property I had not seen."

"Please try to understand. I guess I made a horrible mistake. I thought you would be happy. I always thought that when people are married the husband was in charge. He is supposed to be the breadwinner. He is supposed to provide for his family. The wife is happy taking care of the children, cooking, cleaning, and taking care of the house. The husband knows his duty is to have a good job and make a living for his family. That's the way it has always been. That's the way it was when I grew up. Wasn't it that way in your household when you were a child?"

Stella shrugged, "I guess. I never really paid attention. My sisters and I went to work for the war effort. Afterwards, I went back to school. I couldn't wait to graduate so I could explore and go on adventures."

"I went to war. Those adventures and explorations will haunt me forever," Wills said.

Stella appeared to ignore that when she said, "It just seems all wrong. I thought or hoped that marriage meant equality. I thought we would have ups and downs, but overall, we would discuss things and there would be give and take. I don't understand why the husband should oversee everything. That doesn't make sense to me. Not to mention the fact that I absolutely hate cooking and cleaning!"

Wills took both her hands in his, "I never thought about it like that. I just assumed that was the way it was supposed to be. Since the war ended, though, and now with Kennedy in the White House, the world appears to be different somehow. Maybe we are ready for a little change. I'm willing if you are?"

Stella couldn't think. She couldn't talk. She didn't know

what to say. She wasn't even sure if she was still miffed or disappointed or afraid for the future. She only sighed.

"Will you at least come look at the house?" Wills continued. "I promise you that first thing Tuesday morning I will go down to the bank and put the property in your name. You can then do whatever you want with it – sell it or rent it or live in it. Whatever you want, I will abide by your decision. I am so sorry, Stella. Please forgive me?"

Stella stood silent.

"Do you love me at all, Stella?" Wills asked softly as he looked at Stella and squeezed her arms lightly. He put his hand on her face, then slowly turned around and walked toward the gate. "I'm going down to the Wander Inn for a beer."

"I have always enjoyed an adventure," Stella said. "Ask me again."

Wills stopped, "What?"

"Ask me again."

"Do you love me, Stella?" Wills said.

"Yes."

Wills practically ran to her. He took his wife securely in his arms and kissed her, oblivious to the sighs coming from those watching through the open window.

Chapter 46

1961 – HIDDEN LAKE, OREGON

*A*FEW HOURS LATER, EVERYONE WAS HEADING DOWN TO THE Hidden Lake pier looking forward to the boat ride that would take them to the new property. Stella looked back and forth at all the boats that were tied up to the dock swaying in the gentle breeze. Up ahead she focused her attention toward the worst of the lot. It was a tattered wooden tugboat of an undeterminable age. She guessed it to be about twenty feet long and maybe ten feet wide. The dirty, weathered boat was colorless as its paint had peeled off long ago. Boards were cracked and the roof of the squared cabin appeared to be caving in. It also seemed to be listing to one side. Stella kept up a vigil in her mind, "Don't let it be that one; don't let it be that one; don't let it be that one..."

"Here we are!" Wills said as he pointed at that very one.

Stella and Veronica pasted on their best smiles. The kids jumped and squealed for joy.

"Uncle Wilbur, wow, this is swell!"

"I get the top," Rosie said.

"Since when? That's for boys only," Leon shouted.

"It is *my* boat, so I can sit where I want. You go sit in the cabin!" Rosie shouted back.

"Plenty of room for everyone," Wills said, laughing. "Here's how we will do it today. Older kids on the bow. That means the front."

"I know that," Anton said.

"You did not!" Rosie glared at him.

Will continued giving directions while ignoring the arguing children. "The women can sit in the cabin with the two younger girls. You will be out of the wind that way. Bill and I will be in the stern..."

"That's the back," Anton advised everyone.

"Really?" Rosie said sarcastically.

"I will work the engine and take charge of the tiller," Wills said.

"That's like the steering wheel for the outboard motor," Anton added.

"Lion, would you tell Ant to stick a sock in his mouth before I toss him overboard?" Rosie directed.

Everyone gathered around on the dock in front of the boat. They put down the picnic baskets, tool kit, and the few boxes of what Wills had called necessary items. As each of them wondered what to do next, Merlin flew into the boat in one quick, effortless leap. The boat rocked wildly side to side. Donna clapped her hands and made her happy noises. Stella and Veronica gasped as Bill grabbed the side of the cabin while Wills took charge of the lines.

"Where is Merlin supposed to sit?" Maddie asked.

"Merlin, go to the stern to steady the boat," Wills instructed.

"Wills, I don't think Merlin truly understands English," Stella said.

Barbara laughed, "Don't tell *him* that. Look."

Merlin was sitting at the back of the boat with his paw on the tiller.

"Merlin is smarter than you, Ant!" Rosie said with a smirk.

The boys jumped in next and ran around to explore every tiny square inch of the vessel. Rosie jumped in immediately after them and raced to the top of the cabin ahead of the boys.

"Hey!" Ant objected.

"That's perfect, Ant," said Lion. We can flank her on both sides like military sergeant of the guards."

"Like our toy soldiers," Ant said.

"Yes, so we can protect her when Indians attack with their bows and arrows," Lion added.

"Oh, for goodness' sake! Rosie sputtered. *"Mom!"*

The adults ignored the older children as they handed off the supplies to Bill, who was now also in the boat. He took Barbara's arm and guided her gingerly into the boat and helped her to the loose bench in the square cabin. Next, Veronica held onto Donna as Bill reached for the child and easily swung her into the boat and put her onto Barbara's lap. Then he took Maddie, who struggled a bit but was chuckling when her feet reached the floor of the swaying boat.

"Your turn, my dear," Bill said to Veronica. She hesitated, but Bill grabbed both sides of her waist and easily lifted her inside.

Stella stood back out of Bill's reach. Wills was trying to untie the ropes. "Wills, I'm not so sure I can do this. Bill won't be here all the time and well, I'm not..."

Wills looped the rope back on the cleat and went to Stella's side. "You will be fine, Stella. This will be a wonderful adventure. I will show you how to get in. Just put one hand on the side of the cabin and one foot on this walkway ledge. Lift yourself up and over into the boat. You can do it."

Stella did as she was instructed, but before she actually lifted herself into the boat she stopped and said, "Wills, what happens when Donna gets bigger and can't manage this? She might be too heavy to lift."

"She will be walking by then."

"Yes," Stella said as she grinned and jumped in.

"Bill, start the engine while I untie these ropes. Someone sure made them tight. This may take a while," Wills said.

Bill pulled the engine cord a dozen times without success.

"Pull the choke out, Dad," Ant shouted.

He did so and the idling engine seemed to purr like a snoring cat.

Wills managed to untie the lines and pushed off the dock as he jumped into the boat. He immediately went to the engine and put it into gear. They slowly left the dock and headed toward the middle of Hidden Lake.

Stella twisted her head around. "Wills, I hate to ask, but how much did this tub, I mean tugboat, cost?"

"You will love this, Stella. Not one cent. The owners threw it in with the deal!" Wills said.

"Oh, how nice of them," Stella said as she and Veronica glued their smiles on again.

"Now, Bill, will you please pass out the lifejackets. All children must wear one," Wills said.

Bill went into the cabin first and handed out lifejackets to everyone. "It'll keep you warm, too," he said. He bent closer to Veronica and whispered, "I don't know how to swim."

Veronica said in a loud voice, "Bill and I are going to wear our lifejackets as good role models for the children."

"Good idea," Barbara said. "We all should."

Barbara sneezed as she attempted to wipe the dust off the cabin window. Veronica squealed as she flung a small spider away from her. Donna threw her hands in the air and swatted at a web.

"Wills," Stella called out. "I think this boat needs some cleaning and necessary maintenance."

"Yes. Hey, I have an idea. I haven't actually seen the inside of the house yet, but it might need a little tender loving care, too," Wills said.

"You haven't?" the women increased their smiles.

"How about if the boys work on the boat and the girls make the house all homey?" Wills suggested.

The women looked at each other. "It might not be so bad. We could divide and conquer. We would need to disinfect the bathroom," Barbara said.

"The refrigerator would need to be defrosted," Veronica added.

"Don't forget the stove and cupboards and countertops will probably need to be cleaned," Stella said.

"Sounds like we could handle that easy enough," Barbara said.

"You have a deal!" Stella said, smiling for real this time. "By the way, does this boat have a name?"

"I was thinking that we should call it *The Adventure*."

Chapter 47
1961 – HIDDEN LAKE, OREGON

The Adventure slowly cruised around a peninsula into a cove of clear, glassy water. Stella and Veronica exited the cabin, held onto the side of the boat, and peered toward the land of tall forest trees. Wills cut the engine to a soft idle. "We're here," he said.

Veronica put her hands over her heart and said, "Oh, Stella. This is absolutely stunning!"

Stella was lost for words. She contemplated the unbelievable beauty just a short distance away. From her vantage point, she was overwhelmed by the various intense colors of the hills that were blanketed with more trees than she could count. She gazed spellbound at the sway of the high green grass in a sizable valley that flowed from the mountainous region above. A waterfall tumbled down the sleek rock wall of the peninsula to her left. Its water splashed below into the cove, which caused continual ripples to spread gradually into the bay.

"Do you like it?" Wills asked.

Stella's beaming face was all he needed to know. Stella didn't need to paste a frozen smile on her face this time. "It's majestic," she said.

"Mom, Mom," Rosie cried, "Look at the bird on top of that tree!"

Just as she did so, a giant, white-headed bird swooped away

from the treetop and spread its wings gloriously. Wills grinned and announced to all watching, "That is an eagle. A few eagle families live around these parts. There may be a nest at the very top of that tree."

Stella looked in the other direction and noticed more tree-lined hills and another grassy valley almost symmetrical to the first she saw. The magnificence of the surrounding countryside gradually gave way to an increasingly nagging doubt. "Wills," she asked, "where is the house?"

"We are getting closer. Let me turn the boat slightly. Look straight ahead now. Do you see that rectangular building on the floating dock in the middle of the reeds?"

"That's the house?" Stella gasped.

"No, silly," Wills laughed. "That's the boathouse. The opening is to the side."

Anton turned around and said to everyone, "A boathouse is a garage for boats."

"That's right. But I am not going to put *The Adventure* into the boathouse right now. We will moor up on the side of the dock. I want to make sure it is fully safe first and that everyone can easily get out."

"Look!" Bill shouted. "There it is. The boathouse appears to be parallel to the shoreline. Behind it is a long, narrow wooden ramp at about a 45-degree angle that passes over a watery marsh and up to a landing."

As the boat glided toward the dock and Bill jumped out to tie up the lines, Stella looked in surprise at the long ramp that did indeed rise to a large landing, but the house was hidden from view, apparently tucked back around a corner lost in thick shrubbery.

"No one has lived here in quite some time, so we may have to cut our way through some of these blackberries," Wills said.

"Why hasn't anyone lived here?" Veronica asked, knowing that Stella was thinking the same thing.

"Well, there are a few services that people have gotten used to over the years, but this property hasn't actually been prepared for the twentieth century," Wills replied.

"What?" Stella cried. "You didn't mention this piece of information to me, Wills! What other surprises do you have in store?"

"It sure is warm for this time of year. Maybe we could go for a swim later. Would you like that, kids?" Wills suggested as he wiped his fingers under his shirt collar.

As the children shouted their approvals with a great deal of merriment, Stella peered at her husband, "Wills?"

"Well, umm, well. Okay, the only way you can get here is by boat," Wills admitted.

"I guess I assumed that, but I have to confess I am a bit worried about going back and forth to school by boat in the winter," Stella sighed.

"The winters are fairly mild here. We mostly just have rain and a little fog and sometimes a bit of wind. Nothing to worry about."

"That's not so bad, then. Let's go see our new home," Stella said as Wills took her hand to exit the boat. Most of the children were already out and exploring the dock. Barbara held Donna securely in her arms.

"I'll take Donna up the ramp in just a few minutes," Wills said to Barbara. "It might be difficult getting up the ramp. To the children he said, "Listen everyone, I don't want you climbing up there until Bill and I check it out for safety."

"Boys, help unload the items we brought," Veronica called out to her sons.

Rosie ran toward the ramp and started to ascend, but was stopped short by her mother's call, "Rosie, you too! Come back here and help!"

Soon everyone had something to carry as they made their way up the ramp. Halfway up, Stella panted to Veronica, "This has to be more than 45 degrees."

Veronica just shook her head. Talking was impossible. The children, however, didn't seem to realize that. They ran past the grown-ups and hit the landing with gleeful triumph.

"I wonder if they would mind giving me a little of their exuberance. I need to stop a moment for a bit of a rest. You keep going. I'll be there shortly," Barbara said between breaths, holding tightly to the ramp's railing.

At the top of the ramp, the kids and the men stomped down the high grass to make a path for the ladies. Soon all the supplies were set down and everyone had a chance to see their surroundings. There was an arbor or what Stella thought might even be a gazebo overhead directly in front of them as they reached the end of the ramp. It was hard to ascertain what exactly it was due to the dense vines that strangled the structure. Blackberry vines, thick shrubbery, trees, branches, wildflowers, and grass that looked more like a wheat field obscured the building to the left of them.

"Is that the house to the left of us? I can't quite see it yet," Stella said.

"Yes, yes. Hang on. I brought some cutting shears. They are in the toolbox. Bill, look and see what else you can find to cut with."

"I'll wait back here with Donna until you clear a path to the house," Barbara said.

"That sounds like a good idea," Stella said. "Veronica and I will trudge ahead. Ouch! Oh, no, my nylons. There's a run in them."

"Mine are torn to shreds!" Veronica said.

"Sorry, girls, but I told you to put trousers on instead of your pretty dresses," Wills teased.

"How was I to know that we would be attacked by foliage?" Stella complained.

"We don't own any trousers or hard labor work clothes," Veronica added.

"We will fix that at the Mercantile when we go back," Bill said.

"Fine," Stella whined as she prodded her way through thick straw almost as tall as she was.

"There it is. I can see the house. Let me cut back a few more plants on the steps."

Stella and Veronica stared dumbfounded. Barbara found her way and stopped behind them. "Well, this certainly is an adventure!"

"I never want to hear that word ever again in my entire life," Stella said, still gazing in shock.

"Isn't it a beauty?" Wills exclaimed.

"I think the house is snarling at me," Stella said.

Three broken wooden steps led to an expansive old wooden porch assembled like a patchwork quilt with many areas broken and repaired over the years. Right now, it looked in complete disrepair.

"I better go up first to check things out," Wills said. He jumped over the first two steps and fell through the third. "I can fix that."

Stella, Veronica, and Barbara appeared to be frozen where they stood as they continued to gaze at the enormous structure.

The children came running through the grass. Rosie and Maddie could be heard but not seen. The boys, however, were noticeable by their heads popping up and down, laughing wildly.

"Isn't this swell, Ma?" the twins said in unison.

"Mommy, Mommy," Maddie yelled as she reached her. "That house is made out of trees!"

"Logs," Anton said. "It is a log house!"

The house was indeed constructed of gigantic logs. Directly in front of the steps an open yellow door swung from broken rusty hinges. Two sizable windows, one of which was broken, were perfectly situated a few feet from both sides of the door. An antique-looking rocking chair at the far end of the porch swayed back and forth without the assistance of any noticeable wind.

"Do you think this place is haunted?" Leon howled.

"Don't be ridiculous," his grandmother scolded.

Veronica grabbed Stella's arm and squeezed.

"The first thing we are going to do is paint that front door!" Wills said, pulling his leg out of the hole in the step. He touched the door to determine if it would open further. Without much nudging, the door fell solidly to the floor. A whirlwind of dust puffed up and out the entryway, followed by a few squawking birds. Merlin dashed inside and barked wildly. A couple of squirrels scurried out and headed straight up the closest tree. Merlin ran after them, jumping toward the tree.

"This is wild!" Leon shouted to Rosie. "You are so lucky!"

Stella turned to Bill, who was entering the house with Wills, "I'll trade with you."

"Forget it," Veronica said. "Let's go inside. I think we got the wrong end of the deal. I'm thinking the boat looks pretty good after all."

"Wills," Stella shouted. "All bets are off. You boys are going to help us get this log disaster livable. No arguments. Now, where is the light switch?"

"Well, I've been meaning to tell you about that, but hadn't quite found the time to bring it up," Will admitted.

Although it was daytime, the windows were so dirty that the inside of the house was almost in complete darkness. "Boys, there is a flashlight in the toolbox. Go get it," Bill said.

"There is no power here," Wills said quietly.

"No power? What do you mean?" Stella asked.

"No electricity. No power lines," Wills said.

"Mommy, Mommy, I have to go potty," Maddie cried.

"Wait for the flashlight, then we will find the bathroom," her mother said.

"I'm afraid you won't find it inside."

Veronica thought to herself that it was a good thing Will couldn't see Stella's face now. She couldn't either, but she could easily visualize it.

"Where is the bathroom, Wills? There has to be a bathroom."

"Outside," Wills said.

"Wow, I bet they have an outhouse!" Anton shouted as he raced back with the flashlight and tossed it to his dad. "I saw one in a Western one time. Let's go find it!" The older children were off and running again.

Stella walked back toward the entrance and leaned against the door post. She put her hand on her forehead and said, "I am getting such a headache. I could use some water. I brought paper cups. Let's have some water and think this through."

"Did you bring water?" Wills asked.

"No, I assumed we would just turn on the tap and...oh, no. Please don't tell me," Stella implored.

"There are pipes," Wills soothed.

"Well, that's a good start anyway," Bill added helpfully.

"They are not exactly working. You see, the water comes from a beautiful, cool spring. It is very clean and healthy. That was checked."

"The offsite water spring was checked but not the house?" Stella asked.

"Safety, you see. You have to have fresh, safe water."

"How do we get the water to the house?"

"Carry it."

"How do we cook and bathe and a million other things?"

Bill turned on the flashlight. "Let's go back in and see what exactly is there and what we need to do."

As they followed Bill's flashlight beam, Barbara gave a little scream.

"What is it, Mama? Are you okay?" Veronica asked.

"Why, I haven't seen one of those since my childhood," Barbara mused. "Shine that light back over here. I think we got us a wood cookstove. Why, I never!"

"No range, no oven?" Veronica asked.

"No, child. This beauty is powered by chopped wood."

"*No!*" Stella said.

"No?" Wills repeated.

"*No,* we are going to get pipes, running water, and a bathroom and power and whatever else we need! Do you hear me?" Stella was adamant. She was determined not to let anger, or her increasing irritability, get the better of her. She knew that she could channel this frustration into action. She had to make this work. She would do it. She knew she could because now she wouldn't have to do it alone. She had a family. She had her friends.

"Everyone, pick a task and let's get started."

1961 – Hidden Lake, Oregon | 265

Chapter 48

1961 – HIDDEN LAKE, OREGON

The ragtag group of friends crawled off *The Adventure* moments before dusk. Clearly exhausted, they trudged the short distance to the Mercantile, each of them covered in dust and grime from head to foot. Bill gave every child a dime to pull a soda pop out of the big red refrigerated box located on the store's front porch. The lettering on the front of the container said "Nehi Cream Soda" but each child could choose any flavor from the circulated ice-cold water inside.

As they approached the store, the children ran ahead to be the first to open the pop box, as they called it. Mrs. Armstead was on the porch hollering at the elderly men and pushing them off the benches with a big broom. Stella wanted to run her fingers through her hair to make it look a bit more presentable but decided to just keep the scarf wrapped securely around her head. Veronica did the same.

Mrs. Armstead stopped abruptly when the children raced up the steps and pushed past her. She was ready to give them a good scolding but saw the adults following slowly behind. "My, my, look what the cat dragged in," she said.

Stella gave Mrs. Armstead a look that chilled her to the bone.

"Mr. Armstead," Mrs. Armstead yelled, "You better come out here. You have customers."

"I'm busy," he yelled back.

"No, you're not," she insisted, walking back inside the store.

Bill looked around and suggested that he get the necessary items at the store while Wills took the exhausted group home. Wills agreed willingly as Veronica and Stella just nodded their thanks and continued walking home.

"Please remember to get the paint first," Wills instructed Bill. "That is the most important item. We need to paint your house tomorrow, then we will go back and attack our place. Sam, my brother-in-law, gave us some money to fix up their house and a loan for my place. When I telephoned them yesterday, they told me they were very happy that you will be renting from them and will refuse any kind of payment until the first of the year." He handed Bill some cash and continued, "Please use this to get whatever you think we need. Whatever you do, get the pipes! Stella won't move in until we have running water and a bathroom. Did I ever tell you how happy I am that you are a mechanical engineer?"

"Well, I'm not really an engineer, but I'm pretty sure I can handle it."

"But can you handle the shopping?"

"*That* I'm not so sure about."

"Do you think your mother-in-law could be convinced to cook dinner tonight? She must be exhausted after attacking that cookstove all day. She wouldn't let anyone else near it. She said it was her project. She even named it 'Big Beauty.' Stella called it 'The Big Monstrosity' and refused to go near it."

"Barbara was unbelievable. She even found some kerosene lanterns. She called out orders and told everyone what they were to do and how to do it. She told me that she cannot wait to cook on 'Big Beauty' and wished we had one just like it at the Surly house," Bill said, shaking his head. "Heaven help us all!"

"Sounds like a lot of arguing inside the store. I'm getting out of here fast," Wills laughed as Bill frowned. "Well, you did offer. Good luck!"

Bill trotted up the steps and took a deep breath before

entering the store. Mr. Armstead came through the curtained opening at the far end of the shop and looked directly at Bill.

"So, I have to miss my favorite television show for the likes of you?" he growled.

"I have a list of some items we need fairly quickly," Bill said.

"Do you have any money?"

Bill pulled out the wad of bills he held in his hand and showed it to the shopkeeper. "Yes."

"Give me the list."

Bill handed it to him. "I don't really know how much paint we will need for the entire outside of the house. Can you make an estimate?"

"I suppose." He put on his glasses and scratched his head. "What color?"

"Well, that's the funny thing. Wills said that he doesn't care as long as it's not yellow."

"Look, I'll go through this list and see what I have. I'll give my delivery man a call to pick up the rest. Come back by 8:00 tomorrow morning. Now, leave me in peace so I can watch my show. If only I could get that screech owl to stop her howling!" Mr. Armstead said, marching out.

"But tomorrow is Sunday," Bill called after him. He got no response.

⁓

The Sunday morning sunshine pierced its way through the kitchen curtains, promising a hopeful beginning to the day. Wills looked out the window and said, "I do believe Hidden Lake is having a heat wave. The weather report is calling for sixty to sixty-two degrees with sunny skies today and tomorrow. That's quite unusual for this time of year on the coast."

"Well, let's don't sit around doing nothing. Let's get going while the getting is good!" Barbara said.

Veronica stared at her as if she had lost her mind. "Mama?"

"I'll just clean up these breakfast dishes, then we can go to church. I saw a church not too far away. Don't know the denomination, but it is a house of God and that is all that matters," Barbara added, ignoring her daughter.

"Grandma, I don't think we should go to church. We get to paint the house today," Leon said.

"Church first, house second!" Barbara insisted.

"But Grandma, if we just show up, the whole congregation may have a cow!" Anton pointed out.

"I have no idea what that means, young man."

"Mama," Veronica continued, "we should talk to the pastor first before we just show up. That would be the polite thing to do. These people have not met us yet and it may not be a good idea to just surprise them."

"Well, they might as well get used to the idea that we are here to stay, and I intend to go to church!"

"I am not going to church today or any day," Stella maintained, drinking her coffee.

"Why ever not?" Barbara addressed her. "Ever since you got home last night, you have acted like the world just ended. You have been up and down so many times these last few days that you must be awfully dizzy on that seesaw you are riding."

Wills jumped in, "There's a Catholic church a little distance away. Maybe you would prefer that. It is the only Catholic church nearby. It's very small and right next to the ocean. I think you would agree that it is quite charming."

"I don't care. I'm not going."

"Young lady, you and me is going to have a serious talk!" Barbara said.

"No."

"Yes. Don't you get all high and mighty on me. I have known you since you were barely out of your teens. Your mama told me to watch over you just before we left Chicago and that is what I intend to do."

"When did you talk to my mother?"

"We've been in close contact for years, ever since Veronica and you went on that crazy train trip to California. I asked

Veronica in a letter to send me your mama's address. She did and I found her. We've been friends ever since."

"That explains a lot."

"We both expect you to go back to church."

"No!"

"You better have a good excuse because I am not allowing you to get on the Lord's bad side," Barbara was adamant.

"I think I better help the children get into their painting clothes. Bill is picking up the paint and other supplies now," Veronica said as she put her coffee cup in the sink and got out of the room as rapidly as she could.

"I better go help Bill," Wills said.

"Cowards," Stella moaned under her breath.

"Don't you say those mean words. Do you hear me? Your mama wants you to go to church and so do I," Barbara said, throwing the kitchen towel on the counter.

"I can't. I've been excommunicated."

"I don't believe that. I'm not sure the priest will see it that way, either."

"Well, I can't receive the sacraments because I got divorced and remarried."

"I don't know the rules of the Catholic Church, but you should confess to your priest and ask God's forgiveness."

"Why? God should be asking me for my forgiveness!"

"Do not talk blasphemy," Barbara said. "Why ever should He need your forgiveness? That makes no sense."

"Yes, it does. Have you seen Donna? Have you seen the mess I've made of my life?"

"I have no idea what you are talking about. Donna is the most beautiful creature I've seen in all my born days. It's you who has something wrong with her eyesight. And, right now, the way I see it, your life looks pretty nice!"

"Maybe you haven't noticed, but Donna can't walk or talk, and she is not even allowed to go to school. And, on top of that, all my money has gone into a totally unlivable house that doesn't have plumbing or electricity!" Stella almost yelled.

"You blame God for that?" Barbara asked.

"Of course. He could have prevented it."

"Why should God help someone who doesn't help themselves?"

"I prayed and prayed, but Donna isn't changing. I had hoped to start a new life and get a fresh start. I thought she would have a better chance, but sometimes it all seems impossible."

"I do not believe that God ever expects anyone to do impossible tasks all on their own. People are put together on this earth to help each other build lives that they can be proud of. He is not going to do it for you. People make good and bad choices all the time. Surround yourself with the people that will help you to make the right choices. Ask the Almighty for guidance to help you, but not for Him to do it alone."

"I don't know how to do anything."

"Don't be ridiculous. No more excuses. Get yourself out of this feeling sorry for yourself mood and get busy. *No* more sitting on your hands waiting for divine intervention. The Lord helps those who help themselves!"

Stella hesitated and said aloud what she had been thinking moments ago, "I did pull up my sleeves and got a good start on the house yesterday with everyone's help."

"That you did. It felt pretty good, too, didn't it?"

"What would I do without you?"

"That's what I'm trying to tell you. It is perfectly fine to ask others to help. It is perfectly fine to ask for God's help. It is perfectly fine to visit His house of worship."

Stella's eyes watered up, but she refused to cry. Although she believed everything Barbara was saying, there were times she felt overwhelmed. Sometimes she wanted to crawl up into a little ball and cry. She knew, though, that would be foolish. Stella didn't always feel brave and determined, but right now the support she was being given was all she needed to know. She knew what she had to do. She could be hopeful again. Stella looked up at Barbara.

"You are a very powerful, exceptional young woman, Stella.

have never known someone so stubborn and courageous. I am more surprised when you turn to negativity and feel like you want to give up."

"I never said I would give up."

"Good," Barbara smiled. "We will start there. I still expect you to at least visit your church soon."

"Okay, okay. But only if you take charge of that big monstrosity!" Stella stood up, walked over to Barbara, and hugged her fiercely.

"You have got yourself a deal!"

It wasn't long until Bill and Wills came back with a carload of supplies, including the containers of paint and the painting supplies. Everyone rushed out of the house to greet them. Stella carried Donna and placed her gently into the stroller to watch the activity.

"Open it, Dad. Open it. We can't wait to see what color our house is going to be," Leon said.

"Yes, yes. Hand me that screwdriver, Wills, so I can get the lid off this gallon of paint."

The entire group gathered round in anticipation. When the lid was fully off, there were some gasps, but not a word was spoken. Bill broke the silence, "I ought to take this damn can of paint and the dozen others and dump them on Armstead's head!"

"Watch your language, Bill!" Barbara scolded.

"Wow," Rosie said, "I have never seen such a bright pink paint before!"

"Let's go, Wills!" Bill hissed, "I am going to tell that weasel a thing or two. If he thinks he can get away with this disrespect, why he has another thing coming!"

"I have a better idea," Veronica said as she picked up a paint brush. "What better revenge than to actually use this pretty pink paint? We will have the only shocking pink house in town, just like Elsie's house in San Francisco, and we can praise the Armsteads for making it happen."

Wills added, "A pink boat, too. The remainder of the paint we will use for the boat."

"The fishermen will love it!" Veronica added with glee.

"I don't know. Pretty pink paint?" Stella asked.

"Mommy, Mommy, look. Donna is saying, 'pretty pink paint,'" Rosie cried.

Everyone turned toward Donna. She was moving her lips. She seemed to be blowing wind from her lips as the audible sounds of "papapapa" escaped into the air.

Stella ran back into the house. Everyone stood stunned and wondered why Stella disappeared so quickly. Their quandary was answered within moments. Stella raced back outside and went directly to Donna. She threw a shower curtain around Donna and the stroller. Next, she clipped clothesline pins to the back of the material to secure it into place. Stella pushed the stroller as close to the side of the house as possible. She grabbed a paint brush and dipped it liberally into the can of paint. She put the brush into Donna's hand and said, "Pretty pink paint. Donna can paint."

And she did.

Chapter 49

SEPTEMBER 1961 – HIDDEN LAKE, OREGON

THE MEN LEFT FOR THE EARLY MORNING WORK SHIFT AT THE MILL on the day after Labor Day. The women were in the living room helping each other put the finishing touches on the children for their first day of school.

"I want to wear my pretty dress to go to school," Maddie cried.

"She can take my place," Rosie said.

"Yes. See, Mommy, Rosie said I can go," Maddie cried again as she jumped up and down.

"Well, Rosie is not in charge and needs to behave herself," their mother scolded.

Rosie scowled and Maddie stuck out her lower lip. Barbara picked up Maddie and put her on her lap as she sat down on the couch. "I need someone to help me today, Maddie. I will be alone. What would I do without you here with me?"

"Even Donna gets to go to school, but I don't. It's not fair. Grandma Barbara, maybe we should go to school just like Auntie Veronica and Donna?" Maddie said.

"Did I ever tell you how special you are?" Stella said to Veronica as she tied a large bow on Donna's dress.

"Don't you dare thank me again or I will change my mind," Veronica said.

"No, you won't. I know you. Once you've got your mind fixed on something, you won't change it for anything!"

"That's true enough," Barbara added as she bounced Maddie up and down to make her laugh.

Veronica continued, "The plan is that I will go into the first-grade classroom early. I will put Donna in a desk in the back row and pull up a chair beside her. We know Donna can sit all by herself in an armless chair without help. I will watch and listen to everything the teacher says and does. Then I will help teach those skills to Donna."

"It is certainly worth a try. Maybe you shouldn't mention to the teacher right away that Donna isn't registered for school."

"What she doesn't know won't hurt her," Veronica said laughing.

Leon and Anton ran into the room. "Mama, Grandma is making us wear our Sunday best suits."

"My, my, you two young pups look so handsome," Barbara grinned.

"Mama!" they shouted. "All the kids will think we're sissies."

"You are," Rosie smirked.

"How about a compromise?" Veronica interposed. "Mama, they would look just as nice if they removed the tie and jacket."

Barbara looked unconvinced but acquiesced. "I suppose my big boys will look and do their best regardless of a tie and jacket."

"I shouldn't have to wear my best dress then. It is too frilly. Everyone will laugh at me!" Rosie complained.

"We're already laughing," Leon said.

"Boys! Keep that up and you *will* be wearing the ties and jackets. Besides, one who can look their best tends to be the center of attraction. All the boys and girls will be envious of you, Rosie. You will be the belle of the ball," Veronica said.

"This is school, Aunt Veronica, not a party."

"Rosie, you need to be respectful and behave," Stella said.

"Okay, I will wear my frilly dress so I can be the most beautiful girl in the whole school."

"That'll be the day," Anton said.

"You boys also need to be respectful and behave."

"Grandma Barbara, can I wear my best dress so I can be prettier than Rosie?" Maddie said.

Before Rosie could respond, Barbara stood up and told everyone that they needed to hurry along. Within moments they were all out the door walking toward their first day of school. Barbara and Maddie waved from the picture window.

Stella gave Veronica and Donna a quick hug before opening the door to the first-grade classroom. They went inside and closed the door. The two boys raced over to the tetherball in the playground. Stella caught Rosie by the arm as she tried to run off to play as well.

"What do you think you are doing?" her mother asked. "You can't be running around in the playground. You will get your pretty dress dirty."

"I knew this was a bad idea," she pouted.

"I need to go directly to the office to start work. You know where your classroom is. Go find your desk and wait there until the bell rings," Stella said. "Boys, you too!"

Stella left the children behind, confident that they would do as they were told, as she walked to the office. Rosie shrugged, but decided that this time her mom was right. She stood by the fifth-grade classroom door and smoothed her dress down so no wrinkles would appear. She ran her fingers through her hair and turned her head side to side rapidly so her hair would fly about as she had seen her mother do so often. Once inside the classroom, she looked around expectantly. Several of the other kids were already there. A group of girls stood in the corner laughing. Some boys were pushing each other in a jovial manner. A few other boys and girls were sitting down or looking inside their desks. When Rosie walked in, everyone seemed to freeze. All talking and noise stopped as every eye in the room turned to look at her.

"Well, would you look at this? One of the shrimps of the sea lost their way," a freckle-faced red-headed boy sneered at her. He was about the same height as Rosie, only he looked like a large round ball. His scarlet complexion matched his hair, and he wore plaid pants with a contrasting striped green shirt.

"Who you calling a shrimp, you freckled freak?" Rosie yelled back.

"You should talk, short stuff in a clown outfit!" the boy shouted.

Everyone laughed loudly, which made the boy's face grow even redder. "His name is Freddie," one of the girls said to Rosie.

"Oh, the famous freaky, freckled Freddie," Rosie laughed but got no response from the other kids. They were silent as they stared behind her. She turned around. Leon and Anton came from behind and stood on both sides of her. The girls snickered and talked silently behind their hands to each other. The other boys froze.

"Whoa!" Freddie said. "Hey, would you look at that? Two burnt-out forest trees. My granny always said black people look alike. There's no telling them apart. I thought she was making a joke. It's no joke. They do look alike."

"Oh, for heaven's sake. They are twins, you idiot!" Rosie hissed.

"Why you little creep," Freddie said as he moved toward Rosie and tried to push her.

In a fraction of a second, Freddie was being lifted high into the air, his feet dangling off the floor. Leon held Freddie under one arm while Anton held him up under the other. Freddie's eyes popped wide open in fright.

"Put him down immediately," Mr. Silver roared as he came from outside.

The boys did as they were told and let Freddie drop to the floor, where he bounced once and rolled over.

"Go to my office," Mr. Silver shouted.

"She started it!" Freddie cried.

"No, I didn't!" Rosie yelled back.

"All of you. Now!" Mr. Silver said with a look of anger in his eyes. The four children ran to the office as the others each found a desk and immediately sat down.

"Stay here and read something. I will be back shortly!" Mr. Silver directed.

As Mr. Silver opened the classroom door to the outside hallway, he heard a commotion coming from the direction of the first-grade classroom. "Oh, no," he thought out loud. "It can't be."

Veronica was holding Donna close to her side as she made her way determinedly down the corridor as Mrs. Fox pursued closely behind her.

"Who said you could bring that mentally retarded child into my classroom? This isn't a first-grade class of misfits. Good thing I told Principal Short Stuff that I would teach first grade. I knew that I would need to keep an eye on things around here. You are trying to ruin my school with your fancy big city black ways. Well, I won't have it, I tell you. I won't. We will see about this!" Mrs. Fox screamed.

Veronica did not say a word. She did not race or hurry. Instead she kept her head high and elegantly made her way toward the office.

Mrs. Fox saw the principal just as he was opening the office door. She pushed Veronica aside and jumped in front of her. "Are you aware of what is going on in this school? I'll have you know that they are trying to sneak in a nonregistered handicapped girl without our knowledge! Are you going to stand for this outrage? Well, I for one am not. She cannot come into my classroom. I won't have it. I won't. Do you hear me?"

"I'm pretty sure everyone can hear you. Just come in and settle down. One thing at a time," Mr. Silver said.

"I am sorry, Mr. Silver. We were going to talk to you, but…" Veronica tried to explain but was cut off when she saw a very angry Stella yelling at their children.

Stella was infuriated, "The first day? You are in the office on the first day? You were told to be respectful and to be on your best behavior!"

"But Aunt Stella, it wasn't our fault," Anton tried to say.

"We had to protect Rosie," Leon said.

"I don't need your stupid protection. I can take care of myself, thank you very much," Rosie declared.

Veronica handed Donna to a mystified Mrs. Fox and stood next to Stella. "The first day of school and you three are in the office? I don't believe it! I am so ashamed of all of you! Wait until your father gets home!"

"My father is finally coming home?" Rosie said without thinking.

"That is enough of your smart mouth!" Stella said. "If you ever want to watch television again in your entire life, you will apologize this minute. Do you hear me?"

Rosie nodded but did not say another word. The boys sat ramrod straight and silent. Mr. Silver walked over and said calmly, "Mrs. Rollins and Mrs. Donaldson, thank you for your assistance, but I will take it from here. Mrs. Fox, go back and teach your class."

"I am not done here," Mrs. Fox started.

"Yes, you will be if you do not leave this office immediately! Everyone return to what you were doing," he commanded.

"But what do I do with this child?" Mrs. Fox said stunned.

"Take her with you. Mrs. Donaldson, go with them."

Everyone stood where they were. "Now!" he yelled. They left immediately. Stella went back to her desk.

Mr. Silver stood in front of the students and sighed. "Go back to the classroom and find your desks. There is to be no talking until I get there."

The children did not argue. They were out the door as fast as they could go. But Rosie went to her mother's desk first and said as tears filled her eyes, "I'm sorry, Mommy."

Stella didn't look at her daughter. She only nodded. Rosie ran out the door.

Mr. Silver went into his office, closed the door, and sat at his desk. He took out a piece of paper and a pen. "If there is one thing you know, it's that you never know. And I certainly don't know anything," he wrote.

❦

Ten minutes later, Mr. Silver stood in front of his fifth-grade students. He had an evenly divided class of ten girls and ten boys this year. He looked at their young, worried expressions and smiled. They all sat as still as possible while they waited for him to talk. He paced the floor a few times letting the tension increase slightly. The children were even afraid to squirm. Five more minutes went by. No one spoke or raised their hand. Mr. Silver picked up a piece of white chalk. He held it up high, went to the blackboard, and wrote, "Mr. Silver. Grade Five. Expectations."

"Does anyone know what 'Expectations' means?" Mr. Silver asked.

Anton was the first to raise his hand.

"I can see that a few of you do, a few of you are not sure, and a few don't know at all. That is quite all right. We are all going to learn, but first we will start the school year with a story. I would like everyone to go to the Reading area in that back corner and sit down on the floor," Mr. Silver instructed.

The students did as they were told without a word. As they sat down, Mr. Silver pulled up a chair and sat in front of them. They looked up at him with expectant eyes, unaware of what he was going to say or do next.

"Once upon a time, in a not so distant past, lived a ten-year-old boy in a faraway foreign land. He was very happy and had very many friends. Every day when he went to school, he would learn many things and he would laugh and play with all his friends. One day, he was told that he had to wear a big yellow star. When he asked why, he was told that it didn't matter. He was not allowed to ask questions or take it off. So, he went to school with his new yellow star fully visible to all his friends. All the adults and children at his school and in his town were told that they could not play or talk to any boy or girl who wore a yellow star. His friends turned away and refused to acknowledge him. They would laugh at him and call him names. They would fight and throw things at him. He didn't understand why. They used to have such fun together.

"He decided to be brave one day. He asked his teacher why everyone was ignoring him. The teacher told him that he was different than they were. The boy said that he was the same as he always was. He hadn't changed. The teacher told him that he might feel the same way, but others did not. They were afraid of the others. The teacher said to go back to his desk and not say any more about it.

"The boy got sadder and sadder as he was shunned by the others. At home his mother and father were also being treated poorly by the very people that were once their closest friends and companions. His father ran a bank and his mother took care of the house. One day, his father came home and said that they took his bank away. He could not work there anymore. His mother said that the corner store would not sell her groceries any longer. The boy was told he could not go to school. Soon the boy's family was out of money and had little food left. They were very sad and very scared. The boy overheard his mother and father talking one day. They argued about going away. The boy watched as his mother packed a suitcase, but they did not go.

"Late one afternoon, some men in uniforms pounded on their door. His mother raced to the boy, put the suitcase in his arms, and told him to run. She quickly slipped a letter into his pocket and pushed him out the back door. 'Where do I go?' the boy cried. 'Hide!' was all his mother could say before the front door was broken down. The boy slipped out the back before the big men could notice him. He shimmied up his favorite tree where he would often climb to spy on everyone, hidden from view. He watched in horror as his mother and father were forcibly thrown into the back of a truck with other people wearing yellow stars.

"The boy was frightened. He didn't know what to do or where to go. His mother and father were adamant that he run away. Where should he go? He stayed in that tree a long, long time and cried. The next morning, a little girl from his school stood at the bottom of the tree. 'Little boy,' she said. 'Come down from there. Do you want to play with me?' The boy really wanted to but instead said, 'I cannot. I have a yellow star.' The girl told him that she didn't care about a silly yellow star. If he came down, he could come to her house. Her dad would help him. So, he got down from the tree and ran with the girl to her house. He showed the letter he had in his pocket to her parents. The letter told him that he was loved very much. He was to find a kind family to hide him until the world became sane again. Then he was to contact his uncle Edgar in America so he could start a new life.

"He stayed with her family for two years. Sometimes, her parents made him hide in their attic. He was never allowed to leave the house for any reason. The girl was nice to the boy. She would bring home her assignments from school and teach them to the boy. They became good friends. When the world became sane again, her family found his uncle Edgar, and he was sent to America to live with him. Later, he would go to college and become a learned man. He would have a good career and a good life. But he would always miss his mother and father. He would also miss the friends that never were. The End."

The children sat transfixed. Mr. Silver looked at the faces in front of him. Some looked confused, some sad, and some shook their heads. It was clear that Anton understood the moral without being told. He nodded at Mr. Silver and winked.

"After recess, we are going to talk about what this story means and what it has to do with you," Mr. Silver said.

"Expectations, too?" Anton ventured.

"Yes," Mr. Silver continued, "but first, it is introduction time. I'd like everyone to take turns telling a little bit about yourself. Who would like to go first?"

"I would," said Leon.

Mr. Silver grinned, "Thank you, Leon."

"My name is Leon, but everyone back home in Chicago calls me Lion. My parents said we are home in Hidden Lake now so I should go back to Leon. But I like Lion."

"Is that because you want everyone to be afraid of you?" an

average-sized girl with light blond stringy hair and a thin face called out.

"That is what I used to believe, but not anymore. Not after Mr. Silver's story. I think I like Lion now because it makes me feel courageous and strong. I want to be a leader. I want others to look up to me."

"You are so tall that's it's hard not to," another girl said shyly.

Mr. Silver patted Leon on the back and shook his hand. "Everyone let's give Lion a warm welcome!"

Everyone clapped their hands. Some of the boys clapped him on his back as he sat back down.

"Anton, since you are twins, I think it is only fitting that you go next," Mr. Silver said.

Anton stood up next to his teacher. "My name is Anton, but everyone back home in Chicago called me Ant. So, my brother and I were known as the Lion and the Ant."

"Why?" a nice-looking boy who sat in the back asked loudly.

"I have been told that it is because I work hard and think things through. I am very smart. Or so I tell myself. I guess I want to show the world how smart I am someday. I want to show the world that people who are my color are just as smart as anyone else. Some may even be smarter. Maybe me or someone like me could even be president someday," Anton said confidently.

"He is cute and smart," a girl whispered to Rosie.

Mr. Silver clapped him on his back and shook his hand, "Let's give a warm welcome to Ant."

"Rosie, how about you go next since you are also new here," Mr. Silver said.

Rosie stood up. She wasn't afraid of crowds. She loved them. Being the center of attention was something she reveled in and knew well. "I used to live in California with my mom, sisters, and real dad. My mom and dad got a divorce." Some gasps could be heard, but Mr. Silver gave his famous frozen stare and all the students became silent. They watched Rosie in awe. "My mom remarried, and we moved here. My stepfather is Wilbur Rollins. He is okay, I guess. I'm getting used to him. He's very friendly to me and wants me to be his daughter. I'm going to give it a good try. He bought a cool property up the lake. It's weird, though, because you can't drive there. We must take a boat, even to go to school. We don't even have electricity or a telephone. I feel like a primitive native. I never thought I would say this, but it's kind of fun. My family and Lion and Ant's family are all working together to fix it up. Thank you." Rosie curtsied and sat down.

Everyone clapped as they did for the boys. Rosie smiled widely.

"Jessie, you're next," Mr. Silver said. Jessie was a quiet, somewhat mousy girl. She had very long unkempt dark hair and wore a loose tattered dress.

"It's nice to meet you, Rosie. My name is Jessie. I guess most of you know me, but our new friends don't. You should know that many of us at this school live on the lake. We come to school early because we ride the school boat. That's what we call it. You can't get to our houses by car, either. So Carlton picks us up to drop us off at school, then he gets the regular school bus and picks up the other kids. You might have met Carlton. He is a nice man. He owns the marina, too. Your boat is probably moored there."

The bell rang. "Recess time, everyone," Mr. Silver said. "For today only, you don't have to line up. Go have a good time. But remember to line up outside the door when the bell rings again. Have fun."

"Do you want to play with me?" Jessie said.

"That's a real pretty dress," said Kaye.

The girls linked arms as they walked to the playground. The boys raced past them to the tetherball. Rosie made friends rapidly and easily. A short time later, she strode over with some of her new friends and told the boys that it was the girls' turn to play. The boys didn't argue. They were ready to play a game of basketball. Lion was an instant success. He loved the game. Ant wasn't very athletic, but a few girls were hanging around him and chatting. For the first time in his life he didn't understand why Lion would prefer a sport over having pretty girls surround him. He wondered if there was a book he could read about it. Before they knew it, the bell rang.

Chapter 50

1961 – HIDDEN LAKE, OREGON

The conversation around the dinner table that evening was very lively. Both families were living at the "Pretty Pink House," as they now called it, until the log house was habitable according to Stella's expectations. The men were determined to work on the house a few hours every day after their shift was over at the mill. Wills told the assembled group that he had rented a barge for the coming weekend to move all their belongings. They would have to secure the large barge to the boat and tow it very slowly. The children were quite excited and couldn't wait. The women were not as confident. Stella looked aghast when Wills wondered out loud whether the barge could accommodate a couple of cows and possibly a few chickens as well.

Veronica changed the subject swiftly when she said to the men, "How did your first day at the mill go?"

Bill nodded and said, "I think it will be fine. It didn't take Wills long to blend in as one of the guys. Everyone likes him. I am doing my best, but it may take a bit of time before I can assimilate as an equal. There are a few that don't seem to want me around. Maybe they think I can't do the job or don't belong there. I don't know, but I will work very hard to earn their respect."

"Bill is a good man and a hard worker. He is the only one who knows how to fix that aging plumbing. Some of the men just don't know how to deal with someone who doesn't fit their preconceived image of what a mill man looks like," Wills said.

"Be honest, they don't want a black man around."

"Maybe."

"Mrs. Fox is like that as well," Veronica said. "She has no choice but to allow Donna and me into the class, but she has made it very clear that she doesn't like it one bit. Mr. Silver said that Donna could stay until the school board voted on the issue at the end of the month. He said that the superintendent was very sympathetic, but he had to get permission."

Stella added, "Mr. Silver told me that because there is no law that states a school must take handicapped children, he could not promise anything. We must wait until the school board meeting. It is open to the public, so we can go."

"If Mrs. Fox treats you the same way some of the men react to me at the mill, you must be very upset," Bill said to Veronica as he took her hand and squeezed it.

"I know this sounds surprising, but she said she doesn't actually mind me being there. Every chance I get I try to assist her in any way I can. I'm afraid Donna is the one she doesn't want."

Every head came up as each of them looked toward Veronica. Rosie said what they were all thinking, "How could someone not want Donna?"

"I know this might sound odd, but Mrs. Fox looked at Donna all day today. She never came close to her and never tried to help her in any way. She looked at her with pity, which made me so angry. I just swallowed my frustration and tried to do the best that I could."

"Do you think Donna can learn things there?" Rosie asked.

Veronica sat in silence for a few seconds before she said, "Children learn at different levels. I don't think there is a 'one lesson fits all' timeline. Of course, it has only been one day, but what I really noticed was the reaction of the other children and the incredible positive impression Donna had on them."

"That doesn't surprise me," Rosie said, not looking up.

"Me, either," Anton added as he continued to eat.

"A little girl came over to where Donna and I sat. She touched Donna's face and said, 'She's pretty,' then she touched my face and said the same thing. I touched her face and said that she was pretty, too. The girl looked up at me with big, brown eyes and asked if Donna wanted to play with her at recess. I told her that would be a nice idea. Soon many other children did the same. Donna was the most popular child on the playground. I helped to hold her up or put her in the swings, but they played real games with her. Donna laughed and made her happy noises."

"I believe fifth graders could learn a lot from first graders!" Stella said to the three oldest kids, who became engrossed in eating their dinner without looking up.

Stella and Veronica took turns telling the others about the events that started the day. Bill looked at the three offenders and said to his boys, "I am not happy about this. After your dinner is finished, you are to go to bed. There will be no television. Your mother and I will talk about a punishment."

"The same goes for you, Rosie," Wills said.

"I didn't start it…" Rosie tried to say but was interrupted by that stare her mother was so famous for.

Barbara jumped in for the first time that evening, "You can catch more flies with honey than you can with vinegar."

"What is that supposed to mean?" Rosie said sarcastically.

"Go to your room right now!" Stella commanded.

Rosie flew out of the dining room, ran to her room, and slammed the door. She felt overwhelmed at how unfairly she was being treated. She climbed up to the top bunk and sulked when her mother came in to put Donna in her crib on the far side of the room and tucked Maddie in on the bottom bunk.

Two hours later, Stella walked quietly back into the room that was illuminated by a night light and a tiny flashlight that Rosie was holding to read her book. She sat down on the bottom bunk next to Rosie. "Why aren't you on the top bunk? Maddie is supposed to sleep down here."

"Maddie told me that I had to switch with her, or she would

tell you all the naughty things I have done since she was born," Rosie said.

"I didn't know Maddie could count that high," Stella grinned.

"That's not funny. I bet Maddie won't get in trouble for being a tattletale. I'm the only one that ever gets in trouble. It is not fair."

"What is not fair is when others are called names, or when someone is rude and disrespectful to another. How do you think that makes someone feel?"

"I don't know."

"How would it make you feel if someone was mean to Donna?"

"I would be very mad. I would call them a name!"

"What would Donna do?"

"She wouldn't do anything. She is happy all the time. She doesn't understand."

"No, but you do. You understand that being mean to Donna is bad, right?"

"Yes. It is hurtful. I would hate it," Rosie said.

"So would Donna, if she knew. But she treats everyone the same. She loves the people who love her. You could learn a lot from Donna," her mom said.

"I get so angry at everyone. It's not fair. No one cares how I feel. No one cares that I can't stop the hurt I feel inside because my dad left us. No one cares that I miss him so much I want to scream. I don't like feeling this way." Rosie fell into her mother's arms and sobbed. Stella pulled a handkerchief out of her pocket and wiped her daughter's tears.

"You have every right to be mad and even a little frightened, but you do not have the right to take it out on others. Do you understand that?" Stella soothed Rosie by rubbing her back.

Rosie sniffed, "I know."

"Everyone has problems or things in their lives that affect how they act, but that doesn't give them an excuse to treat others badly. All we can do is look for the best in others so they will notice the best in us. Donna seems to do that naturally. Her happiness makes us happy, doesn't it?" Stella said.

"Yes, but how do I get Freddie to stop calling me names?"

"Stop calling him names. Be his friend instead."

"I don't like him."

"He probably doesn't like you, either."

"What? But I am nice."

"Not to him you're not."

"That's true."

"Think about this," Stella continued, "why do you think a child or even an adult would say or do something that everyone would notice immediately?"

Rosie thought for a moment, then said, "So others would pay attention to them."

"You are a smart girl!" her mother said. "Attention. Everyone wants attention. People want other people to like them. They need it and they will do whatever they can to get it."

"Bad things, too?" Rosie asked.

"Sometimes, yes," Stella said.

"I don't want to be bad."

"Then you have a choice. Do you want to be noticed for appropriate behavior or inappropriate behavior?"

"Does that mean good or bad acts?"

"Yes, maybe," her mother continued, "but I would identify it more as something acceptable or unacceptable for a person who values kindness, compassion, and empathy."

"What does empathy mean?" Rosie asked.

"That will be your homework, but I think you already know. Donna taught you a long time ago," Stella finished as she shut off the flashlight and put Rosie's book next to the bed. She lightly touched Rosie's cheek with the back of her fingers and kissed her forehead. She stood up, walked to Donna's crib, and did the same goodnight ritual. Maddie was too high up, so Stella just blew her a silent kiss.

The next three weeks sped by. Work was going very well both at the mill and on the log house. Wills felt that they should be fully ready to move in completely sometime in the coming month of October. No one showed any apprehension about sharing the Pretty Pink House for the time being. The entire group enjoyed each other's company. The conversations at the evening meals were lively with vivid details of the events of the day. The children were enjoying school, which eased any worrisome tensions they might have once felt. Rosie and Freddie each played with their own group of friends and did their best to stay away from each other. The twins were surprised at their own notoriety. All the other kids seemed to want to vie for their attention, which Rosie claimed made each twin puff up like a bloated peacock. She was quick to tell her mother that that should not be considered name calling. It just happened to be an observed fact.

Tonight, the school board meeting would be held at their school in Hidden Lake. BB, the custodian, had spent most of the day in and out of the office complaining about having to find enough chairs to set up for the meeting as well as how those chairs would undoubtedly scuff up his gym floor. Stella had written a short speech that she had rehearsed for more than a week. Mr. Silver told her that she was on the agenda and would be given time at the podium to talk about her concerns regarding Donna's educational needs. Stella was nervous, but ready to go. Now, she just needed the school day to be over. The speech clouded her thoughts all day long.

The afternoon recess for the older children was louder than normal, and the noise penetrated the office area. Veronica came out of the first-grade classroom with Donna on her hip. She walked down the outside corridor to the playground area and searched for Rosie. In minutes, Rosie ran over to them.

"Rosie, would you mind watching Donna for a little while? I need to talk to your mom in the office," Veronica asked.

"Of course," Rosie said as her aunt Veronica stood Donna

up next to her. "I'll walk her to the four-square area to play ball with us."

"Thank you."

"Merlin, come help me watch Donna," Rosie shouted at Merlin, who always stood close to the blacktop where he could view the entire playground. Merlin jumped up and trotted over to them.

Rosie stood behind Donna in one square of the ball game as a few other girls raced over to call dibs on the other three squares. They had just started their game when Freddie came over and huffed, "Well, well. I don't believe it. So, the talk is true."

"What are you blabbering about, Freddie? You are interrupting our game," Rosie said. "If you want to play, you have to stand in line."

"Why would I want to play this stupid game with stupid girls? Now I know why you don't have a brain. You are just like this no-brain creature sister of yours. You both make my skin crawl. If I get too close, I could get a brain disease from her," Freddie yelled. His face was beet red. He turned around and looked at the other kids and laughed hysterically.

Rosie had a hundred comeback remarks screaming in her head, but instead she sat Donna down and walked toward Freddie to face him. Freddie backed up intentionally.

"You gonna push me again? You gonna call me names?" Freddie yelped.

Rosie looked him straight in the eyes and said nothing.

The Lion and the Ant raced over to Rosie's side, facing Freddie. Merlin jumped in front of Rosie, but she motioned him to go back to Donna. He did so, but his teeth were showing, and he growled. He lay down next to Donna and put his paws on her lap.

Freddie got louder, "What are you going to do? Are your slimy bodyguards going to protect you again?"

Rosie and the twins continued to stare at him but said nothing.

Freddie sneered, "I am going to tell my dad on you. He is

a lawyer. He will sue you. I bet all three of you will go to jail. You wait and see. My dad will take care of you. I bet Lion and Ant will have to go to a black boy jail. Rosie will end up in a no-brain jail!" He turned around toward the other children and laughed. No one joined the taunting.

Rosie took one step forward and pivoted so her back was toward Freddie. She crossed her arms and said nothing. Lion and Ant looked at Freddie, then at Rosie, and turned around as well.

"Scared of me now, aren't you? Scaredy-cats. My dad will take you to court. Yes, he will!" Freddie hollered.

Kaye came from the back of the playground. She pushed her way through the school children who stood and watched. Without a word, Kaye stood next to Lion and turned her back to Freddie. Jessie followed her and did the same. Jack and Timmy came next. They stood next to Ant and turned around. One by one, then in small groups, every child on the playground passed Freddie and turned their backs to him. All the children had their backs to Freddie and remained still.

The only sound came from Freddie, "Hey everybody, it was a joke. Can't you take a joke?" Freddie tried to laugh but no one turned around and no one spoke or made any noise. "I was kidding. Yes, I was. I didn't mean it. Come on, let's go back and play."

Inside the main office, Mr. Silver had left his office and passed Stella and Veronica without noticing them. "This is odd. It is much too quiet. I am going out to the playground. I will be right back."

Mr. Silver watched the entire scene unfold from the time Rosie first turned around. He wanted to observe for a short time rather than interfere. After a good five minutes elapsed, Mr. Silver called out, "Freddie, go to my office now!"

Freddie raced to the office. Mr. Silver looked at the others, who continued to remain where they stood. He said, "Recess is over. Please head back to your classrooms. My class does not need to line up today. Please go to your desks and start reading chapter two in your Social Studies book. I'll be back shortly. Rosie, I would like to see you in my office as well."

Rosie picked up Donna and walked to the office. Merlin followed behind but sat outside the door when she went in.

"I was ignoring inappropriate behavior," Rosie said before she realized that her mother had her head in her arms, face down on the desk. Veronica stood next to Stella with her arm around Stella's shoulders.

Stella raised her head. She was crying.

Chapter 51

1961 – HIDDEN LAKE, OREGON

Every chair set up by BB for the school board meeting was occupied, with many more people lining the back and side walls. Mr. Silver was sitting in the front row with Stella and Wills Rollins as well as Veronica and Bill Donaldson. Stella recognized several faces in the room from her work as the school secretary. She was surprised that they would want to attend a school board meeting though.

Mr. Silver looked around at the murmuring crowd. "I've never seen so many people here. Usually no one attends. These meetings are typically dry as toast."

Stella only grinned. She was more nervous than she thought possible. What Veronica had told her today left her thunderstruck. How would she ever be able to address the board?

Mr. Silver continued making small talk, "The full board will enter in moments. They will sit in those semi-circled desks in front of us on the stage. The superintendent, Mr. Victor, will sit in the far-right chair at the edge of the stage. It won't be long now."

Stella knew that Veronica only wanted to forewarn her. She could not and would never blame Veronica. She tried as best she could.

"Ladies and gentlemen, please welcome our school board," Mr. Victor announced to the crowd. He proceeded to introduce each man that entered the stage and sat down. An elderly white-haired man with an identical white beard and tiny round-rimmed glasses sat at the middle desk. He pounded the gavel with astounding affect. The audience went quiet immediately.

The chairman of the board said to the audience at large, "Thank you, parents, teachers, citizens, and guests. It is so nice to see you take an active role in the leadership of our schools. Please take a seat if you can find a chair. I will remind you that we have a full agenda. We will only welcome comments and questions at the podium during the appropriate time. Please remember to keep your thoughts short and concise. Any grandstanding and you will be ejected from the room."

Mr. Silver whispered to Mrs. Rollins, "That would be a first."

She only grinned. She hadn't heard what was said. She was replaying in her mind the conversation that Veronica and she had earlier that afternoon. Since that time, she went home and did everything possible to compose herself. She showered, selected an appropriate outfit to wear, and put on fresh make-up. She chose not to eat dinner or converse with anyone. Since Rosie had looked so sad, she only told her that she did the right thing. Rosie went to her room and refused to come out.

Stella noticed that the one-page paper she had in her hand was shaking. Wills put her hand in his and said, "Would you like me to hold that for you?"

What did he say? Stella was comforted by his touch, but she was oblivious of anything said around her. Her thoughts were only on Donna.

"Our first agenda item this evening has to do with our aging buildings and our lack of money to fund maintenance projects," the school board chairman started. The crowd moaned. He pounded the gavel down.

Veronica's words earlier in the day continued to invade Stella's thoughts.

"Oh, Stella, I so wanted to come here with good news. I wanted to be able to tell you that everything would work out fine. You need to know before you speak to the board tonight."

"If we are going to be able to fix anything, the voting public needs to..."

"Donna can't do it, Stella. I'm not saying that she can't learn. I believe she can. But not in that environment."

"It's only because Mrs. Fox doesn't want her."

"I wish that were the reason. That is only an excuse."

"She can learn. I know she can."

"She needs to learn at her own speed and at her own level."

"Why can't she do that with other children her own age?"

"I am not so sure chronological age makes a difference. I am not an expert. I want her to be able to learn from these children and from their teacher."

The chairman slammed the gavel down again and the crowd quieted. "We shall table maintenance for the time being. Next item?"

"Are you doing what the teacher is doing and showing Donna how to do it?"

"I wish it were that easy."

"Is it too hard for her? Maybe we should find a topic that is a bit easier until she catches up?"

"Please listen to me. I am going to tell you what Donna is doing. I don't know what she is capable of learning. Only an expert could tell us that."

One school board member responded to a question, "No, I do not think it would be wise for the high school cheerleaders to ride the same activity bus as the football players..."

"I would think that if the children are learning how to write their names, then Donna could have a paper and pencil and practice writing, too."

"Donna throws the pencils and tears the papers. She laughs and all the children turn around and laugh, too. The only ones in the room not enjoying this spectacle are Mrs. Fox and me. It takes Mrs. Fox a while to maintain order in the class."

"What about reading? You could read a book to her or show her pictures and identify them?"

"She throws the books and slaps the desk, making loud happy noises."

"Numbers with her fingers. Two fingers, two pencils – that sort of thing?"

"She stares at her fingers and smiles. You have seen her do that many times."

"Yes."

"Mrs. Rollins? Mrs. Rollins? Come to the podium with your statement now please."

"What can Donna do? How can we teach her? Who can teach her?"

Stella's mind was racing. She was lost in a fog and no one was searching for her.

"Is Mrs. Rollins in the building?" the chairman of the board said to the crowd.

Mr. Silver poked Stella lightly on her arm, "You are being called. Go on. You can do it."

Veronica looked at Stella and smiled fiercely, holding back tears. Stella stood up and walked to the podium. Remnants of old conversations were flying like arrows through the fog. *You should let her go. Go where? She is going home with me. She belongs in an institution. Put her in an institution and forget about her. We will have another baby.*

Stella stood in front of the board quivering. She took a deep breath and stared at the paper in front of her. She couldn't speak. The crowd murmured unintelligible sounds, but various people made shushing noises.

"Mrs. Rollins, are you ready? Maybe you would prefer to address us at another meeting?"

"No" came shouts from the back.

Stella turned around and faced the audience. She saw them look at her expectantly. She now knew why they were all there. Then she saw the faces of Rosie and the twins. Merlin was sitting in front of them. They were soundlessly watching her from the back entrance. They must have escaped from Barbara's watch. No, there was Barbara with Maddie and Donna.

"Members of the board, Superintendent Victor, Principal Silver, ladies and gentlemen of our school community. My name is Mrs. Stella Rollins and I am proud to say that I am Donna's mother," Stella spoke clearly and confidently. The paper she had in her hand floated to the floor.

There was a loud cheer. Stella and her family could not have been more surprised.

The gavel pounded once again. Stella looked at the man and said, "That is a good instrument to have. It tells people what to do and when to do it. I wish I had one of those."

The audience laughed and the gavel pounded out its response.

"Mrs. Rollins, you will be given two minutes to read your statement; then we will tell you what we decided," the chairman said.

"You have already decided something? How do you know what I am going to say?"

"You, dear lady, are twisting my words. I meant that we will discuss the matter afterwards and make our decision," he explained.

"Do you realize how very fortunate you are?" Stella turned around to the face the audience and said to them, "Do you realize how very fortunate each one of you is? You were allowed to go to school. You were educated and given opportunities for futures you could not have anticipated." People in the audience agreed verbally. The gavel pounded its steady rhythm again. Stella waited for the quiet. "Education should be an equal right for all children, yet it is not. Some children are being refused an education. They are being told they cannot go to school. How would you feel if your child or a family member or friend were denied an education? What would you do?" Outcries and noisy audience responses disrupted the proceedings. Stella continued as she turned and focused her attention to the board. The gavel sang out.

"I will clear this room if the audience cannot contain themselves. If you want to speak, you are to go to the podium during the comments from the floor agenda item. Now, Mrs. Rollins, you have thirty seconds left. Be quick about it," the chairman demanded.

"Wait," another member of the board said. The man was in his mid-thirties. He had curly light red hair and smooth skin. He was muscular and movie star handsome. "Stop the clock. I want to hear why children are not being allowed an education. We are living in a time where society should be trying to lessen the impact of prejudice and to fight discrimination, yet how can that happen if we ourselves are the culprits?"

"I can tell you why," Mrs. Fox shot out of her seat and hurriedly walked to the podium.

"*She needs more help than this school can give her.*" Veronica's own words echoed in Stella's head.

"I will concede my time to Mrs. Fox. I know what she wants to say. I will not disagree with her here. I am only asking that the School Board find a way to give my daughter, Donna, an education that makes sense for her. Thank you." Stella turned around to the applause from the audience and sat back down.

"I should hope you give me more than a lousy thirty seconds?" Mrs. Fox growled.

"The clock is running, Mrs. Fox. State your concerns so we can move on," the chairman said.

"Donna has been disrupting my classroom for three weeks now. I see many of the first-grade parents are here. As most of you know, I am first and foremost a good sport. Providing the best education I can for *all* my students is my top priority," Mrs. Fox stated.

Stella almost laughed aloud when she looked over at Veronica, who just happened to be rolling her eyes.

"But that child is Mentally Retarded. She needs to be in one of those Special Education classes, not my normal class!"

"Excuse me a moment, Mrs. Fox, but I would like to address something to my fellow board members," the man with slick combed-back dark hair and a slight mustache said. "Do we know of other children like this particular child that have requested special services from our school district?"

The chairman directed the question to the superintendent, "Mr. Victor, can you answer that question, please?"

"There is a Special Education classroom at the high school," Mr. Victor stated. "They work on what the teacher calls daily living skills like cooking, cleaning, dressing. That kind of thing. I have personally never actually visited the class, however. To my knowledge, no other parents have tried to register a child of Donna's mental capacity."

"Where would the money come from to hire a teacher that would know how to teach this child?" another member asked.

Mrs. Fox jumped in, "That's for dang sure. You won't even requisition money for a sidewalk in front of the school! The children are filthy by the time they are done jumping in and out of the mud puddles. My classroom floors are a mess!"

"Truer words were never spoken! About the floor, I mean!" Mr. BB yelled out. The audience exploded into laughter. The gavel danced to its typical beat.

"Mrs. Fox, would you please finish?" the chairman requested, wiping his brow.

"I have sympathy for that child and her family. Yes, I do," Mrs. Fox continued, "I feel very sorry for her. The children even like her. They play with her and try to teach her things. But she can't be in my class. That child takes up all my time, thereby lessening the amount of time I can give quality instruction to the other children. I tell you she can't learn anything. She does not walk or talk. She cannot even eat by herself. I doubt she can dress herself. I know she can't buckle her shoes. She belongs in an institution, not in a school for normal children!"

"No, she doesn't!" came a shout from a small child in the very back of the gym. "She belongs with her family and in school with other children!"

The chairman banged the gavel once more. "There are no children allowed at these meetings. Where are the parents of that child?"

Wills stood up, "She is our daughter."

"Why am I not surprised?" the chairman said, shaking his head. "Please remove her. And that dog, too! Why is there a dog in here? Mr. Silver, I will talk to you later."

Stella and the others of her group got up and filed down the middle aisle to the exit. She did not turn around to acknowledge the applause that followed her out.

Chapter 52

1961 – HIDDEN LAKE, OREGON

The relationship between Rosie's young adversary and the handsome school board member was now apparent. The father and son were sitting in chairs along the wall in the outer office when Stella came into work the morning following the school board meeting. She hung up her coat on the wall hooks and set her purse under her desk. Mr. Silver had not arrived yet.

"May I help you?" Stella said looking directly at the man.

"My son has something he would like to say to your daughter and to you," the man said.

Stella nodded her assent, "Rosie is outside on the playground right now."

"Frederick, go and ask her to please come to the office," he said to his son.

"Yes, sir."

Once Freddie had left, the man turned to Stella and said, "My name is Daniel Wright. If you don't mind, I would appreciate it very much if I could have a moment of your time for a private conversation after the children conclude their business."

"Yes, of course."

Mr. Silver entered the office. "Mr. Wright, I am surprised to see you. Would you care to come into my office?"

"Thank you, but no. I am here to speak with Mrs. Rollins if that meets with your approval."

"Yes, by all means. I will be in my classroom if anyone needs me. Thank you for coming, Mr. Wright," Mr. Silver said before letting the two children into the office. He squeezed the shoulders of each child, then exited the office, closing the door behind him.

Without further explanation, Mr. Wright said, "Frederick, you can begin."

Freddie looked at his feet and seemed to sway back and forth. His hands clenched open and shut numerous times. Rosie stood erect with her head held high and chin jutted outward.

"I...I...want to say...I am..." Freddie looked like he would cry at any moment.

Rosie wasn't about to help him, "Yes, I am listening. What do you want to say?"

"Not just to you," Freddie began in earnest, "to Mrs. Rollins, too."

Stella looked confused, "Yes, Freddie?"

"I really am sorry. Really, I am. I didn't mean it. I don't know why I said those mean, hurtful things about Donna. Rosie, yes, but not Donna."

"Frederick!" his dad exclaimed.

"I mean. Well, sometimes Rosie makes me mad," Freddie tried to explain.

"Frederick, this is not about Rosie. We discussed this in full detail last night. Continue," his dad instructed.

"Mrs. Rollins, Donna does have a brain. She does. School might be hard for her, but it is hard for me, too, sometimes. Your Donna is a good girl. Everyone likes her. I do, too. I had no right to say bad things. I had no right to be mean to Rosie, either. I want to apologize."

Rosie melted in front of all of them. She looked at Freddie and said, "My dad, Wilbur, said that everyone says things that they might regret from time to time, but the important thing is if you learn from your mistakes and take one step forward to find the good in everyone – even you and Mrs. Fox."

Stella put one hand over her mouth to hide a grin that was trying to escape. "Freddie, I accept your apology."

"Thank you, Mrs. Rollins. Rosie, I hope we can become friends. Well, if not friends, then I promise I will never say a mean word to you ever again."

"Rosie?" her mother said as she watched her daughter closely.

"I'm thinking about it," Rosie said mischievously as Freddie squirmed.

"You are done thinking, young lady. Answer your new friend," her mother scolded lightly.

"I'll try. Well, I'm being honest," Rosie finished.

"And?"

"And, I'm sorry about the first time we met. I'll never say a mean word to you again…I hope," Rosie said, clenching her teeth.

This time Mr. Wright turned away as if he needed to readjust his tie, then turned back again with a straight face, "Now that you two can be friends, please go to your classroom and get ready for school to begin. I would like to talk to Mrs. Rollins."

Once the children had left, Mr. Wright stood up and paced the floor in front of Stella's desk. She waited patiently with her hands folded. "I'm not quite sure how to begin," Mr. Wright started. "Now, I guess I know a little how Frederick must have felt apologizing."

"You have nothing to apologize for, Mr. Wright," Stella responded, confused again.

"That is a matter of opinion, I suppose," he said. "Have you been informed of the details surrounding the school board meeting after you left last night?"

"No."

"I have never seen a meeting so animated before. The line of people waiting to speak at the podium went all the way to the far exit. Each person was given two minutes. I started to worry that we would be there all night. The chairman put a stop to it so we could discuss the matter in a private session."

"I don't understand. These people do not know me. Was it about Donna?"

"The parents of this school definitely know about Donna. The children of our community are extremely vocal. The children of this school voiced their opinions loudly and vehemently through their parents. These children already have a sense of right and wrong at a very young age. I must admit to you that I was taken aback. The impact Rosie had on the others when she silently turned away from horrible remarks from my son sent ripples through the community. Even the first graders have been going home telling tales about Donna in their classroom. Most of these children have never seen a child with any kind of handicap before. This is new territory for them. Even so, I think more people know someone, even if indirectly, who has a disability than are willing to admit. I know I do, and that is why I am here today."

"Go on, Mr. Wright. I am listening," Stella said.

"Ten years have gone by and I have not spoken of this to anyone, not even my son, until last night." Mr. Wright turned away and said slowly, "It's funny. You never truly know how much you love someone until they are not with you. I held Freddie in my arms so tightly that I worried I would break him, but I was the one who broke. I told him the story that I am going to tell you."

Stella watched him intently as he drew up a chair and sat in front of her. He had the look of a lion tamer ready to commence training. She admired his tenacity and his vulnerability.

"Frederick is my only child. His mother died giving birth to him and his twin brother."

Stella could feel a lump forming in her throat. She swallowed and said, "I'm so very sorry."

"If that wasn't bad enough, it gets worse," Mr. Wright said, standing up again and pacing in front of Stella's desk. "I was in the waiting room with a few other expectant fathers. I remember that I had a handful of cigars ready to disburse when a nurse came into the room and called my name. She asked if the doctor could have a private word with me. I stopped and wondered what to do with the cigars. Very strange, I know, but

I just slipped them into my suit pocket and left with the nurse. The doctor sat behind a huge mahogany desk, reading from some papers. He looked up at me and...," Mr. Wright caught his breath for a moment before he could continue, "he said that he was sorry. I asked him what he was sorry about. Mothers have babies all the time. He stopped me abruptly and said that the first baby was delivered without incident. My wife was in great pain, however. The delivery team had just finished cleaning the first baby when a second appeared. This one had the cord wrapped around its neck. The doctor said that he did all he could. The baby lived but had been without oxygen for too long. The baby was severely brain damaged. My wife lost too much blood. They couldn't save her. I remember that I was at a loss for words. I took the cigars out of my pocket and tore them into tiny bits as I flung them around the room. The doctor tried to calm me, but his pronouncements were not over. He told me that I needed to decide about the fate of the second child. I had no idea what he meant. He told me that it would be better if I just let this baby die of natural causes. He would never be able to sustain a normal life. I had a duty to let the child go."

"Let him go where," Stella said softly as if she were talking to herself.

"Exactly," Mr. Wright said. "How did you know? That is exactly what I thought."

"What did you decide?"

"I let him go. God help me, I let him go," he said as he turned toward the back wall, clearly distraught. He pulled a handkerchief out of the inner pocket of his suit jacket. He wiped his eyes unashamedly, sat back down, and continued, "It haunts me to this day. The pain has crushed my heart into so many pieces that I have feared I will never be whole again. Even now there are so many regrets. I never told anyone what happened. My family and acquaintances believed that I suffered from my wife's death. We immediately left Portland to come to this tiny town so I could disappear in my depression. I was never a real father to Frederick. A nanny was hired the day we moved. I lost myself in my law practice and practically ignored my son. When I looked at him, I was seeing two children. I hated myself."

"If anyone can empathize with your plight, it is me. This time I can honestly tell you that I understand what you must have gone through and undoubtedly still are," Stella said in almost a whisper.

"I am not telling you this because I want sympathy."

"No, I know that."

"I am not telling you this because I want you to feel sorry for my son, either."

"No, I know that, too."

"I want you to know that you are not alone. I'll do everything in my power to fight for the Donnas of the world and for Frederick's twin shadow."

"How can you, I mean, what can we do?" Stella asked.

"The board voted last night about whether to accept Donna as a student in this school district. The fierce debate went on for hours. The board fought fervently about their opinions based on what the community had said. Most of the audience last night empathized with your plight. Still, others were adamant that funding is not available for everything. Some felt that priorities must be made and that didn't include this new issue, as they called it. There were even a few people in this community who stated concern that their precious town was changing color."

Stella gave him a look of disbelief.

"I'm only telling you what was said. But, in the end, I was the only one who voted yes. I wanted you to know that. I believe as you do that all children regardless of any feature, color, race, religion, size, handicap, anything, should be given the opportunity to receive an education. This won't be easy, but somehow it has to happen."

"I've been told numerous times that because there is no law that gives children like Donna any rights, I cannot demand that she go to school. I have been told that I would not win in a court of law, either."

"The current law in Oregon is one of permissive legislation.

That means school boards might but are not required to provide Special Education. I say that if there isn't a law requiring all children must receive an education, then…" Mr. Wright started to say but was interrupted.

"Then there should be. When and how do we start?"

Chapter 53
NOVEMBER 1961 – HIDDEN LAKE, OREGON

"Does it ever stop raining here?" Stella wondered as she gazed out the office window.

"A day or two in the spring, I would venture to guess," Mr. Silver said as he took off his raincoat, shook it out, and hung it up on the wall hooks.

"Look at those silly kids. They are jumping in and out of the water puddles spraying mud everywhere. Oh, wait. I changed my mind. Don't look; one of those naughty children belongs to me!" Stella shook her head.

The office door flew open. "Just wait until the principal hears about this!" Mrs. Leechfield warned. "Oh, Mr. Silver, there you are. Would you look at these two? Have you ever seen two more scruffy children in your life?" Mrs. Leechfield, the third-grade teacher, had a fist tightly wrapped around the collar of each child's coat. She was a very tall woman with a thin lined face and mousy brown hair secured in a French twist at the back of her head.

Stella looked back out the window and almost gave a sigh of relief when she noticed that her miscreants were still enjoying the forbidden activity.

"Thank you, Mrs. Leechfield, I will take it from here. Boys, have a seat. No, on second thought, stand over there in that corner. Mrs. Rollins, will you please call for Mr. BB to clean up this mess?"

"My room as well. They spread their mess wherever they could manage," Mrs. Leechfield growled as she left the office.

Stella went to the area used as the school's sick room and took two blankets down from the shelf. "Here, boys, wrap these around you. You are both shivering. I think I better call your mothers to bring you some clean clothes."

"No!" both boys shouted.

"Yes, that's a good idea, boys. In fact, I don't think I really need to talk to you right now. When your mothers come and you can get changed, then you can go back to class." Both boys seemed to melt but nodded their agreement.

It didn't take long for two young women to rush into the office. They were both wearing similarly styled dresses with an apron tied at the waist. Each had a scarf around hidden hair curlers or bobby pins. Stella could tell that one woman had hastily applied some lipstick and blush to her plain face. The other was make-up free but still pretty.

"Thank you, Mr. Silver. Thank you, Mrs. Rollins. It is nice to see you again. I am sorry for your trouble. Melvin, wait until your father gets home!" the pretty young woman said as she gave her son a light tap on his bottom and pushed him out the door. The other woman acknowledged everyone and escorted her son speedily out of the office.

"I think you can handle things in here. Seems like it will be a quiet morning. I need to work on my lesson plans for the day in my classroom. Call me if you need me," Mr. Silver said as he put some papers in a briefcase and headed toward the door. Before he opened the door, he turned back around and said, "Thank you again for your kind offer for Thanksgiving dinner this Thursday. My uncle and I are looking forward to it."

"So are we."

"We want to contribute somehow and would like to know what we can bring or do. I am sure this must be very overwhelming for all of you. You have a large enough family without us barging in."

"Don't be silly. Grandma Barbara, as the kids call her, is in seventh heaven. She loves cooking. She has been prepping all week."

"Well, my uncle Edgar said to leave that envelope on your desk and not take no for an answer. It is a holiday bonus for the men that work for him," Mr. Silver insisted, walking out the door before she could respond.

As he was leaving, Mr. Daniel Wright almost ran into him on his way into the office. "See you for Thanksgiving dinner Thursday. I have no idea how they will accommodate all of us. We may be eating on the porch!"

"Very funny," Stella said. "What is in your hand, Dan?"

"Don't you recognize it? This is quite possibly the largest turkey in the county. I had a client that preferred to pay me in poultry rather than money. The farmer butchered and cleaned the bird very nicely. Don't look like that. He didn't name him. It is all wrapped up and frozen now. Just pretend that I got it from the Mercantile."

"Barbara will be thrilled. Is there any way you could drop it by the house today?"

"Yes, of course. I was just on my way."

"Thanks."

"So, what's the latest count?" Dan asked. "Wills mentioned something about building another wing to Pretty Pink when I saw him last week at the Wander Inn."

"I told him the only wing he was going to claim would be from that bird," Stella grinned. "I also told him the priority is the log house, but I lost that one! He told me I worry too much and things just take time."

"So, when do you anticipate a move-in date?"

"We do manage to live there most weekends. I suppose Rosie and I will need to start using the school boat sometime in the future."

"On another subject and the reason that I'm here, were you able to contact the school districts I suggested?" Dan asked.

"Yes, I made appointments to visit every Special Education elementary classroom within a two-hour drive of here. I believe that I can commute that far every day. Maybe Donna only goes to school three days a week. One of those days, we could stay overnight in a motel possibly. I would have Veronica take over for me here at the school. She has experience as a school secretary. I don't really, but I am managing somehow."

"Don't count your chickens or turkeys before they are hatched," Dan said.

"We will see."

"Who else will be coming to your shindig?"

"Besides the Donaldsons and my family, we invited Simon Silver and his uncle Edgar, you and Freddie, of course, Mr. BB and his wife, my brother- and sister-in-law Sam and Shirley Surly, and believe it or not I even asked Mrs. Fox, but she declined."

"I'm surprised you left out the mayor!" Dan joked.

"I haven't met him yet," Stella said.

"Some things take time. There is no doubt in my mind that you will."

"Maybe so."

"Is there a method to your madness inviting all of us?"

"Quite possibly."

***

The children were nestled in front of the television set in the living room on Thanksgiving morning so they could watch the Macy's Thanksgiving Day parade. The adults were in the kitchen and the large attached dining room putting on the finishing touches for the great feast, as Grandma Barbara called it.

"I told you this family room extension to the kitchen would be a good idea," Wills said to Stella.

She looked at him nonplussed, "I thought the log house was the priority. Bill and you have been working on this project for a month."

"Yes, but look how good it looks and how important it will become," Bill jumped in.

"That's true," Veronica added. "Ever since you put that advertisement in the newspaper seeking out other parents with handicapped children and how you should band together for a common need, you've been inundated with responses."

"You will need a space to have those parent meetings," Bill continued.

"I doubt your little group of ladies will want to boat up to the log house and use the outhouse," Wills said.

"Outhouse? That was your priority! Bill, you said you have been working on the bathroom. I thought it was supposed to be done soon," Stella said as she looked between Bill and Wills.

"These things take time," Wills said as he opened the table to put the extra leaves in.

Veronica went over to Stella and said, "Here, help me put the tablecloth on. You have to admit the family room looks very nice."

"Just in time, too," Grandma Barbara added. "The pullout couch bed will come in handy for our guests and for the twins later."

Shirley said, "I was wondering where we were all going to sleep. You have managed to find a place for everyone even without us inviting ourselves for four days."

"Nonsense," Grandma Barbara continued, "I was getting a little tired of sharing my room with those noisy boys!"

"Thank you for giving us the funds to add on to the house," Wills said to his sister.

"Nope, nothing to thank us for," Sam said. "It just increases the value of the house."

"Always looking to increase a buck," Shirley said to her husband with a smile.

"Bill, someone is knocking at the back door. It's a little too early for our guests. Will you please see who it is?" Veronica said as she and Stella put the tablecloth on the dining room table.

The new family room was connected by a large opening to the kitchen and the dining area. At the far end was a small additional bathroom. An outside door was at the other end. Stella never would understand why it should take two men to answer the door, but both did so.

"Hey, BB, Simon, welcome, welcome. Come in. It doesn't matter that you're early. Love to have you. Maybe Stella will stop complaining about the new family room now that you have arrived," Wills said as he and Bill both shook hands with the other men.

"No, we came to bring over a couple more tables. Kids are never very good at holding plates in their laps. Hey, they are not good at keeping food on their plates when at a table. I should know – I have to clean up their mess in the cafeteria every day," BB said.

"BB convinced me that they weren't being used at school during the holiday, so we could just borrow them," Mr. Silver said. "Come out to BB's truck and help us carry them in."

A short while later, a couple of additional tables were put in the family room for the children. The women continued to work on the meal and set the table as the men walked back out to the truck.

"Thanks again," Bill said as the principal and the custodian jumped into the cab of the truck. "See you in a few hours."

"My wife, Connie, told me to remind your wives that she is bringing her world-famous pumpkin and apple pies," BB said. "I am not sure when they became world famous, but don't mention to the missus that I said that."

※

The Thanksgiving meal was a huge success. Grandma Barbara was pouring coffee as the guests were digging into their desserts. The other women stood up to help clear the table.

"No, no. You sit right back down there. I am more than capable of the clean-up," Barbara demanded. "Besides, I can tell that Stella has been itching to tell you all something. And Mr. Wright over there has been pounding the table with his fingers. Something's on his mind, too, I would venture to guess. *No, no, I've got this.*"

"Can we be excused," one of the children yelled out.

"We have a bunch of games in the living room. I get dibs on the Monopoly car piece," Rosie said.

"Since when?" one of the boys complained.

"Wait a minute, you children bring your plates into the kitchen. Clean up your tables; then you can play your game. First one done gets the car piece," Grandma Barbara said.

The race was on. The children were done in record time and ran to the living room. Stella closed her eyes and shook her head. She just knew that Rosie would somehow manage to get the car. And she was sure Rosie only wanted it because the boys did.

The grown-ups laughed. The conversation was light and easy. Sam and Shirley talked about their teaching experiences. Simon (as he told everyone to call him) recounted humorous anecdotes about being a principal and teacher combined. Once Grandma Barbara got back to the table, Dan Wright stood up and clicked his glass with a spoon. First, a toast to an incredible meal. To Grandma Barbara!"

"To Grandma Barbara!" everyone exclaimed.

"Now, if I could find a woman like her, I wouldn't be so standoffish," Dan laughed.

"Oh, please," Barbara laughed. "A good-looking man like you should have no problem at all finding a good woman. I am surprised they are not flocking around you like chickens to their morning seed."

"I am not well known. I have kept myself aloof toward others, especially women. I know, I know, hard to believe," Dan said and joined in the laughter.

"What kind of woman would you want as a wife, Dan? Maybe someone from Stella's new ladies' group would fit the bill," Wills said.

"If I were interested, I would want a woman who doesn't work for me but stands beside me and works with me," Dan said. "And, if I could find someone that cooks like Miss Barbara, well…"

Stella and Veronica looked at their husbands. Veronica took Bill's hand and said to everyone, "I believe that Dan Wright should be the first guest speaker at Stella's new ladies' group. Just what the world needs – forward-thinking men!"

"The times are changing. Men and women can work together as a team rather than divide their household duties," Stella added.

"Heaven help us all!" Wills laughed.

"What is this ladies' group everyone is talking about, Stella?" Simon asked.

"That is why I asked all of you to come today."

"Somehow I knew it wasn't because we were such enjoyable company," Sam joked.

"Watch it, hubby, or you will be doing the dishes, not Barbara," Shirley said with a wide grin.

"As all of you know, I have been on an endless and sometimes fruitless quest to find an education for Donna," Stella began. "I wish I could tell you that I have met with great success, but I cannot."

"What have you done so far?" Dan asked.

"I have not been able to go to all the Special Education classes yet, but I have called a few and was able to visit one. It has been very discouraging, I can tell you. The ones I've called told me I was welcome to visit, but it was highly unlikely my daughter would get on their roster. We would have to live in their district first, but even if we did, it was not a guarantee. I was told there are two different types of Special Education classrooms. Of the districts I was able to contact, I learned that there is a self-contained Educable Mentally Retarded class and a Trainable Mentally Retarded class. They could not tell me what option there might be for Donna without an evaluation."

Dan finished his pie and motioned to Barbara for another piece, "That doesn't surprise me. The board would make that decision."

"It upsets me that a board would even be involved. Every child should just be able to register like any other child," Stella said heatedly.

"We agree with you," Simon added. "Unfortunately, that is not the way it is."

"No, not now, but why can't it be? That is what I want to talk to you about. It seems we need to change attitudes. Society needs to change its way of thinking about those who are different or don't fit in. Only then can we advocate on behalf of our children. I believe in a real democracy, we are all equal. Look at us around this table. We are different and the same in so many ways. Still, all of us are dependent on others. We must work together to bring about change."

"Stella and I are sisters under the skin," Veronica said. "I am with you all the way."

"When I went to visit a Special Education classroom, I came away feeling like there is an option. I didn't think the class itself was very good, but I am not a teacher so I shouldn't make comments. As a parent, though, I was saddened that nothing particularly educational was occurring. The classroom was segregated from the main school. They were in a basement with stairs. Two of the students were in wheelchairs and must be carried in and out as well as to the upstairs bathroom. What was encouraging, however, was the fact that I was able to talk to some of the adults who were volunteering. Two of the women there were parents. I asked if I could buy them a cup of coffee at the corner diner. The teacher gave her consent and we left for an hour. One mother told me that her family moved eighteen times to find an appropriate classroom for her handicapped child. Eighteen times! The other woman told me that she was a neighbor to the superintendent of her school district. She became friendly with the superintendent's wife, who convinced her husband to let the child into that Special Education classroom."

"Sounds like you have been busy," Wills said. "No wonder you didn't complain as much as I thought you would about Bill and me working on the extension rather than the log house for this past month."

"Oh, I'm still not done complaining about that one. Don't you worry," Stella laughed with everyone.

"Oops, I knew I should keep my big mouth shut," Wills smiled and squeezed Stella's hand.

"I still have a few more visits to make. Some larger districts even have a Director of Special Education, but most districts do not. I have a lot more research to do."

"What does the ladies' group have to do with this?" Barbara asked.

"When I talked to the two women, I realized we had a lot in common regarding our children. I started to think that if I could start a group of parents just like us, we could advocate for our children. Maybe we could figure out ways to change the educational system we have today into something that would work for everyone tomorrow," Stella said.

Dan stood up and put his hands firmly on the table, "That is why I need to make an announcement."

All eyes turned expectantly toward him. "Would you like a third piece of my world-famous apple pie, Mr. Wright?" Mrs. BB laughed.

"Call me Dan. Yes, but no. I need to keep my slim physique if I am to attract those single women."

"Oh, that doesn't matter one bit," Sam said. "Look, I have a bit of a potbelly, but my Shirley doesn't mind one little bit."

"I don't?"

"Ladies and gentlemen, friends, I am going to run for mayor of Hidden Lake," Dan announced.

Simon Silver looked at his uncle Edgar, then at Dan Wright, "Dan, that might be a long way off. We have a mayor right now. The election isn't until next year."

"Mayor Rodger Stout has stepped down effective immediately. A few days ago, he was fishing. He claimed that he finally hooked that enormous devil catfish everyone has nightmares about. I was at the Mercantile when I overheard his wife complaining about the whole ordeal. She said that the old coot was out in the torrential downpour last week. Her husband felt the tension on his line and tugged until that monster pulled him into the lake."

"Oh, my goodness. Is he alive?" Veronica gasped.

"Yes, he was able to swim to the back deck of the Wander Inn. Ted, the bartender, called Stout's wife. She got there after her fisherman husband had finished his fourth beer and the tale got bigger. When he saw his wife, he grabbed his chest and begged her to get him to the hospital because he was having a heart attack. She said that she was going to give him one if he didn't have one already. Next thing I heard was that he needed to step down for a bit of a rest."

"Millie can be quite a terror. I bet he was more afraid of her than any devil catfish," BB laughed with everyone at the table.

"Monday morning, I am going to City Hall to put my name in to run for the interim position of mayor of Hidden Lake," Dan grinned to wholehearted applause.

Chapter 54

JUNE 1962 – HIDDEN LAKE, OREGON

ONCE THE THREE GIRLS WERE TUCKED INTO BED AND FAST ASLEEP, Stella wrapped the cozy handmade knitted shawl that Barbara had given her for Christmas around her shoulders. She gently opened the front door to the porch, hoping it wouldn't squeak like it usually did. She nudged it closed as she gingerly opened the screen door with equal concern. She stood on the front porch in the cool but not unpleasantly cold night air and surveyed the progress that they had made over the last few months. The brush had been pruned back, the grass was mowed to within an inch of the ground, the dead vines were gone off the arbor, and the many bulbs that had been planted in the fall were showing off their greenery. From her vantage point, Stella could now see the ramp as well as the boathouse that occupied a large portion of the expansive dock. She jumped from one large stone to the next on the pathway that Wills had recently installed. At the top of the ramp, she gazed out toward the lake. Stella knew at that very instant she truly did love this land. How could she not? It was beyond beautiful. She glided down the ramp toward the dock. She leaned against the boathouse wall and watched the glimmering stillness of the water. "Wills should be home soon," she said quietly to Merlin, who had followed her down to the dock. Stella sat down in the wooden chair and relaxed the soft shawl around her. Merlin put his big head on her lap as she absentmindedly ran her fingers through his silky fur. Stella looked upward and was overcome yet again by the brilliance of the night sky. The illumination dazzled her every time as if she were looking at diamonds in a large dark cave. She was sure that the quantity of stars outreached actual countable numbers. When she had lived in the big cities, the night sky never appeared so powerful. The majestic awe she felt now filled her with renewed energy and hope for a bright future.

Wills had never been this late before. Stella wasn't particularly worried. She watched the horizon as she thought about how busy they had all been this past winter. Time certainly does fly by when you are juggling so many things. Stella laughed to herself as she visualized holding onto several poles with dishes twirling at their tips. At any moment one or all could fall, and the entire act would end in disaster. She was not doing it alone, however, and that made all the difference.

She wouldn't begrudge Wills a beer or two at the Wander Inn, especially since he was the one who had been recruiting men and supplies from the mill to help build a brand-new sidewalk in front of the school. That had to be why he was so late. Tonight, he was to make the last-minute arrangements and attend to all the final details.

The girls and she took the school boat home after school. Captain Jack Carlton didn't mind adding Donna and Maddie and sometimes Merlin to his passenger list. He was a kind, older man who never complained and clearly enjoyed his work. He often told the children funny or harrowing stories during their ride home. Stella guessed that he exaggerated the factual accounts, but no one seemed to mind. He had worked at the marina his entire life but now in retirement the only thing he truly looked forward to was the daily boat ride adventures he gave the children of his town. It was hard to tell who enjoyed the time more – the children or Captain Jack.

Merlin's head popped up off Stella's lap and he gave a quick bark. Stella didn't need to ask the dog what he saw or heard. In the far distance she could make out a dark vessel that sliced through the still waters followed by a wide V shape of rippling waves. The engine noise surprisingly did not disturb the calm atmosphere as it gradually grew louder on its way to the dock.

"Toss the bow line," Stella called out confidently to Wills as he cut the engine and expertly glided the tugboat into the boat house. She grabbed the line and secured it to the front cleat. Wills jumped out of the boat and did the same with the stern line. Merlin jumped up and put his paws on Wills's shoulders, nearly knocking him back into the boat.

"Merlin, boy, settle down. It is nice to see you, too, but let me greet your mom first."

"I wasn't worried in the least," Stella wanted to say but instead threw her arms around Wills's neck as he touched her face lightly, lifted her chin, and kissed her gently.

"What a day!" Wills said, "But we are all set. Construction of the sidewalk will begin tomorrow morning at eight. So, we will all have to get up very early. Edgar and Warren assigned half the Saturday mill workers to a morning shift and the other half to the afternoon, all keeping their mill salary for the day. To see these so-called adversaries work so hard on a project that has nothing to do with the mill has been nothing less than astonishing. Everyone at the Wander Inn was talking about it tonight."

"That's where I thought you were," Stella said.

"Oh, I'm sorry. I didn't mean to be so late. It is just that they will all be working on this project you have been so adamant about. I could not refuse a drink or two. Bill was there as well. Do you think Veronica will give him a bad time, too?"

"No, no. You worry too much. I'm pleased as punch it's finally going to come together! I simply hope the men will be sober enough to do the job!"

"I am sure the wives will have a thing or two to say about that."

"We need to be there even earlier than eight because I am meeting with the PTA as well as my Donna parent group to set up the tables. Barbara will oversee the food committees for both the morning items as well as the lunch. We also will have a bake sale and a craft booth with the proceeds going to the Donna fund. We have volunteers to watch the younger children and assign tasks for the older ones. Dan and Simon have the design ready to go. The school board has approved it," Stella said. "And we received enough donations from the town to complete the job!"

"You even managed to squeeze money and the needed concrete out of the Armsteads," Wills said.

"I wish I could take the credit for that one. Actually, Barbara is in like Flynn at the local church. She took up the donation charge by passing the hat around. Pastor Powers even gave a sermon in support of community spirit. Next thing you know, the pastor was at the Mercantile summoning up guilt and dire consequences for those who do not attend church services on a regular basis. He somehow managed to sandwich in the school sidewalk and lo and behold, he did the impossible."

"Do you realize how proud I am of you?" Wills said, putting his arm around her as they walked up the ramp. "None of this would have been possible without your stubborn determination and your clever talent for getting what you want."

"I wish that were true," Stella sighed. "Starting the push for a sidewalk was one thing, but I still have not had any luck getting what is really needed, which is an education for Donna and other children like her."

"You have been working at it, though. I'll never forget that first ladies' meeting you worked so hard on. You wrote letters to the editor at the newspaper; you put in an ad about the meeting; you sent home letters with all the children in the school; you put up flyers in every store and on every telephone pole in the county. You and Veronica were unstoppable!" Wills gleamed his approval and his love toward her. They reached the house and sat down on the porch swing together.

Stella smiled in wistful memory and said, "Barbara made enough hors d'oeuvres for an army!"

Wills nodded and they both laughed loudly. "Two women showed up!"

"That was January. We decided to keep at it and to hold a meeting once a month for one, two, or even a hundred people.

"Well, maybe a hundred was a bit of a far-fetched idea, but I can dream." Stella looked up at the stars.

"February was better," Wills took her hand in his and kissed it. "Five."

"Yes, improvement. March there were ten. April and May a full dozen. See, it is just a matter of time."

"Now, it is June," Stella said. "We're still working on a name to call our little gathering. It is not easy to get people to agree on a simple little detail like a name. I thought 'Parents for Donna' would be perfect, but they had other ideas. So, for right now, we all decided that we needed to combine our efforts and do a little research. We need to know what is being done for handicapped children and what is lacking. We need to find out what the laws truly state and what we can do regarding legislation. We also want to find out what other states are doing. We want to write to the various organizations that are already formed and see what they are doing. One woman in our group is a librarian. She loves the research aspect and has given some of her student volunteers the task of finding out statistics and getting whatever information is out there. We have someone else who has a child at the Fairview Institution. She knows quite a few other parents in the same situation and will contact them."

"Little by little it is coming along."

Stella turned to him, "Did I mention that a U.S. census determined there are over four million children not receiving an education in the United States right now?"

"Yes. You said someone in your group talked about that."

"That is appalling. I never realized any of this before Donna. Or even after Donna. I just thought I could register her for school like any other child and the school would have to educate her with public tax funds."

"As I see it, our job is to come together to figure out what we want and work together to get it. This is not a problem or impossible task for you alone. I'll do all I can, and now I believe many others will help as well. I'm sorry I thought it would only be a simple little ladies' group. I was so wrong. This is important for every citizen. We must change how society thinks, not only about education, but about all individuals who don't seem to fit a typical mold. Donna taught me that in such a short amount of time. Her influence and yours have given me a fresh perspective on life, and even my value system has changed immeasurably. I believe as you do that it is time to support all children, not to reject or neglect them," Wills said as he squeezed her hand and squinted his eyes toward her in mock confusion, "But, can we get the sidewalk done first?"

Chapter 55

JUNE 1962 – HIDDEN LAKE, OREGON

"Do you believe that some things are just meant to be?" Barbara asked Stella as they set up dozens of tables on the front lawn of the school on a bright but brisk Saturday morning.

"Not without a whole lot of prodding," Stella said, turning toward her children.

"Rosie!" Stella yelled, "Be careful with Donna in that wagon. I don't think it is safe to tie Merlin up to pull Donna in that wagon. Merlin is not a horse!"

"Why not? They like it. Donna is laughing and Merlin is smiling. Watch, Mommy, he is doing it."

The twins raced over. "Don't worry, Aunt Stella, we will take care of them."

Rosie huffed dramatically and said, "I do not need you to order us around. Merlin and I know what we are doing,"

"Where is Maddie?" Stella looked around.

"I don't want to take care of her, too. I have my hands full."

"I have her," Veronica said as she dropped off another casserole dish on the table and held Maddie with her other hand. "Maddie is going to play with the other children. We have some teenage girls watching them in the second-grade classroom."

"I want Merlin to take me in the carriage!" Maddie cried.

"The second-grade classroom is much more fun," Veronica said. "There are a lot of books."

Maddie skipped off happily with one of the girls that Veronica had signaled over. "Thank you, Aunt Veronica. You are a life-saver!" Rosie said. "Do you think you could work your magic and get rid of your boys?"

"Rosie!" her mother scolded. The children vanished and were rapidly out of earshot.

"I was talking about the weather," Barbara said, returning to the original topic, as she chomped on a donut.

"Oh," Stella said as she also picked up a donut.

"The weather is crisp and dry. The sun is as bright as I can remember in many a day. This is the perfect day for a sidewalk. Some things are just meant to be."

"A day like this was made for building a sidewalk," the principal of the school said as he walked toward the women.

"Why, hello, Mr. Silver. Would you like a donut?"

"I told you to call me Simon, especially now that the school year has just ended. This is the first weekend of the summer and I can feel change is in the air. Even the superintendent is coming. He said that he intends to roll up his sleeves and take part in this great adventure."

Stella creased her forehead and shaded her face from the sun, "I am not so sure this will be much of an adventure."

"Of course it will be. This is all very exciting," Veronica said, putting on her wide-brimmed hat and handing one to her best friend. "My new creation I made just for you."

"Perfect! Thank you."

Mr. Silver glanced around expectantly, "I wonder how many onlookers versus workers will show up?"

"It is still a bit early. Wills said the crew from the mill plan on being here at eight," Stella said.

Barbara surveyed the immediate area and said to Veronica, "Where are those boys when I need them? Come help me get some more items from the house. Where is Rosie's wagon? We could use that!"

"Look," Stella pointed out, stopping Barbara and Veronica in their tracks.

People strolled over from every direction. Some cars parked across the street or in the school parking lot. Most of the people and children just walked to the school. The women were overwhelmed with questions. They started to hand out assignments and orders as if they were in charge. Soon everyone had a task to do or at least waited patiently until they were told what to do. Some people took their own initiative and independently started to work. Mr. Silver immediately went over to help the men with the equipment and supplies.

Dan Wright weaved his way through the crowd with his son. "Hello, Stella."

"Oh, Mayor Dan and Freddie. I am so glad you could make it," Stella smiled.

"Stop that. I told you repeatedly to call me Dan," he said.

"Yes, Mr. Wright, Mayor," she laughed.

"Pastor Powers said that he wants to say a small prayer and give a few words of advice before the actual sidewalk work begins. I better go find him and the other big shots to make sure the stage is ready," Dan said.

"Heaven help us all!" Stella raised her eyes toward the sky.

"A little praying wouldn't hurt you any, my girl," Barbara scoffed at Stella.

Freddie looked up to his father and said, "Dad, I am going to find Rosie and the twins."

"They are wheeling Donna around in the wagon. When you see them, would you please tell them that I said they must untie Merlin from the wagon? He shouldn't be pulling it," Stella said.

"Wow, cool!" Freddie was off like a shot.

Mayor Dan watched his son run off toward town. "You ladies certainly know how to organize an event. Would you look at all this food and the tables with crafts and cakes? Heaven knows what else you have in mind. Is there any way that I could convince you to run the city council?"

"Be careful what you wish for, Mayor."

Veronica took Mayor Dan's arm and said, "Off with you now. Find Pastor Powers and tell him to be quick about it."

"We don't have all day," Stella added.

"Well," Veronica smirked at Stella, "We actually do have all day. We just don't want him to take up the whole day with his preaching."

"I heard that, young lady," Barbara said as she turned around frowning.

"I thought she went back to the house," Veronica whispered to Stella as they hastily headed to the other tables being set up.

The tables were designed with posters that the children had made as well as various items that were being donated to sell for what Stella continued to call 'Donna's cause.' A cafeteria type of table was fully loaded with a wide assortment of food that anyone could take free of charge at any time while they worked. One of the Hidden Lake Elementary School parents brought over a large barbecue. Soon there were three more barbecues lined up together. The men had finished gathering the lumber, concrete, and other supplies that they would need to start the project.

"Ladies and gentlemen, boys and girls," Mayor Wright began. "Thank you all for coming today. First, I would like to introduce you to some familiar faces."

The crowd gathered around and watched the four men that were standing on a small makeshift wooden stage that BB had made the day before. The noises gradually subsided as they waited for whatever these men intended to say. Stella turned to Veronica and whispered again, "I'm not sure why we need all this grandstanding."

"I don't know," Veronica whispered back. "I think it's kind of sweet."

"You would," Stella said aloud.

"I am Mayor Dan Wright as you all know. I want to thank you again for voting for me. It has been a privilege…"

Superintendent Victor moved the mayor over quickly and thanked him as he took the loudspeaker from his grip. He addressed the crowd with his shrill voice, "Greetings, fellow citizens!"

"This ought to be good," Stella whispered to Veronica.

"Sshhh, you are being sarcastic again."

"I am Superintendent Victor. I oversee the entire school district, which includes this tiny hamlet of Hidden Lake."

"Hamlet? Are we in England?" Stella rolled her eyes. Veronica just giggled.

"As you know," Superintendent Victor continued, "we on the school board have been working diligently to get this very important agenda item on the school bond voting ballot. Unfortunately, we couldn't do so, nor we were able to requisition any money for this particular project, but luckily, we didn't need to as it happened. Now, with your cooperation, our hard work has come to fruition."

"Thank you, Superintendent Victor," Mr. Silver said as he took the bullhorn away. "Thank you, everyone. So, let's begin…"

Mr. Silver was not able to finish either. Mayor Wright whispered something in his ear. Mr. Silver said to the crowd, "We will begin right after a quick (and I do mean quick) prayer of good wishes from our Reverend Powers."

"It's Pastor Powers. I am a minister, not a reverend," he said to Mr. Silver as he walked in front of the men. Pastor Powers was a stout middle-aged no-nonsense type of man with thick dark hair that receded at the temples, a clean-shaven face, and dense eyebrows. His eyes were intense as he commanded center stage wherever he went. His voice was known to boom across a large congregation inside or outside of his church. People stopped talking when he looked at them as if he were a classroom teacher of first graders on the first day of elementary school.

"Members of our community, I welcome you!" Pastor Powers bellowed. "If the church is the soul of our village, then the school is its heart."

Stella and Veronica tuned him out as they had to turn away. "Village?" Veronica said as they both tried not to laugh. Barbara glared at them both. They hastily turned back and tried to pay attention.

Pastor Powers was standing tall and at the height of his own personal glory, "Together we can build a town that we can all be proud of. We are all in this together. We can do it!"

Mayor Wright jumped in front of the preacher and yelled, "Let the sidewalk begin!"

The audience clapped wildly and cheered their approval. The men on the stage shook hands. The women unwrapped the bowls and plates at the food tables. Other women at the craft tables set up their wares and announced that they were open for business. Mr. Silver took over a large blueprint plan and unrolled it in front of Edgar, the mill plant manager. Warren, the foreman for the sidewalk construction, looked over their shoulders. Soon Warren started to give orders on the project. Within moments, the men started to build the sidewalk, which would extend from the parking lot at the side of the school and run completely across the front of the building to finish at the far end of the block next to Main Street downtown.

The bustling activity of the townspeople brought about a cheerful cohesiveness. Everyone took part in one way or another. Some people were enjoying themselves just by chatting with their neighbors. Others were fully involved with the actual work on the sidewalk itself. Stella felt like she was being pulled at both ends as she darted from one task to the next while she answered questions repeatedly.

"Oh, there you are, Mrs. Rollins," Pastor Powers said behind Stella.

Stella jumped and almost dropped a large cake she had been positioning on the sale donation table. "Pastor Powers. My, you gave me a bit of a start."

"So sorry. I didn't mean to startle you. I wanted to thank you for your leadership on this very important community event."

"Thank you, but I cannot take the credit. I am not sure that there is anyone in this town who does not want to see a sidewalk built. This is something that has been needed for a very long time and we finally were able to find the time and resources to get it done."

"Thanks to your persistence and efforts, I would say," Pastor Powers said with a nod of encouragement. "If there is anything I can do for you, well please don't hesitate to ask."

"Well, actually there is," Stella said with great confidence and eagerness.

"I was thinking along the lines of saying a nice prayer or a mention to the congregation," Pastor Powers replied, frowning.

"I was thinking about using your church basement once or maybe twice a month," Stella smiled.

"Well, now, let's see. I'm not sure when we could arrange that. Saturday and Sunday are for church events, obviously. Monday is my day off. Tuesday is Bingo night. Wednesday is the Bible reading class. Thursday is split between the crafters' corner and the men's activity night. And Friday is the teen group. That night is the most worrisome. Those kids play the wildest songs on a record player and jump around. They call it dancing. They have even called those so-called dances by animal names," Pastor Powers said. Stella just laughed.

"How about Monday?" Stella asked. "You don't need to be there. This is for the group I am trying to organize to help figure out how to educate children with various handicaps. We had a full dozen people at our last meeting at the Pretty Pink House. I am not sure we could squeeze in any more. Your church basement would work perfectly."

"I suppose that would work, but I need your assurance that your group would clean up afterwards and put the chairs away," Pastor Powers said.

"Absolutely," Stella said. "You are a gem!"

Pastor Powers blushed and turned away when he heard someone call his name.

The day was a huge success. The camaraderie of the community had never reflected such joyous spirit. As the sun started to slide slowly toward the horizon, the tail end of the townspeople picked up their supplies or helped to clean the area. Wills used a trowel on the last foot of concrete to smooth it to a fine even surface. Unbeknownst to anyone he surreptitiously etched the name Stella at the very edge of the still damp mixture.

Stella and Veronica stood close to the school building and

chatted with a few of the other ladies. "Looks like the reverend is about to speak," Stella said.

"He is a minister," Barbara corrected her.

"This must signal the end of our project. Congratulations to all of us!" Veronica said as she lifted a mug of coffee.

Stella turned her head to the back of the assembled group, "Who is that?" she asked Veronica and Barbara.

"My goodness, it's that reporter from the television nighttime news," Veronica exclaimed.

"And a cameraman," Stella said. "Who called them and why are they here?"

Pastor Powers ascended onto the tiny stage to address the townspeople that were still there. "Do not escape now, my fellow community members; we still have the dedication and closing ceremony. I am not done yet! Oh, I see that the news is here. Welcome to our fair city," he exclaimed joyfully.

He received enthusiastic laughs and a few silly comments. Pastor Powers was very good natured, and lighthearted banter never bothered him. "We have a number of people to thank for this amazing feat," he said loudly.

Stella and Veronica tried to pay attention to him but were distracted by a commotion behind him coming from the downtown area. The twins were racing full speed toward them. Barbara immediately noticed them as well. Her eyes opened wide and she gasped, "Good heavens, I hope they don't disrupt Pastor Powers's talk."

Oblivious to the confusion or to the expressions of the people who watched, Pastor Powers continued, "We must never take things for granted. This sidewalk did not get here by itself."

The twins reached their mother and were completely out of breath. Anton whispered in Veronica's ear. She put a hand over her mouth. Stella looked at her with surprise.

The minister was full of steam as he thanked the school and parents and their children and the town and the sponsors. He was getting to the end of his speech when he added, "There is one person that we need to bring up to this stage and give our wholehearted applause of appreciation. She has been tireless in this and so many other..."

He was not able to finish his sentence. Many weeks later he would tell his congregation about how his vision blurred when two women flew over the new sidewalk and raced down the road in a flurry of temper like a wild whirlwind on an unknown fateful quest.

"She did what?"

Chapter 56
JUNE 1962 – HIDDEN LAKE, OREGON

Stella's husband and her closest friends were right on her heels, but she saw only what was ahead of her. Donna sat completely still in the little Red Flyer wagon. Her tiny fingers were wrapped securely around the edges of the wagon. Donna looked flushed like a serene china doll. Her eyes were wide open and darted side to side. Droplets of water fell off her bangs onto her round pink-tinged cheeks. She did not cry.

Rosie sat on the ground next to the wagon with her arms around Merlin as she wiped his wet fur with the sleeve of her blouse. Rosie was crying.

Stella picked up Donna gently and cradled the child in her arms.

"I'm sorry, Mommy," Rosie said between sobs.

Stella put a hand on her oldest child's head and slid her fingers down the silkiness of her hair, then touched her cheek with the back of her fingers. She petted Merlin a couple of times before she turned with a ferocity that she had never known.

Before anyone could say or do anything, Stella darted up the steps to Hidden Hazel's Soda Fountain Café. The fury in Stella's demeanor left the onlookers stunned. Wills started toward his wife to be by her side, but Veronica stopped him.

"Let me go. I have to help her!" Wills yelled.

Veronica gripped Wills's arm tightly. "No, she needs to do

this on her own. We will be there if she needs us. This has been brewing a long time."

Wills knew that he could have easily escaped Veronica's grasp, but he also realized that she was right. He would support his wife no matter what, but this was beyond his control. When it concerned her children, Stella was made of steel.

From the shop's porch came a scream that shredded the gentle fabric of the once sleepy town. Mrs. Lillian Fox stood in the middle of the doorway to her shop. Her hands clutched each side of the open-door frame as if she were holding it up to prevent entrance for anyone.

"Get that creature away from me! It's not fair. She should be in an institution, too!" Lillian Fox shrieked.

"How dare you throw a bucket of icy cold water on my child and our sweet dog!" Stella screamed.

"I told them to go away," Mrs. Fox tried unsuccessfully to explain.

"Are you deranged? What makes a supposedly normal individual do such horrific things? This is beyond contemptible and I won't have it!"

"It is not my fault that your children are misbehaved beasts!" Mrs. Fox yelled even louder.

"The only monster that I can see around here is you!"

Mrs. Fox looked frantic. She glared menacingly at Stella and hissed like an outraged snake, "You and that freak show of yours came into this town and destroyed it. No one wants all your creepy movie extras around our nice, easy-going town!"

"I thought I had seen my fair share of ignorant, simple-minded lowlife, but you are without a doubt the worst creature on earth!"

"You think you are so high and mighty. Those undisciplined horrid children of yours think they can do whatever they want. Well, I will tell you that I for one will not stand for it. They got what they deserved!"

The tone of the argument was at a fever pitch. The screaming insults reverberated throughout the town. Numerous people gathered around to witness the event. Pastor Powers started to walk toward the calamity, but Veronica stopped him as well. He said that he understood and would give it a few more minutes until he had to intervene for the safety and goodwill of all.

"What exactly did my children do that would make you lose your mind?"

"I have not lost my mind. They are not allowed in my store. I have told that despicable short girl numerous times that she was not allowed to read the comic books without buying one first. Did she listen to me? *No.* Did she do what I told her? *No!*" Mrs. Fox was squealing in an almost incomprehensible madness.

Stella was dumbfounded. She narrowed her furious eyes to tiny slits and said, "Are you trying to tell me that you threw a bucket of frigid water on a handicapped child and a lovable dog because Rosie was reading a comic book?"

"Do you ever watch your children and take care of them? They have been pushing that stupid wagon up and down the street all day."

"The town is not exactly large. We knew where they were. They came back and forth to the sidewalk construction area numerous times. They went to the beach with BB for a while, also," Stella explained, clearly confused.

"That sidewalk joke of yours has caused me and all the other honest store owners to lose business and it's all because of you!" Mrs. Fox continued as her face reddened significantly. "I did not make one cent today. Not one cent!"

"Are you blaming that on Rosie? We asked you to come. You were invited many times. You refused. Even the Armsteads came. They donated a great deal toward this project. Lynn Armstead even told me that since they became sponsors, they have increased their sales. We advertised a list of donations. We did ask you. You refused!"

Mrs. Fox ignored her and said menacingly, "That midget girl over there that you call Rosie came into my nice shop and plopped down on the floor next to the comic book section. I told her to get out, but she said that she was trying to decide which book to get. I am too smart for her. I knew she just wanted to read all of them for free."

"Veronica and I gave our children some money to go get a treat because they had been watching Donna all day," Stella tried to explain.

Mrs. Fox continued without regard to Stella or what was said, "Then those Negro boys came up to the porch and stood erect like sentries at a palace guarding both sides of the doorway. They each had a long stick like a branch that they must have stolen from a tree. I don't know what goes on in the vacant minds of those scrawny black boys."

"They were probably pretending to be soldiers!"

"Soldiers. That will be the day," Mrs. Fox jeered at Stella as she noticed Veronica race to the porch, tossing off those that were trying to hold her back.

"I will have you know that my husband, a black man I might add, was a soldier in World War II," Veronica said in her most deliberate tone. "If my children want to have a healthy imagination, then good for them!"

"They are no good, I tell you. I took my broom and tried to sweep them off my porch. Then that mongrel mad dog ran up the steps and tried to attack me! He growled and showed his teeth. As I ran to get a bucket of water to save myself, Rosie ran out the door to escape my wrath. She told that frightful dog to go. Just as I was throwing the water at him, he jumped in front of Donna. It was his fault that she got wet, not mine!" Mrs. Fox glowered at the stunned group.

Stella was beyond anger. She didn't yell, but her fierce demeanor left nothing to the imagination of the onlookers. "Don't you ever do anything to our children again! Do you hear me? Do you understand?"

"Don't look at them. Don't talk to them," Veronica said with equal menace.

"Get out of my sight! You are not welcome in my store!" Mrs. Fox screamed.

"With pleasure. We wouldn't set foot in this sorry place if

our lives depended on it!" Stella said as she shifted Donna to her other hip. Wills rapidly reached her side and took Donna in his arms. Veronica took Stella's arm and both women resolutely walked down the steps into the street as the crowd dispersed in different directions.

Mrs. Fox turned around abruptly and slammed the door of her shop, flipping the closed sign over in the window. The blinds were promptly pulled down so no one could see inside her store.

"I have never been so upset in my lifetime. I don't like how it feels. I need to walk away or catch my breath or something. I don't know. When people get angry at each other, terrible things can happen. It's just not right," Veronica said to no one in particular.

"How can someone be so prejudiced and hurtful against others? I don't understand it," Stella said to Pastor Powers, who came to stand next to both women.

He shook his head sadly and said, "I wish I had a divine easy answer for both of you, but I do not."

"I am afraid it happens more than you know. Discrimination happens all the time and in places you wouldn't expect," Veronica added.

Bill put his arm around his wife. "Veronica made us move here because she could no longer accept the inequality that we saw daily when we lived in Chicago. We thought we could just assimilate easily into a small town that wasn't accustomed to race riots and dissension. This isn't the first time or the last that people will dismiss or be hurtful to someone who might appear different than they are. I'm afraid that not all people are thought of as just another ordinary person equal to anyone else."

"How do you handle it so calmly, Veronica?" Stella asked her best friend. "You are always so nice to everyone. I am the one people should complain about. I am the one with the quick temper and irritating attitude."

"Well, I wouldn't go that far," Wills tried to laugh.

"Oh, don't be so sure, Wills," Veronica did laugh. "I thought I had seen Stella in all of her myriad emotions. I do believe that today was her worst, however."

"Years ago, I noticed some people who treated you poorly for no apparent reason whatsoever. I just thought they were fools," Stella said.

"You got that right," Barbara said as she joined them. "It goes way back, Stella. Prejudice eats at your soul. It happens here, there, and everywhere. It happened to my family and my parents' family and their parents' family and further back. It happens today, too."

Pastor Powers looked at his newly formed congregation, "Our only hope is to teach our children right and wrong. Show the people the error of their ways. Be good role models and rule by example."

"I always thought those who appeared somewhat other than ordinary were by far the more interesting. Doesn't it seem like people would be curious and want to know more about those differences rather than be hurtful or ignore them?" Stella thought first to herself but then said the words out loud. "It is the behavior that should be ignored, not the person. There is always a root cause for any and all behavior. I know that...oh, no. Oh, no. How could I do that? What's wrong with me?"

"Stella, what are you talking about?" Wills said.

"I didn't ignore her. I let my anger take over. I said hurtful things!" Stella looked stunned. "Wills, I want to go to our log house up the lake. Can you please help me get the girls and our things? I want to leave right away."

"We need to help with the clean-up."

Pastor Powers understood and said quickly, "We have so many helpers that I am afraid you would just be in the way. Let us handle it."

Veronica looked at Stella and noticed how shaken she was. "We've got this. You go home."

"I want to go to the log house. I want to get away," Stella answered but didn't look at her.

342 | Uniquely Stella

Chapter 57

JUNE 1962 – HIDDEN LAKE, OREGON

THREE DAYS LATER

"Donna, no!"

Rosie's screech vibrated off the walls of the living room and into the kitchen where Stella and Wills were enjoying a quiet cup of coffee after the breakfast dishes had been cleaned and put away. They looked at each other with wordless exasperated thoughts. Wills wiped his eyes and forehead before he pushed back his chair and stood up. Stella was already at the swinging double door that separated the kitchen from the main room.

"What is going on here?" Wills said as he hastily caught up with Stella and stood behind her.

"Donna hit Merlin! Bad Donna!" Rosie yelled at her sister.

"It was Rosie's fault," Maddie said.

"No, it wasn't, you little baby tattletale," Rosie sneered at her youngest sister.

"I am not a baby," Maddie cried. "Rosie took Donna's hand and made her stroke Merlin's fur."

Rosie looked up at her parents and said, "I was trying to teach Donna how to pet Merlin, but she hit him. Even baby Maddie knows how to pet Merlin."

Stella looked directly at her eldest daughter. "Rosie, you must understand that Donna doesn't understand what you want her to do."

"She probably never will," Wills added.

"Well, I don't believe it!" Rosie jutted out her chin with that stubborn expression she was famous for in her family.

"All the experts have told us that," her mother said.

"Do you believe them?"

"I don't know what I believe."

Wills speedily walked around Stella and the girls to pick up Donna when she started to make loud guttural noises. "Are you all right, Donna?" he asked her.

"She doesn't understand you," Stella said.

"Well, here is what I do know for certain. Donna needs a change. She is wet and a bit smelly." Wills handed the squirming child to Stella.

"I'll give her a bath, change her, and brush her teeth," Stella said.

"Rosie, please take the dog and your sister outside for a little while so your mother can focus on Donna."

"Fine, but this is not fair. Poor Merlin. He will be so confused. First, he gets water thrown on him, then Donna hits him, and now you are making him go outside. He is going to think that no one wants him. Come, Merlin." Rosie deliberately stomped her feet all the way to the outside kitchen doorway. She flung the screen door open and collided with two very tall men. Merlin instantly recognized the visitors and acknowledged them both with his playful high jumps, light barking, and a wild swinging tail.

"Whoa, easy Merlin boy," Bill said as he rubbed Merlin's face and patted the top of the dog's head with his hands.

"Hello, Mr. Wright and Uncle Bill," Rosie said. "What are you doing here? You didn't call ahead to tell us you were coming."

"It's a little difficult to call when you don't have a telephone," Mr. Wright smiled.

"Maybe someone should tell the mayor's office that there are people in this crazy town without electric power and no phone. There should be a law against that. I bet it is dangerous." Rosie glared at Mr. Wright.

Bill cut in rapidly, "Rosie, will you please let your parents know that we are here?"

Rosie opened the screen door and yelled at the top of her lungs, "Mom! Wilbur! Two men who didn't give us prior warning are on our front porch!"

"Rosie, maybe it would be better if you just went to get them?" Bill suggested.

"I don't think so. Wilbur threw me out. I think they want to have an argument."

Wills came around the corner to the side kitchen door toward the front porch. "Bill, Dan, come in, come in. Glad to see you. Coffee is on. Please sit at the table and I will fetch it."

Rosie huffed off as she bounced down the few steps and sulked on her way to a wooden bench that faced the lake. "I didn't want to hear what you have to say anyway."

"Rosie is certainly in a foul mood," Dan Wright remarked as he watched her leave.

"She wants Donna to do more than she is capable of learning," Wills sighed as he returned with the coffee pot and three mugs, "I am not so sure Donna will ever be able to do even the simplest of tasks."

"What does Stella think?" Dan asked as he poured out the coffee for each of them.

"She is afraid to even talk about it. I keep hoping that there will be a breakthrough of some kind to help not only Donna, but all of us. I just don't know. I never realized that being a parent of a handicapped child would be so difficult. Still, I can't complain. The one who must manage all of it and take the brunt of all the backlash is Stella, not me. I want to help, but when I try to handle even Rosie, I end up losing."

"Don't beat yourself up so much, Wills. I am beginning to think that Rosie may be more of a handful than Donna," Bill said.

"Rosie is a big baby," Maddie said as she crawled out from under the kitchen table.

"You are a little scamp. Come here, Maddie," Bill said as he picked her up to set her on his lap.

Dan took a sip of his coffee, then set down the cup, "We came to tell you that there is quite a commotion going on in town. I think Stella and you need to be there to see what is going on."

"I'm not so sure Stella will want to go right now. She is still fretting about her encounter with Mrs. Fox."

"That is what we are talking about," Bill said. "The children of the town have put together a demonstration. They are protesting Hidden Hazel's Soda Fountain Café!"

Chapter 58

JUNE 1962 – HIDDEN LAKE, OREGON

A FEW HOURS LATER

The streets of Hidden Lake never saw much traffic. Today, however, the corner of Main Street and Hidden Lake Road was littered with cars and bikes parked haphazardly in any space they could be squeezed into. Children and adults stood in small and large groups chatting amicably while turning their attention now and then to the fairly large number of children parading in front of Hidden Hazel's Soda Fountain Café. The children, of varying ages, all carried handmade signs decrying their protests of real or imagined slights that they determined had been done to them. A cameraman and a recognizable youthful news reporter stood on the opposite corner to interview anyone and everyone that they could convince to go on the air without compensation.

"Yes, ladies and gentlemen of our extended viewing audience throughout our great county, this is Larry Lowden with an update on the children's strike in the tiny village of Hidden Lake. We are now in the third day of political upheaval as these kids make their demands known."

The cameraman looked up from his camera and rolled his eyes before he twirled one finger in the air swiftly. He pantomimed a quick slice across his neck to indicate that the reporter needed to finish up rapidly. He looked back into the camera lens, hoping it would all be over soon and they could move on to something a bit more important or at least newsworthy.

Larry Lowden was in his element and completely ignored the man behind the camera. His only interest was to stare into the camera lens that reflected his image. "We will be back after these important words from our sponsors. This has been Larry Lowden in Hidden Lake reporting live as the news of the world goes marching by. Back to you, Chester."

Felix, the middle-aged cameraman, shut off the camera and glared at Larry Lowden. "Goes marching by? Are you crazy?"

"Isn't this exciting? We have never witnessed a protest march before! This is one for the ages!" Larry Lowden said.

Felix stared at him with a look of annoyance. "I asked to be put on the national news desk and the next thing I knew a camera was shoved into my hands and I was told to hightail it to Hidden Lake, the backwoods of nowhere land."

Larry's eyes opened wide as he talked into his microphone, "Chester, can you hear me? We have some late-breaking news here. Switch to us immediately. Forget the advertisement. This is more important."

With a quick gesture to the cameraman, Larry Lowden jumped to attention. As the cameraman counted down from five, Larry looked at his reflection and hurriedly patted down his Brylcreem-tamed hair. The cameraman pointed to Larry. "Ladies and gentlemen, we have breaking news. This is Larry Lowden with the latest lowdown. Coming down the street at this very moment in an ultra-fast walk are the perpetrators of this whole calamity. It's anybody's guess whether they will be the strike breakers or instigate further disruption. Felix, turn the camera for just a moment to let our viewing audience see the huge mongrel, the short girl, and her mentally retarded sister as well as the mother who started it all. Let's see if we can get a close-up and hopefully an interview."

The only truth to the whole debacle was that Stella was indeed walking as fast as she possibly could. Wills carried Donna while Bill carried Maddie. Rosie and Merlin ran in front of them and headed directly to the shop, where Veronica and her twin boys were waiting for them.

"What is going on here?" Stella asked Veronica as she tried to catch her breath.

"The kids feel an injustice has been done because of the incident with Merlin and Donna. They also presented more grievances than I can remember to that reporter over there," Veronica answered. "My mother just left to find Pastor Powers in hopes that he might be able to end this."

"Bill, can you find Mr. Silver as well? He has a lot of influence with these children. Thanks. Wait for me here," Stella said as she jumped up the few steps and walked determinedly into Hazel's shop.

Stella's first surprise was that the door was unlocked. The second surprise was that Mrs. Lillian Fox sat perfectly still in the last booth at the back of the vacant, dimly lit store.

Mrs. Fox stared directly at Stella, "I wondered how long it would take you to figure it out."

Stella nodded and said, "It took me longer than it should have. You said the word 'too.' I don't know why I didn't grasp that immediately. Maybe my anger clouded my thoughts."

"I know," Mrs. Fox said with tears blurring her vision. "Why are you here now? Did you come to gloat or bask in my downfall?"

"I came to apologize," Stella replied.

"Why?"

"I let my emotions get the better of me. I reacted without thinking that your responses must have come from a hurt deep within you," Stella said.

Mrs. Fox uncharacteristically let her guard down. She folded her fingers and placed her hands on her mouth, and allowed her tears to drain down a scarred, drawn face.

Stella sat down across from Mrs. Fox and took a napkin from the container on the table. She reached over and handed it to the shop owner. Stella said, "If anyone in the world can understand your grief, I think it must be me. Is her name Hazel?"

Mrs. Fox nodded her head yes.

"Is she at the Fairview Institution in Salem?" Stella asked.

"Yes, Fairview. Formerly known as the Oregon State Institution for the Feeble-Minded," Mrs. Fox said. "I truly believed Eazel would be trained there. They could provide her with training and an education. I was wrong. I was wrong in so many ways and in so many things. I didn't know then, but I know now."

"Coffee?" Stella asked.

Mrs. Fox nodded. Stella walked behind the counter and poured two cups of coffee into the diner mugs. She headed back toward the table and put the drinks down. Stella had pulled out a chair and sat without comment when she noticed that Mrs. Fox continued to sit in a forlorn hunched posture. Mrs. Fox breathed heavily while she wiped her face with the apron that had been tied around her body. She absentmindedly put sugar and cream into her coffee from containers that were on the table.

"Not a day goes by that I don't think about Hazel and admonish myself for what I did – for what we did. For what my husband convinced me to do. Why didn't you put your Donna into an institution?" Mrs. Fox asked without looking up.

"I did," Stella replied.

Mrs. Fox looked at her for a long time without comment, then said, "Can I ask you what happened?"

"Yes, if I can ask the same of you."

"It's not a pretty story."

"Neither is mine," Stella said.

"Did your husband make you, or convince you that it was the only thing you could do?"

"Yes and no." Stella wasn't trying to be evasive, but it appeared that way and she knew it.

"Is it hard to talk about?" Mrs. Fox said without sympathy.

"In my opinion, there is nothing harder than denying one's own child," Stella began.

Another tear escaped down Mrs. Fox's solemn face, but Stella remained steadfast in her resolve to tell the truth of her experiences. She began slowly, "I won't bore you with all the minute details as I am sure you will understand due to your own misguided beliefs or assumptions. When Donna was born, I was told by doctors and other experts that it would be a mistake to take my baby home and try to raise her by myself. Even my family was skeptical at first, but they eventually came around and now they love her maybe as much as I do. Donna had a serious accident one day. This was after my husband had left me for another woman and I needed to find employment. The babysitter did not attend to her as I had hoped she would. I can only blame myself for not being there. She was in the hospital when the doctors told me in no uncertain terms that Donna belonged in an institution so she could receive better care than I could give her. I agreed. I hated myself. I was angry and blamed everyone, even God. I wanted to do whatever was right so I thought if I could just visit Donna often, that would be a good place to start. It wasn't until I brought my other daughter, Rosie, with me to visit Donna that I knew without a shadow of a doubt that Donna had to come home. Rosie said she was not going home, and she would stay there to live with Donna. How could I expect to take one of my children home with me and not the other? How could I deny one child because she had something wrong with her? I created that child, so I was responsible for her. No one else should bear the burden of care – not my family, the government, society, or even God. That is what I truly believed at the time. I needed to raise this child just as much as I needed to raise my other two children. I knew it would be hard. I did not know it would be as difficult as it has been, though. I also know that it won't get any easier. Yet, this is something I must and will do no matter what. What others choose is for them to decide. What society does to accept these children is for all of us to decide."

Each woman took a sip of her coffee and put her cup down. Mrs. Fox started her story immediately without any acknowledgment of Stella's tale.

"Pearl Harbor might live in infamy for the world, but for me I will always remember December 7, 1941, as the day that changed my life forever because that was the day my daughter was born. My husband, Elmer, and I had been married for ten years. We had given up hopes of having a child, so it was a surprise when I got pregnant beyond the typical age of motherhood. I was thirty-two years old. We were so excited.

"Elmer didn't leave my side at the hospital. He brought me candy and flowers and told me that he loved me more than anything in the world. I had never been happier in my entire life. The horrors of the war swirling around the world did not seem to faze us at that moment in time. A few days later just before I was to be released from the hospital, a couple of doctors came into my room. A nurse followed them in with Hazel wrapped in a pink blanket. She handed me the baby. The doctor told Elmer and me to look closely at the baby. Elmer said that a baby was a baby and they start to look like their parents in a few months. The doctors both shook their heads sadly. I was confused. I did not know why they had that strange look on their faces. The next words are a blur in my mind. Elmer got very upset. He yelled at everyone in the room, including me. A big man came into the room and held Elmer back when he tried to punch the doctor who was talking. Elmer turned his anger onto me. He told everyone it was my fault because I gave birth to a mentally retarded child when I was clearly too old to even have a baby. He said that he refused to take this child home. She would destroy our lives and ruin his business. I said he was wrong, but he told me he would make whatever decisions that needed to be made as he was the man of the family. It was not for me to have any say in this matter. I truly don't know if I agreed with him or if I thought I had to do what my husband told me to do.

"I can still hear Elmer's words ringing in my head. He told me that if I dared to bring that deformed child of mine home, then he would leave and never return. Still, against his wishes, I brought Hazel home. Elmer enlisted in the Army. On June 6, 1944, Elmer died on what we now call D-Day. The very next day, I enrolled Hazel at Fairview. I never saw her again, but she lives within my soul. I can feel myself harden day by day with hatred and weakness."

Stella sighed. She grabbed a napkin from the holder on the

table and wiped her eyes. She handed another one to Mrs. Fox and said, "Can I call you Lillian?"

That made Mrs. Lillian Fox laugh, "Of all the things you might have said after my story, I have got to admit that I didn't expect that. I never want to be called Mrs. Fox ever again!"

Stella nodded sadly and glanced around the dreary room. "Where is your brother-in-law Mickey who's usually behind the counter when you are teaching?"

"He's a good-for-nothing lowlife. That's what he is. He deserted me, too, like all the rest. Just like his brother, my husband Elmer. But Elmer lied. He didn't care a whit about anyone except himself. Why did he profess his love and undying devotion? How could someone love me and leave me? He was weak, not like me. I've always been strong." Lillian Fox stopped with a strangled cry stuck in her throat. She looked up at Stella with a lost forlorn look on her wet face and said in a voice that brought a chill down Stella's spine, "If anyone did the deserting, it was me. I was the fool. No, I *am* the fool!"

"Here's what we are going to do," Stella started to say.

Lillian looked up at her in surprise, "I doubt there is anything we can do. I am the laughingstock of my own town; even the children hate me. Worst of all, I have a daughter who does not know me. I am ruined."

"The time has come to change all that. You can start over and erase some of the turmoil of the past. It reminds me of a chalkboard. When you take an eraser and try to wipe off the white chalk marks, a cloudy base remains. It takes a great deal of work and a lot of time to completely clear the board and write brand new information that can be understood."

"I am ready."

Chapter 59

JUNE 1962 – HIDDEN LAKE, OREGON

"Chester, Chester, can you hear me? Patch me in quickly. That minister just finished babbling some thing or another. He is heading toward the door to get the women. I am pretty sure that they are coming out of the diner at this very moment. Okay, thirty seconds for the lousy commercial, but I don't know if I can make them wait until we are on the air. I will cause a commotion or something. I don't know. Just hurry. Also, I believe we should bring to our producer's attention that I really should have a make-up lady following me around. After all, I am looking a bit pale. I need a bit of color on my lips and cheeks. I know I am not a woman. It is called stage and film make-up. Oh, we are on camera?"

The cameraman beamed broadly. He pointed at the news reporter to begin.

"Ladies and gentlemen, welcome back to our continuing breaking news coverage. This is Larry Lowden with the lowdown on the controversial dis-order in the community of Hidden Lake. Coming out onto the porch of Hidden Hazel's Soda Fountain Café to face the wrath of the townspeople are the owner of the establishment and the woman who started this travesty. Let me just push through the growing crowds here so I can bring you my exclusive report and inform my large viewing audience."

Felix continued to follow Larry but shook his head with

obvious annoyance. He, however, was not in front of the camera. He now knew why he preferred to be behind the scenes.

"Excuse me, young man, little girl. Let the news media get up front," Larry urged the children that had been holding the signs in protest only an hour before.

"Hey, watch it," a round, red-headed boy said with irritation.

Merlin jumped in front of the news reporter and growled. Larry turned his microphone toward the dog and said to the camera with a disingenuous smile, "Oh, I found the victim. Mr. Dog, would you like to address our listening audience?"

"Wolf, wolf."

"He is probably a little shy," the reporter laughed and hastily moved away from the dog.

In the meantime, Stella had opened the door to the diner and held onto Lillian's arm as they both appeared next to the railing on the porch. Wills hurried up the steps and stood next to Stella.

"Are you all right?" he asked.

"Yes, yes. I will explain it all later. Now, we need to talk to this crowd. Where is Dan?" Stella asked.

Dan Wright raced up the steps and said, "Here I am. I want to address the people here today, too. You first."

Stella was used to usually being the shortest person in any crowd, but today she felt that it was important everyone saw her and paid attention to what she was about to say. Without asking, Wills brought her a sturdy wooden box to stand on. She looked at all the people standing before her. In her loudest voice, she directed, "Boys and girls, please sit down." She noticed that Mr. Silver had just arrived. He gave a general sitting hand gesture, to which all the children responded immediately.

"I have something very important to say to you today. I hope that you will be considerate and listen with respect. I will be honest with all of you, and sometimes honesty is one of our most difficult but important qualities in life."

"Mrs. Fox threw water on Merlin and Donna," a little girl named Sharon said. "Doesn't that make you mad?"

"Yes!" the other children yelled.

Stella held up her hand for quiet and continued, "Have you ever done anything that made someone else mad?"

A murmur went through the crowd. Freddie proclaimed, "I used to make my dad mad all the time."

Everyone laughed.

"Have you ever done something *because* you were mad?" Stella asked as the crowd agreed verbally and with expressions of approval. "Have you ever regretted something that you said or did and wished that you could take it back?"

More people nodded. Others commented aloud.

"Have you ever felt angry inside yourself, but didn't say anything at all?"

Larry Lowden stopped talking into the microphone and held it out toward Stella and the group assembled on the porch.

"Sometimes that anger can fester inside of a person, which can harden into fury. When someone else says or does something to you that makes you mad, that anger can and sometimes does explode into scenes of despair and regret. That is when bad things happen. You can change that. We as a community can change that. We are going to start to change that now."

The audience burst into cheers and applause.

Stella continued, "I was talking to the children, but now I would like the adults to please listen and try to understand what I am about to say. Mrs. Lillian Fox has a child with the same condition as my Donna. You know Donna. My husband, Wills, is holding her now."

The audience gasped. Audible words of confusion and disbelief were reverberating around the crowd. They had never seen or heard about Lillian's alleged child.

Lillian stood next to Stella but did not need to step onto the box. "Mrs. Rollins is correct. My baby was born on Pearl Harbor Day. On the advice of the doctors and the insistence of my husband who later died in the war, my daughter, Hazel, was sent to live at Fairview in Salem."

The crowd went silent. Even Larry Lowden was at a loss

for words. The cameraman kept a close vigil as he continued broadcasting.

Stella took over, "I believe that pretty much everyone here knows someone or might even have someone in their extended family that has some kind of difficulty or problem or disorder that they just don't want to talk about. You may even have stories that are kept secret for one reason or another. Maybe you have personal experiences that you have kept hidden. This is what happened to Mrs. Lillian Fox. This grief hardened inside of her and made her appear mean. It made her grow old before her time."

Lillian wasn't sure she liked this turn of the conversation, but she took it as part of her punishment. She would do what Stella suggested. She would make amends somehow.

"Mrs. Fox would like you to know that she wants to change your opinion of her. She wants to do what is right. She needs your help. Please show your respect as we allow her to speak," Stella finished, then turned toward her earlier adversary. "Lillian, it is your turn."

Lillian held onto Stella's hands that reached for her. She helped Stella off the box as she herself climbed up, aided by Pastor Powers. She looked at him dolefully.

"It will be fine. This will help," he said in a hopeful, quiet voice.

"Boys and girls, ladies and gentlemen, I cannot believe that I am now going to thank you for being here," Lillian began.

Several people in the audience laughed uneasily but watched her intently. Lillian Fox, the shop owner, took a deep breath before she looked directly at everyone before her. She was overwhelmed. So many thoughts and emotions were screaming in her head. Mostly, she just wanted to go back into her little diner and close the door forever. She knew that was foolhardy. Stella Rollins was right. The hurt inside of her was as lethal as a cancer. If she didn't do something, it would eat her alive. She would do what Stella had suggested. After all, Stella had been through this pain. She told her that it would not be easy, but she had to at least give it a good try. She would.

Why did it seem like the entire town was in front of her

shop? She didn't know this many people lived in Hidden Lake. The town was growing, and she wasn't ready for it. Those thoughts were racing inside her head when she cleared her throat and said, "Thank you for being here today. This has been a difficult time. I am not sure how to start. I did and said some things that maybe were not very nice. Some might perceive them as wrong or hateful. But so did those children."

Shouts came from the group below the porch. Some angry words from a few adults erupted in the back. Pastor Powers put up his hands to indicate quiet and to calm everyone down.

"What I meant," Mrs. Fox continued, "was that we all need to look at how we are perceived by others. What we do and say makes a difference. I have not been very fair. I'm afraid I learned that the hard way. I just looked at how others treated me, not how I acted toward them. I was wrong."

The children continued to watch this surprising shopkeeper in front of them with confusion. Some of the adults nodded their heads in assent. Mrs. Fox closed her eyes and opened them again as if she was ready to start fresh. "I cannot promise that I will be forever changed. I cannot promise that I will never get angry again. I cannot promise to be a perfectly sweet individual who only focuses on what is right and fair. But I will promise right here and right now that I will try. I only ask that you give me another chance. Please visit my shop and spend your money."

Everyone including Mrs. Fox laughed. The tension was over.

"I would like to ask a couple of adults and a couple of the children to please meet with me today. I believe that together we can discuss ways to make this establishment profitable while it provides what is in the best interest of our community," she finished to wild applause and cheers.

Pastor Powers as well as Dan Wright helped her off the makeshift stage. Stella and Lillian hugged with unashamed tears of relief. The audience continued to applaud as the mayor of Hidden Lake stepped up onto the box. He could easily be seen by everyone. He watched the crowd intently as he lifted his arms upward to address the public.

Larry Lowden spoke into his microphone as he grinned with vigor, "Do not go away. Do not touch that dial. This is Larry Lowden with the lowdown as the news of Hidden Lake goes striking by. I can see from my important vantage point that Dan Wright, the mayor of Hidden Lake, is ready to address his constituents. We will return after these extremely quick but essential words from our sponsor. Back to you, Chester."

Larry put his hand over the mic and said to Felix, "This is getting better and better. Maybe we should put together a panel to discuss the implications of this situation? Do you realize that I could very well be in the running for The Coastal Unexpected News Event of the Year Award? This is big. This is really big!"

Felix took out his handkerchief and wiped his forehead. "Do you have any aspirin?" he asked. The camera light went on and he motioned the news reporter to continue.

Larry Lowden, in his best imitation of the popular national news anchor David Brinkley, said, "This is Larry Lowden with continuing coverage of the crisis in Hidden Lake. On the stage is Mayor Dan Wright. Let's listen to what he has to say."

Mayor Wright smiled at his friends and neighbors and projected in words that no one could miss, "Welcome one and all! As you know, I am Mayor Dan Wright. I have come here today to tell you that I agree with both sides of this dilemma and I will support all the people involved."

Bill whispered to Wills, "That's what I like about politicians – they are so decisive."

Mayor Wright seemed to exude power and strength with each word he spoke. "Mrs. Fox said one thing that truly resonated with me today."

"Only one thing, Mayor?" someone from the back yelled out.

"Right here, right now," he answered. "That is what she said and that is what I am saying right now to you. Right here, right now. We will acknowledge that all people are individuals and should be treated fairly and humanely! We as a community and a society have an obligation to all our citizens to understand and accept those that may not fit in, those that are different, those that cannot speak for themselves. In a real democracy all of us are dependent on each other. Social attitudes and social judgments are often made when someone is considered different than we are. We have an obligation, a responsibility to care for each other and help each other. That is how we exist in a safe and considerate world. We do what is morally and ethically right. We must bring about change for the good of all.

"As we have come to accept and welcome the newest members of our community, the Donaldsons, we have been able to see them as neighbors that we trust and value as true friends. As we have come to know and accept Donna Rollins, we see that she is a sweet child who is loved dearly by her family as we all love our own children. Now, we even know about Mrs. Fox's own child, who was unfortunately abandoned by her own family because of fear, which only led to resentment. This is not right! We need to bring national attention to the lack of appropriate educational options, living arrangements, and family support. That is why I am announcing today my plan to throw my hat into the ring. Right here, right now – I want to be your next State Representative in Salem. I plan to run on a platform for the equality of all. I want to work to find a way that *all* children can receive an education that makes sense for them. Right here, right now. I am Dan Wright – your next State Legislator!"

Everyone jumped to their feet, bursting out in cheers and extended applause. The people that surrounded Dan rushed toward him in enthusiastic approval. The women hugged him, and the men shook his hands vigorously. Stella stood in the background with Lillian. Both women leaned against the wall of the building. When the well-wishers had moved aside, Stella walked toward her friend, Dan. She took both of his hands in hers and said not a word. The tears that flowed down her face could not be stopped.

Lillian said loudly from where she stood, "Well, that's two votes you will have for sure!"

Chapter 60

SEPTEMBER 1962 – HIDDEN LAKE, OREGON

THE SUMMER CERTAINLY FLEW BY FAST, STELLA THOUGHT TO HERSELF while she watched the children jump on and over the new sidewalk. She was thrilled that many of them were carrying an assortment of books for the new library that she was ready to establish at the school. A week ago, she and Mr. Silver had sent out a "Back to School" newsletter to welcome all the incoming students and their parents. They suggested a tentative list of upcoming events as well as a request for donated books for the new library.

Stella frowned as she glared through the window at her own daughter and her best friend's boys. They were jumping deliberately into mud puddles that lined the sidewalk or small indentations in the lawn with the obvious purpose of seeing how wet they could get someone close by. She knocked on the window but they either couldn't hear her or were pretending they couldn't.

Mr. Silver walked into the office with gleeful exuberance. He had on a nice new suit and tie. He was ready for the new school year. As he took off his hat and put it on the coat rack, he said, "Good morning, Mrs. Rollins. Are you ready for the first day of school?"

"I am definitely ready and excited to get started, but I'm not so sure how you will feel with the same old miscreants in your classroom again this year. Last year you were the fifth-grade teacher and now you have moved up – or maybe down? – to the sixth-grade level. Would you look at my little monsters? No, on second thought, don't look."

"I love a good surprise," he laughed. "I thought that staying with the same teacher for two years would be a smart move. We will soon see."

Within moments, children started to come into the office to drop off the many books that they had brought from home. "Have you decided where the new library should be?" Stella asked.

"BB has cleared out the storage area behind the stage in the gym. I think you will be very happy. Go have a look. I will tell the kids to take the books directly to that room," Mr. Silver said.

Stella squinted her eyes and tilted her head. "There is a room behind the stage?"

"Yes. It was so cluttered before that even the door was hidden," he said.

Stella left with a pile of books and a few student helpers. BB accompanied her once he saw them heading toward the gym. "Let me help you with that," he said.

The door creaked open to a spacious sunlit room. "Oh, BB, this is unbelievable. Thank you. This is perfect," Stella cried. "You even cleaned every square inch. Oh, my. You are truly a gem!"

The blush on BB's face was unmistakable. "Well now, Miss. You see, um. I need to go unlock the classrooms," he stammered and left quickly.

Stella was overwhelmed. She knew the library would happen now. The children dropped off the books and left when the bell rang. Stella sat on a pile of books to reminisce about the summer that had just come to an end. Like a puzzle, pieces were finally starting to fit into place. No one said all the changes would be easy, yet the difficult, hard work might just have been the best time of her life.

She thought back to the beginning of the summer when Lillian met with her contingent of parents and children to revise the vision of what her shop could become. The first change she made was to requisition a new sign. The name of her establishment was now Hidden Hazel. She decided not to classify it as a diner or a soda fountain café or a craft shop – Lillian wanted it to be whatever the townspeople wanted it to be. The Committee of Change, as they were now called, gave her excellent suggestions. Stella had heard that Anton was the one who came up with the best ideas. Due to his enthusiasm, Lillian hired his mother, Veronica, to help redesign the shop and work behind the counter. Veronica loved it. Lillian was given a contract to again teach first grade. Lillian discovered that she did indeed have a passion for teaching. She told Stella that even she was surprised by that. Veronica would oversee the store while Lillian taught school. They decided to keep the long soda fountain bar with the red vinyl stools. Veronica suggested that they consult with her mother, Barbara, and design a more functional and tastier menu. Lillian agreed. Veronica also went to work on a bright interior with fresh paint and new displays of locally crafted articles to sell on consignment. Even though these modifications were significant and brought in many more customers than ever before, the greatest transformation was with Mrs. Lillian Fox herself.

Stella went back to the office to check on the status of the first day, but so far everything appeared exceptionally quiet, so she decided to head back to the new library to start cataloging the books. She sorted what they had so far by fiction and nonfiction. Next, she alphabetized the fiction by author and put the nonfiction books in various piles by subject. She thought to herself that it might be a good idea to find a book on how to set up a library. Yes, she would do that later. As she worked, she lost herself in thoughts of a summer that she knew she would never forget.

Stella recalled how every week for the last two months Veronica, Lillian, and she had driven to the Fairview Institute in Salem to visit Lillian's daughter, Hazel. Initially, Lillian had tried to go on her own with every intention of finally meeting her daughter. Just as she got into her car, though, anxiety froze her beyond movement. The twins had been downtown one day and noticed that the shop owner had been sitting in her car for well over an hour. They went home and told their mother. Stella remembered how Veronica jumped into action. Barbara would take care of the children. The boys would go tell the men that Veronica and she were on their way to Salem but would be back by dinner.

Sitting on a pile of books, Stella laughed to herself as she thought about the irony of it all. Lillian's husband had believed that having Hazel around would ruin their business. He was sure that they would be ridiculed and ostracized. Today, Hazel lived in the apartment above the diner with her mother. She worked with Veronica during the day. Hazel bussed tables, washed dishes, and did whatever task she was asked to do. Every time the little bell sounded, and a customer would walk in, Hazel would run to the door and hug whoever was there. The town started to call the diner "Hazel Hugs." Instead of losing customers, the diner was always full to overflowing.

Stella wasn't sure if her Donna meetings were fruitful or not. They still had not come up with a group name. She supposed that didn't matter. The group was growing rapidly, and every new person introduced a new idea. More importantly, their personal stories were as diverse as the attendees themselves. Now there were more and more parents or families of Fairview residents. Some expressed concern about what they claimed were atrocities while others felt the individuals were well cared for. Fairview was divided into cottages that housed people according to mental capacity, physical disability severity, age, and sex. Some residents were given small jobs or tasks to accomplish during the day and there were a couple of classrooms in use as well. Sadly, this was a minuscule percentage. The vast majority did nothing at all. One parent said that she and her husband were afraid to go visit because a staff member said that their child would be inconsolable when they left. The families were not in agreement about whether the children and disabled adults were treated well, but they all agreed they were not in an environment where these individuals were loved. They often discussed that the public needed to know what was going on. Stella hoped that in the months to come, the group would be able to work together to advocate for those who could not help themselves. She knew it would take time, but they would do what was necessary to find appropriate care as well as provide an education for all children. Right now, these families needed to tell their stories, and that is what they were starting to do. The fear, insecurity, silence, and even guilt these families had lived with for so many years were slowly disintegrating.

The most overwhelming venture of the summer that completely surprised Stella was her tenacious dedication to creating a pleasant home for her own family. The property on the lake and the log house specifically were being transformed. They all worked long, hard hours and were exhausted in the evening, but Wills, the children, and Stella were happy and content. The grape arbor hadn't blossomed yet, heralding the desired fruit, but it was bushy and vibrantly green. The flowers dazzled in an array of brilliant colors. The house now had running water and a much-awaited bathroom with a tub and shower. A county inspector came to approve the natural spring water supply and helped Bill design the pipe layout. Stella still hated Big Beauty, but Barbara came over often to help cook the meals. Barbara claimed that Stella was hopeless in the kitchen, but at least she tried. Wills was excited that his three cows had arrived by barge. When he brought the animals in from the pasture area, he called it his cattle drive. Stella said that all the eggs that she had been giving away recently were because she finally convinced the darn chickens to do their job or they would end up in Barbara's stewing pot. Yes, things were good.

"There you are," Mr. Silver announced from the doorway. "You have been here for hours."

"Oh, my goodness. I am so sorry. I will go to the office immediately." Stella was instantly flustered.

"No, I wasn't complaining. This is magnificent. It is unbelievable what you have done so far. These things take time, but you obviously don't realize that," Mr. Silver said as he surveyed the area. "I have a feeling that it is going to be an exceptionally productive year."

Stella stood up and wiped the dust off her dress. "You are so right. This is going to be an unbelievably surprising year. I can feel it in the air!"

Chapter 61

OCTOBER 12, 1962 –
HIDDEN LAKE, OREGON

Wills

THE LAST LUNCH DISH WAS DRIED AND PUT AWAY NEATLY INTO the cupboard. Wills threw the kitchen towel over his shoulder as he glanced back at the two girls who were rolling a ball back and forth in the extra-large playpen that he had made for them a few weeks ago. He smiled widely at the girls, his children. Yes, they were his children and he loved them more than he thought possible. He also loved this new domestic identity he had somehow created for himself. If he wasn't careful, he would completely relax into the role of a modern-day housewife. He laughed at his own musings. If the guys at the mill or the Vander Inn ever got hold of this information, they would mock him to kingdom come and back. The arrangement of working at the Mill Monday through Thursday and being able to stay home Friday through Sunday was working out very well. During the week, Barbara was very happy to take care of her babies, as she called them, but Friday was his day to be home with them while he continued to work on the never-ending chores. He looked around at all the changes they had made. Without a doubt in his mind, this home had never seen such loving care. Although he continued to have the occasional nightmares, he no longer felt controlled by them. He had never been happier in his life, and that made all the difference.

Wills looked at his watch and wondered if he should keep the woodstove burning. If so, he would need to go fetch some more wood from the pile along the side of the house. Since it just turned noon, he typically would let it die out and restart the fire closer to dinner time. Still, the wind seemed to be building up and it might start to get cooler earlier. A slight breeze was not unusual off the lake, but he did not like how the tree branches were scratching at the windows right now. The girls stopped playing with the ball. Maddie stood and helped Donna stand as well. She showed Donna how to grasp the top bars of the playpen to steady herself. They stood very still and looked toward the noise at the window. A loud rumbling jolted all three of them to attention.

"Wills, what is that noise?" Maddie said in a frightened tiny voice.

"I bet my woodpile fell over. Sounds to me like I need to learn how to stack wood a bit more securely. I will go check on it," he said. "Maddie, please do not climb out of the playpen. Please watch Donna for me."

"I will," she answered, still watching the window.

Wills threw on his jacket. As he turned the knob on the main room door, it burst wide open with an enormous gust of wind. Wills struggled to close it and was baffled by the enormous power this seemingly typical breeze had. After he finally succeeded with the door, he turned toward the yard and froze in astonishment. Branches and foliage were flying in every direction. He looked toward the ramp. His eyes grew wide as he watched it ripple and sway. Next, he looked up at the sky and shook violently. The unnerving green billowing dense clouds were sliced with slivers of yellow and shades of black. Wills wasted no time. He raced up the steps to the porch and grabbed the door handle. When he attempted to open the door, it immediately flew back and forth, pounding the wall steadily. Wills snatched two jackets and hurriedly put them on each child. He

Lifted both girls out of the playpen and held them tightly under each of his arms.

"Where are we going?" Maddie cried.

"Maddie, sweetheart, I need you to listen to me very closely. Put your legs around my middle. Hold your arms around my neck tightly. Do not let go for any reason. Do you understand?" Wills urged frantically but tried his best to remain calm.

Maddie did as she was told but said, "Wills, I don't think we should go down the ramp. It is moving."

"We must. I will take care of you. Nothing will happen, I promise. I need to hold onto Donna as well as to the ramp railing. Can you hold on to me?"

Maddie was alarmed but nodded her head yes.

Wills knew that he had to get down to the boathouse swiftly for the safety of his children. Any delay would be extremely dangerous. He would not allow them to become stranded here. They must get out now. Wasting time debating whether to stay put or go find the rest of his family was fruitless. Wills knew what he had to do. He stared at the old ramp and wandered how much life it had left, reproaching himself for not attending to that structure earlier. He took one deliberate step at a time as fast as he felt safe. His own safety was never a priority. He gave a quick prayer asking God to save his children and not worry about his own well-being. The dramatic movement of the wooden ramp was fierce. Maddie hid her face in Wills's chest. Donna watched silently with her eyes wide open. Wills imagined himself as a tightrope walker determined to reach the other side. He did so with a triumphant jump to the boathouse. His glee was short-lived though when he noticed the nails of the roof squealing out of their tight wooden enclosure. He raced inside the boathouse and swiftly set the children in the cabin of the boat.

"Maddie, I need you to take good care of Donna. Can you do that?" Wills asked as he quickly untied the bow and stern lines and jumped into the boat.

"Yes, Daddy Wills," Maddie said. "I know what to do. I will put on her lifejacket and mine, too."

"You are a very smart, big girl," Wills said, not realizing what she had said. He only hoped that the engine would start with one pull.

Closing his eyes, Wills whispered the word "please" and took one massive pull on the engine rope. It started immediately. "This is going to be rough, girls. Hang on tight."

Maddie and Donna were both terrified, but neither uttered any sound. Wills urgently reversed the tugboat out of its enclosed dock, then hit the forward throttle to full speed. The boat bounced over the increasingly strong waves and headed away from the shore. Wills glanced back over his shoulder to see the ramp tumble to the ground as the roof of the boathouse lifted into the wind and floated out of sight. He steadied himself securely to the tiller and held it with both hands. The wooden tugboat aptly named *The Adventure* swayed mercilessly as the gusty winds increased in intensity. The boat seemed to cry in pain as it creaked and groaned, but it courageously battled a lake that resembled an ocean with ferocious frothy swells. *What is going on?* Wills thought to himself.

What typically amounted to a 20-minute boat ride took almost two hours in the violent wind and swirling waters of the lake. The gusty headstrong winds beat at Wills and the wooden boat as the waves crashed over the stern. Water poured in relentlessly. Wills knew he had to dock immediately. He could not hang onto the tiller and empty out buckets of water at the same time.

Maddie got up with her little pail to try to help. "No!" Wills screamed over the deafening howl of the wind. "Sit down and hold on, Maddie. I know you want to help, but I need to you hold onto Donna. Can you do that?"

She looked terrified but nodded her head.

Soon they were in sight of the pier. They noticed Captain Jack Carlton frantically waving them away. The wind stole Captain Jack's words, but Wills did not have any difficulty interpreting his screams. He knew that the pier was not safe. He needed to find another place to get to shore. Wills remembered a hidden cove that he once took Stella to when they first moved to the town. There was no pier there, but it was sandy, and tucked inland so the wind might not be as powerful. It could just work. Wills managed to turn the tiller as the wind thankfully pushed them toward his intended destination. He gripped the gears on the handle with all his strength, foolishly trying to force it beyond forward to make the motor respond faster than it was able to do. The boat slammed into the sand until it could move no further. He shut off the engine and jumped out. There was nowhere to secure the boat ties, but he did not give that a passing thought.

"Maddie, bring Donna to me," Wills shouted.

She swiftly jumped up and lifted Donna with more strength than Wills realized that she possessed. He reached over the side of the boat and pulled Donna out easily. "Now your turn," he said to Maddie. She jumped onto the railing and into Wills's arms. He speedily ripped off their lifejackets so he would be able to carry them as he had done before. He had to get them to the Pretty Pink House immediately. He hoped with all his might that school had already been dismissed and everyone was home safely. Obviously, Captain Jack hadn't taken the school boat out, so he was very grateful for that. As the wind raced around them, he focused on the urgency of getting these children to a safe location. Wills watched the debris fly overhead. He noticed trees breaking and bending. Limbs and leaves scattered at his feet. He jumped over and around any and all obstacles. He wondered once again why he hadn't heard any forewarning. Was there one and they just missed it? There was no television at the log house. Surely, Stella would have mentioned it last night and not risked going into school this morning. No, he was sure there had been no warning.

The house was three blocks away. The school was another two blocks after that. He would take the girls to the house first. He would make sure his family and friends were safe, then head over to the school to see if it was secure and all got home without incident. Wills tugged the girls tightly to his side and raced as fast as he was able through the fierce gale-force winds. The Pretty Pink House never looked so beautiful when he gratefully opened the gate and stepped onto the porch. He was not aware of it then, but this was only the beginning of the storm. He would soon find out that the worst was yet to come.

Veronica opened the door in a panic. "Are you all right? Where are the others?"

Wills looked at her anxiously, "They are not here?"

"No," she said, obviously very worried, "We haven't heard anything. We have been watching the trees bang at the windows. My flower bed has been chewed up by the wind. All sorts of debris have flown by. I even saw a swing set tumble down the road."

Wills set the two girls down, closed the door, and locked it. The power flicked on and off until an uncanny darkness descended throughout the house. Wills instantly picked the girls back up and rushed to the hallway. "Where's Barbara?" he shouted.

"I'm in the kitchen," she yelled back.

"Veronica, Barbara, come to the hallway and stay with the girls," Wills instructed. "Has school been dismissed?"

"I don't know," Veronica said grabbing her coat.

"Well, I don't know where you think you are going, but it is not going to be outside. It is too dangerous," Wills ordered.

"If you think I am going to stay here when my children are in harm's way, then you are crazy!" she scolded. "Now stop arguing with me and let's go!"

"Stubborn females. You truly are like my wife!"

"Good," she said, headed toward the door.

"Wait!" Wills looked at Barbara and, in a rush, said, "Please make sure the girls stay in the hall. It is the most secure area in the house. The hallway closet has blankets, pillows, coats, and flashlights. Get them. Also fill the bathtub with water if you are able. The pipes may burst, and the water may shut off. Fill up any pitcher you might have with water but do it quickly and stay away from the windows."

"Don't worry about us. I'll take good care of my babies. Now, go get my other sweet babies!" Barbara said when Wills and Veronica rushed out of the doorway. She pushed the door closed behind them and immediately locked it.

Veronica grabbed Wills's arm steadily. When they reached the gate to unlatch it, an enormous gust of wind yanked it from Wills's hand and tumbled it into the darkening sky. Veronica screamed. The frantic sounds of her name came from the echoes of the whistling winds. Bill sprinted around the corner and swiftly wrapped her in his arms. The wind was at their backs prodding and pushing them all the way. Without words the three of them made it to the school in record time.

Wills opened the office door. Stella was on the phone and put the receiver back into its cradle when she saw Wills and the others standing in front of her. "Mr. Silver just dismissed school and will release the students immediately. I was on the phone to arrange for the buses to come early."

"I don't know if he is aware of the severity of this storm," Wills said. "It's worse than anything I have ever seen."

Bills said promptly, "We need to help."

The four of them raced to the sixth-grade classroom. Stella opened the door to a whirlwind of activity. The lights were out but an eerie glow streamed in from the full wall of windows directly in front of them. Limbs of trees and bushes scratched at the windows like nails on a chalkboard. The howling winds screeched as they blew past.

"Children," Mr. Silver said in his most stern and authoritative voice, "get over to the far wall right now."

"Watch out," Stella yelled as her eyes opened wide.

A large branch crashed through the window, flinging glass shards into the room. The children screamed in panic. Wills and Bill took charge instantly. "Boys and girls," Wills directed, "sit down facing the back wall. Heads down. We will put the desks close to you as a barricade."

"Wills, Mr. Silver has been hit," Stella cried.

A piece of glass had sliced through Mr. Silver's suit jacket and into his arm. Blood was rapidly seeping out. Wills and Stella raced over to him. "It's just a flesh wound. I need to get all the children to safety," Mr. Silver said just before he melted to the floor.

"Bill," Wills called, "give me a hand."

The men picked up the semi-conscious principal and carried him carefully to the far end of the classroom.

"Veronica, go to the health room and get some bandages. Stella, call Dr. Conrad," Will ordered.

Stella said, "I will also call the parents of the children who don't take the bus home to come get their children. What about the school boat?"

"Too dangerous," Will said. "They will have to stay here."

"We need to get them into the gym. It is safer," Mr. Silver tried to stand but Bill held him down.

Veronica came back into the classroom as quickly as she had left it. She had a boxful of medical supplies. Without any unnecessary instructions, she headed to Mr. Silver and took off his jacket. The blood was streaming out steadily now. She tore the sleeve of his shirt and held a folded towel over the wound. "Bill, he needs to go to the doctor right now," she said.

"No," Mr. Silver said in a dazed state. "I need to stay with my children. I will be all right. Just put a bandage on it."

"I'll wrap it up the best that I can, but you must promise me that you will have the doctor take care of it," she demanded.

"Yes, yes, of course," he said weakly. "Hurry. We need to go to each classroom now."

"We can do that," Wills said. "Let's move, Bill!"

Bill spoke to the children before he left with Wills, "Sixth-graders, listen to me. You are the leaders of this school. I am expecting you to be brave and wait here until we help the younger students into the gym. Then we will come back for you."

"We can help, Dad," Leon said bravely.

"No!" Veronica shouted.

"Veronica, they are strong, tall, and big boys now. I think they could be very helpful. I promise to take care of them," Bill said with a loving glance at his boys.

The twins jumped up before their parents could argue, "We've got this!"

Wills was already down the outdoor corridor headed toward the first-grade classroom when he was met by BB. "How can I help?" BB asked.

"We need to get these children into the gym, but it won't be easy. The storm could easily throw these youngsters around. We will have to hold them down and move them rapidly to the gym. Some will need to go to the buses when they arrive. We will have to escort them there as well," Wills said but as he spoke, the roof of the covered play area crumbled before their eyes and smashed to the ground.

"Hurry," Bill screamed over the wind. "We will form a human chain and pass the children one by one. Stay close to the brick wall."

Wills entered the first classroom and told Mrs. Fox what they intended to do. She agreed without complaint. "Children, line up close to the wall by the door. You do not need to be in any order. Go quickly. The adults and some big kids are going to help you get to the gym. Do not head there on your own," Mrs. Fox ordered.

One by one the children were passed from Mrs. Fox to Leon to Bill to Anton to BB. Wills was the last in the line. He picked up each child and hastily raced through the outdoor corridor to the gym and back. The other teachers found their places in the line to assist until all the classrooms were empty and the children were sitting on the gym floor to wait. Soon the buses arrived, and the drivers also helped to assist each child to transport them home. Parents also found their way to the school and helped all that they could. Mr. Silver's arm was wrapped securely, but he refused to go to the doctor until all the children were home. In the meantime, he said that he would remain in the gym with anyone who needed to stay there. Many townspeople and parents came to the gym in hopes that it would be safer than their own homes.

Wills returned to the gym once the last bus had departed. "I will take Rosie and the twins home now," he said to Mr. Silver.

"Mrs. Rollins and Mrs. Donaldson, you both can go, too. Thank you so much for all your help. We are indebted to you," Mr. Silver said.

Mrs. Fox ran over with eyes wide with terror and said, "What about Hazel? Can you get Hazel?"

Stella put an arm around her former adversary and said, "I called the volunteer fire department hours ago. They took her to the fire station but said they will bring her to the gym as soon as they can. She is safe."

Lillian Fox cried with relief and hugged Stella.

"I'm ready to go!" Rosie jumped up and ran to the gym door where Wills was waiting with her mother.

The four Donaldsons and the three Rollinses left the stillness of the gym for the wild fury of the outdoors. "Stay close to the brick wall. When we reach the corner, we will hang onto each other and head for home," Wills yelled above the wailing winds.

When they reached the edge of the school building, Rosie asked, "Were Donna, Maddie, and Merlin scared when they rode in the boat?"

Wills froze.

"Wills?" Stella looked at him with a quizzical expression. "They are all right, aren't they?"

"Merlin?" Wills had a look of horror on his face.

Rosie stared at Wills, puzzled, "Merlin is safe with Donna and Maddie, isn't he?"

Wills inadvertently let go of everyone. He looked around panicky. He swayed side to side. His vision blurred but his hearing became acute. The trees were falling with great frequency. Each broken branch sounded like a gunshot. Every time a tree hit the ground, the earth would shake like a bomb went off. Objects flew in all directions. Leaves were dancing wildly on the ground around his feet. Water sprayed into his face and the wind turned him around. The last thing he remembered was his cry that Merlin was marooned because of him.

A massive tree split in half. Wills hit the ground yelling, "Get down. Take cover!" The tree crashed on top of Wills, pinning him to the ground.

Stella screamed, "Wills!"

Rosie shouted, "Merlin! You left Merlin. You killed my dog! I hate you!"

Rosie yanked herself away from the others and ran down the road toward the beach as she continued to yell, "Merlin, Merlin. I am coming. I will save you!"

Wills shrieked incoherently, "Get to the ship. Hurry. No, don't wait for me. Go!"

"No, Rosie, no!" Stella's shrill voice pierced through the wind as she helplessly watched the gale lift Rosie into the air.

"I am flying. I am going to save Merlin!" Rosie yelled.

Stella looked toward Wills, who was crushed beneath a tree, and then toward her daughter, who was flying away. She screamed. Bill ran faster than he had ever moved in his lifetime. He jumped high and grabbed Rosie by her ankles, forcing her back down to earth. They landed hard onto the ground. Stella raced over and put her arms around Rosie.

"Help me move that blasted tree," she shrieked to everyone.

Wills was oblivious to the current danger. He continued to shout orders to no one in particular, "Leave me stranded. I can handle this island. Those yellow Japs don't bother me. Save yourselves!"

"Wills, Wills," Stella cried urgently, "are you hurt? We are here. We won't leave you."

Everyone in the group, even a sobbing Rosie, pulled and pushed to extract Wills from the tree but failed. "Don't move him," Bill said. "He may have broken bones. We don't want to make it worse. We have to try to get this tree off him."

"We need help," Stella roared over the wailing wind.

Bill shook his head and shouted, "I will get the fire department. Everyone hang onto the tree. Keep trying to break off branches. Maybe that will help. I will be back as fast as possible. And keep your heads down. Stay close to the ground."

"Maybe the children should go home or back to the gym," Veronica suggested, not totally convinced herself.

"No!" they said in unison.

Bill took off rapidly toward the fire station in hopes that he would find someone there. He had a feeling, though, that they were out on numerous calls. He was sure that there must be many others in distress right now. He would get whoever he could find. Then he had an idea.

Stella moved over to get close to Wills without leaning on the tree. "Bill went for help. Be still, Wills. It won't be long."

"Move, get moving. I will be fine. I will hide in the forest. They won't see me. I will put mud on my face."

"No, Wills. You are just trapped under a tree, but you will be fine. You will see," Stella cried, tears flowing freely down her face. Veronica sat next to her as she held onto all three children.

Rain pelted down upon everyone. Huge droplets hit Wills on the face. He tried to move his arm to wipe the water away. He moaned loudly as he realized that he couldn't budge. His confused outbursts were getting more and more frequent as well as illogical. "I will wait in this river until the Japs leave. I can breathe using the reeds. Nightfall I will creep into the woods. They think everyone has gone. I can spy on them. When they don't know it, I will steal into that hut over there and find food. I might have to eat out of the trash, but I will survive."

The fear in Stella's eyes was unmistakable. Her wet hair was matted to her equally wet face. She looked up at Veronica and said, "We need the doctor. I need to go get the doctor right now. It can't wait."

Stella started to get up, but Veronica forced her back down. "No," she cried. "The wind is too strong. You saw what happened to Rosie. You are barely a hundred pounds. Forget it."

Wills shouted louder, "I am responsible. I marooned him. Now I am stranded. Go to safety. Now!"

"I'm going for the doctor now, Wills. Hang on," Stella roared back.

"Boys, do you think you could make it to Dr. Conrad if you hold onto each other?" Veronica asked in a frightened voice.

"Of course," Leon answered.

Anton interrupted, "Yes, we are happy to go, but Dr. Conrad said that he doesn't make house calls anymore. He said that it was old fashioned, and he was a futuristic doctor."

"You tell that fool he better get his fat head over here rapid fire, or he will have me to deal with!" Stella shouted over the howling devastation.

The boys jumped up and were ready to race off when they saw a dozen or more men running toward them as well as the doctor, who had a little black bag and a very tight grip on their dad.

Chapter 62

OCTOBER 1962 – HIDDEN LAKE, OREGON

THREE DAYS LATER

"She did not!"

"She did, too!"

"Did not!"

"Did too!"

"*Mom!*"

The shrill sounds coming from Rosie and Maddie vibrated off the hallway walls into the kitchen where Stella sat reading the newspaper and sipping a cup of tea. She set the cup down and put her hands on her forehead while she massaged her temples with her thumbs.

Barbara was at the sink washing the morning dishes while Veronica dried and put them away. Barbara grabbed another kitchen towel to wipe her hands. She turned to face Stella and said, "Maybe we should try to calm them down a little bit. Rosie has not stopped screaming, sobbing, or arguing for three days now."

Veronica whispered to her mother and Stella, "Maybe a little noise might wake Wills up."

"I heard that," Rosie yelled as she raced into the room. "He isn't asleep. His eyes are wide open!"

Maddie ran in behind her and jumped onto Wills's lap. He did not seem to notice her or anyone around him. He did not wrap his arms around Maddie or cuddle her as he typically would. "Are you awake, Daddy Wills?" Maddie asked him furtively.

Wills continued to stare out the kitchen window. He did not move. He did not respond.

"See, I told you. He keeps looking down the road at nothing at all," Rosie said.

Stella turned her head toward Rosie and said in a calm voice, "Rosie, it is a sunny day. Please go outside and play. Just stay in the yard."

"Fine! I want to go home!" Rosie stomped down the hallway and slammed the front door.

Maddie jumped off Wills and followed Rosie with her own stomp down the hall.

"Maddie," Stella cried after her, "please stay inside and play with Donna. That's a good girl."

"Okay, Mommy," she shouted back. "I can take care of Donna. We will roll the ball. Rosie said she can't do that. Rosie should get in trouble for not believing."

Maddie's whining faded away as the women continued what they were doing.

"The newspaper is saying that it was the strongest windstorm in the West Coast's recorded history," Stella read.

"I can believe that," Veronica commented.

Stella continued to report, "This intense storm was a destructive power outlier which stemmed from Typhoon Frida in the Pacific Ocean."

"I hope we never see the likes of it again. The cold snows of Chicago are sounding better and better to me," Barbara remarked to the others.

"Quite a few injuries and fatalities have also been reported," Stella continued.

"I doubt they can truly measure the significant impact of the storm," Veronica said. "You only have to look at Wills to see the scars that a person never reveals."

"Can you try again to convince your husband to go visit the

Veterans Hospital? They might be able to help him," Barbara suggested as she sat on the barstool next to Stella.

"I keep trying to talk to him," Stella responded, wiping her eyes with the palms of her hands.

The muffled sounds of "Merlin, Merlin" entered the kitchen. "She won't stop," Stella said. "I thought that if I sent her outside, she would help the twins fix the fence. The slats on the picket fence are either missing or hanging loosely. The fence itself is upright in some areas and completely fallen over in others."

Veronica walked over and looked out the window. "The boys are ignoring her. At least she is staying in the yard. She is at the edge of the roadway looking toward the beach area where the town pier is located."

"I suppose she's not doing any harm. She's just noisy," Stella sighed.

"Merlin, Merlin," Rosie's chants continued to be heard but not as loudly as before.

"Oh, look! Here comes Bill with some men," Veronica announced.

A few minutes later, Bill came in the kitchen door with Edgar and Warren from the mill. He walked over to Veronica and gave her a quick kiss on her cheek. The women greeted their guests and invited them to sit down.

"I will make a fresh pot of coffee," Barbara said.

"Hello, Wills. It's a nice day. The sun is out. How are you doing today?" Warren asked. He received no response.

"Ready to come back to work, Rollins?" his boss asked him. Still no response.

Both men looked toward the other adults in the room. They shook their heads to indicate that there had been no change in Wills.

Warren spoke up during a tense moment of silence, "A number of private citizens and various city work crews have spent many long hours on the clean-up."

"It has taken quite some time to clear off the trees on the roads and restore power lines," Edgar said.

"Word is out that you joined the Volunteer Fire Department, Bill," Warren said to Bill.

"Yes, well, I am still in training, but right now I am trying to help by going door to door to make sure everyone in town is okay."

Barbara brought over mugs and the coffee pot. She poured out the coffee as everyone settled around the large kitchen table.

Edgar took a long sip of the coffee before he said, "The reason that we came today is to ask Wills a question."

Wills did not speak, but his eyes moved toward the others. The men knew that he was listening.

"I know what they are going to ask, so let me fill you in first," Bill said. Everyone except for Wills turned expectantly toward Bill to hear what he was about to say.

"As you know, Wills was extremely fortunate. The doctor said that he had only dislocated one shoulder. He gave him a quick examination and could find no other injuries. I might remind you that Dr. Conrad did urge you to take him to the Veterans Hospital for a thorough examination. He claimed that Wills was probably manifesting memories of a time during the war. We don't know for sure, but that certainly makes sense. The morning after the storm, Wills, Edgar, and I found *The Adventure* in good shape in the cove where Wills had successfully moored it. Wills was talking a bit then. He said that he was eager to take the boat up to the lake house to find Merlin. So the three of us motored up there. I did not want to tell you what we saw when we arrived until now. The destruction overwhelmed all of us. We could have been looking at a battlefield. The trees were gigantic toothpicks thrown around like a game of pick-up sticks in crisscross patterns. The boathouse and ramp were gone. We had to climb up the steep embankment through the blackberry vines to the landing. The blackberries appeared to be the only thing that survived. The barn and chicken coop had been ripped apart. The loft of the cow barn collapsed with the weight of the bales of hay stored there."

Stella stared straight at Bill, "The cows and chickens? Are they...?" She couldn't finish.

Bill looked very sad, "I am so sorry. They did not survive the brutal storm. We buried them."

Veronica sniffed. Barbara stood up and took the coffee pot back to the stove to make another pot where her face could not be seen. Tears rolled down Stella's face.

"The grape trellis and gazebo are gone. Your flower and vegetable garden are also lost. The worst, I am afraid, is the house," Bill said.

"I don't think I can hear anymore."

"This is important. Please let me tell you what you need to know."

Stella looked at Wills. A tiny tear dripped from the corner of his eye. Softly she said, "Yes."

"The log walls of the house stood firm. They had not moved, but everything else had. The roof had caved in from the numerous trees that had fallen on it. Parts of the roof and items in the house had blown away. We found various household items scattered throughout the property. All the windows were broken. A few trees extended from some windows as well. The bricks from the fireplace chimney had fallen into the playpen. I can only say that it was a miracle that Wills got those children out when he did."

Stella started to tremble when the reality of the danger to her children hit her. Veronica went to her side and put an arm around her.

"Can I get some more coffee, Barbara?" Bill said. "And maybe a bit of that coffee cake I saw you making this morning?"

"Me, too," Edgar said. "Which brings me to why Warren and I are here. Your property is in complete disarray. I know how hurtful that sounds, but please hear me out. What was a disaster can also be an opportunity."

Stella and the others watched him intently. "What could you possibly mean?" she asked.

"The logs thrown about your acreage are product that we desperately need. We want to buy it from you," Edgar said with a wistful grin.

No one spoke. After a few beats, Warren looked at an expressionless Wills and said, "Well, Wills, can we buy your logs?"

Wills turned to the men and said in a tired voice, "That would be Stella's decision. The property is hers. I put it in her name last year."

Stella put a hand over her mouth. She knew they had argued about that very thing, but she assumed they had forgiven each other and nothing else had been done. Stella was more surprised that Wills did something without discussing it with her first than by what he had done. Maybe he felt they had talked about it. Their argument that day was the discussion. Men!

"So, Mrs. Rollins, I guess we need to ask you. Would you sell us the property?" Edgar asked.

"No," she replied.

Everyone looked stunned. Stella continued, "I have a proposition for you."

"Yes?" Edgar and Warren said in unison.

"I don't know how much the trees are worth or maybe I should say the lumber, but how about a trade?"

"We're listening."

"Would your men be able to fix up the place to its former glory? I know it is a huge task and I don't know if it is financially feasible. I only know that my family and I would be eternally in your debt."

"There would be no debt. We would come out better in the long run," Edgar said.

"No, I think not. We would. What do you say?" Stella asked.

"I say that you will have a grand home and property to match! We will also replace all your household goods, appliances, and furniture."

"What about Big Beauty?" Barbara asked with a catch in her voice.

"Surprisingly, that was the only thing that survived. Not even the Columbus Day Storm could dislodge that beast!" Bill said.

Everyone laughed. Wills leaned closer toward the window and smiled. They thought that he was agreeing with them.

"Pacific Power and Light has been in discussions for years about the need for electrical power up there. We will make sure that happens. You will have a brand-new stove and oven, too," Edgar promised.

"What about Big Beauty?" Barbara said with her arms crossed.

"She can stay. We will have a designer come to figure out how to make it all work," Edgar said. "Well?"

"The cows and chickens?" Stella queried.

"Stella!" Veronica admonished.

"Your new livestock and chickens will feel right at home when it is all finished by Christmas," Edgar laughed. "The cows will have a new barn, the chickens can feast in their new chicken coop, and the hay will be stored in a new outbuilding. We will also throw in grain and seed for the next growing season."

"All that just for a few logs?"

"We will get the better end of the deal, I assure you," Warren said. "Plus, it will give more men work, which is sorely needed right now."

"Wills?" Stella looked at her husband. He continued to watch the road and grin.

"You have a deal," she said.

"Merlin, Merlin, Merlin!" Rosie's chants were getting louder to an almost hysterical sound.

"Good heavens," Veronica said.

Stella jumped up and looked out the window. Wills pushed back his chair and headed to the door. Stella was at his heels.

"Merlin!" Rosie sobbed.

Merlin bounced down the street unaware of anything except the child that raced toward him at that moment. She wrapped her arms around him tightly and sank her face into his wet, furry neck. Merlin barked twice before he gave Rosie a long swipe of his tongue on her cheek. He looked up, licked her once more, and ran down the road toward the man who was standing in the middle of the street. Wills sank to his knees when Merlin glided toward him. The dog put his front paws on Wills's shoulders and licked the tears that ran down the man's face. They tipped over and rolled around on the pavement playfully. Wills got up and led the dog to the grassy yard. The others ran over and threw their arms around each other, except for the three sisters.

"Look at your daughters," Veronica said as she slipped her arm through Stella's. Rosie had walked over to where Maddie was standing with Donna. They pulled Donna up to a standing position and walked her toward Merlin. He escaped the clutches of his long-lost family and sat perfectly still next to the girls with the loving smile that only a dog can convey. Donna looked up at Rosie with a wry grin. Donna's pumpkin doodle eyes twinkled in the autumn sunlight. She lifted her right hand and petted him gently from the top of his head to as far as she could reach for the very first time.

This would be the first of many firsts to come.

EPILOGUE

2018

Nothing was going to restrain an energetic and eager three-year-old Golden Retriever from his ultimate destination – not the leash Rosie was holding, nor the elevator door that was creaking open. Laddie, the dog, flew out of his temporary confinement and sprinted down the hall to the large reception area. Shouts of "Laddie, Laddie" came from all directions. He was oblivious to the various requests and demands to come or stay.

A petite, slightly past middle-aged but still youthful woman with straight straw-colored hair matching the dog's fur, which covered her jeans and pink cashmere sweater, sheepishly walked toward the crowded room. Every space was occupied with walkers, wheelchairs, canes, numerous chairs, and a couple of sofas, all currently holding people of all ages. The woman behind the reception counter held her head in her hands and turned a blind eye to Laddie's shenanigans.

Chaos erupted throughout the room as the playful dog bumped over a lighting stand, which in turn knocked over a man and his large television camera. A stylishly dressed black woman held tightly to a thin, silver microphone as Laddie jumped over the table holding her notebook and pens. As the middle-aged reporter stooped to pick up the items, Laddie decided to greet a few of the elderly residents who lived at the Whispering Winds Senior Retirement Village. They patted his head and stroked his smooth, orange fur. Suddenly Laddie saw his grandma Stella. He squeezed under someone's chair, jumped over another end table, and flipped up onto the couch next to his grandma, where he silenced the crowd by putting his head softly on her lap.

"This is my grand-dog," Stella said to the reporter and to the others around her. Stella was turning 91 today. A few years ago, she had been diagnosed with dementia, but she often forgot that and remained true to herself by being lucid and ready to converse easily with anyone. Everyone could still see the charming beauty she possessed when they looked into her twinkling blue eyes.

"When are you going to teach your mutt some manners?" Maddie scolded her sister, Rosie. "And what took you so long?"

"I was gone a mere five minutes," Rosie retorted. "Nurse Nan said Laddie was barking in Mom's cottage and I had to go fetch him."

The reporter finished gathering her things and smiled at Stella. "Well," she said, "I think we got everything. Thank you, Stella. And, I want to thank all your family and friends for joining us for this exclusive television interview. Your story is quite honestly thrilling. I think our viewers will be amazed."

"You are very welcome," Stella replied sincerely.

"There is one more thing. Could I please take a few more moments," the reporter sat back down in the chair next to the sofa, close to Stella.

"Yes?"

"You mentioned you never once called Donna handicapped," the reporter continued. "So, what did you call her?"

Stella looked directly at the woman as if she didn't understand and needed clarification. After a beat of a second, she simply said, "Why, Donna, of course."

Rosie was quite sure the reporter didn't know how to respond, so she jumped in with what she knew her mother, Stella, would undoubtedly say if she could. "I can explain. Society has a way of differentiating everyone. My mother, though, believes all people are unique and equal at the same time. It's too easy to categorize by color, race, religion, disability, or a host of a hundred different things, but what is harder is to find what we all have in common. That's the challenge society must face. My mother once told me it would take a generation or two before we'd notice any significant changes. Now, it seems the eyes of the world are gradually opening."

"Why do you think that is?" the reporter asked, making sure her mic was still on and the cameraman was continuing to film the discussion.

"Education," Rosie said without having to think about a good answer. "We have to learn how to accept everyone, but we can only do that if we are exposed to it. When you hide people away, fear ensues. Live close to others and you will understand them and build acceptance."

Maddie was determined to add her thoughts as well when she jumped in, "Speaking of which, I heard Gerber Baby Food announced they will have a baby with Down syndrome be their new poster child!"

Stella was clearly following the discussion as she looked up and said, "That would not have happened in my day."

Rosie added, "It would not have happened prior to 1975."

"Why would that particular date be important?" the reporter quizzed.

"It was a pivotal point in the history of education and of our country. That is when Public Law 94-142, The Education for All Handicapped Children Act, was signed. Prior to that, millions of children were denied an education. Now, not only would it become a federal law so *all* children must receive an education, but handicapped children are now guaranteed a free, appropriate public education in the least restrictive environment with their non-handicapped peers," Rosie said.

"Our mother, Stella, was one of the many early parent pioneers in the forefront," Maddie smiled.

"Hence the reason for the news team," Rosie added with pride.

"I know. I was making sure everyone else knew," Maddie said, crossing her arms and scowling.

No one in the room seemed to be paying much attention to the sibling rivalry and bickering. In the back someone yelled out, "Many television shows feature people with all sorts of disabilities."

A man sitting in a wheelchair close to Stella said, "That is for darn sure. I see it all the time. Never would have in my day."

"You're right, Grandpa," a teenager who was holding his hand replied. "In fact, an actor was nominated for a television Emmy for portraying a surgeon with autism."

"There is also an actor who actually does have a disability, cerebral palsy I think, who has the lead in a sitcom," another young individual said.

Another person in the crowd added, "I saw a reality television show all about young adults with Down syndrome trying to make their own independent way in today's world."

A young child in the back stood up on a chair and raised her hand. The reporter looked her way, acknowledging her, "Yes?"

The little girl continued, "I'm in the fourth grade. My best friend is Chrissy. My teacher says Chrissy and another boy in my class have special needs. I don't know what's so especially needy about either one of them. Chrissy and I play on the monkey bars. There is nothing special about that. They both get to go to a fun class at 1:00 every day to learn how to read. She comes back at 2:00 and must do everything the rest of us do. I want to go to that class. Chrissy says she loves it."

A teenage boy with droopy ears due to the huge round earring studs placed securely in his lobes stood up and said, "I got to work in one of those kind of classes for credit. At my school it's called a Resource Room. I helped teach math to a few Special Education students. I got to know a lot of the students who went there. It was cool. A couple of the kids are on the track team with me."

Other people conversed and chatted amicably about how every form of disability was visible in society nowadays. They discussed how all aspects of our lives are filled with a kaleidoscope of individuals. All races, sizes, religions, and disabilities are seen in movies, commercials, sports, workplaces, shopping, neighborhoods, schools, politics, and entertainment every day and everywhere. The conversations became animated and intertwined because everyone apparently knew someone or had a story of their own to tell.

The reporter spoke up, interrupting the chatter, "Ladies and gentlemen, thank you one and all. This has been very enlightening."

The reporter looked up at her cameraman but hastily shifted her gaze to the door far back behind the group. A tall dark man who looked to be in his forties but was closer to his mid-sixties walked into the room. His handsome looks and strong physique gave him a commanding presence. He had black short curly hair mixed with a dusting of gray. His eyes were large, and they appeared to be staring at her. The reporter was at a loss for words.

"Oh, my, ladies and gentlemen, look who just arrived. Senator Donaldson, it is an honor to have you attend our little gathering. Thank you for coming." The reporter stood up and pointed to the cameraman to direct his camera toward the newcomer.

"Sorry, but I'm afraid you've mixed me up with my twin brother, Leon. My name is Dr. Anton Donaldson. I apologize for being late. Traffic from Doernbecher Hospital is horrendous."

"Will the Senator be joining us?" she said, practically dismissing him.

"Yes, yes. He's helping our mother, Veronica Donaldson, at the moment. They should be here soon," he added.

"Well, then. We should wait. I do have a few more questions," she said as she sat back down and directed the microphone back toward Stella.

Rosie met Anton at the door. He turned to her and whispered, "I never understood why a politician should get more attention than a doctor."

"I thought you understood just about everything," Rosie grinned.

"Everything except my brother. He has always baffled me," Anton said.

"More important than a police detective, as well," Maddie whispered behind them.

"Where did you come from? You are always sneaking up on us," Rosie accused her. "Talk about someone I never understood."

"No truer words were ever spoken," Maddie smirked.

Rosie continued to whisper to Anton, "If you want to know who doesn't get any attention whatsoever, let's talk about Special Education teachers, like me."

"You get too much attention," Maddie said. "My vote is detectives, like me."

"Every television show and movie is about some sort of police activity," Rosie whined.

"Well, not quite," Anton interrupted. "If you really want to talk about lack of importance, how about mill workers? You only have to look at our fathers, but I would have to say they had more influence on us and our town than anyone else."

"Housewives!" Rosie and Maddie said at the same time.

"Look," Anton said with a nod toward the reporter. "Looks like Stella is ready to finish up this exposé."

Stella gripped the reporter's wrist while saying to no one in particular, "The world changed because we would not allow our children to be hidden away. The silence was deafening in those days and could no longer be ignored. We all belong together, not apart. The only way to make society cognizant of this is to come together as a group, a team, a family, and even a community. I didn't understand then, but I do now."

Everyone in the crowded room applauded. Stella petted her grand-dog and looked at the happy smiling people around her. "I am tired now," she said, slowly shutting her eyes.

෴

When Stella opened her eyes, she was alone. The artificial electric fireplace cast an uncanny yellowish glow. There were no light stands, no camera, no microphones, no people. Even the dog was gone. Stella looked down the long hallway. She saw a small, dark woman walk calmly toward her using a cane for support. What she noticed immediately about the lady was the unusually beautiful hat she wore.

"Are you ready, Stella?" the woman asked.

"Where did you get that hat?" Stella wanted to know.

"I made it long ago," she answered.

"Can you make me one?"

"I can show you how and we will make it together," she said.

Stella looked up at her, "Veronica?"

"Yes."

"Where is Donna?"

"She decided it was time to see heaven," Veronica answered.

"Where are our husbands?"

"They went to take care of her, of course," she said.

"Yes."

"Are you ready?" Veronica asked.

Stella pushed herself up from the chair and reached for her cane.

"Let's go home."

The End

AUTHOR'S NOTE

*P*ERSONAL STORIES AND EXPERIENCES CAN SPARK COMMUNITIES into political action towards social change. After World War II, millions of people did just that through numerous movements such as the women's movement, civil rights, and the determination to accept marginal groups into the mainstream of American society. Our country is better for the struggle. Yet the struggle for equal rights and opportunities for people with disabilities may be one of the most powerful examples of a lesson about a silent revolution.

A few years ago, I read about a census that was taken in the middle of the 20th century. It stated that over four million children were being denied an education. I shook my head in disbelief but in my own experience as a Special Education teacher and sibling of a profoundly handicapped sister, I knew it must be true. I kept researching. Another study indicated that in 1940, 400,000 children were enrolled in a special school or in a separate Special Education class. The number of children that needed specialized instruction and were not receiving it was closer to four million. By the early 1970s, the numbers had gone up. Four million of a total seven million children were being inappropriately or inadequately educated. Public Law 94-142, The Education for All Handicapped Children Act, was signed in 1975 to mandate for these children a free and appropriate public education in the least restrictive environment with their non-handicapped peers.

The huge gains and significant changes would not have been possible without the support and determination of the parent pioneers, families, friends, and politicians that fought outside the limelight for humanitarian positive values that would ultimately influence our future social attitudes.

There must be a million stories. *Uniquely Stella* is one of those stories inspired by my own family and experiences. This book is not intended to be an in-depth curriculum on the history of the disabled community or of Special Education. I researched and interviewed numerous people to get a feel of the times rather than depend on my own memories. Since this is a work of fiction, it is important to mention that I occasionally mashed together events, characters, and storylines. Any errors in the accuracy of these details are mine alone. As times change so does the terminology and even the way words are used or the emotional connotation. I purposely used the language consistent with the times in the decades I wrote about. My intention was never to cause sadness or hurt with the words that I chose to use.

I believe everyone is unique in his or her own way and we all have our own exceptional inspiration. Mine was one in a million.

ACKNOWLEDGMENTS

My mother always described my sister, Donna, as our silent angel. Many times, I have wondered if I had my own personal silent angel. I have realized there was never one; there were many. The great influences of my book were or have become the best part of my life. These people have unknowingly and unselfishly given me great courage, fortitude, and guidance.

Although this book is a work of fiction, it was inspired by actual events in the life of my mother and my sister. My mother, LaVerne Stella Kossler, has always been my hero. Her bravery and determination is legendary in our family. While I was writing this novel, I would occasionally read a chapter to her. She would smile or laugh and tell me to keep going. I did. Her one request was to keep it hopeful. I did. She told me that this book shouldn't be about her alone because she didn't feel she was anything special. To me she is the most special person in the world.

My sister, Donna Marie Dickenson, taught me about love and empathy. While some people might talk too much, she never talked at all. I wish I could tell her that I wrote this book for her.

My other sister, Judith Dickenson Ackaret, was instrumental in her stubborn insistence that I write a book. She shared with me the overwhelming number of stories I had written over the years that she surprisingly had kept. I had not. As I started writing what I originally called *Silent Angel*, she also started writing her own book *Scored for Life*. Her encouragement and advice pushed me forward. Thanks, Judy – even if you don't think Maddie is anything like you!

Many thanks also to Jerry Ackaret, Judy's husband, who helped me with the technical aspects as well as some research.

I am greatly indebted to the many wonderful friends who read various drafts of my manuscript and gave me excellent comments and suggestions that I was eventually able to incorporate into the book. Special thanks to Julie McGregor and Rick Vandenhole, who read the very first draft of the first chapter and didn't hate it. Nancy Emrick read an early draft and convinced me to divide the book into three parts and pointed out the value of stressing the fierce courage of women. Sue Stoller stayed up all night to read the manuscript and made *me* cry when she said that she was either laughing out loud or had to have a box of tissues next to her. Debbie Dodd was my first line editor. She did an unbelievable job and found 422 errors. I know because my sister told me. Mimi Menenberg graciously read an original draft of Part I and Part II and made me look deeply at my writing. Her kindness, generous heart, and insightful thoughts forced me to dive into the art of writing to learn all that I could.

I must also acknowledge all the incredible advice and help I received at the various conferences and writing retreats I attended. I especially owe a debt of gratitude to Lisa Howe and Scott Stavrou at the Prague Writer's Retreat as well as my new friend Lauren Smith, author of over thirty-five books.

Research became an essential element to the authenticity of my story even though I still have some memories of the times I wrote about. I greatly appreciated the assistance I received from the Chicago History Museum and Coos History Museum as well as the numerous libraries I visited and the people I interviewed.

I've been writing all my life, but what I learned the most as I wrote this book was the value of listening. Layne Lakefish was one of the people I listened to and learned from. Karla Devine gave me valuable suggestions and advice as well. I was also incredibly fortunate to find a great professional editor, Linda

Franklin, who worked with me without changing my voice. She listened to me while calming my fears of editing and guided me through to the finishing touches. Another wonderful surprise was finding Virginia Solan. She has been enthusiastic about marketing and promoting this project. I can see us moving past the business aspect and becoming good friends.

Some of the most heartfelt and surprising encouragement I received was from my nieces and nephew. Maris Menenberg, Dorothy Lee, Mary Lee, and Conrad Lee listened and laughed as I told them stories or read chapters. They asked insightful questions and made me think. I love those kids!

Kids! My students were a big part of my life. I taught Special Education for 36 years. My students and their families and the educational community became my inspiration. I don't believe one truly values schooling until it is denied.

To all the early pioneers that fought for handicapped children and whose shoulders we now stand on, I applaud you. Let us never forget what you endured to give us the gift of education. You are my heroes.

I didn't truly understand what a parent of a special needs child was going through until I became one of those parents. My daughter, Amy Cummins, is the center of my life. She challenges me and keeps me on my toes daily. Amy deserves a huge hug for also continually finding research for this book. I love you, Amy. No matter what.

The main title actor is the last one on stage. A standing ovation goes to my leading man, my unbelievably kind husband, Russell Menenberg. He read every chapter immediately after I wrote it. He encourages and supports me daily. He gives me love beyond measure, which gives me great confidence. How did I get so lucky?

ABOUT THE AUTHOR

Deborah Margaret Menenberg has always been a storyteller. During her thirty-six-year career as a Special Education teacher, she would often tell her students stories then write those tales in letters or emails to friends and family. She also wrote and directed many school plays while also teaching numerous drama classes. Apart from teaching, Deborah toured the inland waterways of Great Britain on a narrowboat performing with the Daystar Theatre Company. When home in Oregon or Washington, she directed or acted in various community theatre productions. Currently, Deborah lives on a floating home in Portland, Oregon with her husband Russell, twin cats, and their Golden Retriever, Flyer.

www.deborahmenenberg.com

Made in the USA
Middletown, DE
16 November 2021